TO DISTANT SHORES

Volume 7 of the Cutler Family Chronicles

WILLIAM C. HAMMOND

McBooks Press

Essex, Connecticut

An imprint of Globe Pequot, the trade division of
The Rowman & Littlefield Publishing Group, Inc.
4501 Forbes Blvd., Ste. 200, Lanham, MD 20706
www.rowman.com

Distributed by NATIONAL BOOK NETWORK

British Library Cataloguing in Publication Information available

Library of Congress Cataloging-in-Publication Data
ISBN 978-1-4930-6900-2 (hardcover: alk. paper)
ISBN 978-1-4930-7132-6 (electronic)

♾™ The paper used in this publication meets the minimum requirements of American National
Standard for Information Sciences—Permanence of Paper for Printed Library Materials, ANSI/
NISO Z39.48-1992.

To my wife Sheree's three grandchildren:

Luka, Chloe, and Esme.

I love you guys.

ACKNOWLEDGMENTS

The completion of any book—fiction or nonfiction—asks much of its author. Not only does it demand a passion for the written word, it demands a commitment that is perhaps unique in the realm of human activity. Day in and day out, the serious writer writes with no time off, no vacation, even when the writer *is* on vacation. At the end of it all, the writer has created a manuscript often with no concept of how it will be received by publishers, agents, and the reading public.

In addition to the above, a special burden is placed on an author of historical fiction. Here, the author is conveying not only a story. He or she is also conveying history that the reader justifiably expects to be *accurate* history insofar as plot development permits. This responsibility especially weighs heavily in our modern age when the subject of history is sadly no longer taught in many schools.

As an author of historical fiction, I have felt that weight, and I have endeavored always to be true to history. In volumes one through six of the Cutler Family Chronicles, the history is American and British history, subjects I have studied extensively including as a double major in college. *To Distant Shores*, however, is set not in America or Europe, but in New Zealand, an island nation I knew little about before moving here in 2016. Nor is its history known to most Americans and even to many New Zealanders (known as "Kiwis" in honor of its native bird). So in telling my story I had to rely heavily on my own research and on the input, large and small, of legions of people who stood ready, willing, and able to assist me. Several of those people and institutions are listed below. First, however, I must acknowledge those individuals who contributed significantly to the creation of this book.

Jess M. Brallier. From chapter one of volume one of the Cutler Family Chronicles, Jess has served on my quarterdeck as first reader and critic of every chapter I have written. An author of a library of titles and a book publisher and marketer of consequence, his wisdom and insights have proven their worth time and again. Such is Jess's knowledge and depth of character, he constantly makes the hard work of writing seem pleasurable!

Melinda Conner of Winston-Salem, North Carolina. In my career as publisher, editor, and publishing sales representative I have met many book editors, both those who freelance and those who work in-house at a prestigious firm. Mindy has been my editor since I began writing books more than twenty years ago. Today I cannot imagine formally submitting a manuscript without her special polish and enthusiasm being added to it. She is among the best in the business.

Richard Curtis of Richard Curtis Associates in New York has served as my literary agent since the publication of *A Matter of Honor*. His business acumen and calm demeanor in what at times can be a chaotic marketplace are qualities any author would cherish. I could ask for no better champion of my literary initiatives and no better guardian of my literary interests.

George D. Jepson is my current publisher. When the winds of change forced me to seek a new publisher three years ago, George was there with a smile and a contract. His enthusiasm for my work is something I treasure.

Sheree Fenwick is my wife and my greatest advocate. A Kiwi of English extraction who was raised not far from where we now live together, she has been instrumental in providing descriptions of various places in New Zealand, including the route followed by the shipwrecked survivors (some portions of which she and I have walked together) starting at Pouto Point, where her parents lived for many years, and ending at Russell in the Bay of Islands. A poet and writer, her command of the language and her sensitivities to the feminine side of things speak to the very heart of this novel.

There are also many individuals and organizations that have offered me advice, answers, and encouragement. Maori customs and history are at the root of many of these entities, including the curator and staff of the Auckland Museum, the Museum of Waitangi Treaty Grounds, the Russell Museum, and the Museum of Dargaville. Special acknowledgment goes to Ngati Kawa Taituha, a worker at the Waitangi Treaty Grounds who spearheaded my introduction to Maori customs and history, and to Stan Parker, a man of letters well versed in New Zealand traditions and history. And I would be terribly remiss were I not to mention the helpful and friendly staff at the gift store at the Pompallier Mission and Printery in Russell. Often they knew what question to answer before the question was asked.

My gratitude to you all is unbounded.

—William C. Hammond III
Puhoi, New Zealand

Author's Note

What you are about to read is a work of fiction. Not every character in the book is a real historical figure. But some are. Similarly, not every event transpired as depicted, or even happened at all. But some did.

As a student of history for more than fifty years, and a writer of historical fiction for twenty of them, I endeavor in all my novels to be true to history as far as plot and circumstances permit. The responsibility to "get it right" is daunting, especially for an author researching people and places with roots far removed from his native New England—places where history is often subject to speculation and interpretation. But having lived in New Zealand for six years now and having married a lovely Kiwi woman of British descent, I have taken on the challenge with gusto. My mission in this novel is twofold: to spin a good yarn and thereby entertain my readers, and to expand the Cutler Family Chronicles to far distant shores and introduce my characters and my readers to these fabled South Seas islands known as Aotearoa, the Land of the Long White Cloud.

I hope I have succeeded in fulfilling this mission. You be the judge.

PREFACE

The decades following the War of 1812, a conflict often referred to as America's second war of independence, were years of introspection for the fledgling republic. Having twice prevailed against the military might of Great Britain, there was now no power on Earth ready, willing, and able to take on the United States. The peace treaty signed in Ghent, Belgium, in December 1814—a month prior to the bloodiest battle of the war in New Orleans and the greatest American victory—ushered in the "Era of Good Feelings," a time when Americans put aside political and societal differences to bask in peace and prosperity.

President James Monroe, having taken the torch from fellow Virginian James Madison in 1816, intended to keep the good times rolling. In his annual address to Congress in 1823 he issued his famous Monroe Doctrine, which in essence declared that the United States would brook no further interference by European powers in the affairs of any country in either North or South America. The days of colonization and puppet governments were over, Monroe declared. Henceforth, the Western Hemisphere was an American sphere of influence off-limits to foreign meddling. Although European leaders may have grumbled over the tone and text of the address, they heeded its warning.

With the two Americas now secured, the first drumbeats of what would come to be known as Manifest Destiny were heard throughout the twenty-four states forming the Union in the 1820s. Manifest Destiny set forth the principle that the United States was destined—by God, its proponents believed—to expand American notions of democracy and capitalism beyond the Mississippi River to the west coast of the continent.

America had no need for colonies elsewhere in the world or for European-style mercantilism. Americans had all they needed in their own backyard. International commerce, the lifeblood of any prosperous nation, was still necessary, of course, but that was a foregone conclusion. The United States had been in the vanguard of global shipping and free trade among nations even before the Revolutionary War.

As America entered the 1840s and began expanding its dominion over North America and opening lucrative overseas markets in Asia and elsewhere, all that was needed to secure its place in the world was an alliance with a like-minded nation with the naval resources to guarantee the integrity of global trade routes and the financial rewards accruing to both parties of such an alliance.

President John Tyler, his cabinet, and every American of sense and sensibility understood there was but one nation to approach, and that nation was Great Britain. The rationale was simple. Although the two nations had squabbled from time to time, Great Britain was the mother country. It had been a critical ally in the war against Tripoli in the Mediterranean, and in the West Indies in the Quasi-War with France. Above all else, Britain and its Royal Navy possessed the wherewithal to forge a global empire that included New South Wales on the Australian continent. From Sydney, the colonial capital, Britain had extended its hegemony over other colonies on the continent and all the way to New Zealand—the two large islands to the east across the Tasman Sea. New Zealand was home to a people who had held sway there since the age of Alfred the Great in England. Its people, the Maori, were quite distinct from the Aborigines of Australia. They were of Polynesian descent, like the inhabitants of Tahiti, Fiji, and other South Sea islands, and they were a proud and clever people. Until the 1820s, when Britain moved to solidify its grip on the two islands, outsiders knew little about them—or even that they existed.

But as Britain and its allies would soon discover, there was much to learn about the Maori, and the lessons could at times be harsh.

CHAPTER I

Washington, D.C.

August 1843

RICHARD CUTLER FELT A TWINGE OF EXCITEMENT AT THE UNUSUAL summons, and yet also an odd feeling of foreboding.

He read the dispatch a second time before folding it and tucking it inside a top drawer of his dark mahogany desk. For several moments he stood gazing out between the twin satin drapes to the three-story gray stone building across the Potomac River, where the dispatch had originated.

Secured to bollards in front of that building were four vessels where yesterday there had been three. The fourth vessel was the approximate length of her sister ships, and like them she was painted black with a white stripe along her gun-port strake. But this newly arrived vessel featured a different sail plan. She had three masts: a square-rigged foremast and a fore-and-aft rig on her mainmast and mizzen. Although her starboard side was largely hidden from his view, he noted what appeared to be the black iron casing of a substantial side-wheeler located amidships just beyond the tall, slightly raked smokestack mounted between the foremast and mainmast. He wondered if her arrival at the Navy Yard was in any way connected to his summons.

From North Street a few blocks away, the first deep, resonating peals of the bells of Christ Church called the faithful to worship. Moments later he saw Roger Offen, the young midshipman who had delivered the dispatch, sitting in the stern sheets of a small ship's boat as two oarsmen rowed him away from the stone quays of the Alexandria waterfront and back across the Potomac.

He heard the door to his study creak open and the soft padding of footsteps and swish of a muslin gown. "Is everything all right, my dear?" she asked in the lilting voice that despite a year of marriage still inflamed him. "I overheard Emma talking to a man who I assume was a dispatch officer. Unfortunately, I was not yet dressed to receive him and could not greet him myself. He delivered the dispatch and took his leave rather quickly, I thought."

He smiled at her, admiring the understated elegance and calm self-assurance befitting an upper-class Englishwoman. Her shining auburn tresses, artfully coiled upon her head, reflected the sunlight streaming in between the curtains to play on her smooth skin, unmarked save for a small dimple on her well-defined chin. The ankle-length sprigged-muslin dress defined her slender body, and the V-shaped bodice accentuated her fine bosom. Despite their year of marriage, he still found her as fresh and beguiling as the first time he met her at the British embassy.

"Well then, my dear," Richard said gallantly, "that was his loss and his error. When a lady is indisposed, for whatever reason, a gentleman, be he indeed a gentleman, should stand by patiently and await her pleasure."

"Thank you for that enlightenment, my love," she chided with a playful touch of irony. "I do appreciate the insights of a true gentleman, and I am always grateful whenever you put my pleasure before your own. However, I very much doubt that the lad gave much thought to paying his respects to me. He had a job to do, and he did it." Her tone changed. "What news did he bring from across the way?"

"Secretary Henshaw has requested the dubious honor of my presence."

"Indeed. When?"

"Tomorrow morning at six bells. That would be eleven o'clock," he added straight-faced.

"Do tell," she parried. "May I remind you that I am married to an American naval officer, and further, that I hail from a Royal Navy family of some consequence. I believe I am well versed in naval time. Why does that pudgy sparrow want with you?"

"I don't know. Dispatches do not normally divulge that sort of information."

"I can't help wondering. It's most irregular, is it not, to send a dispatch on a Sunday morning to request an audience first thing on Monday morning? The matter must be of some importance."

Richard lifted his shoulders. "Perhaps. But I see no point in idle speculation. We'll know the answer soon enough. Besides, although Reverend Davies would doubtless disapprove, Sunday is just another day to Henshaw. I've been told that he often sleeps in his office to be at his desk before sunrise."

She laughed and rested one hand on his arm. "He sounds depressingly like you at times, my love. No doubt his poor wife suffers from the same curse I do."

"What curse is that, pray?"

"Lack of a husband when a husband is most needed."

"Is that so? Be that as it may, I've never heard tell of his having a wife."

"I shouldn't wonder if he sleeps in his office! Whatever business you have with him, please don't forget that we are hosting George and Cassandra tomorrow evening. They were in England for an age, and I am most anxious to see them now they're back."

"As am I." He kissed her cheek. "Don't fret, my sweet, I shall be present and accounted for long before they arrive. It would be most imprudent and undiplomatic of me to gainsay the British ambassador and his wife."

He withdrew a small gold-plated pocket watch from his waistcoat. "Alas, I see we are once again in Dutch with the good reverend. We must leave or prepare ourselves to face his righteous wrath."

She laughed softly. "Despite our sins—or perhaps because of them—Reverend Davies may be inclined to offer a prayer for our safe passage. We may have need of that prayer in the morrow."

At the appointed hour, Richard Cutler approached the Federalist-style façade of smooth red brick and gray stone. He was dressed in the formal blue woolen uniform with gold buttons and facings that identified him as an American naval officer of high rank. At the front entrance to the building, he returned the crisp salutes of two Marine sentries. After stating his name, rank, and the nature of his business at the Washington Navy Yard, he was bidden by the taller of the sentries to follow him.

Although Richard knew the way very well, he followed the Marine down a long, cavernous corridor on the building's ground floor. Their footsteps echoed through the vast chamber, empty but for them so early. The high ceiling had preserved the cool air blown in by the previous night's thunderstorms, which had brought welcome relief from the oppressive heat and humidity of the past several weeks. As he always did, Richard took special notice of the majestic oils that graced the walls, each depicting a single-ship action during the naval history of the young republic. They were all there: *Bonhomme Richard* versus *Serapis in the North Sea*; *Constellation* having it out with *La Vengeance* in the French West Indies; the burning of *Philadelphia* in Tripoli Harbor; the infamous *Chesapeake* affair; *Constitution* hull-to-hull with *Guerrière* off the southern coast of Nova Scotia. His grandfather and namesake, the original Richard Cutler of Boston, had fought in many of these battles—as, in later years, had his father, James Cutler, and his uncle, Will Cutler. And as had his first cousin Seth Cutler, albeit on the British side. The young nation's seafaring history displayed on these walls also reflected Cutler family history dating back a century earlier to when Thomas Cutler sailed with his bride from Portsmouth, England, to the colony of Massachusetts and the seaside town of Hingham.

At the far end of the corridor the Marine stopped before a solid oak door bearing a brass panel emblazoned with the words "Secretary of the Navy." He knocked firmly twice.

"What is it?" inquired a gruff voice from inside.

The Marine cracked the door open. "Captain Cutler to see you, sir."

"Show him in."

The sentry swung the door open, saluted Richard Cutler, executed a sharp about-face, and walked back down the corridor.

Secretary Henshaw rose as Richard entered the room. He resembled a Quaker in his black trousers, black coat, and white shirt with a stiff, upturned collar. His stern expression relaxed into a brief smile. "Captain Cutler!" he exclaimed. "It does me well to see you again, and looking so hale and hearty!"

"As do you, sir," Richard replied. He doffed his bicorne hat, tucked it under his left armpit, and strode across the spartan office to where David Henshaw was waiting with outstretched hand. Richard took it in his own hand and pressed it firmly, looking down at the bald pate of the short, squat official. Henshaw's dark, darting eyes shone with intelligence. The bottom three buttons of Henshaw's embroidered red waistcoat were left undone, the natural consequence of overindulgence. Secretary Henshaw had a reputation as a capable, dedicated, and no-nonsense administrator. Though polite when propriety dictated, he was not a popular man, a judgment of which he was well aware, and which did not seem to bother him in the least.

"Please, Captain, have a seat," Henshaw offered graciously, gesturing toward the two upholstered wingback chairs across from his desk. "Would you care for a cup of coffee? Or tea? We'll enjoy something stronger over lunch, and *that* we'll start off with a spot of your family's rum. I have had several barrels shipped to the Yard. Official business, you understand."

Richard grinned. "The Cutler family is most grateful, sir."

"My colleagues and I are the ones who are grateful. Your family distills a fine rum down in Barbados, and I am looking forward to having another taste of it. For the moment, will coffee or tea suffice?"

"Coffee will do fine, sir. Thank you."

Henshaw picked up a small bell from his desk and jingled it several times. When a neatly dressed young orderly of African descent appeared through a side door, Henshaw placed the order.

"Now then," he said, turning back to his guest, "please do not think me rude if I forgo family news and other pleasantries. We will have occasion to chat about such things in due course, but for the moment, you and I have more important business to discuss."

"As you wish, sir."

"No doubt you are anxious to learn the nature of your summons here today."

"Somewhat curious, sir," Richard deadpanned.

"Quite." Henshaw cleared his throat and then looked hard at Richard. "Then I shall waste no time satisfying your curiosity. You noticed the barkentine on your way here?"

"I did indeed, sir. I first noticed her from my home yesterday morning. As I had not seen her before, and few of her class, I studied her closely on the row across. Midshipman Offen offered what information he could, which wasn't much beyond the fact that she is one of our newest steam frigates. And she appears to be a fine one."

"*Suwannee* is indeed a fine frigate, Captain Cutler, as you will discover for yourself this very afternoon. She mounts—or will mount in a matter of weeks—ten 32-pounder guns on her gun deck, and five 12-pounder guns up on her weather deck. Her engine is a 1,500-horsepower steam engine that will push her along at a good eleven knots. She's just off her stocks in Gosport and was towed here two days ago. As we speak, she is receiving the final touches in preparation of her shakedown cruise."

To Richard's expression of keen interest Henshaw added, somewhat cryptically, "Belowdecks she has every possible amenity. Her after cabin is worthy of a British admiral—or even, I daresay, a lady of noble birth. What is more, the captain's steward, a chap named Torben Larsen, is one of our best. He's a Dane, a meticulous man quite skilled in the culinary arts."

When the secretary paused, Richard offered no comment. There was a reason he was being told these things, and he was beginning to suspect what it was.

"She's yours," Henshaw said abruptly.

Richard blinked. "*Mine*, sir?"

"Yes, Captain Cutler. Yours. You are to be *Suwannee*'s first commanding officer. Does that prospect please you? Ah, I see it does. Then perhaps you will also be pleased with your sailing orders." His eyes shifted from Richard to the side entrance, where the young orderly reappeared bearing a silver tray with matching coffee pot and two bone china cups and saucers. "Our beverages have arrived. Well done, Thomas. Your timing is impeccable."

"Thank you, sir." The young man walked over to the desk, deposited the tray on top of it, and poured out two cups of coffee with the dexterity of an experienced waiter at Gadsby's Tavern. "Will there be anything else, sir?"

"No, Thomas. That will be all."

"Very good, sir."

"Sugar or cream?" Henshaw asked Richard when the side door had clicked shut behind Thomas.

"A spoonful of sugar, if you please."

"A man after my own heart. I will join you."

Henshaw made a show of adding sugar to his cup and stirring it in before placing the small bowl of sugar before Richard. He took a tentative sip, placed the cup gingerly on its delicate saucer, and dabbed at the corners of his lips with a white cotton napkin.

"You mentioned my sailing orders, sir," Richard prompted him.

Henshaw glanced up. To Richard's surprise he was smiling. "So I did," the secretary said. "So I did. Well, here they are, Captain. Your orders are to sail *Suwannee* around the southern coast of Africa to the island of Java. I believe you are acquainted with the Indies and Batavia?"

Richard was, and he knew that Henshaw knew he was. The archipelago encircling Java and its capital city of Batavia had been since 1602 the exclusive enclave of the Dutch East India Company—Vereenigde Oost-indische Compagnie, or VOC as it was more commonly known throughout the world. The quasi-military, fully autonomous, and self-governed VOC was revered in Holland and feared elsewhere. The spice islands of the East Indies were legendary both for their food-enhancing products and for their profit-generating capabilities, and the Netherlands had gone to extremes to defend its monopoly over the global supply of the prized delicacies. In recent years, as the iron grip of Dutch rule had finally yielded to the forces of competition, Richard's family had established a commercial hub in Batavia in cooperation with another prominent Boston shipping family. The progeny of that family and its joint venture had carried on, and today the merchant fleets of

Cutler & Sons continued to ply the waters of Asia in pursuit of ever greater profits generated in the exotic seaports of the Far East. A decade earlier, Richard had sailed on one such vessel to Singapore and had watched with fascination as his cousin Philip Seymour hammered out favorable trade agreements with seasoned representatives of the British East India Company.

"I am, sir," Richard said. "If I may, what are my orders in Batavia?"

"You are to join three ships of the East India Squadron," Henshaw replied. "From Batavia the squadron will sail to Sydney in New South Wales on the east coast of Australia. Between now and then you will learn all you can about New South Wales. What began as a penal colony where Britain shipped its most hardened criminals has flourished and is today on the cusp of destiny. Much as our own country was fifty years ago. Governor Burke is doing a damned fine job making New South Wales a profitable British possession. Nonetheless, the colony is in serious need of the goods and services that other nations can provide. Including, of course, our own nation."

"This is to be a commercial venture, then? To craft trade agreements between the British in New South Wales and the United States?"

"In part. Mind you, these trade agreements—which, by the bye, will eventually include all the British colonies in Australia—will benefit many American enterprises, not the least of which will be your own. In benefiting them, these agreements will also benefit our global commerce and our Treasury."

Richard took a final sip of coffee to buy time to reflect on the implication of what he was hearing. It seemed simple enough, and yet . . . "Sir," he said, "with respect, while I am of course honored to be considered for this mission, I fail to understand my role in it. What do I bring to the table? Yes, my family has strong ties to the region, and I am conversant with the intricacies of trade negotiations. But why me, sir? And why a naval squadron? To my mind, an armed merchant vessel or two would suffice."

Henshaw's brow furrowed as he stared straight into Richard's hazel eyes. "You have a reputation for being a perspicacious man, Captain, and I warrant that your reputation is well deserved. That is certainly one reason why you were selected for this mission. That, and a more compelling one."

"Which is, sir, if I may inquire?"

"Of course you may inquire, Captain," Henshaw said expansively. "You may ask me anything you wish. But don't worry," he quickly continued. "You are not being called upon to conduct negotiations. That work will be the responsibility of a special envoy named David Livermore, a fellow you will meet in Batavia. He has been appointed by Secretary of State Upshur with the full knowledge and support of the president."

"I see," Richard volunteered, although in truth he still did not. When he offered no further comment, Henshaw continued.

"Make no mistake—these trade agreements are vital to our country's long-term interests. But for the purposes of the mission we are discussing, they will serve as a diversion to the main event."

Richard's eyes narrowed slightly in anticipation. Henshaw was finally coming to the point. "A diversion, sir?"

"Of a sort, yes. Trade negotiations are a means of getting our foot in the front door of British foreign policy. These agreements, you see, are as important to the British as they are to us—perhaps more so. But while we are certainly eager to engage in the dance, to the United States government the *real* mission of this expedition to Sydney—and you will hold what I am about to tell you in the strictest of confidence—is to secure the use of Royal Navy bases throughout the western and southern Pacific." He paused a moment to allow that last statement to find its mark. Then: "As you know, it would not be the first time that our navy has been granted access to British naval bases. The past conflicts in the West Indies and the Mediterranean provide excellent precedents. Today, as our country seeks to expand its sphere of influence in the Far East, Britain's cooperation in our initiatives—for the short term only, mind you—would be most appreciated by President Tyler and every member of his cabinet."

Richard thought for a moment. "That's all well and good, sir. But what's in it for the British? What do they get in exchange for our use of their bases?"

Henshaw nodded as though he had expected that question. "I could say the undying gratitude of the United States, but I doubt that would suffice. To answer your question more precisely, the British will get more favorable terms in the agreements than might otherwise be the case. Of greater consequence, they will secure our pledge to become the enemy of their enemies in the South Pacific. That is the real reason we are sending a squadron to Sydney. A show of American sea power will significantly bolster our bargaining position."

"Have you a specific enemy in mind?"

"I do. France."

"France?"

"Yes, France. Britain's ancient enemy. The Frogs are well established in many of the islands of Polynesia. Back in '72, a Frenchman named Du Fresne sailed two frigates into a major whaling center on the northeast coast of New Zealand, a cannon shot from the British colonial capital of Russell. And just last year French Marines landed in Tahiti, marched to the royal palace, threw out the queen, and hoisted the Tricolor over the palace, claiming not only Tahiti for France but the Society Islands as well. British intelligence is now warning that the French have similar designs on islands to the south of Tahiti, including New Zealand."

"New Zealand?" Richard said uncertainly.

"Have you not heard of New Zealand? Well, it's hardly surprising. New Zealand lies on far distant shores. It comprises two fair-sized islands and a host of smaller ones several hundred miles east of Australia. Until recently the islands were administered by New South Wales. Now New Zealand is on its own, more or less. The islands have little strategic value to the United States—only our whalers have cause to lay in there—but they most certainly do have value to Great Britain. The natives there, a Polynesian people known as Maori, recently appealed to British authorities to protect them from French incursions. It seems a Frenchman by the name of Thierry has set up his own little kingdom in the north island. As a result, the Maori chiefs signed a treaty with the British at some place called Waitangi that ceded sovereignty of the islands to Great Britain and elevated the status of the islands to a Crown colony. But that's all background. You needn't concern yourself with it. Just remember: The real threat to Britain in that part of the world is ongoing French meddling in the far bigger prize on the Australian continent."

"Using New Zealand as a stepping-stone."

"Just so. And that's where the United States—and you—have a crucial role to play. Our naval presence in the area will help the British neutralize the French threat, and—perhaps even better—the United States will become an important ally of Great Britain."

Important ally? The irony did not escape Richard Cutler. As a senior naval officer, he was well aware that the military brass in Washington were convinced that America's next war would be fought against England, as in 1775 and again in 1812. The U.S. government was investing a king's ransom in constructing defensive forts in seaports along the Eastern Seaboard—notably in Savannah, Charleston, and New York—as a deterrent to the Royal Navy and an anticipated invasion. Most of this construction was under the direct supervision of a West Point graduate of engineering named Captain Robert Lee. Richard had recently met Captain Lee at a briefing, and they had discussed this very topic. Richard had been impressed by the Southerner's brilliance and courtly manners.

He saw no point in broaching that issue now, however. He ran his fingers through his thick chestnut hair, mentally weighing the pros and cons. "And you think I can help influence the outcome of negotiations with the Royal Navy?" he ventured.

"I do," Henshaw returned, "though perhaps not in the way you might imagine. But you will be involved, I assure you. You and Vice Admiral Reginald Braithwaite."

"Anne's brother has a part in this?"

"Indeed. The admiral can render invaluable assistance to our mutual cause. As the ranking Royal Navy officer in the South Pacific, he chairs the Queen's Council in Sydney. And that council sets policy for the entire region. With Anne's help, I am confident we can make the good admiral and his advisers see things our way."

Richard offered no comment.

"There's more," Henshaw went on. "Anne's other brother, George, can also help. As the British ambassador to the United States, he is highly regarded in diplomatic circles in both Washington and London. Such is his influence in Parliament and the Privy Council that his recommendations are usually implemented without much debate. And of course he has a personal interest in you because of his sister. I've heard that he introduced you and Anne at one of his embassy functions. Clearly he has a high opinion of you and wants you to succeed. Your success in this negotiation will verify that high opinion."

Richard allowed several moments to pass, then: "Sir, forgive me. Although I agree with what you are saying, I don't see how this all connects. My wife and her brother can perhaps be persuaded to lend their support from afar. How much good that will do I dare not speculate. But they will not be the ones doing the negotiations. Nor will they be the ones in Sydney. They will not be coming on this cruise."

Henshaw cleared his throat, as if being forced to acknowledge the simple logic of Richard's words. "You are quite correct about the ambassador," he conceded. "Duty and discretion prevent him from accompanying you in *Suwannee*." Then he smiled broadly. "Fortunately, the same need not apply to your wife."

"My word, Anne. Cape Town? Batavia? Sydney? If you agree to go you will be a diplomat in your own right. Not to mention one of the most widely traveled members of the Braithwaite family. Will you do it?"

George Clarence Smythe Braithwaite looked fondly at his beautiful sister. The third son of Viscount St. John, he, like his older brother Reginald, had left his home in Hampshire to seek his fortune when their oldest brother inherited the title and family estates upon the death of their father. Whereas Reginald had found purpose on the high seas, George had prospered in the diplomatic corps, rising rapidly through the ranks until Foreign Secretary Henry John Temple appointed him ambassador to the United States in 1838. Only thirty-two, he conducted himself with the dignity, wisdom, and aplomb of one considerably older and more seasoned in the art of diplomacy. Like his siblings, George Braithwaite possessed an air of polish and good breeding that, along with his natural charm and good looks, drew people of many different backgrounds to him.

"I'm not sure, George," Anne answered him. "This has come upon us so suddenly. Richard and I have had no time to discuss it. I am certainly not averse to traveling long distances. After all, I have crossed the Atlantic Ocean three times. Nevertheless, I confess to finding the prospect somewhat daunting. I certainly have never gone . . . how far did you say it was to Batavia, Richard? Fifteen thousand miles?"

"About that. And another five thousand from Batavia to Sydney."

"It is a very long way," Anne sighed. "Yet I must admit that I find the prospect of a long sea voyage exhilarating. Rather than watching my darling husband sail away from me, I will be sailing away with him bound for exotic shores." Her voice gained confidence as she continued. "Apparently the accommodations will be more than adequate, and the steward is one of the Navy's best. And a steam-paddler, no less!

"Living in the confines of an after cabin is not every woman's fancy, perhaps, but we Cutlers are an adventurous family. And of course I would get to see Reggie. In Sydney, on the other side of the world!" More seriously she added, "I would also find it difficult to decline a personal request from the president of the United States and his Secretary of the Navy. Among other factors, there is Richard's career to consider. This expedition could advance it quite handsomely, and refusing it might do some harm."

"Regardless of how long you have known about it, you seem to have given this matter a great deal of thought already," her brother laughed. "And I do believe that you have made up your mind."

"I believe I have." She smiled at her husband. He smiled back.

"Bravo!" George exclaimed. "A toast, then!" He raised his glass, clinked it gently against the three other raised glasses, and said, "To my beloved sister and her husband. May they find the same happiness at sea together that they have so clearly found on land."

"What about your mother, Richard," George put in after the meal was resumed and another round of Bordeaux poured, "and the rest of your family in Boston? How do you think they will react?"

Richard shrugged. "They're quite used to my being away at sea, of course. We'll have an opportunity to talk about it when I am in Boston next month for a family conference at Cutler & Sons. It's imperative that I be at that conference in light of the trade agreements we are soon to negotiate in Sydney. Secretary Henshaw is right. Those agreements could be a godsend to the family business. In addition, the family needs to discuss the future of Cutler & Sons. Steam is beginning to supplement sail even in merchant ships, and if we are to keep up with the competition, a considerable investment will be required.

"All that aside, I do have concerns about my mother. She has not been in the best of health recently. She still misses my father, and she is lonely despite having many family members and friends nearby. Still, I infer from her last letter that circumstances may be changing for the better. Apparently, a certain gentleman in town has taken quite a fancy to her."

"Do say! Who is this chap?"

"I don't know much about him, George, other than he is a local merchant. But I intend to find out more when I'm in Hingham." He lifted an eyebrow as he added, only half in jest, "I need to satisfy myself that his intentions toward my mother are entirely honorable."

As George Braithwaite and Richard exchanged grins, Cassandra brought the subject back to the much longer voyage under discussion. "But is this cruise quite safe?" The daughter of a wealthy and privileged family, Cassandra Braithwaite filled the role of an ambassador's wife with distinction. Her beauty and highborn ways combined with a rapier-like wit frequently fired the pens of correspondents at the *National Intelligencer* and other city newspapers reporting on the social scene.

"One hears stories of wretched prisoners starving and preying on one another in the towns and villages of New South Wales whilst hordes of naked savages lurk in the wild. The colony sounds more like a den of iniquity than a Garden of Eden. And before you can contemplate *that*, you first must *get* there. A lot can happen during such a lengthy voyage. Storms abound, and depraved pirates haunt the seaways."

Silence closed around the group like a noose after Cassandra finished voicing her concerns. On a mantelpiece above the hearth, a gold-and-white enamel clock pinged eight times. Finally, George Braithwaite said, "You needn't worry about pirates, my dear. They are scoundrels, to be sure, but they are not stupid scoundrels. They will not meddle with an American warship. Unarmed merchantmen are their prey. As for the prisoners you mentioned, it's true that when the First Fleet sailed into Botany Bay a century ago, it carried a grand lot of British thieves and miscreants who were transported to Australia as punishment. But those days are over. Prisoners are no longer transported there. Today, New South Wales boasts a population of nearly three million people, and its capital, Sydney, is a thriving community of great enterprise and promise."

He looked at Richard. "Is there precedence in your navy for the wife of a commanding officer to accompany her husband on such a voyage?"

Richard nodded. "There is, though rarely in a theater of war, and not always to the good. Captain James Barron, commodore of the Mediterranean Squadron, brought his wife along in *President* during the war with Tripoli. Unfortunately, she proved to be a costly distraction. He was more interested in showing her the sights along the Italian and French coasts than he was in fighting the Barbary pirates."

"That sounds perfectly lovely," Anne remarked. "Good on him for showing such consideration."

"Actually, not good," Richard countered. "Barron was recalled for what was delicately described as 'a propensity for inaction' and assigned to a desk job over there." He pointed in the direction of the Navy Yard across the river. "There are other examples, though, most with happier endings."

"Fair enough. But is Anne's presence in Sydney truly necessary? While I am delighted at this prospect of an alliance between my country and the United States there, and I am proud as punch of my sister, I share Cassandra's concerns for her safety. And I must say, I am not entirely sanguine about your government so blithely using my family to get what it wants."

"I understand, George. As to Anne accompanying me on this cruise, the United States government believes it is advisable. Her presence will benefit all concerned—and myself most of all, of course." He winked at his wife.

"Ah, but you did not answer my question. Do *you* believe her presence is advisable?"

Before Richard could respond, Anne said with a bit of steel beneath her sweet tone, "If you gentlemen do not mind, I would prefer that you not discuss my safety or the advisability of my presence on this cruise as if I were a helpless child. I am a grown woman. I am married to an esteemed naval commander. I have him and his crew to protect me, and should he not be available to do that, I can fend for myself. We all remember what happened on my third voyage across the Atlantic, do we not? In *Dolphin*? That should convince you that I am jolly well capable of taking care of myself in a pinch."

"What you define as a 'pinch,' my dear, was a wee bit more than that," George said lightly. "I believe the two men whose lives you helped to save during that wicked storm would agree with me."

"Right, then," Anne said, closing the subject. "Will someone please have another helping of poached salmon and vegetables? Abigail," referring to a thirtyish woman of mixed heritage who had become a staple in the Cutler household, "went to some lengths to prepare this feast, along with there is a berry trifle waiting in the wings and a delicious port to finish off the meal in grand style. Does that sound good?"

Contented sighs and mock groans of those well aware of Abigail's culinary talents answered her question. George said, "Before we allow our faces to fall into our puddings, may I offer one last toast?" He stood, cleared his throat, and elevated his glass toward Richard and Anne. "May the winds forever be fair and at your back. May your travels prove fruitful, and may you two continue to find, together, all that is good and meaningful in this earthly life of ours. God save the queen."

"God save the queen!" the three others intoned.

"Just come home safely," Cassandra added softly as the four glasses came together a final time.

CHAPTER 2

THERE WAS MUCH TO DO IN THE DAYS THAT FOLLOWED, AND LITTLE time to do it. As the captain of a newly minted frigate, Richard Cutler had to set the pace of a naval rhythm in tune with those on ship and ashore who had a stake in her mission.

When planning the schedule, Richard did what he normally did: He worked backward from the departure date. To avoid the worst of the cyclone season in the Pacific, *Suwannee* was scheduled to sail in late October, two months hence. Everything and everyone therefore needed to be ready to go a week earlier than the scheduled date to address the inevitable delays that plague any such enterprise. The shakedown cruise was a top priority. Richard's father had taught him that if a ship has a flaw, a storm at sea will find it. But before *Suwannee* could battle a storm, Richard needed to muster a crew. And before he could do that, he required the services of an executive officer in whom he had unflinching trust and confidence, one to whom he could, without qualms, turn over command of the ship if need be, and on whom he could rely to anticipate his needs and ensure that his orders were efficiently executed.

That critical piece of the puzzle had quickly been put into place. During his luncheon with David Henshaw, Richard had been presented with a list of senior sea officers currently seeking a position. As he scanned the names on the list, Richard's gaze settled on one name quite familiar to him. Fifteen years earlier, twelve-year-old Richard Cutler and Jack Brengle had entered the first form of Governor Dummer Academy together. The Massachusetts boarding school's list of distinguished alumni included Commodore Edward Preble, a naval hero in the war with Tripoli. At Governor Dummer, in addition to receiving a superb education, Richard and Jack had forged a fast friendship that had carried them through preparatory school and Harvard College, and from there into the Navy.

As midshipmen and later as junior lieutenants, they had served on shallow-draft vessels of the Home Squadron in pursuit of pirates harassing southern shipping lanes. On one occasion, during fierce hand-to-hand fighting on the deck of a pirate brig, Richard Cutler had been stabbed in the back with a cutlass and had collapsed onto the foredeck. Just as the pirate was preparing to finish him off, a well-placed shot discharged from Brengle's pistol shattered the pirate's skull. Several months later Richard returned the favor while leading a raiding party against a pirate stronghold nestled within a complex of mangrove islets off the southwest coast of Florida. Having looked into the dark eyes of death, Jack Brengle later credited his deliverance to the man who, as he put it, "instantly and without question put his own life on the line to save mine."

For exemplary service to the Home Squadron in expunging the curse of piracy in southern waters, First Lieutenant Richard Cutler was promoted to the rank of captain, and Acting Second Lieutenant Jack Brengle was promoted to first lieutenant.

"Is Mr. Brengle truly available?" Richard had pressed Henshaw over lunch. There was a hesitancy in his voice that Henshaw found curious.

"He is," the secretary assured him. "His last appointment was a brief one, through no fault of his own. And as I strongly suspected that you would choose him to serve as your executive officer, I took the liberty of personally verifying that fact. I didn't think you would object."

"I certainly don't object, sir," Richard said. "I hold Mr. Brengle in the highest personal and professional regard. It's just that . . ."

"It's just what, Mr. Cutler?"

Richard took a breath. "Sir, with respect to all concerned, Jack Brengle deserves the honor of commanding *Suwannee* as much as I do. Perhaps more."

Henshaw nodded knowingly. "Your superiors would not necessarily disagree with that statement. But at the moment, you hold the rank of captain and Mr. Brengle does not. I can assure you, his many contributions to our country have not gone unnoticed. His time will come, have no doubts. In the meantime, his most ardent desire is to serve with you on *Suwannee*. I know that you two will make a fine team."

Richard nodded as he cut slowly into a slab of roast beef. "That we will, sir."

With Jack Brengle on board, matters moved forward swiftly. Ted Wheeler, a grizzled seadog with decades of blue-water experience under his belt, was signed on as sailing master. The junior commissioned officers followed, then the warrant officers and senior petty officers responsible for recruiting the junior petty officers and able seamen on whom the proper evolutions of sail and paddle blades would turn. By design, Richard Cutler left that level of decision-making to those who would provide day-to-day oversight to the recruits. He believed that such a laissez-faire approach by the captain ensured respect and loyalty going both up and down the chain of command. It was another lesson taught to him by his father, who had learned it from his own father, who had learned it from John Paul Jones, the legendary Scottish-born sea captain with whom Richard's grandfather had served during the Revolutionary War.

On a morning in mid-September, when the first inklings of a changing season tinged the foliage of the nation's capital, Richard met with his executive officer in *Suwannee*'s stern cabin. At the conclusion of their discussion, he shook Brengle's hand. "She's in your good care, Jack," he said, as their eyes locked. "I'm due to return in two or three weeks' time. She did well on the first leg of her shakedown cruise, and we have every reason to believe our good fortune will continue. We are assembling a fine crew, thanks to your good efforts—the best of the best. Secretary Henshaw has promised to do whatever is necessary to outfit *Suwannee* the way we want and to keep everything on schedule. He will give whatever you and Peter require."

Peter Andrews, *Suwannee*'s recently appointed second lieutenant, was a seasoned sea officer from Stonington, Connecticut, who had a well-earned reputation for quick thinking and decisive action when such were required.

Jack Brengle smiled. Equal in height to his captain at six feet, he likewise possessed the physical characteristics that made many people

consider him a handsome and refined man. There, however, the similar-
ities ended. Brengle's eyes were granite gray, not hazel, and his hair and
short-clipped sideburns were not chestnut but as dark as the coal being
shoveled into *Suwannee*'s hold. "Thank you, Richard," he said. "Peter and
I will see to every detail. You needn't worry about anything. Enjoy your
cruise. Please pass on my best wishes to your dear mother and the rest
of your family."

"With pleasure, Jack."

Of the two weeks Richard had allotted for this visit to his family's home
in Massachusetts, half of that time would be consumed at sea. When not
in his cabin reviewing official dispatches or absorbed in the diaries and
three ships' logs of Captain James Cook written during his explorations
of the Great South Sea, Richard sat up on deck, his back to the mainmast, enjoying the sea air and the warmth of the sun on his face.

All he had heard and read seemed to indicate that Australia was a
land of contradictions—a place where the best and worst of the human
condition vied for prominence, but where former convicts and prison
guards today worked side by side as equals to build a better life for
themselves and the settlers flooding into the new colony. Only the indigenous population seemed to be suffering at the hands of the English,
not so much from strict colonial policies, Richard suspected, as from
state-sponsored neglect and indifference.

Long Wharf in Boston Harbor was the brig's destination, but it was
not Richard's destination this day, even though it housed the headquarters of Cutler & Sons, the family's business and primary source of income
since 1755. Just as it had in his youth, the half-mile length of Long
Wharf comprised a commercial hub that rivaled any seaport in the world.
However awe-inspiring and educational the workstations, warehouses,
and counting houses of corporate America might be to Richard—and
to his family, who were a key component of it—he did not linger there
longer than necessary.

Following a brief meeting with Charles Hanley, director of the Boston office of Cutler & Sons, Richard boarded a company packet boat

bound for Hingham. Before the little sloop raised sail on her single mast, he confirmed to Hanley that he would return to Long Wharf in four days to participate in the family conference planned for that date.

Arriving in Hingham was always a homecoming for Richard. Today, in 1843, it was little changed from the way he remembered it in the days of his grandparents. Snug and well-kept clapboard homes with gable roofs interspersed with white-steepled churches—most of them Congregational in the Puritan tradition—graced the streets and byways of the scenic seaside town first settled by the English two centuries earlier. Although Richard had been born and spent his early childhood in Virginia, he had come to Hingham for family gatherings many times over the years. Hingham was, after all, at the core of his heritage. It was here that he had received nourishment for body and soul following the death of his father. After a ten-year battle, James Cutler had finally succumbed to complications resulting from the loss of his left arm during the British burning of Washington in 1814. With the cooperation of the U.S. Navy, the remains of Captain James Cutler were transported from Virginia to Hingham and interred in the family plot near First Parish Church. The captain's widow and her only child, young Richard, took up residence not far away.

The distance from Crow Point, where the sloop tied up, to the house that was his journey's end was about a mile. Richard lost no time covering it. The day was quintessential New England in autumn: a pleasant sun shining in an endless blue sky, air deliciously cool in the shade of oaks and elms blazing with amber and scarlet leaves that seemed to give off a warmth of their own. He acknowledged the townspeople he recognized as he strode along North Street but did not stop to converse with any of them. Past the intersection with Main Street, he espied the familiar flagstone pathway leading to the two-story dwelling set back from the street.

As he approached the front stoop, he glimpsed the swish of a curtain on a front parlor window. Moments later the door was opened by an elegantly dressed middle-aged woman who hurried outside to enfold her son in her arms.

"My dear Richard! You're home," she cried with joy. "I can't believe it. You are truly home. I have missed you so very much."

"Yes, Mother," Richard said, clasping Melinda Cutler to him. "I'm home. And I have missed you equally as much." He held her away from him to get a good look at her. Her fair hair held a few more gray streaks, but she looked relaxed and happy.

Behind her Richard noted a figure stepping through the front door and onto the front porch. Richard blinked at this apparition: a tall, clean-shaven man elegantly dressed from the black silk kerchief at his neck to the silver-buckled shoes on his feet. His yellow waistcoat of the finest linen bespoke wealth—or the appearance of it. Seconds ticked by as Richard struggled to recall where he had seen the man before. The familiar stranger hung back by the door, his thumbs hooked into his trouser pockets, looking ill at ease despite his efforts to project an air of confidence. He gave Richard a crooked and, it seemed to Richard, insincere smile.

"Richard," his mother said, slipping from her son's embrace, "you remember Mr. Sturgis, don't you? Mr. Harlan Sturgis? He was a dear friend of your father's. And now he is a dear friend of mine. Will you come inside and join us for tea? We've been anxiously awaiting you."

Richard kept his gaze steadily on Sturgis, still wondering. A sudden flash of remembrance brought a past conversation into clearer focus. "Of course, Mother," he said without much enthusiasm. "Of course."

CHAPTER 3

RICHARD WAS STILL CONCERNED ABOUT STURGIS WEEKS LATER, although commanding *Suwannee* required most of his attention. Lying in his cozy bed early one morning, with Anne sleeping soundly beside him, he mulled over his visit to Hingham yet again. Harlan Sturgis was not the man his mother thought he was. He had been an acquaintance of James Cutler, true, but certainly not a friend. His father had, in fact, warned him about men like Sturgis who made a living by preying on newly widowed and otherwise vulnerable women. But for the life of him Richard could not think what to say or do about it. Those few days with his mother in Hingham convinced him that she was finally working through her grief and was now open to the possibility of a new life without his father. Who was he to deny her that? Of greater relevance, Melinda Cutler was a woman of sound intellect and strong moral fiber. He had extracted a promise from her to do nothing rash and to give the relationship time, but other than that he could only trust her to handle the situation.

Another significant matter weighed on his mind as well. The family conference had gone as expected until the end of the meeting when Philip Seymour, the aging director of Cutler & Sons, announced his intention to retire in two years. Speaking for the family, the other directors, and the shareholders of Cutler & Sons, he had asked Richard Cutler to take over the reins of management and guide the company through the challenges of the future. Was he ready to give up the Navy? Richard wasn't certain.

He lay still, listening to his ship. He heard nothing out of the ordinary: no ship's bell, no lookout's cry, no jolt of any kind. All seemed well. The footfalls he heard on the quarterdeck directly above him were controlled and unhurried. His sea senses thus assured him that all was as it should be. The good fortune they had experienced for the past two months continued unabated. If the wind had held steady through the night, as it apparently had, *Suwannee* would be making a comfortable six, maybe seven knots up and over the South Atlantic rollers—another two hundred miles since yesterday, the frigate's average daily run since leaving the Virginia Capes in late October.

He felt Anne stir beside him. Breathing a contented sigh, she reached out and rested her hand on his naked chest. Her eyes flew open. "Richard, you're still here," she exclaimed. "How very lovely."

"Of course I'm here, my love," he said as he turned on his side to face her. "It's Christmas Day, remember? Merry Christmas, Mrs. Cutler."

"Christmas? Ah, so it is." Anne Cutler stretched and yawned. "So that's how it's to be, is it? My Christmas present is you in bed with me for an extra few minutes?"

"Alas, my dear, I'm afraid that is all I have to offer you this year."

"I'll take it, and gladly. You are all I want and all I need." Anne curled up close to him and caressed the side of his face. "Truly I desire nothing more, Richard. Nothing."

"It's the same for me, my darling." Richard reached out for her, a surge of desire overcoming his sense of duty as the captain of a ship at sea approaching land after two months. "Dear God, I love you, Anne. I swear I want you again and again. I shall never tire of you."

"See that you don't," she murmured, feeling the strength in his loins hard against her own mounting desire.

They broke apart when a tentative knock sounded on the cabin door.

Richard made a wry face. "Sorry, my love," he said dolefully. "Duty beckons." He sat up and glowered at the door. "Yes? What is it?"

"Sorry to disturb, Captain," he heard the apologetic voice of Jonty Montgomery, the youngest of the ship's eight midshipmen. His sense of duty and decorum went well beyond his fourteen years, and he was a favorite of officers and crew alike, and particularly of Anne. "Mr. Andrews's compliments, sir, and we have raised Cape L'Agulhas."

"Thank you, Mr. Montgomery," Richard called out. "Please inform Mr. Andrews that I shall be on deck shortly."

"Aye, aye, Captain," the midshipman called back. They heard him walk across the captain's day cabin and then the sound of the outer door closing shut.

"Ah, so we have managed to raise something else this morning," Anne teased as Richard slid out of bed and into a pair of buff trousers meticulously laid out the evening before by his steward, Torben Larsen.

Richard chuckled. "Cape L'Agulhas marks the southernmost tip of the African continent," he said as he adjusted his belt. "Of greater importance, it lies only a hundred miles from Cape Town. Tonight, my dear, we shall dine in style ashore, and after that we will pick up where we left off here."

"How marvelous. Dry land and fresh victuals—now *that* is a worthy Christmas present. May I come up and see?"

Richard finished buttoning his white linen shirt and carefully tucked its hem into his breeches. "My dear lady, why would you not? You have been 'coming up to see' and offer comments since the day we set sail. I shouldn't wonder if the crew sometimes questions who is the captain of this vessel." He shrugged on his undress uniform coat as Anne climbed out of bed.

"Turn around," she said. She brushed the shoulders of his coat with her hand, pausing to push aside his hair and kiss the endearing birthmark on the back of his neck.

"How do I look?" he asked, turning around to face her.

"Hmm." She narrowed her eyes, studied him up and down. "Ready to take on the direst, darkest secrets of Africa, I'd say."

"See you topside," he said grinning.

He kissed her on the cheek and left their sleeping cuddy to walk through his day cabin, where the ship's business was conducted and where they took their meals, often with guests from the ranks of the commissioned and senior warrant officers. When he opened the outer door leading onto the 196-foot gun deck, a corporal of the Marine guard—one of ten Marines and four Marine drummer boys on board—saluted him. Richard returned the salute and hurried up the aft companionway to the weather deck and another in a long string of warm, sunny, breezy days. A steady westerly ruffled his shirt and kept the mainsails, topsail, mizzen, and twin jibs hauled tight as *Suwannee* knifed through the untroubled waters on a broad reach.

His officer corps was waiting for him by the wheel and binnacle. "Good morning and Merry Christmas, Mr. Andrews," Richard said to the senior watch officer. "And a merry Christmas to you, Mr. Brengle. And to you, Mr. Weeks," he said to his third lieutenant. A young bull of a man, Weeks was the one officer Richard had not met prior to this cruise. The lieutenant had five years of service in the Navy, and he came to *Suwannee* recommended by two experienced sea captains and a senator from Maryland.

On more than one occasion while crossing the Atlantic, Richard had wondered what those three individuals had seen in Langston Weeks. In his view Weeks had more sail about him than ballast, and his advancements had more to do with patronage than performance. Still, he did his job. He carried out orders from his superiors and delivered orders to the men in a way that was not condescending. The men seemed to respect Weeks and did what he told them to do without much complaint. For that obedience Richard was grateful, though he wished he received that same level of obedience from Weeks. The third lieutenant carried out his own orders and duties, but far too often with a sullen air bordering on insolence and, on rare occasions, borderline insubordination. Weeks, Richard concluded, had trouble with authority, a taboo in any military service. He kept a wary eye on the young man.

Jack Brengle also had misgivings about Weeks. "I warrant he's earned a visit to Mr. Crocker," Brengle had once remarked in private after Weeks had complied with an order with what Brengle deemed less than adequate enthusiasm. Crocker, the headmaster of Governor Dummer Academy, had meted out stern discipline to unruly students. "Crocker certainly straightened me out."

"And me," Richard added with a grin. "It took some doing, as I recall. We were often hauled in there together."

Anne also had reservations about Weeks. "I would sooner trust a snake under a rock," she had confided to her husband one evening after supper. "I wish he was more like Lieutenant Donahue." She was referring to the steely-eyed captain of Marines, a career officer from South Carolina who was very demanding of his men yet very charming at the dinner table. "Mr. Weeks always looks as though he's about to register a complaint about something."

Richard agreed but saw no point in flogging the issue. There was not much he could do about Weeks unless he crossed a line that demanded disciplinary action. Thus far, he had not.

"Merry Christmas," his officers returned. "To you and to Mrs. Cutler."

"Thank you, gentlemen." Richard looked at his senior watch officer. "What do we have, Mr. Andrews?"

Andrews squeezed the front end of his uniform bicorne hat. "As Mr. Montgomery has advised you, we have raised Cape L'Agulhas. At first sighting I ordered Mr. Wheeler to shape a new course to northward, direct to Cape Town."

"Very well, Mr. Andrews," Richard said. He accepted a long glass from a midshipman and held it steady at his right eye. Satisfied that what he saw was indeed Cape L'Agulhas, he collapsed the glass and handed it back. "At one bell we shall douse all sail and go in under steam. We need to give the engine a workout before we dock. Mr. Jamison," he said to a midshipman, "please inform Mr. Cowles."

"Aye, aye, sir," Jason Jamison said as he hurried off to find Jacob Cowles, the burly, no-nonsense boatswain. To the other officers gathered there Richard said, "Gentlemen, we shall have three days in Cape Town, ample time to resupply and stretch our legs. The men will be permitted shore leave in shifts under the strict parameters we discussed earlier. It will not hurt to remind them that how we conduct ourselves reflects on our ship and our country. Mr. Weeks, I am putting you in charge of the rotations and protocols, as well as any disciplinary measures that may be required. Understood?"

"Aye, Captain."

"Now, gentlemen," Richard said, "if you will excuse me . . ."

Anne had emerged on deck, but as usual she was keeping close to the stern railing, not wanting to distract any man from his duties, least of all her husband. Only when she saw him turn from his officers and walk toward her did she step toward him.

"Do you see those darker waters yonder?" he said to her, pointing eastward. "That is the Indian Ocean. At the moment we are at the point where two great oceans converge. Have a look. Such a phenomenon is a rare sight."

"My word," she said, taking a closer look. "It's as though God himself has drawn a line separating the blue of the Indian Ocean from the green of the Atlantic."

"Just so." He pointed northward. "And do you see the speck of land on the horizon? Just to the right of the jib boom? That, my dear, is Table Mountain. It rises 3,500 feet above a community of twenty-three thousand souls—Dutch mostly, but with a few English, Germans, Spaniards, Portuguese, and others. Are you happy to see land again?"

"Oh, yes," she said fervently. "It's beautiful." She squeezed his hand. "Although I must confess that after being under sail for so long, seeing the coast of Greenland looming on the horizon would please me equally."

Richard laughed and offered her his arm. "My lady, will you accompany me? We are approaching the change of watch, and once the engines fire up, we'll have no more peace and serenity, I'm afraid. In the meantime, I would like for us to tour the ship and wish the crew a merry Christmas."

Three days later, with the exotic flavors of Cape Town lingering in their minds, *Suwannee*'s refreshed crew set sail on a darkening sea. Her course would take them northward beyond the grip of the Agulhas Current off Mozambique, then northeast past the Seychelles and Maldives before turning eastward south of Ceylon. Her destination was the Straits of Malacca, a narrow passageway running between the Maylay Peninsula and the island of Sumatra, from there to the Sunda Strait connecting the Java Sea to the Indian Ocean. With the winds turning fluky as the frigate approached the complex of islands that together constituted the Dutch East Indies, Richard gave the order to switch from sail to steam. The 1,500-horsepower Mehaffy & Company steam engine carried *Suwannee* along at a comfortable eleven knots, each churn of the starboard-side paddles propelling her onward through the Indian Ocean under a long ribbon of black smoke streaming from the tall smokestack amidships.

The use of steam gave the men a respite from working the sails, although that was rarely a rigorous task under the influence of predictable winds and, of greater importance, the eastward-flowing South Atlantic Gyre, an ocean current used for centuries by mariners sailing from North or South America to Africa and beyond. As they had on the Atlantic crossing, *Suwannee's* 209 hands settled into the traditional daily watch bill that clocked a day at sea through five four-hour watches and two two-hour dogwatches in the late afternoon and evening.

Unless weather or sea conditions prevented it, Richard insisted on daily gun drills, which were normally conducted after dinner during the afternoon watch. *Suwannee* carried ten 32-pounder long guns, five on each side of the gun deck. Each was a muzzle-loading gun requiring a crew of six men to service it properly. With the cry, *"Beat to quarters!"* young Marine drummers on the weather deck and gun deck launched into a staccato tattoo that sent the entire crew to battle stations amid the shriek of bosuns' pipes. Peter Andrews, as second lieutenant, assumed overall command on the gun deck, with support from Lieutenant Weeks, six of the eight midshipmen, and a pool of gunner's mates. The objectives of the drill were several, but to Richard's mind two stood out: to exercise the men, and to teach them how to work together as an operating unit in the elusive quest for perfection. Anne Cutler watched the daily practices with special interest and a sharp eye.

"I am most impressed with the crew's progress, Richard," she said one evening after they had dined on the last of the fresh provisions loaded on board at Cape Town. "I am hardly an expert, of course, but I have noted that the men were hard-pressed to complete one or two evolutions per minute when you first began the drills. This afternoon they easily managed three."

Richard twirled the stem of his wineglass between thumb and forefinger. "Which means," he pointed out, "that we now have twice the firepower per minute than we had when this voyage began. I am impressed that you have given these drills such close scrutiny."

Anne shrugged. "I find them fascinating. Besides, there is not much else for a lady to do on a summer's afternoon on board ship. It gets rather warm in our quarters, and the boundaries of what I can and cannot do, and where I can and cannot go, are strictly drawn."

Richard nodded sympathetically. "I know they are, my dear, and I apologize. But it can't be helped. I would do anything for you, but I hardly know what to recommend to relieve boredom at sea. It's something I have never experienced. But take heart. After we reach Batavia, in several weeks' time, we'll be on the last leg of our cruise to Sydney."

"On the outbound voyage, yes," Anne said, adding, "then we'll have to do it all again, in reverse."

"Do you miss home very much?" he asked, not for the first time.

"Yes, and no. I miss George and Cassandra, of course, and our friends in Washington. But home for me is where you are, Richard. That means that, for now, my home is here in this ship's cabin. It may not be my parents' country manor in Hampshire, and it may not be the home my father envisioned for me, but it is my home nonetheless, and I am very pleased with it."

Richard reached a hand across the table. "I want to show you the world, Anne. I want to *give* you the world." He gave her hand a squeeze. "I'm sorry you're bored," he said softly.

"Nonsense, Richard," Anne scoffed. "Who said anything about being bored? Not me. If that is what you think, you are wrong. I am enjoying this voyage immensely. Our time together has been an immeasurable gift. How many married couples have the opportunity to know one another so completely? I am an Englishwoman who in a few months will be returning to my home in the United States with my husband after traversing two oceans and visiting three continents. Far from finding it boring, I find it exhilarating! And the best part? We will be returning home together with our firstborn, a glorious compensation for whatever sacrifices we may have had to endure on this voyage."

She said it so matter-of-factly that it took several moments for the full weight of what she had said to register. Richard sat in stunned silence that was broken only by the rhythmic ticking of the mantel clock and the distant thrum of the engine far belowdecks. "Anne," he managed at length, "are you telling me what I think you're telling me?"

She nodded. "I believe I am, my darling man. We are going to be parents. What do you think about that?" She looked anxiously at him. "Are you pleased?"

"Am I pleased? My God, yes!" he exclaimed, his mind awhirl. "Have you consulted Dr. Green?"

She laughed. "No need for that. A woman tends to know what to do in this situation without having to consult a ship's surgeon—who likely knows next to nothing about it. I assure you, everything is as it should be, including the morning nausea you have been fortunate to miss by being up on deck so early. No, my love, we have a healthy baby on the way. You needn't worry about either of us. But please, if you don't mind, let us keep this a secret until we reach Sydney. There will be enough whispering going on behind our backs on the voyage home when my condition is obvious."

Richard nodded his agreement. He scraped back his chair, came around the table, dropped to a knee, and threw his arms around her waist. "And to again answer you question, yes, I am pleased. You have made me very, very happy." He looked up into her leaf-green eyes. "How far along are you, do you think?"

"I think between eight and ten weeks. For a woman, there are telltale signs after a month, and certainly after two months. I waited to be sure before I said anything to you. We have prayed for a child for so long." When Richard appeared lost in thought, she pulled on his ears. "Making some calculations, are you?"

"I am. We should reach Sydney in less than two months. By then you will be nearly halfway along. I know we had planned to spend only a month in Sydney, but why not extend our stay until the baby is born? We cannot risk having the baby born at sea. My superiors in Washington will understand, especially if our mission is successful, which it will be. After all, it was their idea. In the meantime, your brother and I will move mountains to ensure your care and comfort."

"I know you will," she agreed. Her eyes suddenly lit up. "I have a brilliant idea! If our child is a boy, we will call him 'Sydney!' Sydney Cutler. It has a nice ring to it. And how terribly fitting!"

He stood up, breathing in the fragrance of her signature gardenia perfume. He could not stop grinning. "We'll see, my love. I do like the name, but we will have plenty of time to consider all that. For the moment, we must do something to commemorate this blessed news."

"What do you have in mind?" she asked.

He took her in his arms. "I can think of several possibilities," he murmured, his voice becoming thick with desire elevated by joy, "that have worked quite well in the past."

"Another fine day, Captain," Ted Wheeler remarked offhandedly when Richard appeared on deck later that day. "We've had more than our fair share of them lately."

"Are you complaining, Mr. Wheeler? Getting a bit dull for you, is it?"

The sailing master chuckled. "Hardly that, sir."

The two of them were on the quarterdeck in company with Jack Brengle, Langston Weeks, and two midshipmen. Two quartermaster's mates worked the wheel as the more senior officers, along with the four lookouts high up in the rigging, searched the eastern horizon for the first sight of land. "'Tis just that I've never seen the like of this cruise in all my years at sea. Hardly a foul wind since leaving the Chesapeake. And my sea sense tells me that our good fortune will continue."

As if to prove his point, he glanced up at the cerulean sky dotted with puffs of sugar clouds. The hot yellow sun brought beads of sweat to exposed skin. A lazy westerly breeze provided neither relief nor propulsion, which was why *Suwannee* was sailing under steam.

"May your sea sense prove correct," Brengle remarked by the binnacle. He regarded Wheeler as a good man and an excellent sailor, but also a bit too much of a talker. "We are making excellent time, I agree."

"Your sea sense had damn well better be correct," Weeks put in testily. "The sooner we get to where we're going, the sooner we can head back to where we came from. You'd have to be either an idiot or a saint to live in this godforsaken climate. Give me the depth of winter in Maine any day."

Richard kept his glass steady at his eye. "Mr. Weeks," he said, his voice conveying a warning, "we have been through this before. Too many times. Comments like that serve no purpose. In the future, please refrain from uttering them. Either say something of value or say nothing at all. Do you understand me?"

Weeks said nothing.

"Do you *understand* me?" Richard repeated acidly.

"I do," Weeks retorted.

"I do, *sir*!" Richard snapped.

Before Weeks could speak again, a cry from high atop the foremast crosstrees grabbed their attention.

"Deck, there! Land ho!" Then, a moment later, with a great deal more urgency, "Sails ho!"

Stationed directly below the lookout on the weather deck, Senior Midshipman Thomas Talmadge. Talmadge shielded his eyes and peered up into the fierce equatorial sun. "Where away?" he shouted up through cupped hands.

"The land is ahead, off to port!" The lookout pointed in the general direction. "And sir, I see three sets of canvas off to starboard. One is a merchantman. The other two are lateen-rigged and seem to be in pursuit of her."

"Ensigns? Other identification?"

"None I can make out, sir."

"Very well, Simpson. I shall inform the captain."

The captain has already been informed, Richard thought, having clearly heard the lookout's warning. As he watched Talmadge stride aft toward the quarterdeck to give him official notice, he considered his choices. They were a fair way through the Malacca Strait, so the land that Henry Simpson had spotted ahead was likely the island of Java. These were the waters of the fabled Sunda Strait, the gateway to the 17,500 islands of the East Indian archipelago and the passage through which merchantmen bound for Batavia were inevitably funneled. Which was why the two sets of lateen sails Simpson reported had sinister implications.

"Mr. Zabriskie!" he barked.

The midshipman snapped to. "Sir!"

"Go below to my cabin and advise Mrs. Cutler to stay below until further notice. Then report back here."

"Aye, aye, sir." Hugh Zabriskie saluted and was off.

"Mr. Wheeler," Richard called to the sailing master. "Bring her up to a new course of sou'east, a half east."

"Sou'east, a half east, aye, Captain."

Moments later, *Suwannee* responded to the spin of the wheel.

Brengle sidestepped closer. "Going after them, Captain?"

Richard shook his head. "Don't know at this stage. We need to determine what is happening and if in fact our services are required." He handed Brengle his glass. "I need your eyes up there, Jack. Light aloft and tell me what you see."

Brengle took the glass, returning the salute of Midshipman Talmadge as he strode forward to deliver a report that by now had become superfluous. At the foremast chain-wale Brengle stepped onto the ratlines of the starboard shrouds and jig-jagged his way upward, mindful to keep looking up, never down at the deck growing ever smaller beneath him. At the foretop, he made to transfer to the narrower shrouds leading to the crosstrees at the juncture of the topmast and topgallant mast but decided against it. At this height, he could clearly see the scene unfolding ahead. After a slow sweep with the glass, he slid hand-under-hand down a backstay to the weather deck.

"Pirates, sir," he reported on the quarterdeck. "They're hard after a brig, Spanish by the look of her. They're almost within cannon shot of her and closing fast."

"Very well. Give me full steam. Everything we've got. And beat to quarters."

"It's not our fight, Richard," Brengle cautioned in a low voice.

"To the contrary, Jack, it is. Now beat to quarters. Mr. Andrews, loose the guns, both sides, and stand by."

Brengle took a speaking trumpet from its becket by the binnacle and stepped forward. "We shall beat to quarters!" he announced. "This is not a drill! I repeat: *This is not a drill!*"

Amid a torrent of drum rolls and pipes, *Suwannee*'s crew sprang into action. For most, this would be their first time sailing into a fight. As if to underscore the gravity of what they were about, the first roll of cannon fire sounded ahead in the distance. On both sides of the American frigate, the massive maws of the ship's 32-pounder guns were run out.

"Steady as she goes, Mr. Wheeler," Richard shouted.

"Steady as she goes, aye, Captain!"

Richard strode forward to where the bowsprit began its upward thrust. With the ship running at full tilt—nearly twice the speed of the other three vessels—and the wind whipping up a froth in these less protected approaches to the Java Sea, cresting waves thumped hard against the starboard bow and threw up wisps of spray in tiny rainbows that were visible one moment, gone the next.

Through his glass Richard saw the two pirate vessels, one on the merchantman's starboard quarter, the other on her port quarter, giving the impression of a mammoth nutcracker closing in on its quarry, a vessel flying the yellow-and-red flag of Spain. Ahead lay Cape Tua on the southeastern tip of Sumatra. Charts indicated deep water where they were, but the waters off Java, on the other side of the strait, harbored hazardous shoals and treacherous tidal currents. Could the merchant brig weather Cape Tua on her current heading and then outrun her pursuers? Richard doubted it. The two pirate vessels were fast, and the merchantman was encumbered by the design of her hull and the weight of her cargo. She was built for capacity not speed. Even if she managed to clear the point of land, on her own she was lost.

The pirate vessel gaining on the merchantman's starboard quarter opened fire. The shot glanced off the brig's stern. Another shot rang out from a bow chaser on the other vessel. By now, the Spaniard had only one thing working in her favor, and the pirates had yet to see it. Their eyes were glued ahead at the fruit ripe for picking.

Richard strode to mid-deck and cupped both hands at his mouth. "Mr. Wheeler," he shouted aft, "lay her between the lateens. Mr. Andrews!" he called below.

"Aye, sir," the second lieutenant called up.

"Are the guns ready?"

"Loaded and ready, Captain!"

"At my command!"

By now, the upwind pirate vessel had noticed the threat fast approaching from astern. It bore off, making for the islands of Krakatau and Sebesi hovering low on the horizon before the lush green mountains of Sumatra. The other pirate vessel—whether from greed or bravado or simple ignorance—remained on course in hot pursuit.

"Mr. Wheeler, bear off two points!"

The frigate's bow swung slightly to starboard.

"Fire as your guns bear, Mr. Andrews," Richard shouted, his cry followed a moment later by the strong voice of Peter Andrews: "Number 1 gun . . . *fire!*" Then, in rapid sequence: "Number 3 gun . . . *fire!* Number 5 gun . . . *fire!*"

With thunderous blasts the three forwardmost guns on the starboard side sent 32-pound fists of iron rocketing away. They slammed into the hull of the pirate vessel at a speed of a half-mile per second. The result was devastating. Through a cloud of acrid smoke, Richard and his officers watched in both satisfaction and horror as the volley caved in the port side of their quarry. Falling spars crashed down in a tangled jumble of standing and running rigging. One shot punched through the wooden railing, throwing jagged wooden shards into the air with the deadly force of spears hurled at point-blank range. A distant cacophony of screams confirmed that more than one spear had found its mark. Within moments, a proud vessel had been pulverized into kindling.

"*Cease fire!*" Richard cried down to the gun deck. The order was instantly relayed to the gun crews. The frigate's guns went silent.

"We should finish her off, Captain," the third lieutenant cried out, his dander up. "She's ours for the taking. I say, sink the bastard!"

"Belay that!" Richard shouted back, his voice loud and angry. "We have done our job, and we have done it well. We have delivered our message to the surviving vessel, and now we want that message delivered to the den of iniquity whence it came." He walked aft and nodded at his executive officer. "Take over, Jack. Bring her to half-speed and resume our original course for Peper Bay. I'm going below. An extra round of grog this evening for the entire ship's company."

"Aye, Captain."

Up ahead, the crew of the Spanish merchantman celebrated their deliverance with waving hats and a wild chorus of cheers.

CHAPTER 4

As *SUWANNEE* WOVE THROUGH THE TAPESTRY OF PICTURESQUE ISLETS protecting the approaches to Batavia Bay, those stationed on the weather deck gaped at the spectacle unfolding before them. Save for the frigate's captain and sailing master, none of them had ever sailed in these waters. Only the rhythmic throb of the steam engine and the dull suck of paddleboards disturbed the churchlike hush.

Ahead in the harbor, boats of all sizes and descriptions swung at anchor. Many were two-masted ketches with rounded bow and stern. Others were larger: brigs, brigantines, dhows, and different sorts of coastal traders. Still others were even larger. Of those, three were modern warships, each similar in design to *Suwannee* and each flying high on her peak a flag bearing the twenty-six stars and thirteen stripes of the United States of America. Like *Suwannee*, they were black-painted side-wheelers driven by steam or wind, and each had a white line painted along her two gun-port strakes. Although those ports were now closed, Richard Cutler knew that each ship carried a weight of ordnance similar to that of his own command. Anchored in the lead was *Tecumseh*, a 260-foot, 2,400-ton frigate recently built at the Norfolk Shipyard and now serving as flagship of the East India Squadron. It was on this ship that Richard expected to find Commodore Jason Strong and Special Envoy David Livermore, on whose negotiating skills the success of the upcoming parley in Sydney relied.

Suwannee turned lazily into the wind and tide. At Brengle's command, sailors in the bow let go anchor holds, sending the anchor rode rumbling out through the hawser hole. Seconds later, two great wrought-iron flukes splashed into the harbor. For the first time since departing Cape Town, the American frigate lay peacefully in a port of call.

Beyond the outer regions of the harbor, toward the long commercial wharves, stood a massive medieval-looking stone wall that once had defended the old capital city of Batavia. Save for a few tall wooden church steeples of Dutch colonial design, the ten-foot wall hid most of the city proper from the view of those out in the harbor. Beyond and to the right of the city walls rose gentle slopes of lush tropical rainforests; farther in the distance, jagged mountains capped with wisps of white smoke stood as stark reminders of the island's volcanic origins. It was what lay to the left of the city walls, however, that had caught Anne Cutler's attention as she studied the area through a glass.

The glass revealed a flat, largely treeless area of squalid stone huts and makeshift tents that provided shelter to the island's downtrodden underclass. Men, women, and children clad in ragged half-pants and conical hats seemed to drift about aimlessly like boats becalmed. Skinny dogs and naked, pot-bellied street urchins rummaged through the piles of garbage that were everywhere in evidence. As a child, Anne Braithwaite had not been permitted to witness at close hand the slums and shanties of London, Bristol, Manchester, or any other English city. She had nevertheless read and heard enough firsthand accounts of them to understand how wretched life in such places could be.

"Poor souls," she sighed to her husband on the quarterdeck, well aware of her own privilege. She handed him her glass. "Nobody should have to live like that."

Richard peered through the glass. "No, they shouldn't," he agreed.

"Who are they?"

"Chinese, mostly. I asked about them during my last visit here. They come to the Indies seeking work of any kind. Many surrendered everything they owned in China just to book passage here."

"Let me guess. When they get here, this is the new life they find," Anne said sadly. "Life in Batavia is no better for them than it was in China. Worse, even, because this land and its people and language are all foreign to them. Is no one willing to give them a chance?"

"A handful of the more fortunate ones do manage to find work," Richard said. "Cutler & Sons employs a few Chinese, and we pay them decent wages. Tomorrow, when I take you to Koningsplein, you will meet some of them. But you're right. Most of these poor sods are homeless and penniless. I'm afraid that won't change. We'll see more of this sort of thing in Sydney, you know."

"No doubt we will," she sighed.

Suwannee's entry into Batavia Bay had been duly noted on *Tecumseh* and the squadron's two other frigates anchored several hundred feet away. Her anchor had hardly touched bottom when the flagship dipped her ensign three times. *Suwannee* returned the salute. A half-hour later a ship's boat glided up alongside the newcomer's hull and a fore-and-aft hat appeared atop the rope ladder. When its bearer stepped through the port entry and doffed his hat to salute the quarterdeck, he was met by a squeal of pipes, a roll of drums, a side party of perfectly trimmed sailors, and the ship's second lieutenant and one of two senior midshipmen. The two lieutenants exchanged salutes as the fanfare ceased abruptly.

"I am Forrester Smith, third lieutenant of the United States ship of war *Tecumseh*, at your service. Whom do I have the honor of addressing?"

"I am Peter Andrews, second lieutenant. This young gentleman is Thomas Talmadge. Welcome aboard the United States ship of war *Suwannee*."

Smith bowed. "It is my distinct privilege to be here on the deck of your ship, Lieutenant." He reached into a side pocket of his uniform coat and produced a small white envelope with elaborate red lettering on one side and a red seal on the other. He handed the envelope to Andrews. "I bring an invitation to Captain and Mrs. Cutler to join Commodore Strong and Mr. David Livermore in *Tecumseh* this evening. The captains of the two other warships will also be in attendance. As stated in the invitation, the commodore insists that this will be a strictly social affair. The discussion of ships' business will be deferred until tomorrow morning."

"Understood, Lieutenant." Andrews handed the envelope to Talmadge, who strode aft with it.

"Thank you, Lieutenant," Smith said to Andrews. "I look forward to seeing you in the morning. In the meantime, I wish you a most pleasant good evening."

"And a most pleasant good evening to you, Lieutenant," Andrews said in reply.

The two officers again exchanged salutes. Amid another round of pipes and drums, and with a final salute to the frigate's quarterdeck, Smith descended the rope ladder to the ship's boat.

In deference to the intense heat and humidity, Commodore Jason Strong had relaxed what were normally two strict protocols. Rather than serving supper in his cabin, he had ordered it served on the quarterdeck under a canopy of loose canvas pulled over the mizzenmast boom and lashed to the starboard and port railings. In addition, as stressed in the invitation, guests were permitted to wear white cotton shirts and buff trousers, casual attire normally reserved for off-duty hours. Anne Cutler, delighted to have a chance to dress for dinner, wore a full-skirted dress of blue and cream French linen and a straw hat ringed with ribbons of the same colors. Around her neck hung the string of pearls her paternal grandmother had given to her on her eighteenth birthday. Her frock discreetly concealed the slight swelling of her belly.

The crisp white linen tablecloth featured an array of bone china, cut-glass crystal, and silver cutlery that seemed more in keeping with a state dinner than a casual shipboard supper. Three stewards, one of them *Suwannee's* own Torben Larsen, stood by to serve a variety of fish and chicken dishes, each punctuated with torch ginger, andaliman, and other local herbs and spices. Fresh local vegetables and fruits and choice wines brought up from Commodore Strong's private reserve complemented each dish.

The commodore was a bulldog of a man in stature with the jowls to match. Richard was well aware that Strong had earned every one of his stripes through dedication to the task at hand, a lifelong communion with the sea, and, above all else, an uncanny ability to anticipate the wants and needs of his superior officers.

"Good evening, my lady. Gentlemen," he greeted his guests when they were assembled on the quarterdeck, each standing before his or her assigned place setting designated by a handwritten card. "Please be seated." When his guests complied, he continued, "Tonight we shall dispense with formalities. Tomorrow morning at eight bells we will discuss the business at hand in my cabin. Kindly advise your executive officers that their attendance is, as they say in the Royal Navy, 'requested and required.'" After a round of polite titters died down, Strong concluded, with a bow to Anne, "My sole regret this evening is that tomorrow morning we shall be deprived of the company of so delightful and distinguished a guest as the wife of *Suwannee*'s captain."

Anne blushed prettily, a talent she had perfected long before today when, at the age of sixteen, she had curtsied to royalty and society at the court of King William IV. "Thank you, Commodore," she returned. "I am honored to be included in such august company this evening."

"We could promote Mrs. Cutler for the occasion, sir," exclaimed Terrence Neale, the competent and socially confident captain of *Columbia*. "How smashing she'd look in a captain's uniform!"

That remark set off good-natured laughter around the table, including from David Livermore, who up to this moment had offered the evening little beyond a scowl and studious silence.

"I shall give your proposal prayerful consideration, Captain Neale," Strong promised with a chuckle. "Now then, to equally important matters." He nodded toward the three stewards.

As the food was served and the wine poured, the conversation turned toward England, where young Queen Victoria and her prime minister, Sir Robert Peel, were gaining in popularity. As the wine flowed, further discussion centered on *Suwannee*'s brief engagement with the pirates, a tale that inspired several additional rounds of Bordeaux and tales. Anne Cutler had much to contribute in matters of public policy, diplomacy, and the ways of the sea. When pressed by Strong on the source of her keen knowledge of things nautical, Anne replied that she was from a Royal Navy family and promised that he would learn more about the Braithwaites when he spent some time with her brother in Sydney.

"My brother taught me much of what I know," she said. "My husband has taught me the rest."

"Then the United States is indebted to both men," Strong said gallantly. "I look forward to meeting the good admiral, Mrs. Cutler. Fortunately, that meeting is no longer in the distant future. We should reach Botany Bay in a matter of weeks. We'll accomplish what our government expects us to accomplish, and then *Suwannee* will be homeward bound. I wager you'll be back in Virginia by year's end."

In a movement so subtle that only her husband noticed it, Anne withdrew her hand from the top of the table to place it on her belly, rubbing it soothingly in a circular motion. "God willing," she said with a ghost of a smile.

Shaping a course from Java to New South Wales involved consideration of two possibilities. The first option was to follow a southeasterly course through the Arafura Sea west and south of New Guinea—so named because the island's topography reminded early Spanish and Portuguese explorers of the Guinea region of West Africa—through Torres Strait and the host of smaller islands that formed an umbrella over the northern Australian continent. Although this route was the shorter of the two, it came with challenges. Charts of the area were rudimentary at best, and many of the islands along the route were said to be inhabited by native peoples who practiced cannibalism, something so vile to the Western mind that even jests about it were considered taboo.

The alternate route, the one preferred by Commodore Strong, followed a southerly course along the western coast of Australia before turning east to run along the continent's southern coastline and the fortieth parallel—the "roaring forties" of sea legend. The Dutch seafarer Abel Tasman had hitched onto those strong westerly winds when he explored the Indian Ocean to the south of New Holland, as Tasman called Australia. This route involved mostly open water and thus few of the perils associated with the northern route. It did, however, have a well-deserved reputation for brutal storms fueled by warm ocean temperatures and the violent winds associated with the higher latitudes of the Southern

Ocean. On this route a ship had scant protection or refuge from the elements until reaching the Bass Strait between the island of Van Diemen's Land and the southeastern corner of Australia. Nonetheless, Commodore Strong was confident that no such protection would be needed on this voyage. Late summer was traditionally a season of accommodating weather in the Southern Hemisphere. Moreover, he had great confidence in the seaworthiness of his squadron's ships and the competence of their captains and crews.

"We have hardly had need of a compass or barometer, Captain, but I feel that's about to change," Ted Wheeler remarked to Richard Cutler on the quarterdeck early one March morning.

"What do you mean, Mr. Wheeler?" Richard asked, surprised by the sailing master's vague warning. Overhead, great white clouds of canvas billowed out before all three masts and above the jib boom.

"Only that our long spell of good weather may be nearing its end. The wind has backed and is beginning to kick up a fuss. Nothing serious, I should think, at least not yet. But it's worth keeping an eye on. Those cirrus clouds off to the west have been moving fast and thickening for the past few hours. As you know, that usually spells trouble. The weather may be fine at the moment, and we may be making a good twelve knots, but if this wind gets much worse and those clouds target us, we'll need to shorten sail and be quick about it." As if to underscore his words, a cresting wave of impressive size smacked against the frigate's port side, throwing up white spray and sending a shudder through the fabric of the ship.

Richard rubbed his hands together in the chill air and studied the sky to westward before glancing up at the foremast crosstrees.

Wheeler followed the captain's gaze. "Mr. Andrews has called Stokes down," he said. "We've no known navigational hazards ahead of us, and little chance of sighting another ship other than those in the squadron."

"Mr. Andrews was correct to do so," Richard said. He looked in the direction of land even though they were sailing too far offshore to see anything of consequence. There had not been much to see in that direction since *Suwannee* raised the northwestern tip of the continent. The terrain that was visible seemed incapable of supporting life, though Richard was aware that this rugged, brooding landscape did provide sustenance to man and beast alike. "We'll give it another half-hour," he said to Wheeler. "We may have to rely on dead reckoning if we lose sight of the squadron again. Let's pray we don't. I would certainly not look forward to that prospect."

Only once since leaving Java several weeks earlier had the four frigates become separated. Sailing in a diamond formation, *Tecumseh* held the lead position and *Suwannee* the left flank when the squadron was battered by a series of violent squalls under a coal-black sky that made it impossible to maintain visual contact despite the flags and lanterns set high in the masts of all four ships. By prearrangement, each of the frigates had made it solo to latitude 34 degrees south and longitude 116 degrees east. Although the destination was well defined, the getting there was not, and it was with a sigh of relief that Richard had raised the masts of two of the squadron's ships. The fourth warship steamed into sight the next morning.

At eight bells Lieutenant Weeks joined Richard on deck to assume the duties of senior watch officer. Lieutenant Brengle followed him, although as executive officer he was excused from watch duty.

"Captain," one of the younger midshipmen said in a voice of quiet concern, "I've been below to check the weatherglass."

"And? Is it holding steady?"

"No, suh, it is not," he said in a pronounced Southern accent. "It's at 29.43 and falling right quick. I believe we're in for a blow, suh."

"Just the facts, please, Mr. Zabriskie," Richard snapped irritably. "When reporting to a superior officer, commentary is neither necessary nor appreciated unless specifically requested. It's past time you remembered that."

Hugh Zabriskie hung his head. "Aye, aye, suh. Sorry, suh," he said contritely. "Ah won't let it happen again."

Richard clapped a hand on the youth's shoulder. "There's a good lad."

"It's nothing to worry about, Captain," Weeks interjected cavalierly. "A squall line, nothing more." His lips twisted in a slight sneer. "It's not the first time we've seen one."

Richard's jaw tightened. "A squall line is defined by dark clouds on the horizon, Mr. Weeks," he retorted. "Unless my eyes deceive me, the clouds coming at us are more white than black, and they have been building for some time. Those are the makings of a cyclone. This may not be the season for cyclones, but *that* is what is approaching. We shall brace for heavy weather. See to it."

Weeks rolled his eyes. "The storm will be spent in an hour, Captain. I hardly think such an order is necessary."

"That is your opinion, is it?" Richard snapped, his patience at an end. "Frankly, Mr. Weeks, at the moment I don't give a damn what you think. Either you carry out my order immediately or I shall have the master-at-arms confine you to quarters with all privileges suspended. Mr. Brengle, take note!"

He turned on his heel and went below to his cabin, ostensibly to check the barometer he kept there. In truth, he needed to calm his temper. He cursed himself for allowing his third lieutenant to get under his skin.

He stalked into his cabin, past Anne, who was reading at the desk, and checked his weatherglass: 28.99 and falling. Young Zabriskie was right! Frowning, he tapped a finger against the bulb at the base of the glass tube, as if to encourage the liquid inside to rise and stop its ominous fall.

Anne put aside her book. "What is it, Richard?" she asked.

"Storm's coming," he replied with what Anne recognized as forced equanimity. "We're taking all necessary precautions."

"How exciting! You know how I love a good storm at sea."

"Well, my dear, this one may be a storm only a mother could love."

"That bad?"

"Perhaps. Look through the porthole; you can see what's happening out there. I need to get back on deck. I will have someone check in on you from time to time if conditions continue to deteriorate."

"You will do no such thing!" she exclaimed. "See to your ship and your men. Don't worry about me. I will be fine. Everything down here will be as crisp as crust, I promise you. Besides, I have Torben to look after me."

Despite himself, Richard smiled at her use of a phrase from her childhood. "All right, then," he said, leaning down to kiss her forehead.

When he straightened, he chanced another glance at the weather-glass: 28.92. Never had he witnessed such a precipitous drop. Nor had he ever seen a maelstrom of clouds gather momentum so swiftly. He felt a sickening void in his gut.

Topside, conditions were worsening. With limitless fetch behind them and spurred on by near hurricane-force winds, massive mounds of green water were being whipped to a frenzy, unchecked and untamed, each wave capped with a white crest of spume blown wild by a gale intensifying by the minute. The sky had morphed from a clean blue to a dirty white that packed torrents of rain. But it was not the rain that worried Richard. It was the wind and the impact it was having on the churning sea.

Weeks stepped up to him at the helm and saluted. "The sails and guns are lashed down for heavy weather," he reported, his normal arrogance compromised by something Richard had never before detected in the man: fear. "The storm sails are set, and the hatches are battened down." He paused, then: "Captain, sir, what I said earlier was spoken out of turn and instantly regretted. I was wrong, and I apologize."

"Your apology is duly noted, Mr. Weeks," Richard replied with cold formality. He had to shout to be heard above the shriek and moan of the wind. He returned the salute of Jason Jamison, the signal midshipman, who had approached the helm. "Yes, Mr. Jamison?"

"Signal from flag, sir," Jamison shouted. With considerable difficulty, he had managed to decipher the flapping set of flags run up on the flagship's signal halyard. "The message reads: 'Disperse and proceed on your own to Bass Strait. Good luck.'"

"That's it? Good luck?"

"That's what it said, sir."

Richard looked into the distance and sighed. "Very well. Carry on, Mr. Jamison."

"Aye, aye, sir." The midshipman saluted and forced his way forward.

Brengle stepped close and cupped his hands around Richard's ear. "We could douse all sail, turn on the steam, and come around into the wind. Throw over a sea anchor. Ride it out."

"I considered that," Richard said. "The turn is too dangerous. I've ordered the trail wraps set out instead," he added, referring to a stretch of heavy rope cord cast out from the stern in a giant U-shaped loop, one end of the loop tied to a port stern cleat and the other end tied to a stern cleat on the starboard side. "That should prevent us from being pooped. We'll continue under storm sails and bare poles. We're not far from Bass Strait. My main concern is that we may pass it without knowing we have."

"We have our best eyes posted on the lower yardarms," Brengle said. "We'll sight that island."

Seconds moved grudgingly into minutes, minutes into hours. The dusk of day crept irrevocably into the black howl of night, then, eventually, after an impossibly long, dark age, into the gray, dreary, rain-sodden dawn of a new day. Still *Suwannee* fought on. Up and up each monstrous wave she climbed, hesitating at each peak as though to catch her breath before plunging down into the abyss with a great doleful groan of timbers. In the trough between two liquid mountains she battled for survival as seawater awash on the deck poured out through the scuppers and threatened to destabilize her. Belowdecks, sailors worked feverishly at the pumps to expel the water that was dripping and splashing into the bilge and up onto the orlop, making their best efforts seem futile. And then the frigate began yet another slow ascent into the howling madness to join battle anew against the combined forces of sky and sea surging down, up, and over her battered frame.

Men not required on deck were ordered below. Those needed on deck were tethered to a rope linked to a jackline running amidships from stem to stern. On the quarterdeck, Richard, his two senior officers, and the sailing master took shifts at the helm with two senior quartermaster's mates. Each man was tied by a rope to the mizzen mast and labored in thirty-minute rotations with all the strength he could muster to keep the bowsprit in line with the monstrous roll of the waves, aware that one brief lapse of concentration could do them all in.

Sleep, any sort of escape, was impossible. Although Richard sent his officers below for an hour for every hour served on deck, when the storm unleashed its full fury, conditions on the lower decks were not much better than on the weather deck. Richard did not go below. He worried about his wife but took comfort in her history of confronting violent Atlantic storms calmly.

Late in the afternoon of the second day, the crushing winds moderated sufficiently to allow the cook to prepare simple fare for the crew. Although the great rollers continued their wild eastward romp, a flame of hope began to flicker belowdecks. The misery of the men confined there began to ease along with the rain, although the rancid stench of vomit sloshing back and forth with the sluggish motions of the ship remained.

On the quarterdeck the mood continued bleak. The storm may have moderated, but the sea had not. It remained too threatening to attempt a reversal of course. Worse, Richard and his officers had no clear idea where they were. There was no doubt they had missed Bass Strait, and thus Van Diemen's Land as well. New South Wales and the continent of Australia lay somewhere in the distance behind them. But how far behind them? On what bearing? Where were the other ships of the squadron? The most rudimentary implements of navigation put them somewhere in the Tasman Sea, though their approximate position could not be determined without a reliable noon sun sighting. As the seas finally began to calm, Richard deemed it safe to turn the ship around and attempt a reciprocal course back toward Australia. The turn was executed without incident.

A renewed cranking and clanging of the pumps below signaled renewed hope among the crew.

After a quick word with Brengle, Richard went below to attend to Anne. As he made his way down the aft companionway, he heard it: cries of warning from the crew on deck followed by a thundering rumble somewhere behind the ship. He turned around and hurried back up. As he emerged on deck, he saw it: a gargantuan swash of foaming seawater roaring like every demon in hell was shrieking down upon them.

Richard stood stock still, as awestruck by this sickening sight of doom as the rest of those on deck. Incapable of action, he remained frozen in time and place. Then he remembered himself.

"*Hit the deck!*" he screamed. "*Everybody down! Hang on to something, anything! Hang on, boys!*"

He lunged for the helm and wrapped his arms around its base with a death grip just as the mammoth wave crashed over *Suwannee*'s stern in a cascade of water that lifted the frigate and keeled her over on her beam ends. The force of the impact sprang shrouds and stays on the mizzen and mainmasts. Both masts teetered as the frigate slowly, slowly stood upright, broached to and at the mercy of the boiling ocean. She was still afloat but swamped and taking on water at an alarming rate. Wave after wave stormed over her port bulwark, washed across her weather deck, and careened against the starboard bulwark, creating a backwash that spilled over her starboard rail.

Sputtering and gagging, Richard inched his arms up the base of the helm and with a mighty heave hauled himself to his feet. To his horror, he saw two of his crew off to starboard struggling desperately within a cresting wave. Helpless to save them, he crossed himself and whispered a quick prayer for divine deliverance.

The force of the impact had thrown his two senior lieutenants against the starboard bulwark, where they lay without moving. "Jack? Peter?" Richard called out to them. "Are you all right?" Brengle struggled to a kneeling position, gagging and coughing. He checked on Andrews and nodded at Richard, who began sloshing his way forward. Back and forth, up and down, *Suwannee* pitched and convulsed, no longer able to control a fate that by now seemed beyond doubt. Overhead, dappled sunlight began filtering through tiny breaks in the clouds.

Richard felt a hand on his arm. Brengle was on his feet, wavering and spitting out water and blood. Water dripped from his oilskins and down the exposed skin on his face. The whites of his eyes were streaked with red. "I'll see to the men," he wheezed. "You see to your wife."

Richard nodded. "Thank you, Jack. I won't be long. Break out the boats. We're taking on water everywhere. *Suwannee* can't last much longer."

"Not after that monstrosity. That was the biggest goddamn bastard I've ever seen." He clapped a hand on his friend's shoulder. "We'll make it, Richard," he said. "We've survived worse."

"Have we?" Richard countered. "If so, I don't recall it." As if to underscore his sarcasm, a powerful wave crashed against the hull, throwing both men off their feet as fresh assaults of seawater surged over the port railing to spill onto the weather deck and splash down onto the gun deck.

As Richard climbed down the aft companionway, his worst fears were confirmed. It was steady going despite the roiling ocean, and that was what troubled him. *Suwannee* had stabilized, yes, but that was because her 2,300-ton burthen had taken on so much water. She was a waterlogged slab of wood wallowing in the Tasman Sea. No longer was she going up and over the crests of waves; the crests of waves were now going up and over her.

As he stepped onto the gun deck, he saw what he had expected to see: a mess of ropes, barrels, wormers, rammers, and other gear strewn everywhere. Miraculously, no guns had torn loose from their breeching ropes, and in answer to his query, Midshipman Thomas Talmadge reported that to his reckoning no one had been grievously injured on the gun deck. The Marine corporal on guard duty before the captain's cabin offered the same report.

"Thank Christ for that," Richard said. Then, "Get everyone up on deck. Mr. Talmadge, you and Corporal Hanson take what men you need and go below to make sure no one is left behind. Handsomely, now!"

"The pumps, sir?"

"Keep them going as long as possible. It will buy us time."

"Aye, aye, Captain!" Talmadge said.

As Richard turned to the outer door of his cabin, it opened and Anne stumbled out with Torben Larsen right behind her. She was wet through, her hair was a jumble of tangles, and a cut on her lower lip and a nasty bruise on her forehead suggested she had taken a bad spill.

"Are we going down, Richard?" she asked anxiously.

He took her chin in his hand and gave her face a quick once-over. "Are you all right, Anne?"

"Certainly," she said, straightening her sleeves. "I am quite well."

What a woman she is! Richard thought. He detected a tremor in her voice but said nothing.

"What is happening?" she insisted. "Tell me!"

"You and Torben need to get on deck," Richard said forcefully.

Anne looked past him and saw a line of grim sailors making their way up to the weather deck.

"Torben," he said when Anne hesitated, "please take Mrs. Cutler on deck. Now! I will be up presently."

"Where are you going?" Anne demanded.

"To get my papers. I cannot leave the ship without them. Now, please go, my love!"

Richard squeezed her arm and entered the cabin. Here, too, water flowed across the swaying deck. The water coming in above was quickly finding its way below to the berthing deck, and from there down to the orlop. At his teak desk he pulled open a drawer and retrieved a packet carefully wrapped in oilskins. He undid the straps, unfolded the wrapping, and checked the contents. All there: the commission that identified him as a captain in the U.S. Navy and the orders he was to carry out, together with letters of introduction to those who would assist him. He re-secured the documents in the oilskins and tucked the packet deep inside a side pocket of his trousers. From another drawer he withdrew a small sea-service pistol, a watertight vial of powder, and five rounds of ammunition. These he also wrapped in oilskins before sliding them into the other pocket of his trousers. Only then did he make for the door. He paused briefly for a last look, then, with a sigh of regret, stepped out onto the gun deck.

Richard did not climb up. Instead, he climbed down a separate companionway to the berthing deck. Seawater sloshed down the wooden rungs of the ladder in a steady stream. Nothing of note caught his attention as he descended, either in the deserted wardroom at the stern or in the crew's quarters under the forecastle. He lingered a moment amid the disorder and felt the bow of the frigate turn sluggishly to starboard. He knew what Brengle was doing and nodded his approval.

"Is anybody down here?" he cried out. "Anybody?"

The ghastly moans and shrieks of a ship coming apart and the ominous sounds of water sloshing onto the decks below and above him were the only response.

As he continued down to the orlop deck, his foot slipped on the third rung of the ladder and he nearly lost his balance. Gripping a hand on the hatch coaming, he bent down to take a closer look. The midshipmen's mess, the ship's magazine and coal shuttles, and just about everything else on that lowest deck was either bobbing up and down on the water or submerged beneath it. Debris of every sort and description drifted about in a macabre dance to the rocking and rolling of the ship. He made a quick calculation: Unless the rate of taking on water was slowed—and with the slight turn of the ship he sensed that his officers were aware of that dire need—the frigate had precious little time to live.

Several minutes later he joined Anne and the frigate's crew on the weather deck. The heavy seas continued to batter the ship, but with less violence now. Dirty gray clouds still clogged the sky, but with less menace and with sustained breaks here and there between them. Of greater significance, after judicious and relentless use of the rudder at each wave's crest, giving the swamped vessel a brief surge forward and traction for the rudder, *Suwannee*'s jib boom was now pointed eastward in a following sea. Waves of green water continued to breach her stern, but the ever so slight adjusting of her course had granted the frigate a stay of execution.

Peter Andrews approached. "The boats are ready, Captain," he reported. "And they are provisioned, as ordered. How shall we man them?"

It was not a moot issue. During the past two hours Richard had thought hard about the answer to that question. *Suwannee* had four ships' boats that normally nested upside down in two sets of two boats between the main and mizzen masts. The four boats, now flipped over and slung overboard by a series of pulleys lashed to the booms, could not accommodate the entire ship's complement of two hundred souls in addition to the supplies necessary for their survival. Some of the crew would have to remain on board the doomed ship and take their chances. There was really no chance for any of them, Richard mused, those in the boats or those left on the ship. He would remain on the ship, of course, but what of Anne? Could he persuade her to take to a boat? To leave him behind for the sake of their baby? No, he concluded. She would see the hopelessness of their predicament and prefer to die with him.

Richard was about to reply to Andrews when he heard the cry, "Land ho!"

Midshipman Talmadge rushed forward. "Captain," he cried excitedly, "we have sighted land!"

"Where away?"

"Dead ahead, sir!"

Richard seized the midshipman's long glass and strode forward, feeling the eyes of the ship's complement follow him. At the foremast he climbed halfway up the ratlines and forced his right arm through and around the thick hempen strands of the shrouds before training the glass eastward. Yes, there it was: two jutting headlands with a considerable stretch of water separating them. On the southern headland he saw a high hill, a series of ghostly clouds hovering just above it. To a man, the ship's crew edged forward, as if by that simple motion the frigate could more expeditiously close the gap between them and deliverance.

Richard clambered down the shroud, jumped onto the deck, and strode aft. "Secure the provisions in the boats!" he cried out. "Everything else movable gets tossed overboard! And I want every other gun to blow a hole through its port. Roll the guns into the sea! We can't stop the water, but we can lighten the load! There," he shouted, jabbing his finger forward, "there lies our salvation!"

With a will born from newfound hope, the crew set about lightening the ship. Officers and sailors worked side by side or in relay teams to throw out whatever was expendable, no exceptions. Anne pitched in as explosion after explosion below on the gun deck signaled that the ship's tumblehome was being systematically demolished, in the process lightening the ship by three tons with each thunderous splash of black iron into the sea.

As the low-lying strips of land on the horizon slowly began to draw nearer and assumed distinct shapes and colors, even the naked eye could discern a substantial beach. A row of sand dunes on the northern headland provided a protective barrier for lush vegetation. Repeated sweeps of a long glass revealed no sign of human or animal life, only the occasional gull wheeling and diving in its timeless search for food from the sea.

"Make for that estuary, Jack," Richard said to Brengle at the helm. He pointed ahead at the substantial gap of water shimmering between the two landmasses. "If it's not an estuary, it's either the mouth of a large river or a natural harbor. Either way, we'll go in there and decide which shore offers us the better chance."

"Understood," Brengle said. "It shouldn't take us long to get there." Despite the ongoing peril and uncertainty of their plight, his face broke out in a grin. "See, Richard? I told you we'd make it."

"We're not there yet, Jack," Richard cautioned, adding soberly, "and we don't know what reception committee is awaiting our arrival."

As *Suwannee* edged toward the shore, with the eyes of every person on board focused on the land ahead, the inconceivable happened. A second rogue wave—not as big as the first one but packing a wallop nonetheless—careened down upon the helpless vessel's stern. The giant wave swamped the frigate yet again before plucking her up like a child's toy and hurling her forward in a rush of whitewater until, with a sickening jolt, she hit a sandbar and stopped dead. The sudden impact with the seabed at great speed created a vicious backwash. *Suwannee* lurched forward again, the sudden surge snatching sailors from their lee shelters and sweeping them overboard as the weakened masts snapped one by one.

Cursing himself for his inattention, Richard lunged toward Anne to pull her close and protect her. In those final few life-defining moments, they clung desperately to each other, their eyes conveying, one to the other, the full measure of what was and what could have been. As the wave thundered over them, something substantial struck Richard on the back and sent both of them hurtling across the deck, arms and legs flailing, until they slammed against the starboard bulwarks.

Then, nothing.

CHAPTER 5

IT WAS THE SOUNDS THAT BROUGHT HIM BACK. AS HE SLOWLY EMERGED from the depths of unconsciousness, he could not distinguish the sounds or determine their source. Lacking the strength to lift his head, he stretched out a hand and touched something solid. *Alive. I'm alive.* He drifted away once more into the darkness. When the sounds resurfaced in his consciousness, they seemed closer, more distinct.

He realized that they were bird calls; he was sure of it. He might have been listening to the songs of birds in his childhood home in Massachusetts. Except that he recognized none of the songs. Not one sounded familiar.

His hands slipped off his chest and onto something soft, a bed of some sort. With eyes still closed, he tentatively reached out on either side of him. When his hands touched dry sand, he relaxed and dug his fingers into its warm grains. An image of a Cape Cod beach on a warm summer day flashed into his mind.

Moments later a different image came to him, one that fused the bliss of the distant past with the horror of the present. His eyes flew open, his body convulsed. *Where in hell am I?* "Anne! Anne!" he cried out in confused despair. "*Anne!*"

"He's coming to, sir!" The voice was familiar but out of his view. "It's all right, Captain," the voice said. "It's all right. You're safe."

With those words Richard recognized the voice. It belonged to an officer of a ship. *His* ship, his command. In a sharper tone the man said, "Find Mr. Brengle, Mr. Montgomery. Find him and bring him here. Smartly, now!"

"Aye, aye, sir," a more youthful voice piped. "Right away, sir." Richard heard rapid squeaks of sand as the lad ran off.

Someone knelt beside him, and he felt a cool, damp cloth applied to his forehead. *Oh my God, that feels good.* Richard focused on the face above him. The man was unshaven, and he was dressed in a ragged white linen shirt. The eyes that held Richard's conveyed deep concern marked by undisguised relief.

"Mr. Wheeler," Richard croaked. "Good to see you. Is she here? Is Anne here? Please bring her to me."

"Don't worry about that now, Captain," Wheeler soothed. "Here, take a drink. The water is fresh from the river nearby. We've plenty of fresh water here, thank God."

Wheeler slid a hand under Richard's neck and cradled his head to allow him to sip from a tin cup. Spasms of pain knifed down Richard's spine into his right leg. His arm jerked, spilling the water onto his chest. Cursing the pain and his helplessness, he slumped back onto his bedding, Even that small motion caused him to cry out.

Wheeler refilled the cup from a wooden bucket. "There, Captain," he cautioned, "best not to move much yet." Richard reached out blindly for the cup, his need for water greater than the pain the movement brought. Wheeler again lifted Richard's head and brought small rations of water to his parched lips. Richard spluttered and coughed and gasped for breath, then reached for more. This time, he clung so tightly to the cup, the knuckles of his hands went white. He drank tentatively at first, then steadily, gratefully, greedily, moaning with pleasure.

"That's better," Wheeler encouraged. "But slowly. Drinking too much too quickly is not good for you. You're hurt pretty bad, sir. We don't want you to be sick as well."

Richard grimaced. "How bad?" he asked as he ran the back of his hand over his mouth.

"Don't know for sure. Dr. Green is in bad shape, and no one else knows much about his trade. Near as we can tell, you have one or two cracked ribs. A bone in your leg might be broken. That's what Mr. Brengle thinks, anyway; though you ask me, I'd say it's nothing more than a bad sprain. Something punched a hole in your thigh. Might have been that same spar that knocked you and your lady into the binnacle. Speaking of that, how's your head feeling?"

"Like the Devil's own hammer blows!" Richard drew a deep breath and shut his eyes, willing himself to lie still until the jolts of pain subsided. When he opened them again, he took in what he could see of his surroundings. His vision was restricted by a rough roof of tree branches tied together with fragments of rope. That rope also secured a piece of white sailcloth that provided protection from the elements. Outside the shelter stood a solitary figure with a musket. The shelter was nestled behind a row of dunes, beyond which he could hear the swish of surf. Looking inland, he could see low-lying brush and short, stubby trees. None of the vegetation looked familiar. Clusters of slender trees dotted the landscape. They looked like palm trees but had odd-looking fronds that rose almost straight up rather than drooping horizontally like those he knew from the Indies. Intermingled within these clusters were patches of dense undergrowth that included tall trees that reminded him of the stately pines of Virginia.

"How long have I been out, Ted?" he asked bleakly.

"Coming on two days, Captain."

"Two days? Christ!"

Refreshed by the water, Richard bided his time. He avoided eye contact with his sailing master, who had carefully avoided answering his earlier questions about Anne. When Wheeler looked away, he followed Wheeler's gaze to see two figures approaching at a rapid clip through a break in the dunes.

"Ah, I see Mr. Brengle and Mr. Montgomery coming, Captain," Wheeler said with an air of relief.

The executive officer and Midshipman Montgomery smiled warmly as they entered the shelter. Brengle spoke first. "God is my witness, Captain, it does me good to see you awake."

"Indeed, sir!" Montgomery put in, unable to suppress the joy and relief in his voice.

Brengle addressed the ship's sailing master. "Thank you for sending for me, Mr. Wheeler. If you please, I should appreciate some time alone with the captain. Make certain Webb remains on guard detail.

Mr. Montgomery, please see to food for Mr. Cutler. That flatfish Cowles speared this morning will do for a start. And please fetch more water."

"Aye, aye, sir!" Jonty Montgomery saluted, turned on his heel, and raced away. Wheeler followed at a slower pace.

"How are you feeling, Richard?" Brengle asked when the two of them were alone. His brow knitted with concern as he knelt to look more closely at his captain.

"I've been better," Richard answered dryly.

"Aye. But at least you are alive. I feared the worst. We all did. See those men out there?" He pointed toward the beach. "All of them share my relief. Many of them risked their lives to save you from the wreck."

Richard turned on his side and gripped Brengle's arm. "What of Anne, Jack?" he asked. His voice was desperate. "Where is she? Where is my wife?"

A dark shadow passed over Brengle's face. "What has Ted told you?"

"He hasn't told me anything. He seemed reluctant to talk about it, and I didn't press him. So I am asking you."

"I see," Brengle said simply. He stared down numbly, chewing on his lip.

"Tell me, Jack! For the love of God, tell me!"

Brengle drew a deep breath. "She was swept overboard by that wave, Richard, the same one that got you. She was floundering and, as near as we can tell, got caught in a fast-flowing southbound current. Peter Andrews dove in after her. He tried to save her, but he wasn't much of a swimmer, as you recall. Nevertheless, he gave his all to get to her. Alas, he was caught in that same current and carried out to sea."

"Drowned?"

"I fear so."

"And Anne?"

Brengle shook his head, said nothing.

Richard stared blankly up at the thatched wood roof. "Anne and Peter drowned. What a miserable fate. Is it really true?"

Brengle's continuing silence confirmed Richard's grief. Brengle finally went on: "Others of the crew, those who could swim, tried to help, but none of them could reach Anne. She was drifting away too swiftly.

She had managed to grab onto a spar. It may have been the same one that smacked you. I don't know. In any event, she somehow managed to swim over to it and hang on."

"She could still be alive, then. It *is* possible."

"Anything is possible, Richard," Brengle said gently, "but it seems most unlikely, I am sorry to say. The water is not terribly cold, but the current is swift. And she may have been as badly injured as you. She was a strong woman, but I doubt she could last long in those conditions. I'm sorry, Richard. I am so very, very sorry."

For long moments Richard lay motionless, unable to think, tortured by grief. Brengle waited, searching for words of comfort that were impossible to find. When Richard finally did speak, his tone was not what Brengle had expected.

"How many?"

"How many what, Richard?"

"How many of us survived the wreck?"

"Twenty-eight," Brengle replied, his expression as grim as his voice. "And a number of them are in need of medical assistance that we cannot provide. Some of them won't survive. Most of those able to walk are scouring the beach for salvage or searching for food."

"Dr. Green?"

"Alive, barely, but I'm afraid he's not much use to us. He's delirious, probably from swallowing too much saltwater. I don't expect him to live."

"Lieutenant Weeks?"

Brengle nodded. "He made it to shore." At Richard's grimace he added, "And I must say, he is finally proving his worth."

"God Almighty!" Richard murmured. "Twenty-eight survivors from a ship's company of more than two hundred."

"Just so."

"What about ship's stores? Food? Weapons? Ammunition? Medical supplies? Were you able to salvage the ship's boats?"

Brengle held up a hand. "Don't trouble yourself with such details, Richard. Leave them to me for now. You are exhausted. You haven't eaten in two days. And you have suffered a terrible loss. You should—"

"Enough!" Richard interjected sharply. "Do not presume to tell me what I should or should not do, Lieutenant!" He gave Brengle a look that left no room for doubt that he was serious. "The only thing I *must* do is get our crew safely home. That is my duty as captain, and by God I will do it, whatever the odds, whatever the cost, whatever the number of savages out there keen to slaughter and eat us."

Brengle frowned. "*Eat* us? You aren't serious."

"I am damned serious. We are marooned on a land known as New Zealand, are we not?"

"Has to be. There is no other landmass between Australia and South America."

"Exactly. And Captain Cook makes it quite clear in his journals that the natives of these islands have a penchant for human flesh. So, unless you fancy yourself turning slowly over a spit, I suggest we get on with the business of getting the hell out of here."

Brengle stared at Richard incredulously.

"Anne is gone," Richard said emphatically, although his voice caught. "She is dead. You said so yourself. No amount of grieving will bring her back. We're all in mourning for lost friends and shipmates. Regardless, those of us among the living have a job to do. That job is to survive. Survive and get home. It's that simple."

Not quite that simple, Brengle thought. But his voice was contrite when he said, "Understood, Richard. I'm with you no matter what. You know that."

"I do know that, Jack," Richard said, his own tone softening. "I have always known I can rely on you, and I will be relying on you now more than ever. So, again. Tell me: What is our situation?"

Brengle cleared his throat. "Not as bad as it might be," he said guardedly before itemizing the inventory of ship's stores they had managed to salvage: five barrels of salt beef and pork, hardtack, eight .69-caliber muskets, three watertight cartridge boxes, two pistols, a hundred rounds of dry black powder sealed in tins, fifteen knives, three tomahawks, a handful of nails, a hammer, a tinder box, six blankets, two rolls of sail canvas, a tarpaulin, a copper cooking pot, a store of coffee, several rounds of rope, tin plates and cups, ten oars, a tourniquet, and a compass. "Essentially what we had stored in the boats," he summed up, "and what we were able to grab on our way out."

"A good start. And we have water?"

"Plenty of it. And plenty of food from the sea, it seems."

"Still, it's not much should it come to a fight."

"No," Brengle had to agree.

"What of the ship's boats?"

"We managed to save the jolly boat, although it's in pretty sad condition. It did get you and most of the rest of us ashore, as well as the supplies."

"Can it be repaired?"

"Turner thinks not," referring to the carpenter's mate. He is working on it with salvaged scraps, but he doubts he can restore it to a seaworthy condition. It might get us across to the other side, assuming we want to go there. What we at first thought was an estuary turns out to be one of the biggest natural harbors I've ever seen. We probably wouldn't make it across. This place is alive with sharks. They're everywhere."

"Eaten by savages or eaten by sharks. Seems as though we are on the menu wherever we turn."

Midshipman Thomas Talmadge appeared at the entrance to the shelter bearing a tin plate of food and a cup. Like Brengel, he was barefoot and wore only his uniform trousers and a loosely buttoned linen shirt. "Compliments of Mr. Weeks, Captain," he said cheerfully.

"Thanks, Tom," Richard said, sitting up gingerly and accepting the plate. "Weeks is acting as cook?"

Talmadge glanced at Brengle, who said, "We all are cooks now, Captain, and as you are about to discover, no one is very good at it. This flounder is one of our better efforts. It tastes very much like the flounder we catch back home. They are common in the mudflats at low tide and they are easy to spear. And we are finding beds of mussels and small clams. Other fish are plentiful but hard to catch. The greens, berries, mushrooms, and fruits are foreign to us, so we're leaving them be for now. Best not to risk it."

"Good thinking," Richard said. Tentatively he pulled a piece of tender white flesh from the fish's skeleton and took a bite. "You underrate

Mr. Weeks's culinary abilities, Jack. Even my mother would approve of this, and her fish dishes are legendary." He took two additional bites before setting the plate aside.

"I warrant we'll get right sick of it in due course, but in the meantime we'll have enough food to nourish us." He rose to his feet. "I'm off, Captain, by your leave. Lieutenant Donahue has set up a picket. He and Corporal Hanson and three privates are the only members of the Marine guard to survive, save for the drummer boy, Baker, who is in a bad way. I doubt he'll make it through the night. The other men—those who can work—are fashioning a more permanent campsite. We can't leave here until everyone can walk reasonably well, and I suspect that may take several weeks."

Richard returned the salutes of his first officer and midshipman. "Well done, gentlemen," he said, adding, "Mr. Brengle, a word in private before you go, if you please."

"Of course, Captain."

When the two senior officers were again alone, Richard said in a low voice, "I am assuming that you have organized search parties to look for bodies."

Brengle nodded. "I have a team of ten men searching the beach twice a day. They go northward for five miles, give or take."

Richard propped himself up on an elbow. The pain in his eyes posed the inevitable question.

"We have found a number of bodies," Brengle answered in anticipation of that question. "So far, all of them have been members of the crew."

"I see. In light of what we discussed a few moments ago, it's imperative we give these poor souls a quick and proper burial. Assure the men that I intend to preside over the services as soon as I am able. In the meantime, please see to it."

"Understood."

Brengle stood gazing down at Richard's bloodshot eyes, which had gone vacant and devoid of life. "Is there anything else?"

"There is," Richard said in a strangled voice. "If you find Anne's body, Jack, you will tell me, won't you? Promise me you will tell me!"

Brengle touched Richard's shoulder. "You needn't ask, Richard. Of course I will tell you."

"Thank you, Jack. Thank you." With a muffled groan, Richard turned his head away.

CHAPTER 6

THE REVEREND DANIEL MACKENZIE WAS TROUBLED, DEEPLY TROU-
bled as he walked the mission compound that morning. And disheart-
ened. Reports of the horror at Taranaki the week before, disseminated far
and wide by swift runners from the southern tribes, told of acts so rep-
rehensible that he shuddered to think of them. Had his tireless efforts to
save these people, his preaching, his teaching that each and every one of
them held a divine spark, all been for naught? If what the runner had told
him last night was true—and he had no reason to doubt the youth—his
worst fear since arriving at this far-flung outpost of the British Empire
had been realized.

"How can such evil exist?" he raged. "Why do you allow this, Lord?"

He was not afraid for himself, or for any of the mission staff or those
currently seeking shelter within the mission compound. Te Wherowhero
and other powerful chiefs on the island had solemnly pledged never to
harm any missionary or anyone associated with the mission station, and
he believed them. But MacKenzie was not naive. He understood there
was much more at stake here than the safety of missionaries and those
in their care.

He knew why it was in the chiefs' interests to make such promises.
That reason might have little to do with humanitarian gestures, but that
hardly mattered—not at the moment, at least. No, what troubled MacK-
enzie this morning were the fierce reprisals to be expected following the
butchery at Taranaki. It had happened before, and it would happen again
despite the best efforts of leaders on both sides to curb such violence.

There was more. He strode on, trying to decide what to do. Britain's ongoing violations of the Great Treaty and colonists' illegal seizure of lands owned by the Maori were adding fuel to a fire that was already threatening to rage out of control. MacKenzie knew all too well who would pay the price for these abominations. Missionaries of all faiths had been on the front lines urging the northern chiefs to sign the treaty and comply with its terms. The intentions of the British might have been honorable, but if British authorities continued to ignore and misinterpret those terms, such perfidy was sure to affect the foreigners' fragile relationship with the native population and anti-British chiefs such as Hone Heke. Whether or not what had happened at Taranaki was the result of the land-grabbing to the north, it was an ill omen.

He threw up his arms in frustration and continued walking. At least the weather was fine today. Yesterday's violent storm had finally blown itself out when the wind shifted to the southwest. This morning the sun shone brightly, the offshore breeze was invigorating, and the sea, which yesterday had been a swirling, foaming vortex, sparkled like a treasure trove of diamonds on a vast carpet of blue.

MacKenzie's gaze slid away from the ground before him to rest on that watery carpet. The sweet salt air always invigorated him. Once more he threw up his arms, this time in supplication and gratitude. "Behold God's majesty!" he cried out to the heavens as he gloried in the sublime beauty of his adopted land. It was a far cry from the bleak banks of the River Tyne where he had been raised.

As MacKenzie was about to resume his walk, something in the water caught his eye. "Hello, what have we here?" he wondered aloud. The object in question was not fifty yards away, lazily drifting shoreward on the incoming tide. Its buoyancy suggested it had not been long in the water. Odd, he thought, as he studied the object. At first sight it appeared to be an outrigger broken off a Maori canoe, but he quickly ruled that out. Whatever this was, it was too short and stubby to be off a sleek, hundred-foot *waka*. And no outrigger he had ever seen had a sizable knob on its middle. Was this wreckage from a shipwreck?

As he fumbled in his trouser pocket for the small metal spyglass he had brought with him from Northumberland, he was drawn to the distinctive silvery notes of a tui bird sitting in a tall bush of green flax and dipping its beak into the tubelike red blooms to suck out the rich nectar. MacKenzie had a special fondness for these blue, green, and black birds, which sported a tuft of white feathers at the throat that resembled a parson's ruffle. Although he found most of the local birds fascinating, the tuis were his favorites, especially when they broke into song. He watched the greedy bird for several minutes before turning his attention back to the mysterious object. It was closer to shore now. What *was* that protuberance in its center? Whatever the object was, it was clearly man-made.

He withdrew the spyglass from his side pocket and brought it to bear on the object. He focused the lens and swept the field of view back and forth across the length of wood. He nodded. "A ship's spar, certainly." When the glass settled on the knob in the middle, he held it steady, then, with a sharp intake of breath, dropped it to his waist. He stared out with his naked eyes for several moments, then raised the glass for a final look.

"My blessed Lord," he gasped. He tore off his homespun woolen sweater and tossed it aside. As swiftly as his aging limbs would allow, he leapt from the path, ran through tussocks of reed and seagrass down to the beach, and forced his way through the gently curling surf.

CHAPTER 7

THE DAY BROKE DRYER AND COOLER THAN PREVIOUS MORNINGS HAD been. Strands of white mist hung low over the broad harbor and the far banks, blurring the distinctions between water and land and sky. Awake in his makeshift hut and lying on a pallet set over a bed of spongy moss, Richard shivered in the morning chill and drew the thin blanket up around his shoulders, feeling guilty that he was afforded the luxury of a blanket while most of his crewmen were without. He had neither expected nor requested it. The men had insisted.

The sharp report of musket fire some distance away jerked him upright, thankfully with less pain than before. He held his breath, listening intently for anything suggesting a threatening follow-up to that single shot, but the only sounds were the rustling of wind in the trees, the ever-present trilling of birds, and the distant roar of the surf. Exhaling a long breath, he forced himself to relax. *The men must be out hunting. I hope they bagged something good to eat.*

The camp was astir. During the first week ashore, it had been hastily constructed on a smooth expanse of sand between the high dunes on one side and a seemingly impenetrable barrier of brush, flax, ferns, flowering shrubs, thickets, and prickly-leafed trees on the other. Around its entire perimeter—which was rectangular save for a sideways V at one end that roughly replicated the cutwater of a ship—a four-foot-high pile of tree branches and sun-bleached driftwood protected the compound. The structure was tied together with ropes made of flax reeds and reinforced with rocks lugged over from the beach. Within the perimeter the men had built twelve huts, all similar in size and design to their captain's dwelling. The crude thatched-roofed, open-sided dwellings were arranged in age-old naval fashion: senior officers housed near the stern, Marines amidships, and petty officers and common sailors forward in the forecastle.

When these breastworks were completed, officers and crew surveyed the fruits of their labors with a mixture of satisfaction and the cold, unspoken realization that a two-pronged assault by a determined enemy would quickly overrun this rudimentary fort and the men inside it. Two five-round .38-caliber pistols and eight .69-caliber muzzle-loading muskets did not constitute much of a defense.

Richard could see a few men gathering sticks and other kindling to start a fire with the metal tinder box salvaged from the wreck. As the small talk of early morning drifted into his shelter, Richard listened for a clue that his men might be discussing anything out of the ordinary. But all he overheard was the usual sailors' lament of a lack of rum and women.

Although nearly two weeks had elapsed since *Suwannee* struck the sandbar, Richard's body was still wracked by an unnerving pain that made sleep difficult. He took comfort that at least now the more troublesome pain seemed to be confined to the area around his right rib cage. The constant throbbing in his leg had largely subsided. When he had first stood up to test the leg, he found that the pain was, as Ted Wheeler had suspected, the result of a severe sprain to a thigh muscle, and not a fractured bone. Further, he found he could take the pain, and though walking remained a challenge, with the aid of a crutch fashioned for him by Jim Turner, the carpenter's mate, he was able to stand and managed to hobble an additional step or two with each go.

This morning, as he was reaching for his crutch, he was greeted by Nathaniel Donahue, the square-jawed, sandy-haired captain of Marines, who in some mysterious way managed to present a polished military appearance while the other men were dressed in rags. How Donahue's buff trousers, white linen shirt, black neck stock, and shiny black leather boots had survived the shipwreck Richard had no clue. He sometimes pictured Nate stuffing them inside a kit bag as the waters rose inside the ship, counting military bearing ahead of survival.

"Good morning, Captain," Donahue said amiably as he stepped inside the hut. "Another fine day today. May I offer you a hand up?"

"Thank you, no, Nate," Richard replied courteously. "I prefer to do it myself."

Donahue bowed slightly, taking care not to spill the contents of the cup he carried in each hand. "Of course. Not that I have a hand to spare at the moment."

Richard took a deep breath, waited a moment to steel himself, then used his crutch to haul himself to his feet in one mighty heave.

"Well done, Captain," Donahue smiled. "You seem to have made substantial progress."

"Thank you. It gets a bit easier every time I do it. In another week, or perhaps two, I should be able to move about freely. Then we can get on with the business of finding our way out of here."

"We are already preparing as best we can, Captain." He offered one of the cups to Richard. "In the meantime, Jonty has been busy at his usual morning tasks. May I offer you a coffee?"

Richard edged himself down onto a block of wood next to his pallet and gratefully accepted a steaming cup. He sighed with pleasure as the hot liquid coursed down his throat.

Donahue sat down on one of the five other slabs of wood that constituted the officers' wardroom. "No cream or sugar, I'm afraid. And I regret to report that our supply of coffee is nearly gone. It's hardest on poor Jonty, of course. He'll soon be out of a job. He takes great pride in his coffee."

"As well he should," Richard said before enjoying another sip. "Anyone who can brew quality coffee in a place like this deserves a medal. By the way, a question I have long been meaning to ask: Do you know why he's called Jonty?"

Donahue grinned. "He insists that his name is Jonathan, but I've never heard him called anything but Jonty."

Richard smiled and nodded. "He's a good lad, that one. Someday he'll be a good captain." The smile left Richard's face as he continued, "And I will not let anything happen to that young man." His expression hardened. "I cannot, and I will not," he repeated vehemently. "I care about all of my crew, of course, and I will do my damndest to keep them all safe and well, but there is something special about young Jonty. You understand what I'm saying, Nate?"

"I do, Richard," Donahue said, understanding exactly. "We all do. He was a particular favorite of Anne's," he added.

"Aye," Richard agreed quietly. "Jonty was her favorite." An image crossed Richard's mind of Anne standing on *Suwannee*'s quarterdeck smiling at Jonty as he bowed formally before her, clearly smitten by her grace and elegance. To his dismay, the image quickly faded.

"Are Jack and Lang on their way here?" He asked moments later.

"They are. With Ted. Due any minute. They've been delayed for a reason that I believe will please you. Perhaps even surprise you."

"I would like to hear it, then. I could use some good news."

"All in God's good time, Captain," Donahue said mysteriously. "All in God's good time."

As if on cue, the three officers mentioned arrived together outside the captain's hut. After returning the salute of George Webb, the bearded Marine private standing sentry duty, they were ushered inside.

"Good morning, gentlemen," Richard greeted them. "Please have a seat and we shall get started. Sorry I can't offer you a cup of coffee."

"We've had ours, Captain," Wheeler said hastily.

When *Suwannee*'s five surviving senior officers were seated on the slabs of wood, Richard opened the meeting that had become a morning ritual. Except for mundane matters that could be handled on the spot, everything deemed out of the ordinary was put on the table during these briefing sessions, with time allocated to ongoing discussions on what to do once they were able to make decisions and act upon those decisions. With each passing day, the time to act was drawing closer. The weather was turning cooler, and the supply of fruits and greens that had been determined safe to eat was dwindling. More to the point, they had agreed they had to leave this camp because, as Jack Brengle had recently put it, "Going nowhere is getting us nowhere."

As was true of most mornings, little had transpired during the previous twenty-four hours that warranted serious discussion. That fact was not important to Richard. What was important was gathering the senior officers together as a cohesive unit to share the heavy burden of leadership. Such cooperation was an indispensable component of what Richard considered military routine and discipline, whether at sea or marooned on an island somewhere in the South Pacific. Enforcing such discipline when a laxer routine might seem preferable under these circumstances was the best way to maintain order while at the same time inspiring hope among the crew that their officers were making plans for their rescue.

This morning, all four officers agreed that while food from the sea remained plentiful, the men were being forced to forage farther into the bush for other food. The bush not only seemed impenetrable, it was a forbidding domain in which lurked myriad strange and dangerous creatures. Thus far, they had avoided going too far into it. Until today.

"Tell the captain what you did, Lang," Brengle urged.

"I shot a boar," Weeks said nonchalantly.

"A boar," Richard said, adding, to clarify. "A wild pig?"

"Yes, sir. A big one, too," Weeks said, allowing his pride to show.

"A monster pig," Donahue embellished. "You should have seen him, Captain. Four of my Marines were out with Lieutenant Weeks, near to where we set up the outer fringe of the perimeter, when out of the bush comes this beast, snorting and grunting and charging full tilt for Will Allerton. As calmly as you please, Lang here fired a single shot into the boar's brain and felled him dead on the spot, only a few feet short of where Will was standing, gape-mouthed. Poor boy soiled his pants, I warrant!"

The men laughed nervously, all of them thinking of the destruction a boar's tusks could do to a man's insides.

"Nicely done, Mr. Weeks," Richard said sincerely. "I heard the shot and hoped that it was from a successful hunt. Is Allerton all right?"

"Just had the shit scared out of him, is all," Donahue said with a laugh.

"Good to hear." Richard nodded at Weeks. "The ship's crew thanks you, Lieutenant," he said. "As do I. You have done us all a great service—two great services, in fact. We can ill afford to lose Allerton, and we can ill afford to lose that pig!" After another round of laughter ran through the group, Brengle smacked his lips and said, "Let the cooking begin!"

"It has begun already," Wheeler said with a grin.

"Good," Richard said. "A feast is long overdue, and goddammit, we're going to enjoy it!" His smile faded. "Before we get too carried away, however, we have important matters to discuss. Ted, I take it that Henry has nothing to report?"

Able Seaman Henry Simpson had the sharpest eyesight of the survivors and was responsible for maintaining a lookout on the crest of the highest dune. A seven-foot-high pyramid of wood, underbrush, and other combustibles had been erected there to signal distress to a passing ship. A seaman at the base of the dune kept a small fire burning continuously so the pyramid could be ignited on a moment's notice.

"No, Captain," Wheeler reported. "Nary a glint of sail on the horizon."

"Thank you, Ted," Richard said before casting a meaningful look at Jack Brengle. "Anything new to report from the beach patrols, Jack?"

Brengle understood the question. All those present understood. The search parties sent out twice a day to comb the beach and the harbor's western shoreline had come across seventy-two bodies, most of them washed ashore during those first three days. More recently, body parts—a hand, a foot, a leg shank—had washed up, most of them picked bone-clean by crabs. Or something. The waters off the beach, rich in sea life, were favored feeding grounds for sharks and dolphins. On any given day the men could see fins slashing through the water, which was sometimes stained red. The sight was enough to make stalwart men refuse to wade into ankle-deep water in search of food, let alone venture out to the sandbar at low tide in an unseaworthy boat to gather whatever might still be retrievable from the wreck.

"No new developments," Brengle said somberly. "That makes nearly two weeks now. I pray that some of the crew made it ashore farther down the coast or on the other side of the harbor, and that we'll see no more of them washing up here."

"I pray so, too," Richard said grimly. "We still have a hundred souls unaccounted for."

A respectful silence settled over the gathering. None of the officers, least of all the captain, needed to be reminded that Anne Cutler was among those missing.

"Right, then," Richard said after a moment. He cleared his throat. "That's it for today, gentlemen, unless someone has something to add?"

"I do, Captain."

All eyes swung to Donahue.

"Yes, Nate? What is it?"

Donahue stood up. "We all know that Private Plummer has . . . how shall I say it . . . *unique* abilities?"

"You are referring to his premonitions," Richard replied matter-of-factly. *Suwannee*'s crew had long known and accepted that Garth Plummer possessed an uncanny ability to sense things that others could not. Sailors, by nature a superstitious lot, often believed without question the insights that the mild-mannered Marine from Stonington, Connecticut, offered. And for good reason. Most of Plummer's intuitions and predictions had proven correct. "What of it?"

Donahue chewed on his lower lip before responding. "He believes we are being watched."

"Watched? By whom?" Weeks scoffed. "What nonsense is this?"

Richard ignored him. "If we are being watched, it will be by the natives. What do you think, Jack?"

Brengle shrugged. "Frankly, I'm not sure what to think. I was aware of this but didn't want to bother you. I even went out into the bush with Plummer to see if we could spot signs that someone is out there."

"And?" Richard inquired.

"We did see a few things that might have been caused by human activity: a freshly broken branch here, a shallow footprint there—but nothing definitely indicating the presence of people." He raised a hand to forestall Weeks's next comment. "Yes, I see your reaction, Lang, and I agree with you. It is at this point speculation. Yet I would not bet against Plummer. He has been spot-on too many times."

"What do you suggest?" Richard asked.

"I suggest, Captain, that we take the matter seriously. To do otherwise, in my judgment, would be folly."

"I agree," Richard said. "So the natives likely know we are here. And in that case, we can expect the pleasure of their company in the near future."

"That would be my hunch as well," Donahue said. "We'll have to prepare for it, though there's not much we can do beyond what we have already done. We might take a few of them down with us, but the bitter truth remains that we live pretty much at their mercy."

"I disagree!" Weeks blustered. "Let them come. Those savages will be no match for us."

Donahue shook his head but said nothing.

"All of which suggests we should leave this peninsula immediately," Wheeler said.

"And go where?" Weeks demanded.

"North," Richard answered immediately. "There lies our salvation. I have read enough of Captain Cook's journals to know two things." He held up a finger. "The landmass we are on is not a large one." He held up a second finger. "There are areas on the northern fringe of this island where Europeans have settled, and they are visited by whalers from many nations, including the United States. Captain Cook called that area the Bay of Islands. Cheer up, gentlemen, and trust me. A Harvard man is never wrong." He grinned at that sally, but only Brengle grinned back. "In any case," he said firmly, "we are going to the Bay of Islands."

"And do you have any concept of how to get there?" Weeks asked sarcastically.

Richard ignored the sarcasm. "I do, Mr. Weeks. First, we break camp. Then we take out our compass and start walking. That way."

He pointed northward up the beach.

CHAPTER 8

TE WHINA PRICKED UP HER EARS AT THE SOUND OF LOW SOBBING IN the next room. The young white woman Mister K had found in the sea two days ago moaned and tossed fitfully whenever the Maori woman bathed her with cool water, but no matter what Te Whina said or did, the woman would not wake. But this sound was different. Te Whina set down the basket she was weaving and peered through the open door of the mission's infirmary, where she served as *nehi*. What she saw made her turn on her heel.

"Mister K, Mister K!" she shouted to the man working at the edge of the vegetable garden on the opposite side of the compound.

The man swiped at his forehead with his shirtsleeve. "What is it, Te Whina?"

"The lady awakes, Mister K. She awakes!"

"You're quite certain?"

"*Ae*, Mister K. This time I am certain. *Haere mai koe kia kite!*"

Daniel MacKenzie got to his feet as quickly as his aching knees would allow and hurried to the white-boarded house. The five-room cottage was one of seven buildings in the horseshoe-shaped mission compound, which overlooked the great harbor to the west at its open end. He climbed the three steps to the front veranda and hurried inside. Te Whina was sitting on a chair beside a four-poster bed, speaking softly to the woman lying supine on the bed beneath a linen sheet. Te Whina could have been attending a young child as she smoothed back loose strands of the woman's auburn hair. The woman's eyes flashed open, taking in her strange surroundings and the nurse's foreign words. "*Ka pai koe*," Te Whina kept repeating. "*E arohhaina koutou.*"

When MacKenzie approached her bedside, the woman settled her gaze on him. "What is she saying?" she rasped.

MacKenzie gave her a warm smile. "She is saying, 'You are safe here, dear one, and you are much loved.'"

The woman relaxed and offered a timid smile. "How lovely. She is a native woman?"

"She is. And she is right. You are quite safe here. No harm will come to you as long as you remain here."

"Where am I? Who are you? Who is she?"

MacKenzie chuckled. "So many questions. I will answer them one by one. But first, Te Whina will bring you food and water. You must be very thirsty and very hungry." He turned to look at the nurse.

"Of course, Mister K. I am warming soup in the cooking pot. I will bring bread and water, too.

"Perfect."

MacKenzie sat patiently while Te Whina fed Anne. On several occasions she made to talk, but each time he shook his head and pointed to the tray on the bedside table. Only when she had finished did he speak.

"Better?"

"Much better. Thank you." Her voice sounded stronger.

"You are welcome. I must say, you sound much better. Now," he smiled, "as to your questions. I'll answer them, and then perhaps you will oblige me with some answers of your own. We shall keep this brief because I know you are not yet recovered from your ordeal." He patted her hand. "And no doubt you are bewildered as well."

She nodded.

"Very well. The answer to your first question is that you are in a Wesleyan mission on the west coast of New Zealand. We are not far from the city of Auckland. Have you heard of Auckland?"

She shook her head.

"Auckland is the new colonial capital of New Zealand. The British colonial government resides there, as do units of the British army and navy.

"As to your second question, my name is Daniel MacKenzie, and I am—I pray I am—a man of God. I am the director of this mission, which at the moment is playing host to a most intriguing guest—of British descent, judging by her accent—who has drifted in from the sea to grace us with a visit."

Despite herself, Anne managed a small smile.

"This woman is Te Whina. She is trained in Maori ways of nursing. We are blessed to have her here in the mission as our *nehi*. She will take good care of you, just as she takes good care of us all. And you will be pleased to know that she is also an experienced midwife. So you needn't have any concerns over your . . . condition."

The woman quickly brought her hands to her belly. "*My baby!*"

MacKenzie covered one of her hands with one of his and gently squeezed it. "Your baby is fine. Te Whina tells me that you carry a feisty little urchin. 'Twould seem that two lives were saved on that day." He smiled at Anne, and when her panic had subsided to profound relief, MacKenzie went on. "For the past two days, when you have not been delirious, we have been giving you sips of a tea called *kawakawa*, which is both nutritious and good for just about anything that ails you. It's good for the child, as well. The natives swear by it. They've been using it for generations, to good effect. Do you recall us giving it to you?"

"No. I've been dreaming, I think."

The woman's eyelids were beginning to droop, but suddenly they flipped wide open and focused on MacKenzie. She struggled to sit up. "My husband!" she demanded. "What of my husband? Tell me, I beg of you!"

"Richard, is it?"

Her eyes widened. "Yes, Richard! You know him? Is he here?"

MacKenzie shook his head. "You have been calling for him in your sleep."

"But where is he?"

MacKenzie shrugged sadly. "I do not know your husband's where-abouts, my dear. I found you quite alone drifting in the water just off the beach, clinging to a broken ship's spar. I did notice other debris in the water. Was there a shipwreck? Is that what befell you and your husband?"

"Yes, a shipwreck," the woman whispered, slumping back onto the bed. Her voice was trailing into exhaustion. "My husband's ship. A naval ship."

"A Royal Navy ship went down?" he said in horror. I have heard nothing from Auckland of a shipwreck." MacKenzie glanced questioningly at Te Whina, who had returned to the room with a fresh cup of tea. Perhaps the woman's delirium had returned? He returned his gaze to the woman, who was shaking her head in frustration.

"What is your name, my dear?" he asked kindly. "What do we call you?"

"My name is Anne Cutler," she replied wearily. "My husband's name is Richard Cutler. He is the captain of the American frigate *Suwannee*."

"Your husband is a naval captain? An *American* naval captain? My word! Well, Mrs. Cutler," MacKenzie soothed, "that's enough talk for now. After you sleep we will talk some more. A great deal more. Sleep now. You are safe here. No harm will come to you or your baby."

"I must look for my husband," she insisted, her voice weakening with each word. "*We* must look for him. We must look for him *now!* He is alive, I know he is!"

"We will do all we can to find him, Mrs. Cutler," MacKenzie promised in his deep, soothing voice. "Please, do not worry. We will find him. At the moment, what you need is sleep. You are among friends who will care for you. You need your strength for what lies ahead. Your baby needs you to be strong. Your husband needs you to be strong. Pray, go to sleep now."

"Yes," she murmured. "Yes, you are quite right." Moments later she again slipped into unconsciousness.

CHAPTER 9

FROM BALTIMORE TO RICHMOND AND EVERYWHERE IN BETWEEN, THE BALL AT the British embassy was sure to be the jewel in the crown of a most satisfying social season. Even the heat and humidity and the fetid odors of summer in the nation's capital could not dull its glamour. All haute société *was anticipating the gala, and fortunate those among them who were included on the list of invitees, which defined America's upper crust: the first families of Virginia and Maryland, members of Congress and the president's cabinet, legendary war hero General Winfield Scott, literary and theater luminaries, along with others with a finger on the social pulse of Washington, D.C. It was widely rumored that even the newly inaugurated president, John Tyler, would make an appearance, a prospect that sent the event's organizers into a delighted frenzy. It was indeed a glittering gathering, which was why Richard Cutler questioned the invitation delivered to his Alexandria residence direct from the British embassy on Massachusetts Avenue. He had not met the new ambassador and knew precious few of those whom common sense dictated would be in attendance.*

There was no question of his accepting the invitation. To decline or ignore it could ruin his naval career. So at half past eight o'clock on the prescribed evening he went, dressed in his finest dark blue dress uniform, hoping that the receiving line would be short by that time.

Ambassador George Braithwaite nodded knowingly and smiled on hearing Richard's name. "Your reputation precedes you, sir," he said.

Surprised, Richard could only bow. He entered a room filled with lavishly clad guests sweeping and swerving gracefully past him through the magnificent ballroom that dominated the embassy's first floor. He felt like a buoy placed there to help the grandees navigate toward the quartet of musicians who were testing the first dulcet tunes of a Loeillet composition.

He caught the eye of Secretary David Henshaw, who was in conversation with a man Richard recognized as a senator from North Carolina. Henshaw nodded before resuming his conversation with the senator. The signal was clear. Wait.

"So be it," Richard sighed. Leaning against a Doric column, he folded his arms across his chest and contented himself with observing the dazzling spectacle. Although fascinating, it was the stuff of someone else's dreams. Adding to his feeling of unease was the presence of Miss Mary Custis, a member of the Old Guard of Virginia whose great-grandmother Martha Custis had married George Washington. She was fanning herself while eyeing him intently from across the room. Richard had no interest in Miss Custis, despite her pedigree and obvious interest in him. It was not that he found her unattractive. Despite her plumpness and her unflattering corkscrew ringlets, Richard found her looks pleasing enough. It was her haughty conviction that her bloodline entitled her to whatever she wanted whenever she wanted it that put him off. Now, at eighteen, she was of an age to claim her desires, and Richard feared that he was one of them.

He instinctively took a step backward when he noticed Mary leaving the company of three young gentlemen to head in his direction, her intention obvious. Just then he noticed a far more appealing apparition approaching him from a different direction. She was walking arm-in-arm with the ambassador, a dashing figure clearly born into the aristocracy. His noble bearing, finely chiseled features, and exquisitely cut clothing left no doubt of that. The young lady on his arm, dressed in an ankle-length, rose-colored damask gown, showed similar traits of culture and breeding that captivated not only Richard but nearly everyone else in the ballroom, from what he could see. He was astonished to realize that the pair was clearly approaching him, their gazes firmly fixed on him. He glanced behind him to see who instead might be the object of their attention, and the woman smiled at him when he looked back at her. Her sea-green eyes and the graceful sweep of her long auburn hair gathered at the back of her head in a French-style chignon took his breath away.

As the couple glided past an astonished Mary Custis, Richard stood transfixed, barely able to breathe and unable to take his eyes from the most beautiful women he had ever seen. Those soft eyes seemed to convey a message to him. He saw interest and kindness, yes, but something more, something—dare he believe it?—more promising.

Stop this, *Richard sternly chided himself as the couple drew near.* You don't know this woman; you cannot possibly tell what she is thinking, and besides, she is from a realm far beyond your reach.

After an age, the couple stood before him. When Richard, still transfixed, was slow to react, the ambassador coughed discreetly into a fist. "I have a special favor to ask of you, Captain Cutler. This lady requires a dance partner. As no doubt you have noted, the harpsichordist is signaling all dancers to take their places for the first dance. Would you oblige me by agreeing to dance with her? We would both be ever so appreciative."

Richard heard every word the man said, but he could not pull his eyes away from the woman. She owned his heart without ever saying a word. He swallowed hard. "Sir," he managed, "it would be my great honor to serve as the lady's dance partner this evening. I pray I am worthy of such an honor."

"Indeed you are, sir," the ambassador laughed. "I have no doubt on that score. And besides, the lady insists." He took the woman's hand and gallantly offered it to Richard, who took it in his own hand. After a quick peck on the woman's cheek and a polite "pleasant evening" to Richard, the ambassador bid them adieu and walked away to another group of guests.

"Hello?" the woman said into the awkward lull as Richard stared after her escort, who took the hand of a woman waiting nearby and led her toward the dance.

Richard blushed. "M-my most sincere apologies, my lady," he stammered. He bowed low in courtly fashion. "I am Richard Cutler, a captain in the United States Navy."

"I know who you are, Captain. And it was unaccountably rude of my brother not to introduce us."

"Y-your brother? Are you not the ambassador's wife?"

For the first time he heard her deep, rich laugh. "Good heavens, no! I would never marry a fuddy-duddy like George. I am Anne Braithwaite, his sister, and I intend to marry someone far more dashing than George."

He laughed out loud, then caught himself. "But I don't understand. You wanted to meet me? *Why?" Anne merely smiled and squeezed his hand. "The musicians are ready to begin, and I believe you have agreed to dance with me, Captain Cutler—*

"Sorry to disturb, Captain, but might I have a word with you?"

Richard sighed in quiet frustration as the pull to duty destroyed those sweet remembrances. For an extra moment he sat motionless on the beach, unable to wrench himself back to reality.

"Good morning, Lieutenant," he said finally. "Another fine day, it seems, after the rain of the night."

"Good morning, sir. Aye, a fine day indeed." Weeks pointed out to sea. "A good memory out there, I take it?"

"Yes," Richard said softly. He seized that final moment to savor the magic of what once had been before discreetly brushing his hand over his suddenly moist eyes and turning his full attention to his third officer. "Please sit."

"Thank you." Weeks sat down on the sand beside him.

"What's on your mind?"

"Tomorrow," came the forthright reply.

"What about tomorrow?"

"You are leaving here, as planned?"

"Yes. *We* are leaving here as planned."

Weeks shifted nervously. "Captain, I ask on behalf of myself and five of the crew that we be permitted to remain behind."

"Remain behind?" Richard said incredulously. "Here? You want to remain here on this peninsula? That was never part of our plan. Why do five of you wish to stay?"

"Six of us."

"Very well, six of you. Good God, man, *why?*"

"I—we—believe that we have the best hope of being rescued if we remain here."

"And how did you arrive at that startling conclusion?"

"It was not hard," Weeks replied. "I realize that we have not sighted a ship since we've been here, but that may change any day now. We all agree that the harbor out there is one of the best natural harbors any of us has seen. Surely other mariners know of it and will be putting in here during the winter months. In the meantime, we have plenty of fresh water to drink and food to eat. Just as we have been doing. It's a waiting game, and the six of us are willing to take our chances by waiting here on the peninsula. When a ship does come in and picks us up, we will sail north to find you. And if you find that township of yours . . . what is its name again?"

"The English call it Russell."

"If you do find Russell and the Bay of Islands, you can find a ship and come back here for us. As you say, there are likely to be whalers and even Royal Navy vessels in such a place. So you see, Captain, if the six of us remain here, we have two good alternatives for being rescued. If we all go north, we have only one."

"What of the natives? They may not take kindly to you lounging about on their land, and they may decide to do something about it." To this point he had not broached the subject of cannibalism to anyone but Brengle, and he was not about to broach it now. "What chance would six of you have against them?"

Weeks waved that away. "We haven't seen a single savage. Plummer's intuition seems to have failed him in this case. For all we know, the natives may be concentrated in the north. Are you not just as likely to encounter them as we would be if we stayed here?"

Richard bit his lower lip. He could not refute the logic of that question. "Perhaps. But if you stay here at the tip of the peninsula, you will have no place to go if you are attacked." After a moment he asked, "Who are the other five?"

"Able-rated seamen Chatfield, Killcullen, and Blackford; quarter-master's mate William Kehoe; and Jacob Cowles."

The first four Richard knew to be good sailors, hard-working and hitherto loyal crew members, but he was jolted even more by the last name. "The boatswain? He's in on this? I would not have suspected him."

"With respect, Captain, Cowles isn't *in* on anything," Weeks exclaimed indignantly. "He simply agrees with me that dividing our resources increases our chances of rescue. Frankly, Captain, I resent your implication. This is no mutiny, and I certainly intend no disrespect to you or to anyone else."

"I believe you don't." Richard rose to his feet and brushed sand off the seat of his breeches. Weeks followed suit. "Nevertheless, my answer must be no, Mr. Weeks. Emphatically no. Your proposal does have some merits, but under no conditions will I permit my command to be split in two. We're weak enough now, and dividing us, in my opinion, would lead to disaster. Nor can I afford to lose the services of an officer I have come to respect and value. I mean you, Mr. Weeks. Whatever differences you and I may have had on *Suwannee* are trivial in light of your performance since we landed on these shores. You have proven yourself to be a fine officer, and I am fortunate that you are with us. Further, you are the best shot among us, and the men respect you. They would be devastated if you were to abandon them."

Richard shook his head. "Think on it, Lang. This place may have water, but as winter comes there will be no fruit or vegetables save for kelp on the beach. Without them you will get scurvy, your health will decline, and you will be at risk of other diseases—and helpless if you should be attacked. We must find a way to save ourselves, and stagnating on this spit is not the way, I promise you."

When the lieutenant offered no comment, Richard said, not in anger, "Request denied, Lieutenant. I will hear no more about it. We stay together. Understood?"

"Understood," Weeks said dully. "But with respect, Captain, let the record show that I believe your decision is wrong. I believe you are making a serious mistake that could jeopardize us all."

"Duly noted," Richard assured him.

The wind shifted that night from the prevailing southwesterly to a more easterly flow. With it came clouds, rain, and heavy ocean air. The next morning the rain continued, as it did the morning after that and the morning after that, in the form of heavy mist one moment, heavy wind-blown downpours the next. The cold, miserable dampness seeped into clothing, bedding, food, and mood. It was impossible to find a dry spot, impossible to find comfort. Not until late afternoon of the fifth day did the misery ease with indications of better weather ahead.

Sure enough, the next morning the low, dark clouds yielded to dirty white clouds interspersed with splotches of pale blue sky and, increasingly, shafts of yellow sun that lit up the deep green forest glades and the slate gray of cresting waves. It was time to move on.

Richard had shaved carefully the night before, using his fingers to guide his razor in the darkness. He had tied his shoulder-length chestnut hair back in a queue and gathered together his few possessions, paying special attention to his identification papers and sidearm, all carefully wrapped in oilskins. Early the next morning, as he was tucking his three-and-a-half-pound revolver into the waistband of his worn buff breeches, he was startled by the sudden appearance of his executive officer. Brengle looked haggard from worry and lack of sleep.

"Weeks is gone, Richard," Brengle said abruptly.

"What do you mean, gone?"

"Just that. He and his five cronies must have crept away sometime during the night."

"Any trace of where they went?"

"Just footsteps leading into the bush."

"The fucking bastard!" Richard drew a deep breath. "What did they steal from us?"

"Thankfully, very little. One musket and a few rounds of ammunition. A few other items. Nothing of great consequence."

"Well, I suppose we should be grateful for small favors."

"I suppose we should. So what do we do now? Go after them? Bring them back?"

Richard shook his head. "What's the use? We'd never find them. Even if we did, we can't stand guard over them like prisoners, day and night. They'd just run off again. No, they are well hidden somewhere in the bush by now. When we are well away they'll come back here and wait. For what, God only knows. I fear it's likely to be a spear in the gut."

Brengle nodded grimly. "So we move on?"

Richard nodded. "We follow our plan. We've been held up too long as it is. We're ready to go, so we'll go. Assemble the men. I want a word with them before we head off."

Minutes later, the remaining twenty members of *Suwannee*'s crew were standing together at ease on the beach where they had washed ashore. Even in that informal setting, military protocol prevailed. Jack Brengle, Ted Wheeler, and Nathaniel Donahue stood beside him facing a ragged company of men consisting of three midshipmen standing in front of nine sailors, who stood beside another group of four Marines. Overhead, the sun was already beating down, heating the soft white sand and forcing the barefoot men to retreat to the cooler, harder sand near the water's edge.

"Gentlemen." Richard spoke just loudly to be heard by all. "Some of what I am about to say to you I have said before. But it bears repeating." He paused. "We have been through hell together. We have sailed together halfway around the world, and together we have suffered the loss of our ship and of too many of our shipmates. We have managed to survive on a land unknown to any of us.

"Now we confront a still greater challenge. Although our future remains uncertain, we now have something we lacked before: hope, real hope. We have chosen to seek our salvation rather than sit here passively on our duffs and wait for rescuers who may never appear. That is not the way of the United States Navy, of whom we are proud members. I am telling you what should be apparent to you all by now: Our salvation will not be handed to us. We must seek it out." He paused to let that simple statement sink in. "Not everyone may agree with me on how best to proceed. I can accept that. Indeed, if any of you has an opinion or a suggestion, I will listen to you and I will discuss what you have to say with my officers. Nothing is off-limits as long as what you have to say points to a positive outcome. Whether you are speaking on behalf of your shipmates or your concern is of a personal nature, I will listen to you and I will give you my best response. As your captain, however, I will give no countenance to suggestions I deem foolish or dangerous. You must have faith in the decisions your officers make. We will get you home.

"A few of our company have chosen to abandon us. It grieves me to say it, but we must leave them behind to their fate. It will be a cruel one."

The reference to Langston Weeks and the veiled warning to others who might follow his example were unmistakable. Although many of the men nodded in apparent understanding, Richard's words sparked no comments or rumbling undertones. He pointed up the beach.

"That is the way home. A town of consequence lies there. It exists! The town is called Russell, and it is the colonial capital and the seat of English authority in New Zealand. As such, it contains units of the British army and a squadron of the Royal Navy. What's more, whalers of many nations pull in there, American whalers among them. Our countrymen, lads! And we will find a ship's master of one of those whalers who will take us back to America. A whaling ship's master does not defy the United States Navy! No one does!" He was shouting by the time he finished the last sentence.

Cheers, laughter, and resolve surged through the slim ranks. When the din quieted, Richard held out his arms expansively, as if to embrace them all. "There you have it, men! There you have my sacred pledge to return you to your loved ones! I can do this! *We* can do this, together! Are you with me?"

Henry Simpson raised a fist in the air. "We're with you, Captain! We all are! I say, three cheers for the captain!"

His shipmates complied, with gusto.

"Thank you, men," Richard said when silence returned. "Thank you very much. Now, let us get on with the task at hand, shall we? Pick up all the food and gear you can carry, and we are off."

Although their progress was slowed at high tide when they had to slog through the softer sand, they remained by necessity on the seemingly endless beach. Their pace was set by the slowest among them—those who had not yet fully recovered from the shipwreck. Two men carried revolvers, seven others had muskets. Others carried the rest of the arms available to them: a sailor's knife, tomahawks, belaying pins. Every man, including the officers, carried all the food and supplies he could manage.

On the first day they walked for six hours and covered somewhere between seven and eight miles. They made similar progress each of the next few days. For all that distance the indigenous flora changed little. Lush tangles of scrub and underbrush bordered the beach. Now and then they passed dense thickets of tall, thin-trunked trees rooted in reddish-brown clay soil. Twice they tried to hack their way through the underbrush, neither attempt getting very far or yielding anything of value. It was simply too difficult. So they remained on the beach for the time being.

The terrain became hillier as they ventured farther north, and the long, continuous beach became a series of smaller beaches in between majestic headlands jutting out into the sea.

Eastward in the interior, trees of gargantuan height appeared, towering over the underbrush. Neither Richard nor any of his crew had ever before seen trees as tall as these, although he had read about trees of unimaginable height and girth in accounts written by Lewis and Clark during their 1804–1805 expedition to the Pacific Northwest. Those trees were thought to be more than a thousand years old, mere seedlings at the start of the Plantagenet dynasty in England. Gazing up in awe, Richard suspected that these giant New Zealand trees shared a similar timeline.

As they trudged along, every sailor and Marine remained vigilant for the sight of a ship to seaward or a movement in the bush that might signal some form of human activity. Private Plummer remained convinced that hidden eyes were watching them, a prospect that unsettled them all. But they came upon little to substantiate Plummer's claim. Men saw things that seemed real at the time, but on reflection were dismissed as imaginary. Nonetheless, sleep did not come easily, and those standing watch during the night were especially on edge.

During the days on the march and at night while trying to snatch what oblivion he could, Richard reviewed again and again what he knew of New Zealand, specifically the Bay of Islands. Despite the confidence he had projected to his crew, he knew precious little. His studies of the Great South Sea had focused on Sydney and New South Wales. Other areas had received little more than passing interest. Much of what he knew about New Zealand was anecdotal information that came from seafarers and from the published writings of Captain Cook and Tupala, the English-speaking Polynesian navigator and interpreter Cook had taken with him from Tahiti. The facts seemed clear enough: The British had established hegemony on these islands following the Treaty of Waitangi five years earlier. Of the existence and general location of the town called Russell, Richard had at least a working knowledge. He had not lied to his men, he convinced himself. By all accounts, Russell was a well-known port in the South Pacific that catered to traders and whalers, and as such enjoyed a reputation for grog and easy sex.

Secretary Henshaw had told him that the French had designs on these islands. If they did, other European nations likely did too. All well and good. It mattered not at all to Richard if he and his men stumbled upon an Englishman, a Frenchman, a Spaniard, or an Italian. Any European might offer a way home. It was not the Europeans in New Zealand that gave him pause. It was the natives.

Another concern was his physical condition. The wound festering in his right thigh since the wreck continued to worry him. During the day, the degree of pain varied from dull to acute, and walking on the soft sand made it worse. But there was nothing for it but to keep going.

On the afternoon of the ninth day out, they came to a dangerous cut in the beach carved by a swift-flowing stream. While they had been wading across the waters between the headlands, this was a different matter. The water looked deep and threatening. A wide gully inland scarped into steep, muddy hillsides. Judging from its shape, Jack Brengle reckoned that the gash in the landscape had been carved by a tidal river whose source was somewhere upstream. Their choices were limited. They must either wade across the strong current at dead low tide or venture inland into the bush to find a safer place to cross upstream.

Because they were currently at half-tide on the come, Richard decided to wait until the following morning to get a better feel for the lay of the land. Here was a good place to pitch camp for the night, he decreed. The waters off the beach promised food, and a cluster of small lakes just inland contained clear, fresh water. That night, for the first time in many days, the men slept soundly on a protected beach. The breeze was sufficiently strong to keep away the mosquitoes and the dreaded sandflies that had tortured them relentlessly on their march north.

Early the following morning, Richard awoke refreshed. First, as on every morning, he ventured to the water's edge and scanned the horizon for a glint of white canvas. As on every morning, he saw nothing but empty ocean. Fancying a swim in one of the freshwater ponds, he invited the three midshipmen to join him.

As the four men were shedding their clothing, young Tom Talmadge posed a question to him. "How do you do it, sir, if you don't mind my inquiring."

Richard gave him a bemused look. "How do I do what?"

"Well, sir," Talmadge began. He looked at Hugh Zabriskie and Jonty Montgomery for reassurance. They nodded. "What I mean is, you have suffered so much, sir, and lost so much, and yet you manage to keep your chin up and our spirits up as well. We all look to be captains someday, too, sir. So how do you do it? We'd very much like to know."

"And you are still limping, sir," Montgomery put in, "quite badly. Yet you never show that you are in pain. How do you manage to keep going?" He looked at his two comrades before going on. "We continue, and we all act as though rescue is certain, but in truth we fear it is not."

Richard swallowed hard. It took him a moment to summon an answer. "I appreciate your concern, lads. Truly I do. Please don't worry about the limp. It's nothing. The wound will heal with time. To answer your question, Tom, I keep my spirits up and encourage all of you because I don't know what else to do. I am no Captain Bligh, nor would I ever choose to be like him. Every captain has his own style of leadership, his own way of managing the responsibilities of command. *I* believe that captains lead best by showing the way, not by driving their men before them. It may not be the best way, and it may not be your way when you rise to high rank—which each of you will do someday because each of you will have earned it. Whatever your way may turn out to be, I have every confidence that it will be a good one. And a fair one."

"Yes, sir. Thank you, sir." Talmadge took a breath and again glanced at his shipmates. Rapidly, and in a slightly sheepish tone, he said, "It's just that we—that is, Hugh, Jonty, and myself—want you to know how much we admire you, sir. You have always been very kind to us. Stern, but fair and kind. We want you to know that we'd sooner be here on this island with you, whatever might happen, than anywhere else on land or sea."

When Richard did not respond, Talmadge buried his hands in his trouser pockets and stared down at his bare feet. A shock of blond hair tumbled over his forehead. "I'm sorry, sir," he mumbled, "if I have spoken out of turn."

Richard walked over to Talmadge and placed a hand on the boy's shoulder. "You have not spoken out of turn, my boy, and you certainly have nothing to apologize for. I am deeply touched by what you said. A moment ago you asked me how I do what I do. You just answered your own question. Truth be told, I could not do much of anything without you three and Mr. Brengle and Mr. Wheeler and Mr. Donahue and all my crew to help me. However experienced and learned a sea captain may be, he cannot act alone. He is no god, despite what Mr. Bligh may have thought to the contrary. He can only do what his officers and crew *believe* he can do. Do you understand what I am trying to tell you?"

Talmadge smiled. "Yes, sir, I believe I do."

"Jonty, Hugh? Do you understand?"

"We do, sir," they said together.

"Good. Remember it when you are walking the quarterdeck as captain of your own vessel someday. Now, let's get that swim in before we head back to camp. We have another full day ahead of us. This may be the day we turn eastward across the island."

As the four were emerging from the cool water, washed clean of salt for the first time in days, they heard shouts in the distance. Marine private Will Allerton crested the summit of a large sand dune and struggled through the brush to reach them. "Captain! Captain!"

"What is it, Private?" Richard called back. He struggled into his clothing as Allerton raced toward them, then waited as the young Marine summoned enough breath to speak.

"Quick, Captain, please come quick!" Allerton wheezed. "We have made contact with the natives, and they seem none too pleased to make our acquaintance!"

CHAPTER 10

ANNE HAD BEEN NAPPING FOR NEARLY AN HOUR WHEN SHE FELT A hand gently shaking her shoulder. She opened her eyes to see Te Whina and Maude MacKenzie, the mission director's Kentish-born wife standing next to her bed.

In their brief chats Anne had learned that the ample-bosomed, motherly Maude had also been born into a family of means. Unlike Anne's family, who had given their daughter a liberal education and a degree of freedom unusual for that time and place, Maude's parents demanded strict obedience in all matters filial. When they arranged a marriage with a man she despised, however, Maude defied her heritage, took up with and married a zealous young minister, and sailed away with her husband to devote her life to the English Missionary Society of New Zealand. Together, she and Te Whina were responsible for the physical well-being of the mission's staff and the Maori converts who lived on or near the mission.

"No, no, Anne dear," Maude said. "Please don't feel you need to get up on my account. You are not yet recovered. Te Whina said that you wished to see me, and here I am."

Anne sat up anyway and slid her legs to the side of the bed. With Te Whina's help she put her feet on the floor and walked to a rocking chair placed nearby. Once Anne was settled, Maude wrapped a woolen shawl around Anne's shoulders to shield her from the autumn chill.

"I do not get up on your account, Maude," Anne said, "but on my own. I think it best that I move about as much as I can."

Maude nodded approvingly. "I cannot disagree. It's best for you and it's best for your baby."

"It must be," she agreed ruefully. "The baby is growing more active every day. I may not get much sleep these next few months." She reached up and took Maude's hand. "I have you and Te Whina to thank for the fact that I can feel him at all. I shudder to think what the outcome would have been were it not for your care."

Maude smiled. "It has nothing to do with us, my dear. It is our pleasure to care for you, but it is God's will." She squeezed Anne's hand, then turned it over to feel Anne's pulse. After a moment she glanced at Te Whina. "*Kei te haere ngara o re ra. He pai ahau,*" she said to her.

Te Whina nodded knowingly. "*Karite ki ahau, tuahine,*" she said, adding further comments equally foreign to Anne's ears.

"What are you saying?" Anne asked. "Is it something you don't want me to hear?"

Maude MacKenzie's smile remained. "I apologize, my dear. Speaking Maori has become so natural to me that I often do it without considering my audience. I was saying to Te Whina that you are getting stronger by the day, and that it pleases me greatly. We are also pleased to note that you are walking more steadily than before. She says that all the meat and vegetables you are eating are speeding your recovery. Your healthy appetite bodes well."

"You have been so kind," Anne sighed. "The Maori people have certainly benefited from your presence. How many missionaries are here?"

"Here in New Zealand? One hundred thirty-two at last count. Here in this mission? Nine, including our staff. You have met most of them."

Anne's eyes widened. "My goodness. I hadn't expected there to be so many missionaries in the colony."

"There are, and that number includes only Wesleyan missionaries. It does not include those of the Anglican, Catholic, and other faiths. There are quite a large number of them, as well. Now then, Anne, what can I do for you beyond checking your vital signs? Why did you wish to see me?"

Anne pursed her lips. "I need your help, Maude."

"Of course, Anne. What do you need from me?"

"I need information," she said earnestly. "I want to know when your husband is planning to dispatch a search party to find the survivors of my husband's ship. If I survived, others must have survived as well. And yet, days have passed, and I have heard nothing about a search for them. I am going mad with worry and frustration. Surely you understand that I must find out what has happened to my husband," she said urgently. "If I could go myself, I would."

Maude nodded slowly and took both of Anne's hands in hers. "I cannot imagine the pain you are suffering, my dear, and I am so sorry for the cross you have had to bear."

"I am not looking for sympathy, Maude. I am looking for answers." Tears filled her eyes. "Please help me."

"Have not Daniel and Jonathan explained the situation to you?" Maude asked quietly.

"To an extent," Anne said impatiently. "I am told, time and again, that there is danger out in the bush, and I understand that it is forbidden for anyone to leave the compound. But I do not fully understand why this is so. Nor do I understand how long this edict is to remain in effect. Your husband won't tell me, though I have begged him to do so. Jonathan will tell me nothing either. So I am turning to you, a lady I have come to trust and respect. Please help me, Maude. Please tell me what you know."

A shadow passed over Maude's face. "My dear," she hedged, "I am not at liberty to discuss such things. Those sorts of decisions are not mine to make."

"I realize that," Anne said, her frustration mounting. "I am not asking you to reveal great secrets. I am simply asking for the truth. Given who I am and where I am and what I have been through, I believe I am entitled to it. Do you not agree?" Her voice had been steadily increasing in volume, and those last four words were a shout.

"Anne dear, please. You must not distress yourself. The baby . . ."

"Yes, the baby!" Anne exploded. "Exactly! The baby has a father whom he may never know, God forbid. His father may still be alive and dying of starvation. Or he and his crew may already be dead. I am sick of living with fear and the dread of not knowing. I am sick of feeling like a prisoner, and I am sick of waiting. Please, Maude. I am not accustomed to begging, but as God is my witness, I am begging now. I want my husband, and I want to board a ship with him, and I want to go home! For the love of God, *help me!*" She buried her face in her hands and sobbed.

Maude stood silently looking at her with a pained expression on her face.

"I am sorry, Maude," Anne said when she regained control. "None of this is your doing. You have all been so kind to me."

Maude gestured to Te Whina, who hurried from the room. "I will help you, Anne. As God is *my* witness, I will help you. Please wait here. I will return soon."

Within the half hour, Daniel MacKenzie entered the infirmary in company with Jonathan Riggs, the mission's assistant director. Both men were dressed in the traditional black serge with a clerical white stock tied at the throat. Jonathan Riggs was the younger of the two, not a handsome man with his aquiline nose, closely clipped brown beard, and neatly queued hair, but gentle and kind. MacKenzie's faded blue eyes showed deep sympathy and concern.

"How are you, Anne?" Daniel asked cautiously.

Anne looked up at him from her rocking chair. "I am doing as well as can be expected under the circumstances," she returned evenly. "May I assume that Maude asked you and Jonathan to come?"

"She did. And I have rarely seen her so perturbed."

"You know why?"

"We do," MacKenzie said. "Truly, we have been expecting it."

"Expecting it? Then why did you not speak up sooner?" Her tone was demanding but calm. "Why put me through this wretched misery?"

"It was not from lack of caring, as I have told you before. And it was not from a lack of sensitivity."

"What, then?"

MacKenzie sighed. "It's difficult to explain something that to the European mind is inexplicable. And terrible."

Anne's expression hardened. "Try me."

MacKenzie pointed toward the bed. "May I sit down?"

"Of course. You too, Jonathan."

The two missionaries sat side by side on the edge of the bed and looked forlornly at Anne, who continued to rock while eyeing them closely.

"I am listening, gentlemen," she said when neither man spoke. "Please tell me what you know. And please, hold nothing back."

"Very well," MacKenzie said with a resigned sigh. "I'll start. The truth is, there is precious little in any of this that makes sense. Even those of us who have been many years in New Zealand find it difficult to understand what is happening. The situation is complex."

"So you have already said, Daniel. Can you simplify it for me?"

"We will try. I must begin by warning you that some of what you are about to hear is not for delicate ears. Or faint hearts." MacKenzie paused to allow Anne to absorb his words. When her expression remained unchanged, he said, "The fact is, some of it is downright shocking."

"Especially to well-bred women," Riggs added pointedly.

"Please do not concern yourself over my sensibilities, Jonathan," Anne said sharply. "I come from a noble family, it is true, but I possess the grit and perspectives that often go hand-in-hand with that privilege. I do not panic, and I do not shock easily. I am strong enough to hear anything you might say."

Riggs grinned to concede the point. "Everyone in the mission has commented on those qualities, Mrs. Cutler."

"Right, then." MacKenzie cleared his throat. "You have asked on several occasions why no one is allowed to leave this compound—a most logical question. The short answer is that out there"—he held up a hand and waved it in a full circle—"a war is raging. It is not a war between the British and the native people. It's a war pitting Maori against Maori, tribe against tribe. They are fighting over land and trading rights and muskets. Why? Because land and trading rights translate into prestige and power, and muskets safeguard that power and respect. Plus, and just as important, they add to a warrior's *mana*."

"*Mana*? What is that?"

MacKenzie held up a hand and said kindly, "That is a subject for a future discussion. It's an important concept. For the moment, here is what you need to know: Power and prestige mean everything to a Maori chief and his tribe. To them, land and trading rights are worth killing for, and worth dying for. Are you with me so far?"

Anne nodded slowly. "I believe so. The desire for land I can understand. And I can understand that the greater a tribe's ability to seize and hold land, the greater its perceived status. But trading rights? Are you telling me that the Maori trade with each other?"

"With each other and with anyone willing to trade with them, including this mission. Where do you think we get the kumara and meat you enjoy, and the wheat to make bread? Certainly not from this compound. Our modest grounds can produce only bare necessities. But as a trading post we can garner all we need. But we are getting off the subject. Let's agree to save this topic for a future discussion as well, shall we?"

Anne nodded. "Very well. But tell me this: Where is this war being waged?"

"Everywhere," Jonathan told her.

"That would include the area where my husband's ship went down."

"It would."

"How long is the war likely to last?"

Jonathan shrugged. "It's difficult to say. Intertribal wars are quite common in New Zealand. The actual fighting does not normally last for long, but these wars can be fierce. There is a Maori word called *utu*. Remember it. Essentially, *utu* means exacting revenge. If one tribe has been harmed in any way by another tribe, it will seek revenge on that tribe, usually by inflicting a much greater harm. Which can lead to another round of *utu*. And so on and so on, sometimes for generations."

"Until everyone in one of the two tribes is killed?"

"Precisely. Like two men in a duel of honor, one of them will receive satisfaction by killing the other."

She sighed. "How dreadful. Are we in danger here? In the past you have denied that we are."

"I still deny it," MacKenzie replied. "Since they first came to these islands, missionaries have been regarded as *atua*, as gods. Maori chiefs trust us. They give us food and other things we need, and in return we teach them English and other disciplines. But our first mission is to teach them about Christ and salvation. The Maori listen. We have converted many of them to Christianity. One such chief is Te Wherowhero of the Waikato tribe, one of the most powerful chiefs on this island. He is a king in his own right who has chosen to ally with the Crown. For services rendered to England, he has been awarded one of the finest homes in Auckland for his personal residence."

Anne shook her head. "I must confess that I find it hard to take in all of this. And despite what you are saying, I seem no closer to finding out about my husband!"

"We understand, Mrs. Cutler," Riggs said, "and we are coming to that. Thus far we have but scratched the surface. But you must understand the fundamentals of what is happening here to understand why we cannot conduct a search for your husband at this time."

Anne rubbed her temples. "Go on."

Riggs continued, "Te Wherowhero is a close friend and ally of another great chief in the Hokianga region north of here. That chief's name is Tamati Waka Nene, and he is a chief of a powerful Ngapuhi tribe. Seven years ago he converted to the Wesleyan faith and was baptized. He also speaks fluent English."

"How on earth did he learn to speak English?" Anne asked, caught up in the narrative. "Who taught him?"

"Ah. Yet another topic for a future discussion." He looked at MacKenzie, who said, "The point is, Anne, we live among powerful friends who have pledged to protect us."

"What about the other tribes on the island who are not so enamored with British rule? I assume they exist?"

"They do," MacKenzie acknowledged. "A good number of them."

"Are they at war with the two chiefs you mentioned?"

"Some of them are, yes. It depends on one's allegiances. Some *iwi* stand with England and the perceived economic, military, and religious benefits of such an alliance. Other *iwi* chiefs have taken a different stand. They may lead smaller tribes, but in the aggregate they amount to a sizable force. They don't always agree on policy, but on one goal they do agree. They want every white man and woman off this island."

"Including you missionaries, who are gods to them?" she said tartly.

"Including us. Though they would not harm us unless we were to do something bad to them. Or unless the social structure on this island is turned upside down."

"I think I see," Anne said, although she was not sure she did. "But one thing puzzles me. Does this so-called protection extend beyond the mission? If it does, what is to prevent us from sending a search party to the north?"

"We will send a search party as soon as we can. But I'm sorry to say, that won't be for a while. As I have indicated, until now the Maori have let us be. Their quarrel has not been with us or even with white settlers—*pakeha*, as they call them. Their quarrel has been with each other and with the colonial government they believe stabbed them in the back following the Treaty of Waitangi."

"The Treaty of . . . ?"

"Waitangi. Everything hinges on that treaty. But we can't get into that now. It's too big a topic, and Jonathan and I have already burdened you with too much information. The point, for now, is that the Treaty of Waitangi—along with other events—makes this civil war different from the others. It is more complicated and more volatile, and thus more uncertain and more dangerous. If we were to send a search party to look for survivors of your husband's ship, it could be only with Te Wherowhero's knowledge and permission, which thus far he has refused to grant. It would be his warriors doing the searching, you see, and he will not put them deliberately in harm's way. So we must wait to see how this civil war unfolds and if it spreads to include the *pakeha*. If it does, we will be forced to evacuate this post and seek refuge in Auckland. Our exalted status as deities would then be compromised. Do you understand?"

"I'm beginning to," Anne said guardedly. "But something about all this doesn't add up. Why have things suddenly changed? I understand that tensions are rising. But something must have happened to involve the white settlers in the tribal conflicts, which in turn has put everyone under lock and key. Am I right? If I am, is it just the treaty and its aftermath that has caused this? Or is it because the white man is the source of muskets?"

"Not only is that a perfectly reasonable assumption," Riggs allowed, "it would be true, if all things were equal. Unfortunately, all things are not equal."

"Then why . . . ?" Suddenly, shreds of muted conversations she had overheard came together and a light dawned. Up to this point, these confusing pieces of information had meant little to her. Now they made sense. "Something dreadful has happened, hasn't it, Jonathan? Something so horrible it has turned everything upside down, as Daniel put it."

MacKenzie and Riggs looked at each other, and then at Anne.

"What is it?" Anne half-whispered. "What has happened?"

"We warned you, Anne," MacKenzie ventured in a low voice.

"Yes, you warned me. But tell me, please. It's all right, I can take whatever it is."

"Very well." MacKenzie heaved a sigh of resignation. "You are quite right. There was an incident, south of here, in a whaling station called Taranaki. It involved whalers. British whalers."

"Yes? Go on, Daniel," she said impatiently.

"The whalers crossed the Maori in a bad way. I don't know what they did or why they did it. But whatever it was, they paid the ultimate price as a result."

"They were killed," Anne said in hushed tones.

"Worse than that, I fear."

"What could possibly be worse than that?"

MacKenzie's expression looked as wretched as his voice sounded. "Mrs. Cutler . . . dear Anne . . . the Maori slaughtered the whalers, and then they . . ." He stopped, unable to say the words.

"They did what, Daniel? Tell me! What did the natives do to the whalers?"

MacKenzie closed his eyes. "They slaughtered them, and then they . . . consumed them."

CHAPTER 11

RICHARD AND THE THREE MIDSHIPMEN WERE HALFWAY BACK TO CAMP when they heard gunfire followed by incoherent shouting and a sweeping volley of musket fire. The shots were followed by screams and two high-pitched reports that sounded to Richard like pistol shots. Richard ran faster, trying to ignore the crippling pain in his thigh. Struggling to keep going, he dug his feet into the sand and dragged himself up the steep dune. When he was just short of the top, he dropped onto his stomach. With chopping motions of his hand, he signaled the three midshipmen and Marine private behind him to get down. Then, crawling on his elbows and knees, he edged his way to the summit and peered over the crest.

The scene below was not encouraging. His men had taken refuge in a shallow gully perhaps fifty feet away. Their backs were to him, and they were all looking toward a large group of what he assumed were Maori who had taken position within the bush that began another fifty feet beyond the gully. In the open area between the gully and the edge of the bush he saw three bodies. Two of them were not moving at all; a third was writhing, still alive but clearly injured. He could tell that all three were members of his crew, but at this distance, without the aid of a spyglass, he could not identify them.

"What do you make of it, Captain?" whispered Thomas Talmadge, who had slithered up beside him, with the other two midshipmen and Private Allerton following behind. "What can we do?"

"You can stay put and stay low," Richard hissed. "And be quiet."

Richard watched intently as those of his crew brandishing muskets finished reloading them—ramming powder and ball down the smooth-bore barrel and inserting a percussion cap in the breech. Brengle and Donahue directed them up against the gully's waist-high eastern side, where they rose to a kneeling position and took aim at the bush. Nate Donahue swung his pistol back and forth in front of him, searching for a target.

Richard considered what his military training had taught him as he surveyed the arena of combat below. It did not look good. Enemies had been defined; lines of battle had been drawn; and the killing had begun. Blood lust was up on both sides, and the odds against the Americans looked overwhelming.

"What do we do, sir? There must be some way we can help," Jonty whispered.

Richard ignored him. He stilled his thoughts to allow his instincts and experience to fill the void. An incident that occurred while he was serving with Jack Brengle in the swamps of Florida during the Seminole Wars came to mind. It had worked then. Would it work again? Turning on his side, he pulled out the pistol he had tucked under the waistband of his breeches. He checked to see that all five chambers were loaded. Satisfied, he rose to his knees and from there to a full upright position.

"What are you doing, sir?" Hugh Zabriskie gasped.

Richard replied by raising the pistol high above his head, aiming the barrel straight up, and firing a single round into the air. A second shot, then a third, fourth, and fifth. Complete silence followed. Those in the gully below him and those in the bush gave him their full attention. With all eyes fixed upon him, Richard heaved the pistol far up the beach, then started walking down the dune toward the gully.

"Follow behind me," he called over his shoulder to the others. "Walk slowly, stay calm, and do exactly as I do."

As he made his way toward the gully, Richard held his hands out, palms up, and kept his eyes steadily on the bush. The Seminoles had recognized the gesture as an offer to parley; would these natives regard it the same way? It was a gamble born of desperation; at any moment he expected to feel the burning sting of a metal ball ripping into his stomach. His heart raced, beads of sweat formed on his brow and under his armpits, and still he walked on.

"Captain, thank God!" exclaimed Nate Donahue when Richard reached the gully and descended into it. "We didn't think you would make it back alive." He watched slack-jawed as Richard limped on without pause across the dry bed of the gully to its other side. He gave Brengle a small nod and motioned to the midshipmen and Private Allerton to stay put before he hauled himself up to stand alone at the top of the expanse, facing the dense bush.

Donahue was about to leap up to bring him back when Jack Brengle grabbed his arm. "Leave him be, Nate," he said softly but forcefully. "The captain knows what he's doing."

"You men," Brengle called quietly to those with muskets, "throw your weapons up onto the sand. And make sure they see you doing it. Do it, *now!*" he hissed when the Marines, to a man, hesitated. Grudgingly, one by one, they did as they were told. "You too, Nate," Brengle commanded. "Lose your pistol."

"Bloody hell!" Donahue cursed as he stood and hurled his pistol up the beach.

Richard started walking again and kept walking until he stood beside the body of Henry Simpson, the sailor from Connecticut prized as the ship's best lookout. Richard crouched down to feel for a pulse. There was none. He moved on to the next body and winced. Judging from the small red patch in the center of his white shirt, Ted Wheeler's death had been swift. Richard crossed himself twice and moved on to the third man down.

When he reached Garth Plummer, he dropped slowly to one knee and scanned the bush to the east, his eyes riveted there in a silent plea. "I'm sorry, Captain," the Marine breathed, grimacing in pain. "I'm to blame for all this. I panicked when I saw them and shot at one of them. I'm sorry."

Richard gently lifted Plummer's head and settled it on his knee. "I know you are, Garth. It's done. Don't think on it. It does no good."

"I'm better than that, Captain," he pleaded. "I'm better than that."

"I know you are, Garth," Richard soothed again. "You're one of our best."

Engrossed in the moment, Richard ignored what was happening around him. When he reached down and probed a finger inside a hole in Plummer's trousers above the kneecap, Plummer cried out in agony. Uncertain what to do next, Richard stroked Plummer's head gently until he sensed someone kneeling beside him and felt a hand on his arm firmly pushing it away from the wound—a slender brown hand. To his astonishment, a young woman with long black hair was kneeling next to him. If she was Maori, she was the first he had ever seen. He took in the expertly crafted black tattoos on the rich brown skin of her arms and legs, and the four vertical black lines on her chin. The young woman motioned him to lean back to create some space. She clearly knew what she was about as she scrutinized Plummer's leg. As her fingers gently probed into the wound and up around his thigh and groin, Plummer twitched but did not cry out or protest.

"Who are you?" Richard asked her. Everything about the graceful young woman was strange to his eyes. She was wearing a loose-fitting cloak woven from plant fibers, a decorative pendant around her neck, and a green skirt-like affair made out of the same plant as her cloak. She was astonishingly beautiful. In some way Richard did not understand, the tattoos enhanced that beauty.

The young woman ignored him. She continued her ministrations, occasionally nodding at something she found. At one point, Plummer smiled up at her. That, too, she ignored. At length, satisfied with her diagnosis, she glanced at Richard.

"We will heal him," she said forthrightly. "He will be well in time." She pointed at Richard's thigh. "We will heal you, too. And the others. Not them," she pointed to where Simpson and Wheeler lay dead.

Questions raced through Richard's mind as he struggled to make sense of it all. In the end all he could come up with was, "You speak English?"

The look she gave him questioned his intelligence. "Yes."

"Are you Maori?"

The narrowing of her eyes suggested she had just been asked another inane question. "Yes."

"Are you the leader of these men?"

She shook her head. "No." She pointed. "He is *ariki*."

He followed her gesture and saw a wall of brown-skinned warriors standing shoulder to shoulder at the tree line. Many were brandishing muskets—some of them were old-style flintlocks, but most were the recently introduced percussion cap muskets. Other warriors gripped spears, long-handled axes with evil-looking serrated edges, and wooden clubs. The men were dressed much like the woman, in short kilts that wrapped around the waist. Those who were not bare-chested wore cloaks that seemed woven from flax reeds. All of them sported tattoos of grand design seemingly from head to foot. Some men wore sandal-like shoes. Most were barefoot.

Still cradling Plummer's head, Richard watched as six of the armed warriors broke ranks and approached. The man the woman had pointed to and called *ariki*—a stocky, muscular, handsome man—walked ahead of the group. His cloak was more intricate than those of the others. Three colorful bird feathers woven into his long, thick hair further marked him as the leader. A study in coiled fury, he stopped in front of Richard and folded his arms across his chest. The young woman rose to her feet to stand beside him, her expression blank.

The *ariki* scowled at Richard. "You English? French?" His voice was deep, gruff, threatening. He looked as though he was about to spit in Richard's face.

Richard carefully placed Plummer's head upon the sand. He then stood up and locked eyes with the *ariki*. "Do you understand my language?" he asked him.

"Enough," the man grunted.

"Good. Then you know I am not French."

"English?"

"American." Richard went on, "I am an American naval officer. The men you see with me are members of my crew. Our ship was lost south of here. We are looking for an English settlement called Russell. Do you know of it? Perhaps you can tell us where it is. Perhaps you can take us there."

The *ariki* looked at the woman for clarification.

"Kororareka," the woman said, then continued speaking to him, apparently translating what Richard had said.

As the Maori woman spoke, the *ariki* sneered at Richard and flared his nostrils, then took a menacing step toward Richard. Richard stood his ground.

"We're here, Captain!" Nate Donahue called from the gully.

Richard held out the flat of his palm behind him: Stay calm.

"*Kaua e kino kia ia,*" the woman said.

Whatever that meant, it angered the *ariki*. "*Na te aka ahau i kino ai ki a la?*" he thundered. "*He ana tana korero ki a la?*"

"*Ko te tangata te rangatira nui.*"

"*He rangatira?*" he spat, his voice incredulous.

"*Ae.*"

"*Kaore au e whakapono atu!*"

"*He pono.*"

For a moment the *ariki* appeared more confused than angry. When he finally spoke to Richard, his tone had lost much of its edge. "You come with us," he snorted before turning on his heel and walking away.

"You call your men," the woman told Richard. "Come."

"What did you say to him?" Richard asked her as she turned to head for the bush.

She offered no reply.

"Whatever it was, thank you," he called after her.

Richard signaled to his men to join him. An hour later, after a detail of American sailors had buried their dead and the Maori warriors had collected the weapons discarded on the beach, a makeshift litter was fashioned from the strong branches of a prickly *manuka* tree, and the Maori and Americans set off inland.

CHAPTER 12

LONG TENTACLES OF SUNLIGHT WERE CLINGING TO THE TREES WHEN the Maori finally called a halt in a woodland clearing that, judging from the trampled earth and ashes strewn about in its center, had seen previous use. The Americans were told to sit down. Since leaving the beach they had covered but a few miles while following the course of a meandering river.

Grateful for the rest after the long, stress-filled day, Richard sat down with his back to a tree and closed his eyes for a few moments. The cool breeze transported him in his mind to Massachusetts. On just such a cool, sunny day he would stroll beneath the autumn leaves to the quays on Crow Point to gaze longingly at the activity on ship and shore as sailors, merchants, dockhands, and others brought the business of the day to a close. It was there, in the seaside community of Hingham, where Thomas Cutler in 1756 had established a commercial foothold in what would become an epicenter of the global carrying trade. The thought of Hingham also brought back the worry about his mother being wooed by a man his father had avoided for reasons his mother either would not or could not recognize. If he survived New Zealand, retired his commission in the Navy, and followed his family's wishes as expressed during last year's conference in Boston, he himself might one day live in Hingham.

Brengle came and sat beside him. "What are you thinking, Richard?" The two had walked together for most of the day but had not spoken much. "Have you figured out the affairs of the world? Or at least what the hell we're going to do about the situation we find ourselves mired in?"

"No, to both questions," Richard confessed as he massaged his right thigh.

"So you're telling me that we're fucked? Don't you have any plan at all?"

Richard smiled glumly. "Certainly we're up against it. I don't think these fellows like us very much. That goes double for their leader."

"He looks fierce, that one," Brengle agreed. "But I suspect he may be more sail than ballast. Not all of them are like him, thank the Lord. Some of them seem decent enough. And that woman, my God, she knows her business when it comes to healing. She's not very friendly, though."

Richard snorted. "I agree."

"Quite frankly, though, I don't give a damn what their *ariki* thinks of us as long as he doesn't invite us for dinner." Brengle nudged Richard. "Speak of the devil, here he comes."

The *ariki*, accompanied by two armed warriors, stopped before them. "You stay here," he grunted, indicating a swath of ground on the northern third of the clearing. The yellowish-green grass that covered it looked comfortable enough to lie upon—more comfortable, Richard noted with interest, than the ground cover apparently allocated to the larger number of natives.

"You not move," the man growled. "Next day, we stop."

Richard took that statement to mean that tomorrow they would reach their destination. During the day's march he had inquired of several Maori, through a combination of broken English and sign language, where and how far away their destination might be. His queries were met with polite shrugs. Either they didn't understand him, didn't know, or were unwilling to say.

He had not asked the young Maori woman. Beyond his wound, she seemed to have no interest in him or his history. Throughout the day she had deliberately avoided him save for those brief moments during a rest break when she attended to him, Garth Plummer, and others of the crew with minor ailments. On one such occasion Richard had stood beside Plummer's litter and looked on as the woman briefly inspected the wound before smearing a paste of some sort over it and then gently massaging it into and around the wound.

"What is that?" he had asked her.

"Healing medicine," she answered.

"Yes, but what is it?"

Without another word, she got up and walked away.

Another opportunity arose during supper that evening. Richard and his men had been anticipating a good meal ever since a Maori hunting party had walked into camp earlier in the day carrying dead birds they had snared. A number of the birds looked very much like the common pigeons he knew in America, except that these birds were twice the size and far more beautiful, with gray-and-white plumage and an emerald-green head and chest. "*Kereru*," the young Maori plucking the birds called them when Richard asked.

The young Maori cook wrapped the dressed carcasses in large leaves from a cabbage tree along with a vegetable that looked like a sweet potato. On top of the concoction he spread a layer of grubs plucked from under the bark of trees. Each bird was then wrapped in fern fronds and placed in a fire pit started by rubbing *kaikomako* sticks together. As the fowls began roasting, fresh dirt was spread over the flax cover that held in the heat and protected the food. After what seemed a very long two hours, supper was ready.

Each of the Americans was handed a plump fern leaf bursting with savory meat and juices. Accustomed to fish and little else, the men dove into the meal and ate hungrily with their fingers.

Richard unwrapped his bird slowly, savoring the aroma before taking the first bite.

"Goddammit to hell, this is delicious," Nate Donahue said in astonishment. "At least these damn savages are good for *something*. Best food I've had in ages."

Toward the end of the meal, a Maori youth of perhaps sixteen walked up to Jonty Montgomery and held out a fern frond to him. With his other hand he rubbed his stomach in the universal signal of tasty food. Montgomery glanced over at his captain, who gave a brief nod.

"Thank you," Montgomery said, returning the Maori's smile and accepting the fern. "Thank you very much."

The Maori youngster nodded and then pointed at the midshipman's makeshift hat fashioned from flax reeds.

"You want to wear it?" Montgomery asked. He took it off and held it out. "Here, try it on."

The boy shook his head. "*Kore, e kore e taea e au*," he said, keeping his hands at his sides.

"Here, please," Montgomery insisted. "I want you to try it on." To demonstrate, he put the hat on his own head, and then took it off before holding it out encouragingly to the youth.

The young man took the hat and tentatively placed it on his head. The older Maori men who had been watching this interchange broke into raucous laughter, and the boy blushed and hurriedly handed the hat back to the midshipman.

"You keep it," Montgomery said, indicating his offer by sign language. "Please, I want you to keep it."

"*Kao, ka mili*," the young man said shyly. He stepped back, waving his hands back and forth in front of him. "*Kaore ahau whakatauki.*"

"I can only imagine what that means," Donahue said cuttingly.

"Whatever it means," Richard remarked, "what that lad just did was a gesture of goodwill. He wouldn't have done it without the *ariki*'s knowledge and approval. Remember that, Nate, and be grateful for it."

He scanned the cluster of Maori to whom the boy was returning. They were sitting around a second fire that popped and crackled agreeably, fueled by sticks collected from the forest floor. The young woman was sitting alone on the periphery, gnawing on a *kereru* leg. When her eyes met his across the distance, she averted her gaze.

Richard got up and limped over to where she was sitting. Although she did not invite him to join her, he sat down near her and waited. When she made a show of ignoring him, he said, "I want to thank you."

The woman finished sucking out the sweet marrow and tossed the bone aside. "Thank me? For what do you thank me?"

"For saving my life," Richard said.

The woman made a face. "You lie. I not save your life."

"Aye, you did," he said. "And please don't get up," he added when she started to stand. "I want to talk to you."

"Why?" she asked coldly. But she sat back down. "You want to talk? Talk."

Now that he had her full attention, a boon he had not expected, he found himself at a loss for words. He asked her the first thing that came to mind. "That man, your leader, the one you call *ariki*. Is he your husband? I mean no disrespect," he added quickly.

She shook her head emphatically. "Not my husband. He is not healer."

"Your husband is a healer?"

"No husband!" she barked. "I need no husband."

"I understand. What I mean to say is, when the *ariki* and I were talking earlier, I thought he didn't like me. In fact, I thought he wanted to kill me. I am hoping you can tell me why."

"Why was Manala angry?" she snapped back at him. "We were sent to help you, and you tried to kill us!"

"You were sent?" Richard asked eagerly. "Who sent you? The English?"

She looked away. "That is not for me to say. But you are right. Manala no like you. Manala no like any *pakeha*."

"I see. But what did you tell him? Why did he turn away without harming me? I could not have stopped him."

She shrugged. "I tell him you are *rangatira*."

"*Rangatira*? What is that?"

"A great chief."

"Good lord!" Richard blurted.

She looked at him closely. "You are chief, yes?"

Richard nodded slowly. "Well, yes, I suppose I am a chief, of a sort. But I am not a great chief." He gestured toward his encampment. "As you can see, my tribe is very small."

She allowed a faint smile. "Number in *iwi* does not matter. What matters is, you are their chief, yes? I did not lie."

"No, you did not lie."

She got up.

"No, wait, please." He made to reach for her but thought better of it. "Tell me, where did you learn to speak English so well?"

When she was silent, he said, "May I at least ask your name?"

She stared down at him. The light cast by the dying flames reflected off her slender body and waist-length ebony hair. She seemed at once a bold jungle princess and a blushing young maiden.

"Ataahua," she told him. "My name is Ataahua."

"Ataahua." He repeated the name softly to himself. "It's a lovely name. Does it have a meaning?"

She hesitated. "It means 'beautiful,'" she finally said.

He watched her as she walked away. "Of course it does," he said when she was too far away to hear him.

When the light from the two fires died away and yielded to the ethereal glow of a third-quarter moon, Richard did what he had done most evenings since he had recovered sufficiently to move about freely. He visited the members of his crew, tonight clustered together within the small clearing assigned to them. The morale of his men was crucial, and he did not stint on the time he spent with each man.

"How's that rib coming along, George?" he asked George Webb, a nineteen-year-old Marine private from Savannah, Georgia. A rib cracked while Langston Weeks dragged Webb from the sinking ship had not yet fully healed. Rest and a proper diet would see to that, but meanwhile he was in considerable pain. Webb was popular among the crew and officers for his wit and sunny disposition.

"Comin' along smartly, Captain," the lad replied with a forced grin. "The pain's not so bad, really. I'll soon be back to normal, makin' a damn fool of myself like always."

"Looking forward to that, George. We'll soon be getting proper medical attention for you and everyone else."

"That includes you, Captain, I hope. That limp of your'n shows you ain't doin' so good neither."

"Perhaps not," Richard had to agree. "But like you, I'm managing. It's getting better. We need to keep our chins up and our wits about us, eh?"

"Aye, Captain. You can bet we will."

Matthew Shields, a gunner's mate from Narragansett, Rhode Island, inched over to join the conversation. His father was a successful merchant captain and an old acquaintance of the Cutler family. "Captain," he asked, "do you think these savages are taking us to that English settlement you've been talking about? Russell?" His broad face was alive with hope.

"First off, Matt," Richard said sotto voce, "I must caution you once more not to refer to them as savages. It could land us in a heap of trouble. Besides, it must be clear to you by now that these people are not savages. Savages do not offer food and shelter to strange white men. You saw what that Maori boy did."

"Aye, Captain, I did," Shields admitted.

"More to the point, these Maori carry percussion cap muskets that are not yet standard issue even in European armies. Until we know where they got them, who is supplying them with powder and shot, and who trained them, we must be very careful what we say. It could be the English or the French or someone else altogether. And who are they using them against? So many questions and so few answers. Until we have those answers and we know what and who we are dealing with, we should accord them the same respect we would give to any strangers. We should base our opinions on what we see, not what we want to believe. And what we see seems to indicate that these people are highly intelligent. I realize that Lieutenant Donahue does not see things that way, but don't be swayed by what he says. He is entitled to his opinion, but he may be wrong. And assuming that he is wrong, our chances of getting off this island alive and well are greatly enhanced. Do you understand?"

"I do, sir," Shield said contritely. "I confess, I hadn't considered it that way."

Richard nodded. "As to where we are being taken, I have no better notion of that than you do. We'll have to see what Fate has in store for us. Whatever it is and wherever it is, we'll deal with it, just as we have dealt with everything else. Stay positive and get some sleep now. Good night, men."

"Good night, sir," they both returned.

The rounds continued—to Jim Turner, the carpenter's mate; Cyrus Payton, boatswain's mate; Josh Sturgis, a native of New Hampshire rated able seaman. Man by man he spoke to each—Will Allerton keeping watch over Garth Plummer; Elijah Howe, the oldest of the survivors, who had sailed on a whaler out of Nantucket and who knew the ropes at sea as well as any man afloat; and Henry Spaulding, the ship's purser, a man of frail frame and quiet disposition who suffered from minor ailments and was often cold and sickly but put on a brave front to deflect attention away from himself.

Eventually Richard ended up where he had started, in the company of the three midshipmen, Nathaniel Donahue, and Jack Brengle.

"Well, gentlemen," he said wearily as he settled back against the same tree trunk he had hauled himself away from earlier, "let us hope that tomorrow provides some answers."

"Let us hope so indeed," Donahue said testily. "And that the answers are to questions we want answered."

"Sir," Montgomery prompted, "about those men standing over there." He nodded toward a group of well-armed Maori men standing along the eastern and western fringes of the clearing. A third of them were facing outward toward the bush. The rest were facing inward, their eyes seemingly fixed on nothing.

"What about them?"

"Well, sir, I was just wondering, are they guarding us or protecting us?"

"Protecting us?" Donahue scoffed. "Protecting us from what? Those bastards are guarding us, my boy, bet your last dollar on it. Though for the life of me I can't figure out why. Where could we possibly go where they couldn't track us down? There's no escape from here."

Behind them, the bush had gone quiet save for the *zig-zigs* of cicadas, a good deal louder here than near the coast, and the occasional "*more pork!*" call of some unidentified creature in the woods. The clouds that had blocked the sun earlier had dispersed, leaving the heavens clear and the landscape aglow with the moon's amber light.

"I'm not sure, Jonty," Richard replied. "It could be a combination of both, though I am as baffled as Mr. Donahue about who or what we might be protected against. I expect we'll know soon enough."

As the Americans slept and the Maori took shifts on sentry duty, clouds gathered overhead once again. By daybreak a thin, chilling rain was falling. After a quick breakfast of leftovers from the previous evening, they were on the march. Their route continued to follow a well-defined path hacked out of the bush. Although clearly much used, the path was so narrow in places that they had to walk single file behind the *ariki*, who led the way. Ataahua and the bulk of the men followed immediately after him, then the Americans and another band of armed warriors who brought up the rear. The pace remained slow but steady, and to Richard's relief, Ataahua was not the only one of the Maori helping the American having difficulty walking.

Despite the strangeness of his surroundings and the pain in his leg, Richard did his best to study the landscape they passed through and the other footpaths that crossed over or veered off from the main pathway. Casual discourse with his officers was difficult, and it was impossible to speak with his men except on breaks, so they walked in silence while Richard noted landmarks that seemed unusual enough to serve as guides—an especially large *kawakawa* tree with its bright orange fruit spikes or an old gnarled trunk of a *karaka* tree. Even though the flora was strange to him—or perhaps because of it—the landmarks stuck in his mind.

The rain ceased in late morning, and the murky gray sky cleared. The *ariki* held up a hand for the column to stop and called up two young men to run on ahead, presumably to alert those waiting for them to arrive.

Half an hour later, the party rounded a bend in the now considerably wider path, and there it was. Richard was astonished at what he saw. Stretching out before them to a distant line of trees that seemed to shimmer in the sunlight like a mirage was a clearing of far greater size than the one where they had spent the previous night. It seemed more a plain than a plateau, and it contained a massive square fortress that combined elements of a U.S. Army frontier fort, an English medieval castle, and something probably uniquely Maori. A five-foot-high palisade of stakes and heavy logs draped in what appeared to be large green carpets surrounded the structure. Outside the wall were clusters of simple thatched dwellings that presumably housed those who tended the fields, which lay fallow in late autumn. Richard was impressed by the setting. The modest river they had been following provided irrigation to the fields, water to the fortress, protection on the fortress's flank, and a waterway to the abundant sea life in the ocean some distance away to the west. A hill of considerable height rose above the bark-covered palisades, its mesa-like summit sufficiently large and level to accommodate several buildings, including one of impressive size. The hill was terraced from top to bottom in a series of well-kept concentric circles featuring a fair number of what looked to be thatched-roofed huts of similar size and design. Those near the summit appeared more commodious. The entire compound reminded Richard of a drawing of an Aztec temple in one of his old schoolbooks.

Richard presumed that the sturdy-looking wooden tower that rose high above the other structures served the same function as a crow's nest in a sailing ship. Indeed, standing lookout atop the structure were two bare-chested men. One was holding a musket at the ready, and the other held what looked to be a giant conch shell. In the far distance, between the eastern wall of the fort and the tree line beyond, clouds of white smoke rose into the air. Richard could make out the scent of a burning wood fire. Brengle caught Richard's eye and cast a look that was both questioning and grim. Richard lifted his shoulders slightly and kept walking.

"Mae haere, e te tangata ma!" the *ariki* abruptly demanded. Richard understood the meaning of those words when he was jabbed in the back by the blunt end of a short-shafted spear.

As the ship's crew and their Maori escorts moved out from the cover of the bush into the open plain, the lookout blew loud, hollow tones on his shell trumpet, apparently to announce to the villagers the party's return. Men and women tilling soil in the fields stopped what they were doing and stared curiously at the white men walking by them. "Eyes forward!" Richard called to his men as they trooped past.

Ahead, twin gates on the fortress's western wall swung open to allow entry. Before the group reached the gates, the Americans noted something unexpected: parallel lines of earthen trenches, each slightly higher than the one before it, all of them six to ten feet deep and set ten feet apart, giving the impression of a series of empty moats encircling a castle wall. The stakes that formed the wall were tied together by ropes made of flax, with enough space between them to thrust a spear or bayonet through the narrow opening. A dozen or so high wooden platforms similar in design to the lookout platform, but smaller, were placed above the wall.

As they neared the open gates, Richard was surprised to see that the fortress was surrounded by two walls, and what they were approaching was the outer wall. The inner wall was constructed in the same design and dimensions as the outer wall, only smaller, and was separated from the outer wall by about forty feet of open grassland. On each of the four corners of the outer wall, the Maori had constructed a frontier-style blockhouse.

As he was taking all this in, Richard felt a tug on his arm. "Look there, Richard," Brengle urged him softly. Richard followed Brengle's gaze to the top of one of the inner wall's main supports. Not only was the stake intricately carved in the manner of an Indian totem pole, at its peak was a shriveled human head. Richard had read of shrunken heads but had dismissed their existence as absurd. Now he wasn't so sure. Was it real? It certainly *looked* real. He felt a primeval terror surge through his veins. *Have they brought us here to eat us?*

The apprehensive Americans passed slowly through the second gate, which closed behind them. Their fear and dread bordered on panic as they entered the heart of the fortress and saw what lay ahead of them.

CHAPTER 13

ANNE WAS SITTING AT A TABLE IN THE SCHOOLROOM WHEN THE FIRST pains hit.

Daniel and Jonathan had convinced her that keeping busy was the best way to pass the time until the baby came—and, equally important, until the situation was stable enough for Chief Te Wherowhero to send a search party to look for Richard and other *Suwannee* survivors. When Jonathan had suggested that she might teach in the mission's school, she quickly agreed. The energetic Maori children who raced about the compound were enchanting, and she had a lot to learn about raising a child. Any experience would be helpful.

Although she had been uncertain how to proceed when faced with a room full of adorable but rather undisciplined children, Jonathan had offered guidance and support. After a day or two, she discovered that she had a natural talent for teaching.

The children were progressing quickly in their lessons now, and Anne was learning Maori in the process of teaching them. She had no plans to stay in New Zealand, yet she was becoming increasingly comfortable at the mission. If Jonathan seemed to be becoming a little too attentive, well, she could deal with that.

She doubled over when the first labor pain jolted her. "Get Te Whina," she gasped.

The morning mist that frequently blanketed the coast during the winter months had dissipated, and brilliant golden sunshine lit up the landscape.

Reveling in a burst of unbridled joy, Anne Cutler settled back into the white wicker rocking chair on the front veranda. She raised her face to the sun and smiled into its delicious warmth. She rocked slowly, breathing in the sweet honey fragrance of *karaka* trees and listening to the frantic *tui* birds fighting over the *karakas'* berries. Other birds in the bush were singing gentle lullabies surely intended solely for her pleasure. Moved by the magic of the moment, she started humming a tune that her mother had once sung to her. Remembering the familiar lyrics, she broke into song herself, taking great delight in changing the words at the end of each stanza from "my fair lady" to "my fair son."

The baby cradled in her lap opened his eyes and gave her a toothless grin. He beat his tiny clenched fists in the air lustily until she carefully gripped him under his shoulders and lifted him up to kiss him once, twice, on the forehead before lowering him to her breast. "Hungry today, aren't you?" she laughed as he began greedily suckling on her nipple. "Then again, why should this morning be any different from the others? Keep this up, little boy, and you will grow to be a strong and magnificent man just like your father. I'll have to shoo the girls away, and your father will have to . . ."

She stopped. Despite the time that had passed, tears welled in her eyes every time she allowed herself to think of Richard and what might have been had he lived. Her hope of finding him alive was fast dwindling. She gazed down at little Jamie, now fast asleep on her lap, as memories swirled through her mind. The embassy ball in Washington. The whirlwind courtship and sudden proposal of marriage. The rapture of their wedding night and then setting up house in Alexandria. So many blessed events leading her to where she was today, stranded on a distant shore cradling the cherished gift of their union.

"Protect him, Lord," she implored the Almighty as she gazed down at her sleeping son. "Protect, guide, and preserve him. And watch over his father, who is forever in my heart."

She heard approaching footsteps and the familiar voice of Te Whina. "She is here, Mister K, on the west veranda of her hut."

"I'm with Jonathan at the moment," MacKenzie called out. "I'll be with her shortly."

When Daniel appeared beside her with an unusually cheerful greeting, she looked up a bit warily. "Good morning, Daniel," she replied. "I was just taking the air with young James here."

"Good on you. How fares our handsome little prince this lovely morning?"

"He fares as well as anyone who has naught to do all day but eat and sleep and be rocked to his heart's content by his doting mother. Would that all our lives could be so pleasant."

"Indeed."

The mission director's smile seemed as forced as his tone had a moment earlier. He glanced at Te Whina and then at Anne, who understood from the exchange that something big was afoot. "Might Te Whina take Jamie from you for a few minutes?" MacKenzie asked politely but firmly.

Anne shook her head. Smiling at Te Whina, she said, "I would trust her with my life, but I prefer to keep Jamie near me for now." She stroked the infant's cheek before settling him into the cradle next to her chair.

"Very well, if I cannot persuade you." He nodded at the Maori nurse, who turned and left. MacKenzie watched her go in silence.

"What is it, Daniel?" she asked him. "What is troubling you? I can see it on your face. Whatever it is, I fear it is not good."

His expression was somber when he replied, "No, my dear, I'm afraid it is not."

"Tell me."

"Just a moment, Anne."

MacKenzie walked down the veranda to retrieve a straight-backed chair, which he set near to Anne. He sat down, took a deep breath, and gazed into her eyes. "We have word from the warriors Te Wherowhero dispatched to the peninsula to the north."

Anne drew a breath. "Yes? And?"

MacKenzie paused. "They found six bodies there," he finally said. "Six only, mind you. They were lying together inside a crude enclosure constructed from local materials that seemed built to accommodate more than six people—considerably more. Therein lies the puzzle. We don't know who these other people were or where they might have gone. Te

Wherowhero's party scouted up and down the beach and into the bush, but they found no clues, unfortunately."

"What about the six men?" Anne said unsteadily. "Do you know who they were?" She had stopped rocking and was leaning forward in her chair.

"We are not certain," MacKenzie replied slowly. "Though they had been dead for some time, it was still possible to identify the bodies as men of European extraction. No specific identification was found on any of them, nor much of anything else, for that matter. They died violently, I'm sorry to say. Whoever killed them took everything, including the men's clothing. The bodies had been stripped naked."

"Was it the Maori?" she heard herself ask.

"We must assume it was."

Anne's lips trembled. She took a deep breath and resumed rocking the baby and stroking his back. For agonizing moments she said nothing, avoiding the critical question.

Anticipating what she wanted to ask, MacKenzie said, "No, Anne, they didn't find it. I was quite specific when I told Te Wherowhero and his *ariki* about the birthmark on the back of your husband's neck that would identify him without question. The *ariki* assured me that he and his men had carefully examined all the bodies and found no birthmark on the back of anyone's neck. We can safely conclude that Captain Cutler was not among the dead there." He patted her hand and reached down to caress the baby's head. "We can also speculate that a number of men— more than those six—survived the shipwreck and were there at least long enough to build the enclosure and a few huts. Your husband may well be among those. So you see, the news is not all bad. There is still hope; I would say more hope than I had before."

Anne nodded, lost in thought. At length she glanced up. "What did they do with the bodies?"

"They buried them. Apparently there was a makeshift graveyard near the camp where others had been buried. The Maori had the decency to lay the dead sailors next to their shipmates."

"*What?*" Anne blurted out. "What are you saying, Daniel? There were others? Did they dig up the graves to see who is buried there?"

MacKenzie looked shocked. "Of course not! The Maori would not do such a thing, Anne. To them it would be a desecration."

Beyond reason now, Anne sobbed, "Maybe so, but they should have anyway! Oh, if only they had! Then we'd know for certain. Now we'll never know!"

"Steady on, Anne," MacKenzie cautioned. "I realize how difficult this is for you, and you have my sympathy. But as I have told you, the Maori are a spiritual people. Never in life would they contemplate digging up a grave. They would view such a thing as a sacrilege, to God and the living, as well as the dead."

"Damn and blast, Daniel!" Anne exclaimed as her baby started crying. "That is nonsense! How can you be so naive?" She picked Jamie up from his cradle and clutched him so tightly that he squalled in protest.

"Why do you call it nonsense, Anne?" he asked defensively.

"Spiritual!" she spat. "These people are not spiritual. They are savages! Spiritual people do not kill people and then *eat* them!"

She buried her face in Jamie's hair and wept. Jamie, frightened by his mother's violent emotions, cried all the louder. Anne finally managed to compose herself sufficiently to quiet him.

MacKenzie pushed himself up from his chair and moved to Anne's side. He placed a hand on her shoulder. "There's still hope, my dear," he half-whispered. "Trust me, there's still hope. Never, never lose heart. God is with you, and I feel He is with your husband."

She shook her head despondently as MacKenzie turned and walked slowly across the veranda and down the steps to the gate. Jonathan Riggs met him there.

"Did you tell her?"

"Yes, Jonathan. I told her." MacKenzie's shoulders sagged. "I didn't share all the details of the massacre with her. I could not. But I told her enough. No doubt you heard her reaction."

"I did. My heart bleeds for her, Daniel. Did you mention anything about the other matter we discussed?"

"No. I want to give the poor woman a day or two to absorb what I just told her before I tell her that."

"I agree," Jonathan said. "We can't do anything about it right now in any event, except to proceed with the plan we have in place."

"Yes. We mustn't dally. Lives are at stake. Our superiors will support our plan, as will Admiral Braithwaite. His sister is no longer safe here—none of us is safe here—and he will demand immediate action when he learns that. This business with Hone Heke has caused matters to deteriorate far more rapidly than any of us could have foreseen. It was already bad enough, but cutting down the flagpole in Russell amounts to a declaration of war. We must prepare for the worst. As soon as the soldiers arrive from Government House, we will abandon this mission and leave for Auckland."

CHAPTER 14

MANALA HAD BEEN INTIMIDATING ENOUGH WHEN THE AMERICANS had first encountered the *ariki* on the beach the week before. The man striding down the hill toward them now was downright awe-inspiring. He was closely followed by Manala, Ataahua, and four other men clearly of high status. They were shielded within a phalanx of heavily armed warriors. Their path took them through clusters of thatched huts whose inhabitants stood quietly in front watching them pass. Men, women, and children alike were dressed in simple but well-made cloaks and skirts that suggested modesty and propriety.

Richard wondered if these people were more interested in the new arrivals or their chief's reaction to them. Their stolid expressions revealed few clues. They appeared to have witnessed this sort of thing before.

As the distance from the base of the hill to the gates of the inner wall decreased, Maori guards moved in behind the Americans, effectively sealing them inside. When Richard overheard Nate Donahue mutter, "Not that we'd have any place to go, you bastards," he let the remark pass. They were all on edge. He glanced back at Jonty Montgomery, who straightened his shoulders and gave him a fleeting smile. *Brave lad*, Richard thought.

When the procession reached the group of sailors and came to a halt, the impressive man at its center stepped out of the phalanx and into the open. *This must be their* rangatira, *their great chief*, Richard thought.

The chief, if that's who he was, was taller than most of the other Maori the Americans had encountered, although an inch or two shorter than Richard Cutler. Nevertheless, Richard had the impression that he was the one looking up as he took in the man standing before him. The chief wore a body-length cloak woven out of long grass and adorned with bird feathers and animal skins. His dark eyes seemed old and wise, and the skin on his hands and face was leathery, like that of a sailor who had spent years at sea exposed to wind and sun. His ebony hair was tied back to reveal a wide face with thin lips, a square jaw, pendants dangling from his earlobes, and tattoos on his cheeks and forehead. These expertly applied markings were nothing like the colorful streaks of red-and-white war paint American Indians applied before a battle and washed off afterward. These delicately crafted designs were permanently etched in black and yellow into the weathered skin of his face. The chief wore a headdress of bird feathers similar to the one Manala wore but larger, and other feathers were woven into his hair.

Richard Cutler, in stark contrast, sported a three-day growth of beard; shaggy, shoulder-length hair; and dirty buff breeches and cotton shirt. He felt like a pauper standing in a royal court.

For several minutes the two men stood face-to-face, each taking the measure of the other. Time seemed to stand still as the chief, his expression grim, stood regally with arms folded across his chest. Richard had at least a notion of what was coming. Earlier in the day, on the march, Ataahua had given him a piece of advice.

"Stay firm when you meet our chief," she had warned him. "Stay firm. Do not show fear, and do not turn your back. All will be well," she assured him.

He had appreciated the advice, as much for her willingness to give it as for its content. Now, with his men behind him, depending on him, and life and death hanging in the balance, he wondered if she had told him enough.

Richard was taken aback when the chief suddenly bared his teeth, rolled his eyes, and repeatedly stuck his tongue out like a viper striking at its prey. The chief's honor guard did the same thing while pumping muskets in the air and waving spears and stomping their feet on the ground. It was a gruesome and brazen assault on the senses. As Richard felt his knees begin to buckle, the chief bellowed out, "*Nau mai ki tenei pa! Tena koutou ko te tinomihi ki knonei!*"

Good Lord! Richard thought. *Am I supposed to do the same thing?* For a fleeting moment he had to repress a surge of laughter that would have doomed them all. Instinctively, as if to fend off a mighty blow, Richard took a step backward and said, struggling for calm, "I'm sorry, I don't understand what you are saying."

The chief, seemingly infuriated, took two steps toward him. "*Nau mai ki tenei pa!*" he screamed.

Heart racing, Richard held out his hands, palms up, as he had on the beach. Marshaling the remnants of his courage, he kept his face expressionless, as though he were witnessing a child's temper tantrum and wanted no part of it. He allowed a small smile that belied the terror he felt and seemed to catch the chief off guard.

"*Nau mai ki tenei pa!*" he screamed again, with such violence that flecks of spittle hit Richard in the face. Then the chief raised his right arm.

As quickly as it had started, the din ceased. In the eerie silence that followed, Richard glanced at Ataahua, who gave him a tiny smile and a brief nod. Others were smiling as well, including, to Richard's stupefaction, Manala and the other *ariki*. Richard shifted his gaze back to the chief, who motioned to Ataahua to come forward.

"*Nau mai, haere mai*, Captain Richard Cutler," she said pleasantly. "The *rangatira* said to you, 'Welcome to my *pa*.'"

"Surely he said more than that," Richard ventured guardedly.

At that, the chief's face broke into a broad smile that revealed fine white teeth. When Ataahua added, "And the *rangatira* says, 'You and your men are most welcome here,'" the man shook with laughter, both hands at his ample belly, which was apparently a signal to his tribespeople to join in on the hilarity. The plain and surrounding bush rang with shrieks of laughter. The eighteen Americans watched the goings-on in stunned silence.

When the laughter died down, the chief stepped forward to offer Richard his right hand. Richard took it in his own and was astonished when the chief began speaking clear English. "This is how *pakeha* express friendship and greeting, *ae*?"

Richard nodded dumbly. "Aye," he replied, feeling the pressure of the chief's firm grip.

"This is how Maori express friendship and greeting," the chief said. Still holding Richard's hand, the chief pulled him in closer until Richard could feel the chief's warm breath on his face. Tilting his head slightly upward, the chief touched his forehead to Richard's and appeared to be about to kiss Richard either on the cheek, in French fashion, or on the lips. Instead, he touched the tip of his nose to the tip of Richard's nose and pressed gently against it. Stepping back, he said, "It is called a *hongi*. It is to honor Mauna Kore, the creator of the universe who breathed the first breath of life into you and me and us all. You like?"

"Well, your customs are very different from ours," Richard hedged.

"Naturally," the chief said. "*Pakehas* come from lands in Europe. Maori come from a land called Hawaiki, very far from Europe. We are different peoples. Yet we are all very much the same, no?"

Richard nodded. "May I ask, sir," he said formally, "whom I have the honor of addressing?"

The chief drew himself to full height and balled a fist over his heart. "My name is Tamati Waka Nene," he replied with equal formality. "I am *rangatira* of this Ngapuhi *iwi*. He held out his arms to indicate the entirety of his domain. "Ataahua informs me that you are not English?"

Richard bit his lip. Unaware of the chief's allegiances, he was unsure how to proceed. Sensing the eyes of his crew on his back, and imagining them holding their collective breath, he decided to simply tell the truth. "Ataahua is correct," he said. "I—we—are not English. We are Americans. My name is Richard Cutler, and I am—was—the captain of the United States ship of war *Suwannee*. These men with me are members of my crew. Several of them require medical attention. I respectfully request your help for them."

"*Ae*, I can see they do need help. Do not worry. We will tend to them. Maori medicine is strong medicine. It will heal your men. But I must ask: You are friends of the English?"

Richard committed himself. "Yes. Many of us here have ancestors who are English. My wife is English."

"Your wife? She is in America?"

"No," Richard said, swallowing hard. "She came with me on the voyage to Sydney. You know Sydney?"

"Of course."

"We were to confer with British authorities there and sign an agreement with them."

"What kind of agreement?"

"An agreement to trade things—buy and sell things—to each other. Do you understand?"

"Of course. We trade with English in Sydney."

That got Richard's attention. "You trade with Sydney? In whose ships?"

"Our own ships," Nene replied as if it were nothing out of the ordinary. "Now tell me why you are here and not in Sydney."

"A big storm carried us out to sea. My ship struck a shoal off a peninsula south of here. My wife perished in the wreck. Most of my crew perished with her."

"I see," Nene said quietly. "I am sorry, for the loss of your men and I am very sorry for the loss of your woman. I have suffered such a loss. It is difficult for a man to accept. But do not despair, my friend. The pain will ease with time. Papatuanuku knows what is in your heart. She listens to you and she will bring comfort to you."

"Forgive me. Who is Papa . . ."

"Papatuanuku. The Earth Goddess. She is listening to you, and if your heart is pure, she will protect your wife in the world of spirits until you are called to join her."

Richard stared hard at Nene. "Thank you for those words," he said. "I believe you."

"That is good." He clapped his hands. "Enough talk! We have great matters to discuss, you and I, Captain Cutler. But that is for tomorrow. Tonight, we have special *hangi*. You and your men are honored guests. When the sun sets, we sit together and give thanks to Tane for the bounty of the forest. Then we feast. But first, we find you huts to sleep in tonight with full bellies!" He clapped his hands again, sending his tribesmen scurrying off to their duties.

"Well, God damn me to hell," Richard heard Nate Donahue murmur behind him. When Brengle retorted, "Most likely He already has, Nate," for the first time in a long time, Richard Cutler burst out laughing.

The *hangi* that evening was similar to the feast the Americans had experienced on the march inland, but far greater in both proportions and portions. It was held outside the *pa*, eastward toward the bush, and everyone in the village was involved in some way: preparing the food, collecting *mahoe* branches off the forest floor for the fire, or providing entertainment. The amount of food the villagers carried out to the fire pit seemed almost sinful to Richard, and he wondered how the deep, rectangular pit, as big as it was, could accommodate it all. But it did. As soon as the fires had heated what seemed like a quarry's worth of flat stones, pigs and birds and freshwater eels all went in, and the pit was covered by leaves and dirt. Soon delicious aromas wafted up from underground. While the adults worked feverishly at their tasks, children of all ages happily chased each other in the games common to children of all times and nations, including one similar to the hoops Richard had enjoyed as a boy. Early on in that game, the three midshipmen were invited to join in.

That night the Americans slept deeply, relieved for a time of the worries that had haunted them the previous days. The next morning, as previously arranged, Richard Cutler, Jack Brengle, and Nate Donahue met with Chief Nene in the *whare* assigned to Richard. The little house was located near the top of the hill, a stone's throw from the chief's own residence and from the *wharenui*, the meeting house that was the focal point of the *pa* and its largest and most elaborately adorned structure.

Chief Nene arrived at the appointed time, accompanied by Manala and another formidable-looking *ariki* named Hohona who carried a large green basket covered with a white cloth. After removing their footwear and washing their hands in a wooden tub placed outside the entryway, the three Maori men joined the three Americans waiting inside.

The hut was a cozy two-room structure fashioned out of materials gathered from the bush—bracken, rushes, bark, long grass, and *toi toi* for the thatched walls and roof, and timber for posts and ridgepoles. Having never developed metal-working technology, and thus lacking nails, the Maori bound the materials tightly together with flaxen twine and ropes.

The interior of the hut contained little more than two floor pallets woven of flax, two chairs of European design, and a roughly hewn square table on which had been placed a two-foot-high human-like figure carved from wood. This *tiki*, Richard later learned, was a sacred image representing an ancestor who was revered in his day and who would protect and nourish those in the hut and throughout the *pa*.

Of greater interest to Richard was the leather-bound book Ataahua had left for him on the table the previous evening. Although exhausted by his journey and almost too stuffed with food to move, he had picked it up and flipped through the fine linen pages. The beautifully crafted book was written in a language that Richard assumed was Maori. He made a mental note to ask Chief Nene about it when an opportunity arose.

After reciting a brief prayer, Chief Nene sat down, folded his arms across his chest, and with a single hand motion invited the three Americans to sit on the pallet opposite the one he and the two *ariki* occupied. "*Tena koutou*," he greeted them formally after they were all seated.

As he began speaking, the cool mist that had blocked the sun that morning turned into heavy rain. The thrumming on the thatched roof made the inside seem even cozier, although a bit cool. The Americans pulled the flaxen cloaks they had been given around their shoulders for warmth.

Richard bowed his head in response to the greeting. He had assumed the same crossed-legged pose as that of the chief and the *arikas*. Brengle and Donahue, one on either side of him, followed suit. "It is good to see you this morning, Chief."

"Good. You are learning our ways," Nene said. He unfolded his arms. "Now we get down to business, as you *pakeha* like to say. But first, as I promised you at the *hangi*, I will allow you five questions." He held up his right hand, its fingers outstretched. "So, begin. Ask the first question."

"Thank you," Richard said, "I will. But before I do, I want to thank you, on behalf of my officers and my men, for your hospitality last evening. The fish and pork were the best I have ever tasted. And that chicken . . ."

"*Pukeko*," Nene corrected him. "Not chicken, but the English say that it tastes like a chicken."

"It was delicious, whatever it was. And the welcoming display your people put on for us was superb. What a fascinating culture you have! It shames me to say that Americans know nothing about you. My men and I are very much in your debt."

"*Ae*, you are," Nene said, unexpectedly. "We will discuss that debt later. Your first question, please."

Richard cleared his throat. "Yes, of course. My first question is, how do you come to speak English so well? You speak it better than many Americans I know."

Nene smiled, as did the two *ariki*. "I expected that question. The answer is, I am related in marriage to Hongi Hika, the greatest Ngapuhi chief ever to rule. I am chief of this *iwi* because of him. Years ago, Hongi Hika sailed to England. For five months he studied your culture and your language. He had tea with the English king at Windsor Castle and explained Maori culture to him. There, too, he acquired muskets from the English and the French in return for giving them land here in Aotearoa, as the Maori call New Zealand. The guns he brought home with him have made us strong. You look surprised," he added when Richard raised his eyebrows.

"I am more than surprised," Richard admitted. "I am dumbfounded. How did Hongi Hika get to England?"

"On a ship, of course. On a British whaling ship. It is not so unusual. Other Maori chiefs have sailed to England to study English. Tuai of the Ngare Raumati tribe studied at Cambridge."

Richard's jaw dropped. "Cambridge University? In England?"

"*Ae*. It is what I just said."

"My God," Richard said, chagrined at his ignorance of this land and its people.

"He studied Him too," Nene chuckled. "On his voyage home to Aotearoa, Hongi Hika brought with him two teachers from London. These teachers agreed to teach English to those in my village who wished to learn."

"So, you learned English from these teachers?"

"No. Not from them. It is not proper for a Maori chief to learn from *pakeha*. I learned from Ataahua."

"Ataahua?"

"*Ae*. She is a very smart *wahine*. She makes her people proud. She learned English and taught me and others in our tribe. Missionaries helped, too. But I learned only from Ataahua. She is like a daughter to me. Her mother and father are dead, so I adopted her. The entire *iwi* adopted her. We are very fortunate to have her. We all love her. We rarely send out a hunting party or war party without her."

"Indeed, you have every reason to be proud of her. Tell me, is Ataahua a medicine woman? A healer? Do you understand what I mean by that?"

"I understand. *Ae*, call her what you like, that is what she is. So was her mother before her and her ancestors going back in time. What she knows, she learned from them. It is a respected position in any *iwi*. She is skilled in her work."

"I've noticed. Mr. Plummer, the man brought in on a stretcher, is now able to walk a little. Two days ago, when we first met Ataahua, he was in great pain. Last evening he enjoyed the *hangi* almost free of pain."

"I told you yesterday, Maori medicine is strong medicine." His eyes danced with laughter. "Ataahua and I have learned your language. Now you must learn ours. I will ask her to teach you."

When Richard hesitated, Jack Brengle said, "I'm afraid you will be disappointed, Chief Nene. Captain Cutler is not good at learning languages. He failed Latin in school, and he barely passed French."

Nene's belly jiggled with laughter. Manala and Hohana laughed too, although perhaps not certain what they were laughing about.

"Thank you for that insight, Lieutenant," Richard muttered under his breath. "I am certain Chief Nene is pleased to be enlightened." He surprised Brengle by saying, "I would be honored to have Ataahua teach me your language, Chief Nene."

"Good. You begin today and you learn every day." He waved his hand in the air to dismiss that topic. "Next question."

"Very well. That book on the table. Is it written in the Maori language?"

"*Ae*."

"How did you come by it?"

Nene grinned. "That is two questions, but I will treat them as one. A church man in Kororareka has them printed and presented to Maori tribes as gifts. The book tells of the teachings of the Church. We are pleased to receive these teachings. I am a good Christian, did you know?"

"I did not know," Richard confessed, "and I am pleased to learn that you are. This official, is he Anglican?"

"No. He is Catholic," Nene said impatiently. "Next question."

A Catholic official—a priest, certainly—who prints books for the Maori, Richard marveled to himself. *What is this cleric doing in Russell?* Aloud he said, "I shall allow my executive officer to ask the next question," he said to Nene.

"Chief Nene," Brengle said deferentially as Nene's gaze shifted to him, "yesterday, when we arrived here, you and your people took us in without question or hesitation. We are very grateful that you did, of course, but we are somewhat baffled as to *why* you did. What convinced you to accept us without knowing anything about us?"

"You think we know nothing about you?" Nene grunted. "We know much about you. My warriors followed you for days. They watched you from the bush. They saw how you treat each other. They saw how you help each other. They saw the love your men have for you and the love you have for them. They saw the bravery of your captain when he stood alone without weapons. My men watched you. Ataahua watched you. They learned what they needed to know, what they needed to tell me."

Brengle recalled Garth Plummer's warnings. "We saw little evidence of you following us."

"Of course not," Nene said indignantly. "And what you cannot know, because you are *pakeha*, is that a Maori can see into a man's heart. He sees what is there. We trust what our own hearts tell us. Manala and Ataahua think much of you."

Richard shot a surprised look at Manala, whose expression did not change.

"They think much of you especially, Captain Cutler," Nene concluded. "Because they do, and because of what I see for myself, I do as well. Next question."

Richard nodded. "What is the closest English settlement to your *pa*?"

"Kororareka."

"I have heard of it. It is also called Russell, yes?"

"Yes."

"How far away is it?"

"Not far. Two days walking. Then a short journey by boat from a village called Paihia. It is where the treaty was signed. Kororareka was once a beautiful place, but it is now a place of sin."

"Sin?"

Nene nodded. "Much sin there. No good. The English promised Maori chiefs they would make those sinful men leave, but so far they have not. Sin is now worse than ever." He frowned impressively.

Richard decided not to pursue the subject. "The British army is there?"

"A small number. Kororareka was the English capital. But no longer. Auckland is the capital now. Most soldiers have gone there. Kororareka gave much trade to northern chiefs. Now that trade is gone. Not good."

"Will you take us there?" Richard asked bluntly.

"We shall see." Nene waved his hand. "You have asked many more questions than the five allowed. But I shall grant you one more."

"I have one," Nate Donahue spoke up.

Nene held out his hand inviting Donahue to speak.

"Those shrunken heads stuck on the posts by the gate: Are they real?"

Richard shook his head slightly as Nene and the two *ariki* glared at him. "Some are, yes," Nene answered coldly. "Those are the heads of our enemies. No more questions. Captain Cutler, I wish to speak with you alone."

"I apologize for the words of my captain of Marines," Richard said when he and Nene were sitting across from each other in the hut. "He offended me, and I fear he also offended you."

"I took no offense," Nene replied. "He meant no disrespect. He is curious, that is all." Unexpectedly he asked, "Why do you call him 'captain'? Does he also have a ship?"

"No. Mr. Donahue is in fact a lieutenant. But because he was the highest-ranking Marine officer on my ship, he is given the courtesy rank of captain, just as a midshipman is called captain when he is on a vessel with no higher-ranking officer."

Nene nodded. "In that same way, when Manala came upon you on the beach, he was *rangatira*, chief of his warriors."

"Yes, exactly."

"We have much to teach each other," Nene said. In a sharp change of subject, he added, "Tell me, is this Donahue a good leader of men? A good soldier in battle?"

"He is an excellent leader," Richard said readily. "And I suspect he is an excellent soldier, although I have not seen him in battle. My country has been at peace for a long time. But I know him to be brave and fair, and intelligent. As you have noted, however, he is not a diplomat. He sometimes speaks his mind before he thinks. But in a fight, I would want him on my side."

"That is good. And Lieutenant Brengle?"

"The same is true for him. Lieutenant Brengle and I have been friends since we were children. I would trust him with my life, and I have done so on more than one occasion. You can rely on him, always."

"That is all good," Nene exclaimed. "There is a saying in Maori that the quality of a *rangatira* can be seen in the quality of his *ariki* and the loyalty of his tribe. You must have a similar saying in English. It is true in your example. What you have said about your lieutenants pleases me greatly. We need men like them. We need men like you."

Richard narrowed his eyes. "I'm afraid I don't take your meaning, Chief Nene. Need us in what way?"

"You will find out soon enough."

He seemed about to say more when an older woman appeared at the open doorway. "Ah, Kaia," the chief greeted her, "*tomo mai.*"

The woman was one Richard had seen earlier that morning sitting outside Chief Nene's hut. Wrapped in a worn blanket, she was holding the stem of a short clay pipe, the sort that whalers preferred. She had it clenched between her teeth, and she seemed lost in thought. When

Richard wished her a good morning, she turned her attention from the white smoke curling upward from her pipe and smiled at him.

"*Morena koe*," she replied, raising her pipe in salutation. "Good morning to you."

When she entered Richard's hut now, she flashed him a smile of recognition. She was bearing a tray with a bowl of a hot liquid, two crudely fashioned tin cups, and another, larger bowl. She ladled the liquid from the smaller bowl into the cups, then handed one to the chief and the other to Richard.

"Drink," she urged him. "Good medicine." After another warm smile at Richard she left the hut.

Richard looked at Nene before drinking. "She is a good woman," Nene said, "a beloved elder of the *iwi*. She works hard, and she enjoys her tobacco!" They shared a chuckle. "This drink is a tea made from the *kawakawa* leaf. And Kaia is right, it is good for you. It cures everything. It is the heart of Maori medicine. You and your men must drink as much of it as you are able."

Richard took a sip. "It tastes good. Ataahua has made it for me, and I have enjoyed drinking it."

Nene nodded and sipped from his own cup.

Richard took a healthier sip. "And this?" He pointed at the larger bowl, which contained a mixture of plant shoots, a small mound of orange and red berries, and what appeared distressingly to be fat maggots.

Nene made a show of surveying the contents of the bowl. "The greens are *pikopiko*, he said. "They are the ferns you have seen in the bush. The *huhu* grubs are important to good diet and digestion. Go ahead. Eat one."

Steeling himself, Richard picked one up and popped it into his mouth. To his surprise, it had a pleasant, nutty taste. He downed another one.

"You like them!" Nene declared with obvious delight. "Now do not ignore these," he added, pointing to the fruit. "They are dried *karaka* berries. Do you like them?" he pressed after Richard dropped several into his mouth.

"I do," Richard professed.

"Good. They are poisonous."

When Richard gagged and spat out the berries, Nene roared with laughter. "Not now," he laughed. "Not now. They are not poisonous now. We have made sure of that!"

Richard wiped his mouth on the sleeve of his shirt. "I'm glad of that. Still, if you don't mind, I'll stick to the greens and grubs."

"As you please," the chief said.

They finished eating in silence. When the food was gone and they were on a second cup of tea, Richard said, "I don't wish to be rude, Chief Nene, but I am curious. What did you mean a moment ago when you said you could use men like us. Use us for what?"

Nene finished his drink and placed the cup on the floor mat. His expression turned sober as he collected his thoughts. "Captain Cutler," he finally said, "your arrival here at my *pa* is most fortunate."

"How so?"

"A war is coming. If my spies are correct, it will soon be upon us. This will not be a war with a small battle here and a small battle there. It will be a war in which many people will die in their homes."

"Whose war? Do you mean the Maori will fight the British?"

"Yes and no. The matter is complicated. I shall try to explain it to you. Years ago, before *pakeha* came to these islands, Aotearoa was not a Garden of Eden, as in the Christian Bible. There was war. Maori were fighting Maori for the same reasons all men fight with each other: for power and dominance. Smaller tribes with fewer warriors sought the protection of the larger tribes. These small tribes became *hapu*—controlled and protected by the more powerful tribe. Here, in the north, two powerful chiefs emerged in the Ngapuhi tribe. I am one, and the other is a *rangatira* named Hone Heke. I know Heke very well, and in some ways I admire him. He is intelligent. He is wise. He loves his people as much as I love mine. But although we have much in common, he sees the British differently. At first he was their ally. He was the first chief to sign the Treaty of Waitangi. You have heard of this treaty?"

Richard nodded. "My superior in Washington mentioned it to me, and I have read about it. My understanding is that the treaty granted the British Crown sovereignty over New Zealand in return for the Crown's agreement to protect the Maori against the French and other invaders."

"Your understanding is flawed, but it will do. What is important for the moment is that Heke accuses the British of bad faith and of using the treaty to justify their seizure of Maori land."

"Do you also believe the British have acted in bad faith?"

He sighed. "Yes, I do. What most *pakeha* do not understand is that before the treaty was signed, Aotearoa was an independent Maori nation. All European nations attested to this fact, including Queen Victoria and the British government. So, in our view, the treaty was an agreement made between equals. But we were not treated as equals after the treaty was signed. Governor Hobson did not keep his promises."

"So Hone Heke is right," Richard said. "The treaty was a ruse to allow Britain to add New Zealand to its empire?"

Nene thought for a moment before answering. "In part, yes. But what the British have done does not make them our enemies. We need their trade and rule of law and the prestige they bring us. And we need their protection, for reasons you will better understand over time. I shall always regard the British as my friends and allies. They have treated me and my people with respect, and I will fight to the death for them.

"Against your own people?"

Nene shook his head sadly. "My friend, the Maori have been fighting each other for many, many years. The treaty did not change that."

"And you think war is coming here? You think your *pa* will be attacked?"

"I do."

"By Heke?"

"No. Not by Heke. We are of the same tribe, remember."

"Who, then?"

"Several other chiefs. First of all, Heke's Ngapuhi ally, Te Ruki Kawiti. With many from another tribe, the Ngati Whatua. They are a confederation of four *hapu*, smaller tribes related to each other by blood and by common goals. We have fought them many times over the years, and we have defeated them. But Maori do not forget or forgive any insult, especially one that involves a defeat in battle. The Ngati Whatua demand *utu*. Now, by allying themselves with Heke, they gain power and see their chance."

"What is *utu*? Revenge?"

"*Ae*, revenge. A cruel and bloody revenge. It may take a Maori weeks, months, or even years to get *utu*, but they will get it. Or die trying to get it."

Richard considered that. "It must work both ways," he said. "Has your tribe not sought revenge against the Ngati Whatua?"

"Yes. Many years ago, they attacked Ngapuhi at a place called More-monui. The Ngapuhi had flintlock muskets. The Ngati Whatua had clubs and spears. Before our Ngapuhi warriors could reload their muskets, the Ngati attacked, slaughtering almost all the tribe. And for that we demanded *utu*."

"Did you get it?"

"More than once. Now the Ngati Whatua are demanding *utu* on us. Back and forth we fight; back and forth." He looked old and wise and sad. "In the end, everyone loses. Very foolish."

Richard paused to consider the implications of what Nene was say-ing. "So it would seem that Hone Heke has just what he wants. He can act the statesman and revered leader, a friend and ally to all, whilst others fight for him and achieve his goal?"

"Yes. But understand: Heke *is* a revered leader to his people. And he is a man of many gifts. But I believe what he secretly wants—his goal, as you call it—is for all *pakeha* to leave these islands. That includes the missionaries that my ally Te Wherowhero and I have vowed to protect."

"Who?"

"Potatau Te Wherowhero is *rangatira* of the Waikato *iwi*, south of here. He is as strong and loyal an ally of the British and British mission-aries as I am."

Richard ran his tongue over his lower lip. "Tell me: How do the British authorities view all this?"

"The British are doing what they can to avoid war. War does not serve their purposes. So far they have been able to avoid it. But for how long? Heke professes peace. He has written a letter to Queen Victoria asking for her guidance and blessing. But all the time he plots against her and all *pakeha*. Just recently he chopped down the British flag where the treaty was signed. That is an act of war in your country, yes?"

"It is. My country went to war against Tripoli after its ruler ordered the American flag chopped down and tossed into the Mediterranean Sea. My father fought in that war. What preparations have you made for the war you think is coming?"

"I have sent messengers to Kororareka to request British army soldiers."

"Will the authorities send them?"

"If the messengers arrived, I believe they will. The British are our friends. How many they will send, I cannot say. It is my belief that the Ngati Whatua will attack before such help can reach us. Your presence here, on what the Ngati Whatua consider sacred ground, has made them very angry. They know you are here. They are watching, always."

Richard let some time pass before speaking further. He understood why Chief Nene was telling him all this. His purpose was clear. What Richard could not come to grips with was the extent of his own obligation to Nene and his people. They had saved his life and the lives of his crew. Yet they were so close to reaching their destination. Richard's desire to take the next step toward home was almost overpowering. Could he abandon Nene and his people? In the end, he supposed, the question hardly mattered. There could be no leaving the *pa* now. His small company would have no chance against the powerful enemy lurking in the bush. For better or worse, the fate of the survivors of *Suwannee*'s crew was now inexorably linked to the fate of this *iwi*.

Having reached this conclusion, he asked, "How can I help?"

Nene exhaled slowly. "First, I must ask you, do you *want* to help?"

"I do."

"And your men?"

"They will follow my lead once I explain that this is the only way to repay our debt to you. And," he added ruefully, "the only way we will get to Russell."

Nene smiled. "*Kia ora, a taku hoa, me te hoa rangatira*," he said. "It means: 'Thank you, my friend and ally.' In return for your assistance, as soon as it is possible, my warriors will escort you and your men to Kororareka. From there you can board a ship that will take you to America."

Richard nodded. "I believe we have an alliance."

"*Ae*. And because we do, I can now return these to you."

Nene retrieved the basket that Hohana had brought with him that morning and handed it to Richard. Richard removed the white cloth cover and found the two revolvers that he and Brengle had discarded on the beach. All five chambers of both revolvers were loaded.

CHAPTER 15

THAT VERY AFTERNOON, MANALA AND HOHONA BEGAN FAMILIARIZING the American officers with the *pa's* defenses. The midshipmen joined them after Richard explained to Chief Nene that despite their youth, the three junior officers were well versed in the military arts. Plus, the older seamen trusted them and deferred to them. Nene had grunted his approval.

At the end of the day, the Americans were left with two contradictory impressions. The first impression was that this fortress had been in place for many years and had successfully withstood numerous attacks. The second was that what had succeeded in the past might not succeed in the future.

Nate Donahue went further: "This fort belongs in the last century."

"How so?" Richard asked him.

"For close fighting," Donahue declared, "these defenses are brilliant. No West Point engineer could have designed them better, and that includes your friend, Captain Lee."

That was high praise. Robert Edward Lee was hailed in American military circles as the finest engineer of his age.

"As you are aware," Donahue continued, "Lee has stressed the critical importance of interior lines within a defensive position. This place has more interior lines than I've seen anywhere else. Nene's warriors can fight from trenches at two different locations. If the enemy does manage to reach the outer wall—the *pewhairangi*, I believe Hohana called it—the defenders can use firearms or jab spears at them through gaps in the palisades. If by some miracle the enemy is able to breach that wall, the defenders will have retreated to the space between the walls and can pick them off as they come over the wall." He continued ticking off points on his fingers. "If necessity demands, they can retire inside the inner wall while those on the platforms give the attackers a hot dose of enfilading fire. If the enemy manages to force entry into the *pa* itself, they are met by defenders in a second set of trenches. If the attackers get past those trenches, Nene's people can retreat up the hill and fight from the advantage of high ground. And if all else fails, they can use their interior lines to flee into the bush and fight Indian style from there." He shook his head in wonder. "This was designed by a genius!"

"You sound awfully impressed, Nate," Brengle said.

"Damn right I'm impressed," Donahue declared flatly. "Twenty, thirty years ago I would have declared this fortress to be impregnable. Today, I would not say that."

"Why not?"

"Cannon, Mr. Talmadge," Donahue replied succinctly. "A remarkable invention. These walls may be strong enough to withstand musket fire, but even a dullard wielding a six-pounder could chew them up in no time. On the other hand, the attackers would need to address the defenders in the rifle pits before they could swarm inside the *pa*, and I can assure you that would be no small matter."

"That same thought had occurred to me," ventured Hugh Zabriskie. "But the enemy we're expecting won't have cannon, will they?"

"Not likely, Hugh, but possible," Richard said. "We need to prepare, in case. Who knows what the Ngati Whatua might have traded with the Europeans to get them?" He looked at Donahue. "What do you recommend, Nate?"

"Two things," Donahue said after a bit of thought. "Both of them depend on the firepower we have at our disposal. How much powder is here, do we know?"

"Jack and I have a revolver each, with perhaps thirty rounds of ammunition between us. There appears to be a good number of muskets available in the *pa*, including our own that we discarded on the beach. The supply of powder and shot is unknown."

"A rather important consideration, Captain. I suggest we find out."

The next few days passed without incident. With no immediate indication of hostile activity, life in the *pa* settled into its normal comfortable rhythm. Slowly, inexorably, the sailors began to blend their daily routines with those of the Maori villagers. Save for the communal rite of preparing and eating food, however, day-to-day affairs were still being conducted at arm's length, as if all were attending a grand ball where everyone was enjoying the music, but no one had yet summoned the courage to invite someone to dance. The Maori seemed to enjoy the easy company of the Americans, and vice versa, but largely limited their interactions to a shy smile here and a nod of recognition there. Most of the warriors kept their distance, offering the Americans little beyond a grunt or a few words of broken English. Neither Manala nor Hohana spoke at all unless directly addressed. But the Maori took keen interest in the Americans' daily drills on the plain, sometimes participating in them, sometimes simply watching.

The children were another matter. They were neither afraid nor shy around the Americans. They followed them everywhere, taking special delight in the three midshipmen, who were not much older than they and who openly encouraged their affection. On one occasion, the boy warrior who had brought food to Jonty Montgomery that first night approached him and invited him through sign language to slide down the hill with him and his mates on a *nikau*, a large, spoon-shaped palm fern capable of gathering impressive speed on the slippery mud banks. Montgomery was delighted. He had been watching the game longingly, recalling New England winters and sledding down snowy hillsides. That look of yearning had apparently prompted the invitation.

"You're on, Irangi!" Jonty shouted. Down the hill he went in his own pod, delighting watchers with his shouts of glee. Not to be left out, Tom Talmadge and Hugh Zabriskie grabbed their own pods and followed him down the hill.

Just after noon on the seventh day in the *pa*, Richard Cutler sat alone on the pallet in his hut, deep in thought. He did not know what day of the week it was, or even what month, and he found himself caring less and less about such details. He thought of Ataahua, and the mere thought of her made him smile. And more. Much more. He knew he had no future here, but for now, after what had happened last night, he was loath to see the present pass by too quickly, his keen sense of guilt notwithstanding.

On the plain below, Nate and Jack were conducting the daily drills, doing what they did best. He appreciated now more than ever their ability and willingness to stand in for him when necessary and lift the burdens of command from his shoulders. *Hell. They are doing a better job of it than I could do.*

He closed his eyes and took a deep breath, allowing the pleasures of the previous night to seep back into his consciousness. Once there, they proved impossible to block or ignore. They assumed a life of their own, pushing aside the moral barriers imposed by a strict Christian upbringing, the sanctity of love and marriage drummed into him from an early age, and the certainty of eternal damnation if God's laws were disobeyed. Since childhood, he had felt secure within these parameters, and he had tried his best to honor them. And he believed he had done just that until last night, when the barriers had come crashing down, exposing his sin and hypocrisy. He had known that would happen from the moment she crept into his hut, knelt beside him, and put a finger to his lips. She had then caressed him gently, intimately. He had not tried to stop her, had not pushed her away when she mounted him. As she sat astride him, her hands gripping his fiercely, her breasts heaving up and down above his face, her hips working back and forth, wave after wave of exquisite sensations coursed through him. He could not fight them, did not want to fight them. Only when it was over and she had crept out of the hut into the darkness did anguish and guilt sweep through him, escaping in one heavy, heartfelt sob.

With an audible sigh he opened his eyes and stared out the open window. The palm mat that served as a curtain had been pushed aside to admit shafts of sunlight and a view of the plain to westward. Beyond the plain he could see the tree line and the exact spot where, a week earlier, he and his crew had first emerged from the bush. Had it truly been only a week? It seemed to him a much longer span.

He listened intently to the commands of his officers directing the Maori warriors in the evolutions of continuous fire, a battle tactic forwarded by Lieutenant Donahue. He did not hear the reports of muskets, nor would he. Dry powder was far too dear to permit live practice, especially in light of what Nate Donahue had in mind to do with it. His plan was audacious and risky, and it took some doing to convince Chief Nene and his *ariki* that the risk was worth taking.

From the angle of the sun, Richard estimated it to be early afternoon. The drill had ended, and the gurgling in his stomach indicated the reason why. It was time to join the others for the noon meal. He hauled himself to his feet, draped a cape around his shoulders, and was making for the front entrance when a graceful figure loomed in the open frame. She was wearing a colorful wrap that covered her from neck to knee; a green fern waved in her waist-length hair, which was enhanced with the sweet lemon-scented resin of leaves from a *tarata* tree.

"*Ra pai*," she greeted him, stepping inside. "*He pai te kite atu ki a koe.*"

"*Ra pai*," Richard returned, his eyes resting comfortably upon her face. As she approached him, he caught the now familiar scent of her. "Thank you," he added in response to her declaration. He did not understand what she had said, but he inferred from the inflection of her voice and the look she was giving him that it was an endearment. Then he remembered himself. "Forgive me. I meant to say, *Kia akamai takila kotou.*"

Ataahua laughed, a pleasing, joyful sound that stirred his loins. "You should have," she agreed. "But that was good. You are learning. The *rangatira* will be proud of you. And of me, for teaching you."

"You are a good teacher, Ataahua," Richard said, holding her gaze. "And not just a good teacher of language. You are a woman of many talents."

She smiled. "*A ko koe haki*," she said softly. "*Te tangata rongonui au.*"

He blinked and shook his head. "I apologize. I didn't understand what you just said."

"Perhaps not yet," she said coyly. "With time, you will."

"I fear I have much to learn."

"Do not fear learning, Richard," she said seriously. "Our purpose in life is to learn. And to love. Nothing is of greater importance."

"I have to agree." He felt a rush of tenderness wash over him and reached for her hand. "Ataahua, we must talk . . ."

"No!" she hissed. She brought a finger to his lips and her lips to his ear. "No talk," she insisted. "No talk, Richard, please, no talk. We enjoyed each other, yes?" When he nodded in helpless surrender, she said, "I will come to you tonight."

It was not a question.

The days rolled by. Nothing in the bush indicated danger. Each morning, Chief Nene dispatched scouts to prowl near and far in search of anything suspicious. Each afternoon they returned to the *pa* with nothing to report. No sign of the Ngati Whatua, but also no sign of a British relief force. About the latter Nene was disappointed but not surprised. Runners sent east to the port of Russell reported that Major Blackwell, the ranking British army officer in Paihia, while professing his love and respect for Chief Nene and his Ngapuhi *iwi*, had stated in no uncertain terms that he had his own concerns and could not spare soldiers from the Russell garrison at this time. He pledged to send what relief he could when he could, but as the days passed with no word and no soldiers, it seemed an empty promise. And Richard had his own problems.

"The men are getting restless," Jack confided to Richard one afternoon as they took their daily walk around the compound's outer defenses. "We're going into our third week here, and nothing is happening. We're marking time, is all, and the men want to know why. There's no end to it in sight. They want to go home."

"You've told me this before, Jack. Which men are you referring to?"

"Not just one or a few, Richard. All of them. Even Turner and Templeton are speaking out, and I can't recall either of them ever piping up about anything. The mids are doing a good job keeping the lid on the discontent, but even they are getting out of sorts. They aren't scared. They're bored, which is worse, and they see no point in staying here. They want to leave, too."

"And go where?"

"Russell. And from there, home."

"What do you make of our chances of getting to Russell alive?"

"Good, if there's no threat out there and we are provided with an escort."

"And if it turns out there *is* a threat out there and we are *not* provided with an escort?"

Brengle shrugged. "Not so good."

"I'd say abysmal. Jesus! We have two revolvers, a handful of shot, and a few muskets. That's it. And we won't have an escort until Chief Nene consents to give us one." He glanced up. A halo had formed around the sun, a sure sign that foul weather was imminent. His gaze shifted to the lookout tower rising high above the *pa* and to the platform secured to it halfway down from the top. Kauri stood on sentry duty, ready to pound on the thick wood to warn the *pa* of approaching danger. Richard waved to him, and Kauri waved back. All was quiet. The only sound was the sweet music of wind and songbirds in the bush.

"Look, Jack," Richard said in a calmer tone, "you have to agree that there's not much we can do until Chief Nene gives us permission to do it. And you and I both know that won't happen until he is convinced that the immediate danger to his *pa* has passed. I believe he sincerely cares for our well-being, but he also wants our help. To violate our pledge to him would not only be dishonorable, it would be foolhardy. The men might not understand that, but I would expect you to."

"I do undersatnd that," Brengle said earnestly. "At least, I did. Chief Nene is a reasonable man. And an educated man. Surely he understands the need to adapt to changing conditions. The war he had predicted was his justification for keeping us here. But that war hasn't happened. And may never happen. So what are we to do? Sit around for weeks or months and wait? We are not his slaves, or his prisoners. We are his friends, and we can do more for him and his people in Russell, negotiating with the British on their behalf, than rotting here. Do you not agree?"

"Your reasoning is sound, Jack. I don't disagree with it. But I am quite certain Chief Nene would."

"Can we at least go and talk to him about this?"

"I already have."

"You talked to him about our leaving?"

"Just so. I was testing his reaction."

"What was his reaction?"

"What I just told you it would be."

"Damn!"

When they reached the tree line, they wheeled around and headed back. A few days ago, Donahue would have had the Maori warriors and the sailors out drilling in the plain at this time of day. But they had learned what they needed to learn, including how to lob a hand-sized flaxen ball filled with dirt. These days, drills were limited to "keeping the edge," as Donahue liked to put it. What these men needed now, he added, was the signal to start killing the bastards.

When they reached the first trench, which was screened by ferns and underbrush, Brengle, his gaze firmly on the ground ahead of them, said hesitantly, "Could it be, Richard, that you have found a reason not to leave? That something has happened to keep you here?"

Richard, too, kept his eyes averted. "Is that what you think?"

"I think it's pretty damn obvious," Brengle answered. "Any dullard looking at you two can see it. This has happened quickly, I grant you, but in matters of the heart, time is of little consequence. I can say nothing against it," he added. "Anne is gone forever, and whether or not you decide to stay here, you are beginning a new and different life." He lowered his voice. "And my God she is beautiful. Rarely have I seen the like of her, or even dreamed of a woman like that in my schoolboy fantasies. And like Anne she is beautiful inside as well—kind and loving. We are all in her debt. What your relationship with her may mean for the rest of us, time will determine. For now, I want you to know that I am happy for you, and for Ataahua. God knows you deserve that happiness."

"And the men? Are they happy for me?"

"I'm not sure I would say happy. Jealous as hell is more like it, although a number of them have established their own liaisons with the *pa*'s *wahines*."

Richard laughed. "I am thinking that Henry Spaulding is not among that number."

"No indeed," Brengle said. "The purser has no interest in lovemaking. Numbers are his only passion."

Richard shook his head. "And you, Jack? Are your needs being met?"

Brengle avoided the question, although Richard suspected that he did not spend his nights alone either. "This is not about me. It's about you and Ataahua. At least your romance gives the men something to gossip about."

Richard chuckled. "Please tell the men to keep the sordid stories to a minimum. I don't want anyone to be offended by idle gossip, especially the chief. Ataahua is like a daughter to him."

They walked silently along the narrow pathway leading across the series of trenches and were nearing its end when Richard turned to his friend. "Thank you for understanding, Jack. It means a lot to me. I wish I could explain what is happening in some way that justifies my actions. The truth is, I can't explain it even to myself. Emotions are swirling inside me. Yes, it will be hard to leave here. I have found something in Ataahua I thought I would never again find in a woman. What's more, I have become very attached to many of the people here. Even Manala has become my family. So, I don't know how to stay, and I don't know how to leave, although leave I must. You can tell the men I said that. I fear my leaving will be very hard on Ataahua, and that saddens me." He added softly, "It will be equally as hard on me."

"I'm sure it will be. I see her watching you when you're not aware of it, and the look on her face says everything. I'm no Romeo. I was never as popular with the young ladies as you were. But I am experienced enough to recognize the look of a woman whose heart is full. And any lubber can see that Attahua's heart is overflowing. She is very much in love with you."

"Your mind wanders, Captain Cutler. Shame on you. You are teaching me more English these days than I am teaching you Maori. The *rangatira* will not be pleased. He will have your head for supper." Her arch, frisky tone made clear that she was teasing him. "*Kia tupato kei tahuri ranei ahau ki te aroha ki a koe!*"

Richard smiled sheepishly. "I'm sorry. I fear you have me there."

Ataahua shook her head in mock disgust. "I said, 'Pay attention, or I shall be forced to *hanga aroha ngakau nui*'!"

"Does that mean what I think it means?"

She smiled. "Probably."

"In that case . . . where were we?"

"He wairangi tena," she scoffed.

"I agree. It is silly."

She eyed him closely. "You understood me," she said, her tone serious now.

He reached across the table and took her hand. "I understood your words, Ataahua. What I have trouble understanding is what is in your heart. And what is in mine."

She squeezed his hand and nodded, acknowledging his confusion. For a space of time they sat together in Richard's *whare*, their eyes locked, neither willing to speak. It took a harsh shout from Nate Donahue on the plain below to shatter their trance.

Ataahua stood and held out a hand to him. "Richard, will you come with me?"

"Of course. Where are we going?"

"Out to the river. We must get water to add to our storage containers. Then maybe we take a walk together."

"Won't that get people's tongues wagging?"

She narrowed her eyes. "Wagging? Like a dog wags its tail? But you mean something different, I think."

"Yes. I mean, won't people gossip about us if we go off alone together away from the *pa*? We have never gone outside the walls except with others."

She shrugged. "My people have no more to say about us. Their questions have already been answered."

"I take your point. Give me a moment and I'll meet you in front of the meeting house."

After Ataahua left, Richard set about tidying himself up. He added water to some dried *kumarahou* leaves and flowers, the same mixture Araahua had applied to Garth Plummer's wound and the same compound he used to wash his clothes. He stirred the blend vigorously until it thickened to a frothy paste, then dabbed it on his face and rubbed it in. Holding his knife firmly, he stroked downward and scraped away whiskers. When he was satisfied that his face was as smooth as it would get, he set out to meet Ataahua.

The day was warm by his standards, a typical early fall day in New England. Although Richard could see his breath in the morning—if it wasn't raining—and welcomed an outer wrap to ward off the chill, it hardly seemed like winter. By midday, if the sun was out and the wind light, Maori men often went about their business bare-chested and barefoot, dressed only in the traditional kilt-like *rapaki*, which covered the body from the waist to the knee.

Ataahua led Richard down the well-trampled path from the outer gate between two of the four trenches cut into the plain and on to the southern bank of the river. When they got there, she brought out a skin fashioned from the hide of a *kuri*, a native dog. Nearby was an array of canoes displaying impressive carved designs that created something marvelous out of ordinary wood. Downstream, where the river met the sea, he knew, sat a fleet of much larger *wakas*, war canoes, which were also used to transport people and cargo on long voyages. Although Richard had never seen one, descriptions he had heard indicated they must be at least a hundred feet long. The technology involved in the single mast, square sail, outrigger, and tapered construction apparently made them seaworthy under even the most challenging conditions. It was on such vessels, Manala had once explained to him, that his Polynesian ancestors had sailed to Aotearoa from far distant shores to the west, navigating by the sun and stars.

After the skin was filled and their official mission accomplished, Richard helped Ataahua to her feet. "Let's leave the water here and pick it up on the way back," he said.

She held on to his hand, and they followed the river upstream as it curved eastward through the thick bush. When the path ended, they carried on in silence through the subtropical vegetation that crowded the river's edge, in particular a tree fern Ataahua called *ponga*, which she loved for the silver underside of its emerald-green leaves.

"Is all Aotearoa as beautiful as this?" Richard asked.

"What I have seen is much like this," Ataahua replied. "It is a beautiful land. South of here, on another island, are high . . . *ayunga* . . . mountains. People say that it can be very cold, and there is . . . I forget the word." She fluttered her fingers up and down.

"Snow," Richard laughed. "It snows there."

"*Ae*. Snow. Have you seen snow?"

Richard grimaced. "More times than I care to remember."

"It is beautiful?"

"It can be."

"I would like to see snow," Ataahua sighed. "And I would like to see the mountains."

He squeezed her hand. "I hope you get to see them one day, Ataahua. I wish I could show them to you."

Intermittent flashes of sunlight through the scattered clouds cast diamond sparkles upon water so clean and clear that they could make out the colors and shapes of mottled rocks on the riverbed halfway across to the opposite bank. When Richard stopped and pointed at a sizable eel swimming lazily with the current, he turned, grinning, to point it out to her. The look she gave him in reply had nothing to do with eels.

"Ataahua . . ."

"No talk, Richard. We promised. We will talk later, when we must. Now, we make love."

He inhaled sharply when she began working the buttons of his shirt and trousers. She looked up. "I want you, Richard. You want me. It is enough." He moaned softly as he untied her skirt and let it fall to the ground.

"You do want me," she managed, her tone deep and husky. Her gaze slid downward and then back up again. "I see your desire. You want to make me your woman!"

"God help me, I do, Ataahua!" He gasped as guilt and passion again crossed swords. "How could I not? How could any man resist you?"

"*Naku mai, e taku aroha*," she whispered urgently. "*Haere mai ki ahau.*"

Quickly he spread out his clothes on a bed of soft green ferns. She lay down and pulled him down beside her, arching her back. Taking him in her hand, she deftly guided him toward her, and cried out when he entered her with a single thrust and then again and again without slaking his desire. Their movements had become less urgent and more artful, each moment, each movement, bringing him to heights he had never before experienced with Anne. At the critical moment, he lifted himself on his elbows and stared into her dark eyes as he poured his seed deep into her.

He rolled to the side and held her tightly against him until her tremors had subsided. When she was again breathing normally, he closed his eyes to the sun and allowed every fiber of his being to wallow in the sublime afterglow of ecstasy.

"Do I please you?" she whispered.

"Yes. You know you please me. Do I please you?"

She turned to him and kissed him hard on the lips. His mouth opened in response, and their tongues dueled.

"I like this kissing," she sighed contentedly, snuggling closer.

"It's better than rubbing noses?"

"*Much* better," she answered, and her fervor made them both laugh. She laid her head on his shoulder as he covered her nakedness with their discarded clothing. Lazily, he traced with his finger the four vertical lines tattooed on her chin and around her lips.

"Was it painful, getting this?"

"Yes, very."

"I hate to think of you in pain."

She caressed his cheek. "Sometimes pain is necessary. *Moko* is very important to Maori. It is part of us—very spiritual, very mystical. Someday, when I have better words, I will explain it to you."

As Richard continued to stroke the firm flesh of her back and buttocks, Ataahua sighed and asked, "How long do we have?"

He kissed her forehead. "Do you mean how long do we have here today? Or how long do we have before I must leave the *pa*?"

"Before you leave the *pa*. I know you must leave." She pulled away from him and looked sadly into his eyes. "Do not worry. I will not try to stop you."

"Why?" he asked, not to protest but to understand. "Do you not want me to stay?"

"Of course. But your *tauihu*—your fate—is not here in Aotearoa. It is in America. I have always known that. The memories of your wife are not here. They, too, are in America. I know you love her still, Richard. I sometimes hear you cry out her name when you sleep."

"I know I have done that," he said, moved by her words and feeling another sharp jab of guilt. "I'm sorry."

"Do not be sorry," she said. "Your love for Anne and the time you spent with her has helped make you the man I love." She added, "and your *mana* is not in Aotearoa."

He shifted position to get a better look at her face and to pull the clothes more tightly around her. Overhead, the sun was sinking toward the tree line. Long, cool shadows were fingering toward the entwined pair. "My *mana*? You have not yet explained what that word means either."

With her free hand she stroked his chest and abdomen. "*Mana* means everything to Maori. It is hard for *pakeha* to understand *mana*. It is the heart, the spirit, the soul, a supernatural force that makes Maori—every one of us—who we are."

"How does a man acquire *mana*?"

"He gets it from his ancestors. And he gets *mana* by how he lives and from those around him: his family, his friends, even his enemies.

"His enemies? How is that?"

Ataahua paused. "You have heard, I think, that once, not very long ago, Maori sometimes ate other people."

"Yes. And I must confess," he added apologetically, "that my men and I were concerned about that when we first arrived here."

She laughed and smoothed his hair. "You need not have worried. The practice is all but gone today. It was a tradition, a rite based on respect."

"Respect? What do you mean?"

"It was believed that if a Maori ate the body of an enemy warrior, that warrior's *mana* would be added to his own. He would then become a better warrior, a better man. It is difficult for *pakeha t*o accept, but to a Maori it makes great sense. I tell you this because I want you to understand our culture and our traditions."

"Well, I am relieved to know that the tradition is dead." He paused. "It *is* dead?"

"It still happens," she admitted, "but it is very rare. If it is done, it is done for spite, for *utu*, not for *mana*. No one in my *iwi* would ever do such a thing."

"So, when you told me that Chief Nene would have my head for supper, you were joking?"

Ataahua laughed. "Yes, joking, of course," she laughed again.

"That's a relief." He rubbed her back to warm her and looked into her eyes. "Do I have *mana*, Ataahua?" he asked seriously.

She nodded. "You have good *mana*, Richard. Nene thinks much of you. He says you are one of us, a warrior. He pays you a high compliment."

"I am honored to be considered one of your people. I will try to deserve such praise. But now, Ataahua, it is getting late and you are cold. We had best return to the *pa*."

She nodded and rolled away from him. "Yes. But we will return here. And later, after you are gone and I am alone, I will return here many times."

He noted a glint of tears in her eyes. "Will you? Why?"

"To remember, of course. I may not always have your body, Richard. But here I will always have your *wairua*—your spirit. And here," she added, placing the flat of her palm on his chest, "*Ka mau tonu toku ngakau.*"

He placed his hand over hers. "As you will always be in my heart, Ataahua."

Nine days later, as Richard was meeting with his increasingly restless officers and crew, they heard the unmistakable sound of wood being frantically pounded in warning.

"Well, gentlemen," Nate Donahue announced with a dramatic flair, "methinks that what we have been discussing has just become moot."

CHAPTER 16

"SORRY TO DISTURB YOU, MY LADY. THERE IS A GENTLEMAN HERE KEEN to see you. He and Mr. MacKenzie await your pleasure in the front parlor of your cottage."

Anne turned her eyes away from the rolling surf of the Tasman Sea to see Rachael Brown, the youngest of the mission's staff. The comely young native of Bradford-on-Avon had bid farewell to England—and to an avid suitor—to serve God and country in a remote colony. Though far from home, she remained English to her core and was so deferential to Anne's noble lineage that she acted as though the modest accommodation at the mission station were a royal palace, and she a lady-in-waiting to a princess.

"Who is he?"

"I wasn't told his name, ma'am," Rachael replied. "I believe he is an army officer come from Auckland."

"Thank you, Rachael. What of James?"

"He is taking his nap, my lady. Te Whina is with him."

"Very well. Kindly inform our visitor that I shall be there presently."

"My lady." Rachael curtsied and left.

Not yet ready to leave her favorite retreat, Anne took a few more moments to gaze out to sea, soothed by the gentle lullaby of waves. With a sigh she gathered up her skirts and made straightaway for her cottage. *This is it*, she thought. In a day, maybe two, she would be leaving the mission station, a prospect she accepted with a blend of great anticipation and considerable regret. She had friends here; her son had been born here; she had made a home here; and yet here it was: the first day in the process of going home, whatever "going home" might mean for her now. This would be the last day of holding onto a cherished dream that, despite all, her husband would emerge from the bush, alive and well, to claim her.

She shook her head to dispel the demons of false hope. She suffered no illusions. Such a miracle was impossible. Five months had passed since the wreck of *Suwannee* a few miles to the north. Anne had never tried to visit the scene of the disaster. There was nothing for her there but shattered dreams and a broken heart. Even had she wanted to go, it was still too dangerous to venture there.

When she entered her cottage, the two men who had been conversing in the front room stood up. Daniel MacKenzie in his modest black clothing faded into insignificance against the young army officer dressed in crimson frock coat, buff trousers sporting a yellow stripe down each leg, and glossy brown leather boots. The bottom two buttons of his white waistcoat were left fashionably undone. His dark eyes scrutinized her as she entered the room, and she was highly aware of her dowdy dress. The mission did not run to fine attire and fashionable accessories, only the castoffs that people back in England felt virtuous in giving away.

But like the lady she was, Anne walked coolly up to him and extended her hand, which he lightly kissed in the courtly fashion. "Charmed to meet you, Mrs. Cutler," he exclaimed gallantly. "Charmed indeed. Imagine my surprise and delight on learning that such a lovely noblewoman was stranded in this desolate place."

"I would hardly call this place desolate, sir," Anne admonished. "I find it charming and shall be sorry to leave it. The good people here saved my life and the life of my little son."

"Yes, of course. I understand," he said patronizingly. "I merely meant—"

"I know what you meant, sir," she said stiffly. "Now, if you please, who are you and what is the purpose of your visit?"

The officer went ramrod stiff. "Forgive me, madam. I meant no offense or disrespect, I assure you. I forgot myself in the joy of finding that you are indeed alive and well. You had long been given up for dead." He bowed stiffly. "Major Henley Packard-Smythe of the 99th Lancashire

Regiment of Foot, at your service. I am here at the behest of Sir Robert Fitzroy, the royal governor, who desires me most earnestly to see to your safe conduct to Auckland. There, you will stay in comfort and safety until we are able to arrange passage for you to England."

"If England is where I choose to go," Anne said. "I don't believe that decision has yet been made."

The major's eyes widened, and his ample jowls jiggled. "Yes, of course, Mrs. Cutler," he flustered. "If I have made a false assumption, I apologize. All will be as you wish, of course."

"Thank you. Will those attached to this mission accompany me to Auckland? I have no desire to leave without them, and I understand that they will be in considerable danger if they remain."

Packard-Smythe gave MacKenzie a meaningful glance before responding. "I understand, ma'am. Be assured that the royal governor is most grateful to Reverend MacKenzie and those in his charge. They are doing God's work, and Sir Robert is most concerned about them all. However, my orders are to provide for you and your personal attendants only. That is all I can guarantee at the moment. I had presumed that you had been informed of this."

Anne looked hard at MacKenzie. "Does this mean you and Maude and Jonathan are not coming with me, Daniel?"

MacKenzie shook his head. "Not at this time, Anne. Rachael and Te Whina will accompany you. Jonathan and Maude and the others will remain here with me to serve the mission and its dependents. We cannot abandon them."

"But you told me it was too dangerous for anyone to stay."

MacKenzie waved that away. "And so it was, when I told you that. The danger has lessened somewhat since then. We have received further assurances from Te Wherowhero that he will guarantee our safety in this mission for as long as necessary."

"How long will that be, do you think?"

"We cannot know at this stage. We will leave only when the sick among us are able to travel."

Silence prevailed until Major Packard-Smythe said, "It is not just the Maori chief who will be protecting the mission. The British army will be doing its part. A lieutenant and ten regulars will soon be joining us and will remain until the mission is abandoned. I myself will remain on station until reinforcements arrive in Auckland from New South Wales and are sent here. Sir Robert is offering such protection to all British mission stations during these difficult times." He bowed to Anne. "This particular mission is granted special dispensation due to its distinguished guest."

Anne nodded in acknowledgment before turning her attention back to MacKenzie. "You *will* be coming to Auckland, Daniel? Promise me you will. I cannot bear the thought of leaving you behind."

"I will join you in Auckland as soon as I am able, Anne," MacKenzie assured her. "We all will. That is a promise."

"Thank you. That is some relief. If it must be this way I shall go, but you know I should prefer to remain here at the mission with you and the others."

"I do know that, Anne," MacKenzie said carefully. "But I cannot permit it, nor can the major. You heard him. He has his orders."

Anne bowed and turned to Packard-Smythe. "So, Major. I am being forced to flee. What are my marching orders? If you are not to command those responsible for my safe conduct, who is?"

"Captain John Shilling will have that honor, madam."

"And who, pray, is Captain John Shilling?"

"The captain is a Royal Navy officer who is held in the highest regard by your brother, Admiral Braithwaite. The admiral would be the first to agree with me that Captain Shilling is one of England's finest and most experienced officers."

"And how does my brother know him?"

"I believe Shilling served under him as a midshipman and then through the ranks to first officer."

"Go on."

"The admiral thought enough of him to sponsor his promotion to post captain. Later, he recommended that Governor Fitzroy take on Shilling to advise him on military matters. The captain possesses a brilliant mind, and he has been of enormous service to the colony despite his relatively short time here. Now, as divine Providence would have it, he has been given command of a ship-of-war out of Auckland. Captain Shilling is a superior sea officer whose expertise we may sorely need in the days and weeks ahead. Does all this answer your question?"

"Quite adequately, thank you. I am humbled that my brother has selected a man of such stature to serve as my escort to Sydney. It appears that we all are in safe hands. Where is Captain Shilling now?"

"He is on his way with horses, two wagons, supplies for the mission, and twenty Royal Marines. He should arrive sometime this afternoon. Today is Tuesday. You and your attendants will be departing at daybreak on Thursday. If the weather and our luck hold, you should reach Government House that evening. It will be more a forced march than a casual ride through the countryside, you understand. The terrain will be rough."

"I am quite accustomed to enduring rough terrain, Major," she said with a wry smile.

Later that afternoon, as Anne was bathing Jamie in a big wooden basin half-filled with water warmed over a fire, the clatter of hooves and the rumbling of wagon wheels drew her attention to the central courtyard. Horses whinnied and snorted as chickens squawked and men shouted. A firm voice stilled the commotion with a single command.

Anne wrapped Jamie in a thick towel and hurried over to a front parlor window. Pulling aside a curtain, she saw Major Packard-Smythe, closely followed by Daniel and Jonathan, striding to where two army service wagons had drawn to a halt. A squad of marines wearing blue uniform coats adorned with pipe-clayed crossbelts disembarked. At their head, a young man bedecked in rich blue cloth featuring twin rows of gold buttons and a gold-fringed epaulette on each shoulder sat astride a stately roan.

Anne watched in admiration as the officer swung a leg over the roan's neck and slid easily to the ground. Despite what must have been an arduous ride from Auckland, he might have just walked off a parade ground. In the man's relative youth—she had expected to see someone considerably older—and fine military bearing she saw a striking resemblance to Richard. The thought occurred to her that, like her husband, this man possessed the qualities of command that My Lords of the Admiralty in London desired in all their sea officers.

The officer removed his fore-and-aft bicorne hat briefly to coax back a shock of blond hair. After replacing the hat just so, he squeezed the front tip of it in salute to Major Packard-Smythe and bowed genteelly to the two directors of the mission. Although she could not hear what was said, they carried on a short conversation. When MacKenzie pointed to Anne's cottage and Captain Shilling shot a glance in that direction, she felt a flood of sensations that she found oddly exhilarating.

She drew the curtain closed and stepped away from the window.

CHAPTER 17

ALTHOUGH THE LIGHT RAIN MADE FOOTING TREACHEROUS, RICHARD lost no time clambering up the lookout tower, past the platform, now abandoned, and on up to the top, as high up as a crosstree on a 74-gun ship of the line. Nate Donahue was right behind him.

Below, on the plain outside the outer wall, Manala, Hohana, four other *ariki*, and the three midshipmen were already directing the *iwi's* warriors and *Suwannee's* sailors into the defensive rifle pits that surrounded the *pa*. Each defender carried a musket along with cartridges and shot to service it. A few brandished long flint-tipped spears.

Breathing heavily, Richard scanned the distant bush. "What, Tane?" he said to the lookout, who had ascended from the watch platform after sounding the alarm. Seemingly oblivious to the rain and chill, Tane wore only his usual kilt. Richard followed Tane's gaze to a particular area in the bush.

"I don't see anything," Richard told him, looking harder at the spot where Tane was pointing. "*Kaore au e kite i tetahi mea.*"

Tane slowly shook his head. "*Ka haere mai roto i nga wa katoa, e Kapene!*" he exclaimed with a sweeping motion of his arm. His normally soft voice was agitated and edged with grave concern.

"What's he saying?" Donahue demanded.

"I don't understand all of it. Apparently he sees the enemy everywhere. They have us surrounded."

"Good," Donahue said. "More of the bastards to kill. Although I have to admit that I don't see a damn thing," he added.

"Neither do I. Tane does, and that's all that matters."

"So how do we proceed?" Donahue's tone was cool, professional.

Richard took a moment. "Exactly as we drilled. I'll take the back trenches. You take the forward trenches. One round of continuous fire, then back inside the outer wall."

"Agreed. What about the surprise we have in store for them?"

"Save it. We may not need it. I hope we don't. It will use up most of our powder."

"Got it!" Donahue saluted, grabbed the taut rope leading down, wrapped his right leg around it, and slid hand under hand as though descending to the weather deck from a foretop.

Richard pointed a finger at the Maori and jabbed it downward once, twice. "Come with us, Tane," he insisted. "Get down. You're too large a target up here. *Takahia iho!*"

Tane nodded. As he hurried down the steep, wet wooden platform, Richard surveyed the distant bush a final time. He still saw nothing and cursed his lack of a long glass. He followed Donahue down the rope. Once on the ground, he strode through the *pa*'s rear gates, across the grassy space between the two walls, and out onto the plain.

Jonty met him there with a salute. "It's all prepared, Captain," he said in a voice fraught with fear and excitement.

Richard returned the salute. "Very well, Mr. Montgomery. Take position and await my orders."

"Aye, aye, sir!" Montgomery offered another salute and was about to leave for his post when Richard called him back.

"Jonty!"

The midshipman turned, gave him a questioning look. "Sir?"

"Keep your head down."

"Yes *sir!*"

Richard took position in the outermost of the three rifle pits. Fifty Maori warriors and five sailors crouched with him along a line that faced east and curved around to the north and south sides of the *pa*. Behind him, in the parallel middle trench, Manala held ground with fifty additional warriors. Behind Manala, in the trench nearest the outer wall, Jonty and an *ariki* named Ihaka crouched against the dirt sides of the trench. In the westward-facing trenches halfway around the *pa* on the side facing west,

Nate Donahue, Hugh Zabriskie, and Hohana commanded the three trenches with an equal number of warriors. Inside the *pa*, Jack Brengle and Thomas Talmadge were overseeing final preparations in company with Chief Nene and the bulk of his Ngapuhi defenders.

All was ready. They could only wait.

It started as a low, guttural growl that came at them from all directions. The growl became a chant that increased in volume and intensity until it filled the air around them, the earth below, and the sky above. The chanting continued, growing ever louder, until it morphed into blood-chilling screams.

Richard knew the significance of that. They all did. On their first night in the *pa*, during the *hangi*, the sailors had witnessed a scaled-down version of the *haka*, a war dance not unlike one American Indians might dance on the eve of battle. Chief Nene had explained that the purpose of the *haka* was to instill terror in an enemy while whipping the attackers into a killing frenzy. The Ngati Whatua, Chief Nene had told Richard in private, would bring everything they had to bear against the Ngapuhi. And if victorious, they would show no mercy. They would slaughter every man, woman, and child and defile their bodies. *Utu* was demanded, and they would have their revenge whatever the cost.

Although Richard had taken pains to keep that piece of information from his officers and men, he suspected that most of them had an inkling of what lay in store if the battle was lost. The Ngapuhi, all of them, Ataahua included, would choose death over capture. So, Richard resolved, would he.

"Stand firm!" Richard cried out, his gaze focused on the bush before him. He could not see the Ngati Whatua yet, but he had no trouble hearing them. As he heard his command echo down and across the lines, he pulled out his revolver and checked its chambers. Nothing had changed since he last checked five minutes ago. Glancing to his right and left, he noted that the Maori warriors in the trench with him appeared unfazed by the chants and screams. If anything, they seemed to be enjoying the spectacle. These men, Richard knew, were among the tribal elite. To a man, they held positions of high status within the *iwi*. They were battle-tested and battle-hardened, and as such they were not easily frightened. Their seeming indifference to the unholy din coming at them helped to temper his own fear and slow the racing of his heart.

In a perfectly choreographed maneuver, the Ngati Whatua suddenly began emerging from the bush. Only the north side of the *pa* remained empty. There was sparse cover there between the outer wall and the river, and the distance was too short for an effective charge. From the other three directions, however, they came on, chanting and screeching, their cries now accompanied by the harsh sounds of body-slapping and foot-stomping. Each warrior carried his musket a-tilt at his chest and wore a flaxen bag around his waist, presumably containing extra shot and powder.

Peering carefully over the top of the trench, Richard tried to calculate their number. There were hundreds of them, certainly. Thousands, more likely, depending on the number still concealed in the bush. However many there were, they held a significant numerical advantage, and they were as well armed as the Ngapuhi. Several of them—their *ariki*, no doubt—gripped swords of European manufacture, their steel blades glittering in the sunlight filtering through broken clouds.

"*Hold!*" Richard cried out. "*Hold firm!*"

On and on they came, step by step, their cries and screams growing ever more ferocious as they narrowed the gap to the *pa*. They slapped their flesh and stomped their feet, bared their teeth and flared their nostrils. Richard felt hot bile rising in his throat.

Suddenly, eerily, the noise stopped. Seconds ticked by as the Ngati Whatua gathered strength in numbers that now stretched all the way back and into the bush. Then, again in perfect synchrony, with a collective scream that seemed to summon all the dark forces of hell, they charged. On three sides they charged, sprinting and screaming.

Richard jumped to his feet. "First line, make ready!"

Maori and sailors in the first trench stood up, took aim.

"*Fire!*"

Fifty-five shots rang out. A score of Ngati Whatua leading the charge collapsed where they were or staggered forward to fall face-down.

"*Fall back! Reload!*"

Those in the forward trench fell back over the middle trench to the innermost trench. Once in the pit, each warrior bit off the end of a cartridge, poured powder into the muzzle of his musket, inserted a ball, rammed it home, placed percussion caps into the breech, and made ready to fire again.

"*Raina tuarua, kia rite!*" the bold voice of Manala rang out. "*E te ahi!*"

A second volley of withering fire dropped another score of enemy warriors. It was hard to miss a target. The range was fast becoming point-blank.

"*Fall back! Reload!*"

Those in the middle trench fell back through the open rear gates of the outer wall.

"*Third line, make ready!*" Jonty shouted in a powerful voice remarkably unlike his usual soft Southern drawl. "*Fire!*"

Those in the third line, reinforced by those from the first line, opened fire on an enemy who had advanced to a few yards short of the outer trench. The effect was devastating. It was a hammer blow, an onslaught of hot iron that slammed into what was fast becoming an army in disarray.

"*Fall back!*" Richard commanded.

Jonty stood rooted to his place in the trench, either stunned or enthralled by the havoc his command had wrought. Richard grabbed him by the arm. "We don't need heroes today!" he shouted at the midshipman. "We need leaders!" He pulled him toward the twin outer gates, which closed behind them as they and Manala ran inside.

Outside, on three sides of the *pa*, the Ngati Whatua had taken control of the outermost defenses and were gathering for a coordinated assault. Ngapuhi warriors thrust musket muzzles through gaps between the stakes of the outer wall and fired into the enemy mass. Each musket fired was replaced by one freshly loaded. The bloodbath raged on.

Yet the assault did not waver. The plain had become a killing field littered with the dead and dying. But the Ngati Whatua came on and on. Some took cover in the abandoned trenches and shot at any target they spotted. Others advanced to the wall, determined to turn the tables in what up to now had been a one-sided battle. Despite the terrible attrition they were suffering, a good number of Ngati Whatua reached the wall and plunged their weapons between the gaps, firing blindly. A Ngapuhi warrior standing near Richard dropped to his knees. A warrior next to him spun around, doubled over, and fell.

Through the open inner gates of the *pa* a company of Ngapuhi warriors ran out with six-foot spears and rammed them through gaps in the outer wall into the flesh of those attempting to scale the wall. When a Ngapui was cut down by random musket fire, Richard picked up the man's spear, ran to the wall, and shoved it through a gap. He felt the tip enter flesh and heard a grunt of pain, so he pushed harder, and harder still, until the writhing ceased and the body was a dead weight at the end of his spear. Only then did he release his grip on the spear and reach for his pistol.

Enemy warriors were breaching the wall. Despite the crossfire from the corner blockhouses, several Ngati Whatua had pulled themselves up to its spiked top and had dropped over it and onto the grassy space. With club or axe in hand, they savagely took on all comers. One of them swiped at Tane and knocked him down. As Tane lay helpless on the ground, Richard stepped up, pointed his pistol at the temple of the Ngati Whatua, and squeezed the trigger. The bullet exploded through the warrior's brain and out the back of his skull, spraying blood and bits of brain over Tane and into the air.

Richard offered Tane a hand up. "Can you stand?"

"*Ae.*" He wiped at the gore on his bare chest and *kaura.* "*Kia ore, e Kapene.*"

"*Tena koe.* You're welcome." Richard pointed at the open gates. "*Haere ki roto i te pa.* Get inside. We can't hold out here much longer."

As if to underscore his words, he noted the motionless body of Will Allerton a few feet away. The Marine private lay supine, his face bashed in nearly beyond recognition.

"Go with God, Will," Richard muttered as he rejoined the fray. Despite what should have been catastrophic losses, more and more Ngati Whatua warriors were scaling the wall. Incredibly, streams of fresh warriors continued to emerge from the bush.

The two sets of massive gates leading into the *pa* had to be closed to allow the Ngapuhi to regroup inside their last and strongest line of defense: the *pa* itself. But shutting the gates would cut off the Ngapuhi and sailors fighting the enemy in hand-to-hand combat between the two walls and those who even now were charging out from the *pa* to join the battle and form a human barricade at the gates to keep the attackers out. During their strategy sessions Chief Nene had insisted that the decision of when or whether to close the gates was Richard's to make. Failing him, it was Donahue's. But Donahue was nowhere to be seen.

Richard glanced at Chief Nene standing stoically, arms folded, at the base of the hill, the very spot on which he vowed to live or die this day. He nodded at Richard when their eyes met and calmly held out the flat of his right hand, as if to say that he was prepared to accept whatever decision Richard made. Richard nodded his understanding and looked desperately for Brengle. To his relief, he saw his executive officer weaving toward him through the confusion and commotion.

"We're ready," he said when they were together.

"Good. Where's Nate?"

Brengle shook his head. "He's down. It's bad, but I don't know how bad. He was hit trying to save Manala. We managed to drag him back inside the *pa*. Ataahua is tending to him in his hut."

"Was he able to save Manala?"

"No. Manala is dead."

"Damn!" He shook his head to clear it. "Okay, let's do it. We have no choice. Unleash hell."

Brengle hesitated. "All of it?"

"All of it. Every goddamn last bit of it. There's no point in holding anything back. If the grenades don't do the job, we're out of options. See to it, Lieutenant!"

"Aye, Captain!"

As Brengle ran off to set the desperation plan in motion, Richard took stock. What he saw in and outside the *pa* was not a battle. It was a melee devoid of any sort of military discipline. Although they fought heroically, the Ngapuhi warriors were being overwhelmed just as assuredly as the giant wave had overwhelmed *Suwannee*. The enemy controlled the plain and, increasingly, the space between the two walls. Soon they would start swarming through the human barricade at the gates and into the *pa*, where the fight would be fierce but hopeless. Military doctrine dictated that he order the gates closed. His battle plan dictated the opposite.

Richard checked the chambers of his revolver. Three bullets left. He had no others. He whirled around and checked the nearest of the six fires blazing around the perimeter of the *pa*. The first hollow reeds stuffed with powder were being lit. Maori and sailors were making ready.

He looked up again and saw what he was hoping to see: the first wave of flaxen balls stuffed with powder and small, sharp objects: shards of flint, wooden splinters, shattered oyster shells, any sort of shrapnel that could cut flesh and muscle and create havoc. Each ball was coated in *kauri* resin, which served as both a sealant and an accelerant. The balls looked like shooting stars as they flew upward.

Richard closed his eyes and counted backward. "Three . . . two . . . one."

The first grenades were followed by others, exploding one after another as wave after wave of flaming balls flew up over the walls of the *pa* and down onto the enemy on the plain. The result was inevitable. The screams and cries of men being blasted apart stunned the invaders to their core, blowing their will to fight right out of them.

The first explosion was the signal to the Ngapuhi inside the *pa* to attack. With cries of rage they streamed out through the two sets of inner gates, slashing at the stunned Ngati Whatua with spears, knives, swords, tomahawks, anything sharp that could flay skin and tear muscle. Like berserkers smelling blood, they hacked, pounded, bashed, shot, and speared their way from the inner gate to the outer gate, making short work of the stunned enemy's meager resistance.

Outside the outer wall, on the plain, the roar of explosions was replaced by the higher-pitched *zing* of musket fire. Ngapuhi warriors in the corner blockhouses and up on the hill and lookout tower were taking aim at Ngati Whatua fleeing back into the bush. It was a turkey shoot. One after another was hit in the back and staggered forward a step or two before collapsing on the ground. Scores of dead, dying, and wounded lay on the plain and in the trenches surrounded by the acrid smell of smoke and the gut-wrenching stench of blood and urine and feces.

"Cease fire!" Richard shouted. "*Ka mutu te ahi!*" As the order was relayed, the slaughter ceased. The plain went quiet save for the pitiful pleas of the wounded and dying.

Richard spotted Brengle talking with Chief Nene at the base of the hill and walked over to them. "Well done, Lieutenant," he said, offering his hand.

Brengle shook it. "Thank you, Captain. But the credit goes to Nate. The plan was his. All I did was follow instructions."

"*Ta matou, ka mate ki a koe,*" Chief Nene said, his voice thick with emotion. "*I a tatou te Atua.*"

"It is our honor," Richard assured him. "And I agree, God was with us today."

After the *rangatira* left, Richard said to Brengle, his voice low and grim, "I'll want the butcher's bill when you have it, Jack."

"I'll get it. I know of four of our own dead. Likely there'll be more."

"Allerton and who else?"

"Turner, Zabriskie, and Webb. Rand is badly wounded. He won't make it."

Richard knew these men as well as any commanding officer knows men he has sailed and fought and survived with despite the odds. Their deaths pained him greatly. But one death struck especially deep and hard. "Hugh? Oh, Jesus!" He crossed himself multiple times. "He was a good lad, and he would have made a fine captain one day."

"It came close to being all of us," Brengle reminded him.

"You think I don't realize that?" Richard spat. "Keep me posted, Lieutenant."

"Aye, aye, Captain," Brengle said curtly.

"Wait, Jack. I didn't mean to snap at you. That was uncalled for. I apologize."

"All sins forgiven on this day," Brengle said with a hint of a smile.

When Richard reached the hut assigned to the Marines, he found Ataahua kneeling by Donahue. Even from the doorway he could tell that Donahue was dying. The rank odor of perspiration and blood blended with the sour smell of urine. When she saw him, she rushed over to embrace him.

"*Kia ora te Atua kia ora koe*," she murmured, close to tears. "You are alive!"

"And you," he whispered in her ear. He released her hold around his neck and held her at arm's length. "Nate?" he asked, nodding toward Donahue.

She looked into his eyes and shook her head slowly. "I am sorry, Richard. There is nothing my medicine can do for him. The wound is here." She patted Richard's chest.

Richard stared down at Donahue. He looked peaceful enough, and unmarked save for a red splotch at the center of his cotton shirt. Donahue's breath rattled as he struggled to breathe, and his eyes were closed. They flew open when Richard knelt down beside him and placed his hand over the wound.

"Is the day won, Captain?" he rasped.

"It is, Nate. Your plan worked perfectly. It was brilliant."

Donahue managed a weak smile. "Good. Then I have done my duty."

"That you have, Lieutenant," Richard assured him. "That you have," adding, under his breath, "God rest your soul, my friend."

Chapter 18

There was no *hangi* that evening to celebrate the victory. Throughout the *pa* the mood was somber. Even the children showed no interest in play or food. The faces of Tom Talmadge and Jonty Montgomery as they kept watch over the body of Hugh Zabriskie summed up the emotions of everyone in the *pa*. The corpses of Maori warriors also awaiting burial lay next to him, their bodies anointed with *kokowai* and oils. Later, Richard was told, the *tupapaku*, the corpses, would be exhumed and the bones washed and hidden in secret places. The sailors watched the preparations in respectful silence, even if they did not grasp the implications. It was a ritual that stirred Richard deeply. The Ngapuhi laid out on the ground were not just fallen soldiers to him. They were men and women who had sacrificed their lives to save his life and the lives of his men. Just as he and his men had done for them. He was proud of them all. His heart was full. And he ached for the loss of Nate Donahue and the other four slain Americans, just as he mourned the loss of every man dead among *Suwannee*'s crew, whether killed in battle, washed up on the beach, or gone in secret into the bush. He sorely missed their skills and counsel.

The heart-wrenching and backbreaking work of burying the dead began the next morning. The previous evening, Ataahua had not come to him. Nor did she come on this night. He understood why. She had her own grief to address. Although he missed her terribly, he was grateful for the respite. His own considerable grief was coupled with guilt. He was too fond of this woman, too fond of this land. Was he in love with her? He could not say for certain. To the best of his reckoning, six or seven months had passed since the wreck of his ship and the loss of his wife, his beloved Anne, whose face, he was shocked to discover, he was having difficulty remembering.

His mother, he knew, would be scandalized by their relationship. Nor would his father have approved, notwithstanding the tolerance for all that he had often expressed during his lifetime. No one in polite society in Massachusetts or Virginia would give him the time of day if he brought her home with him. Yet this wonderful, loving, gifted woman had pledged her body and soul to him. Her *wairua*, her spirit, had spoken to him, and try as he might, he could not deny the message it conveyed. If his family, friends, and acquaintances did not endorse their union, well, so be it. *Brave words*, he said to himself, but he knew it was not that easy. He could only hope that his forthcoming mission would provide answers.

The next morning, by prearrangement, Richard led the remaining eleven sailors under his command to the *wharenui*, the *iwi*'s meeting house at the crest of the hill. It was a sacred place used only for special occasions. Every piece of wood used in its construction, and every nook and cranny within it, had been polished with flat stones and then carved in intricate detail. This was true especially in the *poutokomanawa*, the central part of the large space that served as a cathedral to the *iwi*'s ancestors. How such immaculately crafted artistry could be fashioned using only stone and crude wooden implements, Richard could not begin to fathom.

The eleven men he led up the hill were a sorry-looking lot. Having endured many months of fear and uncertainty, wearing disintegrating shirts and trousers, several of them suffering from battle injuries, they nonetheless walked with dignity and pride. These men were survivors. They had faced the worst and they had endured. Since the cyclone and shipwreck those many moons ago, they had met the enemy on the enemy's terms, and they had prevailed. At the entrance to the *wharenui* they removed their shoes and washed their hands in a wooden tub, then walked inside to sit together on the floor, surrounded by the beautifully carved images of the tribes' ancestors mounted on the four walls.

Sitting nearby were the tribe's *ariki* and other senior warriors. Chief Nene sat before them on an ornately carved high-back chair with armrests. The dimly lit space was filled with the savory scent of freshly woven flax.

When all was quiet, Nene stood. "*Tena koutou*," he said in greeting. He went on to speak to his people in tones that were at once passionate and mournful. Richard understood the gist of what the chief was saying, but because only a few of his crew understood any of it, he waited until Nene had said what he had come to say before betraying any emotion. When Nene ended his speech, the Maori warriors pounded their fists or the ends of short, stout sticks on the floor.

When the noise had abated, Chief Nene rose to his feet. He stood regally, surveying his audience with arms folded across his chest. He wore a thick ceremonial cloak of flax interwoven from shoulder to waist with bird feathers, many of them, Richard had come to understand, the brown feathers of the indigenous *kiwi*. He held out an arm to Richard, then to his crew, and said, in the resonant tones of a professional statesman, "I have told my people that we, the Ngapuhi tribe of Chief Tamati Waka Nene, acknowledge with humble gratitude the services and sacrifices of Captain Richard Cutler, Lieutenant Jack Brengle, Lieutenant Nate Donahue, and the brave men of their command. Your valor has earned our eternal gratitude. Your deeds will long be respected. Your dead will forever be remembered. Your debt to us has been paid, many times over. You are now free to leave us. Tomorrow morning, Ihaka and Tane will take you to Kororareka. There they will ask the British to help us, and you will be free to pursue your lives unburdened by any obligation to us."

After the speech, as the sailors stole glances at each other, Chief Nene walked to Richard and offered him a hand up. When they were face-to-face, he pressed his nose hard against Richard's nose. Stepping back, he proclaimed in a loud voice, "I am proud to call this man my brother! I am proud to call all of you my friends. We are no longer Maori and American. We are one people!"

Again the tribesmen pounded fists and sticks on the floor in enthusiastic approval. Richard bowed in acknowledgment of the accolades, then said, with a sweep of his hand to include every sailor and Marine, "We of the United States Navy are proud to be brothers-in-arms with Chief Nene and his brave warriors of this Ngapuhi *iwi*. May the friendship and support we have created together these past few months endure. I pledge everything I am and everything I have to ensure that result!"

This time it was the Americans who pounded their fists on the floor. After Chief Nene had translated Richard's words, his warriors launched into a final round of thumping applause and the session was declared over.

Outside the *wharenui*, Ataahua and a host of men, women, and children who had come to bear witness to the unusual proceedings were waiting. The somber mood continued as word passed from one to another that the Americans would soon be leaving the *pa*. Recognizing what that meant to Richard and Ataahua, the throng around them quickly thinned. Only Chief Nene paused before them. Placing one hand on Ataahua's shoulder and the other on Richard's shoulder, he stared meaningfully into the eyes of one, then the other, before motioning what Richard took to be a blessing over them. Then he walked away, having uttered not a word.

"*Haere mai, e taku aroha,*" Ataahua half-whispered after Nene had gone. "*Me haere tahi tatou.*"

"*Ae, taku aroha.*"

Where she wanted to go was a foregone conclusion. Neither of them spoke as they walked hand-in-hand along the pathway by the river to the familiar clearing. Overhead, the sky was partly overcast. Dark gray clouds loomed to westward, while to eastward, ribbons of white clouds floating within a pale blue sky bore witness of better things to come. The temperature in September was warm and welcoming, much like what Richard would expect in Virginia in early April. Layers of clothing were no longer necessary even for those sensitive to chill. The songs of exotic birds echoed through the woods, and the red flax flowers and delicate white and pink blooms on *manuka* shrubs and trees pleased the eye and perfumed the air.

Today, such sensory delights did not evoke giddy delight, as they often did when in Ataahua's company. They were sad reminders of what he would miss were he to leave this land and this woman. He could already feel the emptiness that would accompany him home to America and throughout his life.

Ataahua broke the silence between them. "I am sorry I did not come to you last night, Richard. I wanted to come. I always want to be with you that way. But I thought, maybe we both needed time to be alone, to sit and remember people we have loved and lost. I hope you understand."

Richard moved aside a low-lying branch to allow Ataahua to pass. "I do understand, Ataahua," he said when they had passed by the branch and he let it swing back behind them.

"I include your wife among those people you remember with love, Richard."

He stopped and sighed softly. "I know you do, Ataahua."

Moments passed in silence. Then: "Does it trouble you when I speak of Anne, Richard?"

"Trouble me? How could it possibly trouble me?"

"You have been so quiet," she said. "And I know you are troubled."

"I was thinking."

"About Anne?"

"No. About you."

When they reached the clearing, he gripped her shoulders and turned her toward him. "Far from troubling me, Ataahua, your willing-ness to speak about Anne and my love for her is one of the things I love about you. You are never jealous about my life with her. You honor her memory and you honor the years we shared together. Sometimes your unselfishness is hard for me to accept. Not many women would say what you said."

She placed the flat of her palm on his cheek. Her eyes glistened with unshed tears. "You say . . . you love me, Richard?"

He held her gaze, unblinking, for a long time. "Yes, Ataahua, I love you. *Aroha ahau ki a koe.* It may have been the battle, it may have been the loss of so many I hold dear, but I have realized that I cannot lose you. I feared maybe I had. I feared that maybe you had died in the battle. I could not bear the thought of it. I could not bear the thought of living the rest of my life without you."

A single tear rolled down her cheek. She raised a hand to wipe it away, but Richard caught the wrist and kissed the tear away himself. "But now you leave?" she said.

She allowed him to seat her comfortably on a bed of soft moss before speaking again. "Your voice tells me you must go. But your eyes tell me different."

He sat down beside her, drew his knees to his chest, and clasped his arms around them. "Yes, I am leaving, Ataahua."

She looked away.

"But I am coming back."

She looked at him. "Coming back? You will come back?"

"I am going to Kororareka to meet with British authorities there. The matter is critical. The *pa* is nearly out of powder and shot. That makes it defenseless and puts us at grave risk. The Ngati Whatua will likely attack again when they have recovered. When they do, we must be prepared. To be prepared, we need British arms and ammunition. We can no longer depend entirely on ourselves. We need British help, and we need that help as soon as possible. So I am going to get it. If I can."

"Does Chief Nene know this?"

Richard nodded. "He and I devised this plan together. He has asked me to lead this expedition, and I will not refuse him. I cannot."

"Your men will go with you?"

"Yes, all of them. As their captain I have a duty to them. They have been asked to sacrifice too much. They will not return to the *pa* with me, and I must see them safely on a ship sailing to America before I can come back. I cannot rest peacefully in your arms until they are homeward bound."

She looked away again and for a while simply watched the swift river swollen by the heavy spring rains. He was gently massaging her back when she said hesitantly, "Richard, my love?"

"*Ae, e toku aroha?*"

"I understand why you must go. You are leaving for your people and for mine. I love you for doing that, and we will say no more about it. You have also told me that you are returning to the *pa*. That fills me with more joy than I can express. But what then, my love? What will you do then? You have many obligations in America, do you not?"

He pulled her close and kissed her hair. "Yes, I do. I have given it a lot of thought." There was his heritage and legacy to consider. His career as a

186

naval officer and his obligations to Cutler & Sons, regardless of whether he decided to follow his family's wishes and take control of the company. And he had obligations to his family and friends in Massachusetts and Virginia. What about them? What about so many others? His life had been mapped out from his youth, he realized, and until now it had been lived according to the plans of others. To forsake the pillars of his existence, so meticulously forged, seemed unthinkable. And yet, did *anything* in life truly matter beyond the love of a man for a woman, and the love of a woman for a man?

"Ataahua," he said in a voice muffled by her hair, "please, can we wait to talk about this until my return from Kororareka? You were the one who never wanted to talk, remember?"

"I do remember, but all I want to do now is talk to you. But I will do as you wish. Also know that I would come to America with you, if that is your wish."

"You would?" he said in surprise. "You would come with me to America?"

"Yes, if that is your wish."

"But what of your family, your home, your *iwi*?"

"*You* are my family now, Richard. You are my home, my *iwi*!"

She was choking on her words. Tears ran down her cheeks, and she shivered and clasped him tightly as if she were cold. Never having seen her so vulnerable, his heart filled, and he felt any remaining resistance evaporating like an early summer mist over Hingham Bay. He pressed her close, kissed her cheeks, her lips, her forehead, whispering in her ear, tasting the salt of her tears. "Ataahua . . . Attahua, I love you. How could I possibly leave you!"

She clung to him. "I want my life to be with you, Richard. I want to see the mountains and the snow with you. Only with you."

"*Mau, Ataahua. Te fafau au nei au e. Kei te hoki au ahau ki a koe.*"

She pulled away from him and held him at arm's length. "*Fafau koe?*" she exclaimed in disbelief.

"*Ae, Ataahua, fafau ahau,*" he replied with fierce resolve. "I promise I will come back to you. And when I do, I promise I will take you to see the mountains and the snow. You and I will go there together. These promises I make to you upon my sacred honor!"

Then, with a low groan, he took her eager body in his arms. Later, as they lay naked in the warmth of the late afternoon sun, they talked softly, tenderly, about the promises the future held for them.

CHAPTER 19

THE ROAD FROM THE TASMAN SEA TO THE COLONIAL CAPITAL OF AUCK-land on the opposite coast of North Island was more a track than a road, used mostly by missionaries and Maori taking supplies and information back and forth to the missions and homesteads. It had been widened in places by men wielding machetes and hacking at overgrown bushes, tree limbs, and shrubs, but spring downpours gushing down the hilly terrain had cut narrow gullies across the track. The three women and four Royal Marines riding with them in the two military wagons had a difficult and uncomfortable passage.

They had planned to leave early on Thursday morning, but the torrential rains had kept them at the mission for another three days. During that interval Anne saw little of anyone save for Te Whina and Rachael. On several occasions Daniel MacKenzie had dropped in to drink hot tea and chat with Anne about Auckland and the road she would travel to get there. Just after his arrival, Captain Shilling had come by to formally introduce himself and announce his orders, which were to accompany Anne Braithwaite Cutler to Auckland, and from there to the British naval compound at Sydney.

"Does that mean you will see me to New South Wales?" she had asked.

"It does, my lady," he replied. "Your brother the admiral insists on it. So yes, I shall see you to Sydney. Bad luck for you, I'm afraid," he added with boyish charm. He bowed gallantly and smiled at her as he came upright. Anne found herself returning his smile.

Today, as the two wagons rattled and rumbled eastward under an escort of six marines on horseback and two in each wagon, Anne divided her time between tending to Jamie on her lap and observing a world full of wonders. Despite having been in New Zealand for half a year, she had seen only the well-groomed mission compound. The landscape had a stark beauty, although her sadness at having to say farewell to Daniel and Maude MacKenzie, Jonathan Riggs, and the others at the mission who had served her and her son so well marred her enjoyment. The morning air was chilly, but the sun promised warmth to come. Sure enough, as the morning progressed, the sullen pewter overcast of previous days broke apart and gave way to a brilliant blue sky.

Lulled by the rocking motion of the wagon and the warmth of the sun, she was startled when Jamie awoke and cried, whether for attention or food, Anne was not certain. "Why are you fretting, my little one?" she crooned to him. "Are you hungry? Can you be teething so soon?" She reached into a basket at her feet and withdrew a slice of apple wrapped in muslin. When she brought it to her son's lips, he clutched it with tiny fingers and began sucking greedily. The muslin covering allowed him to draw out the sweet juice but prevented the crisp fibers and seeds of the apple from breaking into bits and possibly choking him.

Captain Shilling cantered past the wagon on his roan just then and touched the rim of his hat to Anne as he rode by, smiling wistfully at the charming sight. She watched him ride on for a moment before shifting her attention to the Royal Marine sitting next to her. On the sleeve of his red uniform coat he wore two gold chevrons. "Excuse me, Corporal," she said to him, "where is the captain off to? He seems in a bit of a hurry."

The corporal glanced ahead. "A routine check, ma'am. Nothing more, I expect. He wants to talk to the scouts he sent ahead. Just making sure of things. Leaving nothing to chance. That's his way, ma'am." His tone held genuine admiration when he spoke of his captain.

"Is he looking for hostiles?"

"Just making sure, ma'am, like I said. I doubt he expects to find signs of hostiles. Ain't many of 'em around these parts. Least not since the Royal Marines arrived here," he said with obvious pride.

"Why is that?"

Before the corporal could answer, the driver shouted a warning, yanking on the reins as the wagon lurched to the left. Both horses reared up as the two left wheels jounced into a large sinkhole filled with water. Anne clutched Jamie as the right side of the wagon rose off the road, its wheels spinning in the air. For several raw moments the wagon teetered on edge.

The two Marines riding in the wagon lunged to the right, their weight helping to bring the wagon back down with a dull thump and splash. There was no longer any danger of the wagon overturning, but the front left wheel was deeply mired in the hole.

The Marines who had been riding in the two wagons jumped out onto the soggy ground. Two of them pulled on the horses' reins and harnesses while the other two put their shoulders to the back of the trapped wagon. Two Marines on horseback dismounted to add their considerable brawn to the task. Pulling and pushing and cursing, they managed inch by inch to move the wheel forward until, with a harsh sucking sound, it rolled free and onto solid ground.

The driver turned his head to look back at his passengers. "Everyone all hale 'n' hearty back there?"

"We're fine," Anne called out, although she was unable to disguise the quaver in her voice.

"Sorry to frighten you and the wee one like that, ma'am. All that water in the hole fooled me into thinkin' it was just a puddle. Fooled me right good, it did."

"I warrant it did," Anne said kindly. "Pray carry on, but please be mindful." She returned her gaze to the corporal, who, now wet and muddy, had climbed back on board the wagon and retaken his seat. A crack of a whip, and they were again under way.

"What is the reason, Mr. . . . . Congleton, isn't it?"

"Yes, ma'am," he said. "Samuel Congleton." He touched the rim of his hat to her. "Now what were you asking me, ma'am?"

"I asked you, what is the reason there are no Maori in the bush out here."

"Oh. Well, beggin' yer pardon, ma'am, that's not quite what I said. There are Maori out there, all right, you can bet yer last shilling on it." He winked and jerked his head at the captain, clearly delighted at his pun. Anne suspected it was an overly used one. "You just can't see 'em, is all."

Anne ignored the humor. "But they are not hostile?"

The corporal shook his head. "Not these ones, ma'am. They're our allies. We treat 'em nice. We trade with 'em, we give 'em muskets and nails and tools and whatnot, and they're our friends."

"You're quite certain of that?"

"As certain as a fellow can be, ma'am. Ask Captain Shilling. He'll tell you."

"I will do that, Corporal. Thank you."

The Marine again touched the rim of his hat. "Happy to oblige, ma'am."

On an impulse, Anne asked one more question. "You're quite fond of the captain, aren't you, Corporal?"

"That I am, ma'am," he replied without hesitation. "I'd give my life to save his, and I'd be proud for the privilege. Every man jack here would do the same if it should ever come to that."

"Admirable," Anne said quietly. "How like Richard."

"Ma'am?"

"Nothing, Corporal. Sorry. I was musing."

As the sun began to dip below the treetops, the entourage pulled up beside a crude complex consisting of a building next to the road and a smaller outbuilding on the edge of the bush. Anne was expecting to see it, even knew the building had two small rooms, because Daniel had told her about it. According to local lore, MacKenzie had explained, shacks had been put there during the Musket Wars, some twenty years earlier, to serve as a trading post of sorts. European gun-sellers displayed their wares inside and either bought them outright or bartered them for the bounty of land and sea the local Waikato tribes brought in to trade.

"Is that how Te Wherowhero became so powerful?" Anne had asked.

"No question," MacKenzie replied. "The percussion cap muskets he acquired there were the newest arms available anywhere, state of the art, as the saying goes, and just what the chief needed to build a powerful kingdom in central North Island. He declared himself king of that little realm. To him and his subjects, he was on a par with Queen Victoria.

He even wrote her a letter and addressed it 'From the king of one island realm to the queen of another.'"

Anne had chuckled at that. Imagine a native king considering himself equal to an empress! But she added, "If he is as strong as everyone seems to think he is, I am relieved to know he is on our side."

"You are not alone in that, my dear!" MacKenzie had replied.

Although the colonial capital lay only ten miles ahead, Captain Shilling ordered a halt at the compound. He dismounted near the wagon where Anne still sat and announced that they would stay the night here and continue to their destination tomorrow. The wind was picking up, he informed her, and menacing gray clouds were advancing from the east, blocking out any light from stars and moon.

He assigned the women and baby Jamie to one of the rooms and ordered the Marines to build a fire in the grate and bring in whatever makeshift bedding they could gather from the wagons. "My apologies for these less-than-luxurious accommodations, my lady," he said to Anne as the room was being prepared. "I'm afraid it's the best we can offer. If it rains, and if the roof does not leak, at least you will be dry during the night."

These were the first words he had spoken to her that day, though their eyes had met on numerous occasions as he rode back and forth along the route. Anne had felt a growing attraction with every glance. The handsome captain reminded her so much of Richard in his bearing and his easy relationship with command.

"Thank you, Captain," Anne replied. "I do hope that you and whomever else you select will take advantage of the other room. This is hardly the time to stand on ceremony or be hostage to social conventions."

"That is most gracious of you, my lady," Shilling said, "but my men and I will stand guard outside. We will take no chances until we have you safely ensconced in Government House. That will be by midday tomorrow, I assure you."

"May I bet my last shilling on that promise?"

He grinned. "Oh dear. You have heard that one already, have you?"

"On several occasions."

"So much for decorum. It amuses the men, and I have no real objection." He turned to go and then turned back. "Someone will be along with supper for you soon. It will be simple fare, I fear, but adequate." He bowed. "Good night, my lady. I wish you a pleasant night's sleep."

"Good night, Captain," Anne said, adding in a more serious tone, "I am very much indebted to you."

"Nonsense, my lady," Shilling returned. "I am the one indebted—to your brother, for honoring me with such a pleasant duty, and to you for allowing me to fulfill it."

"Well put, sir."

After he left, Anne wrinkled her nose at the dank, musty smell of the room the Marines had prepared for her, hoping the fire would dry it out enough to keep Jamie from catching cold. Taking her son from Rachael, she settled down to breastfeed him and to chat softly with her two attendants. At length, with little Jamie contentedly asleep beside her, she too managed to drift off.

Mere moments later, it seemed, she was awakened by a gentle yet persistent shaking of her shoulder. "Please wake up, ma'am. You must wake up! Please!"

Anne opened her eyes. "What time is it, Rachael?" she inquired, yawning. "Surely it is not dawn yet."

"No, my lady, it is not. It is the middle of the night."

"Then why . . . ?"

"Captain Shilling insists that we leave now. Right away!"

Anne raised her arms and stretched her still aching back. "He insists, does he? Why, pray tell?"

"I am sure he will explain, ma'am. Quickly now, we must go!"

"Where is Jamie?" she asked anxiously.

"Te Whina has already taken him to the wagon. Come now, please!"

"I'm coming!" Anne scrambled to her feet and followed Rachael out the door. Having never undressed, she had only to slip on her shoes. The menacing clouds were gone, and stars and moon cast weak yellow light upon the landscape.

"What is it, Captain Shilling?" she demanded to know when she spotted him waiting impatiently by a wagon. "Why all the to-do?"

"There is no time to explain in detail. A Maori war party is approaching from the west." He pointed down the road whence they had come. "Trust me, please. We need to leave *now!*"

"From the west? That's the direction of the mission. Have they attacked the mission?" Her voice was edging on panic.

"I do not know, my lady, and I am in no position to find out. Into the wagon now, please. We must go!"

She took a step back. "My friends are there! We cannot abandon them!"

"We can, and we will. Think of your child if nothing else!" He took her hand and, ignoring her protests, helped her up into the wagon to sit beside Te Whina. He wheeled the roan and galloped ahead, waving to the driver to follow. The wagon lurched forward.

Chapter 20

THE WAGONS HAD GONE ONLY A SHORT DISTANCE WHEN THE HARSH clopping of hooves approached them from behind. Shilling raised his hand to signal a halt and turned in his saddle as his sergeant of Marines burst into view, riding at a hard gallop. The sergeant's white-brimmed hat shone in the dim moonlight.

"What is it, Sergeant Wiggins?" he asked the heavy-set Marine when he pulled even and reined in his horse. The horse reared up in protest at the sudden stop.

The sergeant saluted smartly. "It's the natives, sir! They're coming fast."

"How far away are they?"

"A mile, sir, give or take."

Shilling did a quick calculation of time, distance, and speed. They had a good ten miles to go before reaching Government House in the city center, nine miles before they were within the strong defensive perimeter the army had established around the outskirts of the city. At their current rate of speed, barring a miracle, they would not make it. And Shilling put no stock in miracles. Although he could do nothing about either time or distance, he could influence their rate of speed. But speeding up on this wretched stretch of road ran the risk of a wagon wheel again falling into an unseen rut or sinkhole. If that happened, all four unmounted Marines and the three women would have to ride in the remaining wagon, a less than satisfying prospect where speed was paramount. No, there was but one option open to them.

"Marines, dismount!" he ordered the five Marines a-horse. "You four, out!" he ordered the four Marines riding in the two wagons.

His gaze swung to the nearest wagon. "Anne," he said urgently, "did you bring a sling for the baby with you?"

"Yes, I think Te Whina has it. She made me one some time ago. It is a marvelous way to carry a—"

"Good," he interrupted. "Get it and put it on. Put your baby in it. You will ride with me." He shot a glance at the other two women. "Can you women ride?"

Rachael nodded. So, to Anne's surprise, did Te Whina.

"Right. You will each ride one of those horses." He pointed at the five riderless horses. "Pick one. Quickly, now! Mr. Smithwick! Mr. Johnson!" he barked at the two wagon drivers. "Unharness your teams. Stay with them. Don't let them run off! Turn each of the wagons on its side and barricade the road!" He turned his attention to his sergeant of Marines. "Wiggins, I need you to come with me. Pick two Marines to join us and have them mount up. Handsomely now! We've very little time!"

As people scurried to comply with his orders, Shilling faced the seven Marines being left behind. "Corporal Congleton is in charge now, gentlemen. When the natives appear, give them a full round. One full round! Then toss your weapons, get on the unharnessed horses, and get out of here! Ride bareback or double up if necessary, but get out of here!"

"Understood, sir!" Corporal Congleton answered. He saluted Shilling and gave Anne an encouraging smile before he turned away, well aware of his danger if she was not.

"Here, Anne, let me help you up!" Shilling urged her. Anne took the sling that Te Whina had hurriedly produced from the baggage, put it around her neck and over her shoulder, then reached up to take the captain's hand. She put her foot in the stirrup and let him pull her up behind him. Te Whina handed up Jamie, and Anne carefully slipped him inside the thick cotton pouch. She slid the pouch around behind her and made sure it was secure, then wrapped both arms around Shilling's waist.

"Are you secure?" he tossed over his shoulder.

"Yes," she assured him, tightening her arms.

"Jamie?"

"Also secure. If he wakes, he'll think he's in some grand adventure."

"He is, by God!" Shilling cried out. "Right, then. Everyone ready?"

Before anyone could answer, a scattering of musket fire erupted down the track. Shilling listened intently to the distant shouts of those caught unaware and those catching them unaware. He could not detect a word spoken in English.

"Sounds like our Waikato friends are coming to our rescue, Captain!" Sergeant Wiggins cheered.

"Could be," Shilling agreed. "I hope so." He consulted the gold Rotherhams watch he kept in a side pocket of his uniform coat. "It's just on three o'clock, Corporal," he said to Congleton as he tucked it back in the pocket. "Give us a twenty-minute head start if you can. Then mount up and follow us. If you see a way to lend support to the Waikato during that time, do so. But under no circumstances are you to take unnecessary risks. I want to see every one of you and every horse back at the base tomorrow."

"Aye, aye, Captain! And good luck, sir. And to you, Lady Anne."

Anne lifted an arm briefly in salute as the riders set off, then slipped it back around the captain's waist. Shilling picked his way carefully along the rutted, potholed road, frustrated by the need to go slowly. It occurred to him that soldiers on foot who knew the road—especially Maori warriors, who, in his estimation, possessed an uncanny stamina—could easily outstrip a wagon and even a horse. Who these particular Maori were, and why they were pursuing them, he did not know. Nor did he care. His orders were to deliver Anne Braithwaite Cutler safely to Government House in Auckland, and by God he intended to do just that!

Again he consulted his watch: 3:10. Even going at this slow pace, Private Cunningham's mount had stumbled into a hole, crippling the beast and rendering it useless. With hardly a pause Cunningham took the revolver offered by Shilling and administered the *coup de grace* into the head of the stricken animal. He returned the pistol, then doubled up behind Private Walsh.

Shilling's recollection of the outbound journey indicated the road would soon improve and they would be able to increase their speed.

But not soon enough. The battle raging behind them was now almost upon them. Their Maori pursuers, sensing the weariness of their prey, were making herculean efforts to catch them, pushed on by savage cries that chilled the blood.

"John . . ." Anne quavered into his ear.

"Don't look back, Anne. Don't look back!" He squeezed the roan's flanks with his knees and flicked the reins. With a sudden burst of power, the roan broke into a fast walk and then into a comfortable lope. The four horses carrying Rachael, Te Whina, Wiggins, and the two Marine privates followed suit. Shilling held his breath, expecting at any moment to hear a whinny of anguish as a horse went down or a cry of pain as someone took a bullet in the back. But the seconds crept by without incident, and the ground beneath them became firmer and drier. The horses accelerated from a lope into a gallop, and onward to safety.

John Shilling returned the salute of the barrel-chested British army sergeant posted at the gigantic U-shaped barricade of dirt, logs, and rocks that barred entry into Auckland Town. The barricade was sufficiently high to provide minimum cover for soldiers in the event of a frontal assault, but sufficiently low to allow maximum firepower and maneuverability for the cannon positioned along its entire length. These juggernauts, placed fifty yards apart from the northern anchor of the U at the army barracks to the southern anchor beyond the shipyard at Merchants Bay, were the mainstay of Auckland's defenses. Most of them were capable of hurling a 32-or 64-pound iron ball into attackers advancing across the open farmland that supplied food for the city. Were the enemy to broach the barricade, Auckland's defense would rely on the large contingent of army regulars garrisoned inside the perimeter. Seaward of the city, four ships of the Royal Navy stood ready to blast the enemy with broadsides—or, in a dire emergency, to evacuate the city.

"Blessings of the morning to ye, Captain!" the sergeant said genially. "And welcome back. It seems your mission was a grand success." He sketched a bow at Anne, who returned the gesture with a blank stare. The sergeant cleared his throat. "How may I be of service to you, Captain?"

"You may be of service by letting us through," Shilling said curtly.

"Right away, sir. As I was just about to do. My apologies, sir." He motioned to two soldiers stationed at the gate, which now swung open, allowing the party of seven individuals on five horses to file past.

"There may be others behind us," Shilling informed Crowell in passing. "They may be in trouble, so make ready a rescue party. Send word to Colonel Crenshaw to that effect. Tell him I will be with him as soon as possible. Under no circumstances should he wait for me before dispatching the rescue. Is that clear?"

"I understand, sir," the sergeant replied soberly. "We'll keep a sharp eye out for them, have no worries, and we'll send out a rescue party pronto if we don't see them ridin' down that road in a few minutes."

"Thank you, Sergeant." The two men exchanged salutes.

Shilling's roan led the way along a well-managed dirt road. Anne kept her arms tightly around his waist but felt safe enough to take in her surroundings. Jamie had yet to stir from a sound sleep. Small groves of cabbage trees dotted an open landscape gently rolling downhill toward the harbor, a significant stretch of water. The harbor in turn was a small adjunct of the much larger harbor of Auckland, which opened into the vast Pacific Ocean. As the road descended toward the harbor and into the city proper, the open landscape gave way to homes, shops, and white steeples of various denominations. It looked very much like a small English town.

Shilling's gaze swept the waterfront ahead. Yes, there she was, his temporary command, HMS *Hazard*, an 18-gun *Favourite*-class ship-rigged sloop. He slowed his roan to a walk, then came to a full stop.

"Is that your ship?" Anne asked, finally loosening her tight grip. She was amused to feel him take a deep breath. Apparently, her grip had been a bit too tight.

"How did you know?"

Anne laughed. "You forget, Captain. I have been keeping company with naval commanders most of my life. A captain catching sight of his command from a distance goes still, as you just did. But tell me," Anne went on, "isn't it unusual for an officer of your rank to command a sloop of war? I should have thought that you would command a first or second rate, and not a, what, fifth rate? I don't mean to be rude. I'm just curious."

"Well, you have certainly put me in my place, my lady," Shilling retorted good-naturedly. "But you are quite correct. A post captain would normally be given command of a larger ship, but there are no such ships in these waters, and precious few naval ships of any kind. Soon after I arrived in Auckland, I was offered temporary command of *Hazard* when Captain Bell, her former commander, drowned in an unfortunate mishap. I suspect the governor saw more value in me as a naval officer than a military adviser," he said ruefully. "So he gave me a ship when one came available. Her executive officer will assume command when we leave Auckland—you will recall that I was sent here to fetch you and return you to your family."

"We'll go in *Hazard*?"

"I suspect so." He nudged his horse onward, and for several minutes Anne did not speak. "Are you quite all right, my lady?" he said over his shoulder.

"Yes," she replied. "Though I confess that I am fatigued, and Jamie will certainly need his breakfast soon. I'm astonished he managed to sleep through all this. Have we much farther to go?"

"Not far at all. See that building down there? The one between the two roads?" He pointed ahead at a single-story white wooden building that stood near the base of a large, triangular compound formed by three buildings. "That is Government House, our destination." He tried to sound cheerful, but his tone conveyed little enthusiasm. Nor were his words received with enthusiasm.

"You will have aid sent to those we left behind, won't you, John? Right away?" Anne said moments later, her voice taut with worry.

"Of course," Shilling answered. "You heard what I said to the sergeant. Those are my men out there. I will see to their rescue as soon as I see you to Government House."

"And the mission? Will you send help for those left behind at the mission?"

"Yes!" he said impatiently. "My men are stationed there as well, remember?"

"I'm sorry, John," Anne said. "I don't mean to doubt you. You have been so kind. It's just that . . ."

Shilling shook his head. "I know. Please forgive my outburst. If *my* nerves are frayed, I can't imagine the state of yours. Now that we are out of immediate danger, we can turn our thoughts to the others."

After another half-mile they arrived at the apex of the triangle. From there, Princess Street ran off on a slight diagonal to the left and Queen Street to the right. Shilling called a halt and addressed the two Marines doubled up on a chestnut mare. "Privates Walsh and Cunningham, you are to proceed to Barracks Point and report there. Please inform Colonel Crenshaw that I wish to add to my report. The matter is most urgent. I will be with him shortly."

"Aye, aye, sir," the two Marines responded.

"And then get some food and rest," Shilling shouted after them. He turned next to Te Whina and Rachael.

"Rachael, you will accompany us to Government House. Te Whina, over there"—he pointed to his right at what looked like a miniature *pa* perched high up on a hill—"is a *marae* of the Ngati Whatua tribe. I assume you will want to lodge there."

Te Whina nodded. "*Ae*, Captain Shilling."

"Very well. See to that immediately. Tomorrow, please attend Mrs. Cutler at her lodgings."

Te Whina inclined her head in assent. "I will do so, Captain Shilling."

"*Tena koe, Te Whina*," Anne called after her. "*Kia pai te mihi.* Please join me and little Jamie when you can." Anne knew that Te Whina must be at least as exhausted as she was, yet she sat easily and confidently on her horse. She was, after all, on land originally owned by her people. Daniel MacKenzie had once explained to Anne that the capital was built on land owned by the Ngati Whatua and given to the British colonial government to build a city for their mutual protection and benefit. The British had their own small communities within the city limits, their locations based on the degree of wealth or influence the inhabitants wielded. The Maori population lived, by tradition, on the highest ground.

Shilling followed Anne's gaze. "You speak Maori? Who taught you?"

"Te Whina did," Anne laughed. "She is a good teacher and also a skilled nurse."

As Te Whina disappeared between parallel rows of *harakeke* and *toi toi* bushes, Shilling and Anne continued down Queen Street, Rachael following behind. Although the morning was still young, the citizens of Auckland were emerging from the simple dwellings that lined both sides of the street—going to work at the shipyard, on the quays along Commercial Bay, in the haberdasheries and other shops along the water-front, or in the homes of the rich and powerful near Official Bay. Few of them paid much attention to the dusty British naval officer and the two bedraggled women accompanying him. Their appearance notwithstanding, these three individuals clearly belonged to a higher social stratum than any of them, and therefore played no role in their mundane lives.

At the intersection with Shortland Street at the base of the triangle, Shilling nudged his horse to the left, and left again when they reached the entrance to Government House. Two army privates posted at the entranceway offered a sharp salute to Shilling. As they entered the outer complex of the building, several people emerged from inside to offer assistance.

Anne carefully removed the sling that had kept Jamie safe all this time, taking a deep breath as the weight lifted off her back and she was finally able to straighten up. She handed him down to a kindly looking matron who handed him back to Anne after another Maori woman had helped her off the roan. An officious-looking civilian appeared at the top of the stairs leading from the veranda and began to descend with mincing steps. He gave a brief and, it seemed to Anne, dismissive wave to Shilling, as though seeing him alive and well after the perilous mission was unworthy of note.

The man approached Anne and bowed formally. "I am Charles Scott, my lady, the major domo, if you will, of this humble establishment. On behalf of Governor and Mrs. Fitzroy, and their entire staff, and on behalf of the citizens of Auckland, I bid you welcome. If there is anything—anything at all—that you desire during your stay, you need only send for me. For the present, the governor and his lady wife invite you to make yourself at home here in Government House in accommodations that have been prepared for you. Today, please rest and see to yourself and your son. Tomorrow, if it pleases you, they request the honor of your company at evening tea."

"Thank you, Mr. Scott," Anne returned, feeling the last of her strength ebb away. When her legs buckled beneath her, Shilling gripped her elbow with one hand and held it firmly, supporting Jamie's weight with the other, until she had restored her balance. "I'm afraid I am indeed in need of rest and sustenance. May I request a hot bath and a change of clothing? And for my son as well, if clothes are available for him."

"Yes, of course, my lady! The governor and Mrs. Fitzroy have four children, including a little boy about the age and size of your son. I am certain they will be happy to lend you everything you need. I will see to your requests immediately."

"That is most kind. And please inform my hosts that I gratefully accept their invitation for evening tea tomorrow. And please ask them, for me, to include Captain Shilling in their invitation."

"Captain Shilling, my lady?" Scott sniffed prissily.

"Yes. I think it quite appropriate. Were it not for Captain Shilling's gallantry and bravery, I daresay I would be in no position to accept *any* invitation from anyone."

CHAPTER 21

RICHARD'S PATIENCE WAS WEARING THIN. HE SAW NO JUSTIFICATION for the wait. He and his men and their two Ngapuhi escorts had arrived in Paihia two days ago. Surely the major had read the reports he had handed to the man's orderly. He must also have heard from local authorities that the matter was most pressing. Yet Richard had been waiting nearly an hour in this small, bare antechamber for admittance into the inner sanctuary, and the day was now drawing to a close. He picked a piece of lint off the new pair of buff trousers he had been issued upon his arrival in Paihia and flicked it onto the rough wooden floor. Heaving a sigh, he stood up and began pacing about like a lion in a cage. His frustration mounting, he walked to the window facing east toward Russell and gazed out across the mile-wide harbor to the peaceful-looking port town. From this distance it seemed undeserving of its widely held reputation as the hellhole of the Pacific.

Two evenings earlier, while dining at the home of his new acquaintance Henry Williams, he had learned much about this hot spot of debauchery, known for lawlessness, escaped convicts, and drunken sailors and whalers. Taverns and fleshpots sat cheek by jowl on every corner, one business happily fueling the revenues of its neighbors.

Williams had a great deal of information to offer on other local subjects as well. And he seemed a reliable source. Richard discovered that Williams was a veteran of the Napoleonic Wars who had come to Paihia two decades ago as the leader of the Church Missionary Society, a subset of the broader Anglican Communion. When informed of the American sailors' arrival in Paihia, he had used his considerable influence to arrange comfortable lodgings for them. Richard Cutler was invited to his home for tea that very evening and offered accommodations for the duration of his stay in Paihia.

More important for Richard, each member of *Suwannee*'s crew was issued soap and water, clean linens, a tot or two of rum, a fresh change of clothing, and enough food to satisfy any appetite. For the first time since they had dragged themselves ashore in this alien land, they were in surroundings they recognized and where they felt at home. Most, though not all, immediately set about putting the past behind them and getting on with their lives.

"What a tale you have to tell, Captain Cutler," the square-jawed, white-haired missionary had said after Richard shared the high points of his saga during supper that first evening. "What a tale indeed. I am most sorry for the loss of your wife," he added sympathetically, "although I know she is in a better place than this world can offer. I take great comfort, however, in seeing you sitting here at my table, having emerged from the bush in such good health. As for the future, it rests entirely in God's hands."

"It does," Richard readily agreed, although with a heavy heart.

Williams's smile carved deep wrinkles in his tanned skin. "It is not often we see an American naval officer in these parts, or an American official of any sort save for whaling captains. And how fortunate it is that you managed to safeguard your papers during all the events you have described. The authorities here might otherwise not have believed your story. And who could blame them? Such an adventure!"

As Richard concentrated on his plate of fresh fish, kumara, and greens picked from Williams's own garden, Williams in turn studied him. He saw a youthful-looking man who clearly had suffered greatly and yet had shown impressive maturity and strength of purpose in bringing his men to safety. He picked up the crystal carafe containing a delicate Bordeaux that was the crown jewel of the meal. Richard politely held his hand over the top of his wineglass. "No more for me, thank you, Mr. Williams, although this is truly an excellent wine."

"Come, my good man," Williams admonished. "You must be at your ease now. You're among friends here."

"The wine is excellent," Richard repeated, "but this is the first alcohol of any sort I have had in nearly nine months, and it has affected me more quickly than perhaps it should have." His words were slightly slurred.

Williams chuckled. "We have more to discuss, I think, and this will make your words flow more easily. Do allow me." Williams held up the wine bottle again. Richard paused, then shrugged his shoulders and with a crooked grin removed his hand.

"What are your intentions now, Captain Cutler?" As he posed the question, Williams removed his spectacles and meticulously cleaned the lenses with a handkerchief. Richard smiled inwardly. It was Williams himself, at the start of the meal, who had mentioned Richard that the local Ngapuhi chief and his wife referred to him as *e wha hga kanohi*—four eyes. No disrespect was intended, Williams was quick to emphasize. The term was used with affection by the couple who had donated the land on which the mission and the village of Paihia were built.

"My intentions, Mr. Williams?"

"Yes. Where do you intend to go from here?"

Richard took a sip of wine and slowly replaced the glass on the table. "My first objective is to find a ship's captain willing to take my crew home to America. My executive officer is scouring the Russell waterfront as we speak."

"And enjoying himself in the process, no doubt," Williams remarked dryly. "It should not be difficult to find a ship," he added. "American whalers frequent these shores in considerable numbers, and as you might suspect, given the . . . pleasures these shores have to offer, the captains are often in need of experienced hands to replace those who jump ship. I would not be surprised if there are several such ships riding at anchor out in the bay, making ready to sail."

With his knife he slid the last morsel of snapper onto his fork and brought the succulent white flesh to his mouth. He dabbed at his lips with a linen napkin before reaching for the stem of his wineglass. "And you, Captain? You will sail with your men, I presume."

"I think not," Richard hedged, "although I may follow them later in another ship." He waved off a pesky fly buzzing around his head.

The missionary's jaw dropped. "Later? And in another ship? In heaven's name, *why*? After all you have been through, I should think you would be eager to go home!"

"I have unfinished business here."

"Here? In Paihia?"

"No. Out there." He pointed westward. "I am returning to Chief Nene's *pa*."

"Alone?"

"I would prefer to go alone. My executive officer insists on accompanying me despite my efforts to dissuade him. There are rumblings that others of my crew want to come as well."

Williams slowly put his glass on the table. "My dear sir, I mean no disrespect, but have you taken complete leave of your senses?"

"No, Mr. Williams. I have not taken leave of my senses, although as soon as possible after I confer with Major Blackwell tomorrow, I will be taking leave of your gracious hospitality. And I expect to be leading a troop of British soldiers carrying enough muskets and powder and shot to keep Chief Nene, your loyal ally, in good standing for a long time."

"Well, I never," Williams laughed, shaking his head in disbelief. The evening ended soon afterward on a note of forced good cheer.

The next morning, following a deep, alcohol-induced sleep in the unbelievable luxury of fresh sheets and feather pillows, Richard slowly made his way downstairs to the kitchen. A pleasant-looking young Maori woman pointed to a pot of coffee hanging above the fire. Apparently she had heard him stirring upstairs, because she was in the process of heaping a plate with eggs, pork strips, and freshly baked bread for him.

"*Kia mihi*," he said to the woman as she placed the plate before him at the kitchen table. Abigail, his cook and housekeeper at his home in Alexandria, would have done exactly the same for him. For an instant he was back home in Abigail's kitchen and the past fifteen months had never happened. He and Anne had never left Washington. There had been no shipwreck. Anne was upstairs in bed waiting for her breakfast to be brought up to her. The instant passed, and it came to him with a sickening blow that Christmas was nearly upon them. Just a year ago he and Anne had celebrated the day together in the intimacy of *Suwannee*'s after cabin. "Anne," he murmured woefully. "Anne."

"*Kaore koe e pai ana?*" the Maori woman said with concern. She pointed at the largely uneaten food on his plate. "You no like?"

The familiar lilt of a Maori woman's voice snapped him back. "*Ae*, I do like it. *Tino pai.*" He patted his stomach.

The woman returned his smile. "You speak Maori?"

"A little," he acknowledged before elaborating. "*He iti aku korero o te Maori.*"

Her smile broadened. "You speak good. You have good teacher."

His smile faded. "The best," he said, and turned his full attention to his breakfast. "Where is Mr. Williams?" he asked when he had finished and she was clearing the table.

"He visit Mr. Busby. You meet him soon, I think."

Richard was introduced to James Busby at his home later that day. A Scotsman, Busby had served as an ad hoc ambassador of the British government to help Governor Hobson forge the treaty that on February 6, 1840, was signed by thirty-four northern chiefs and by representatives of the Crown. Busby and his family lived in a comfortable home several miles away from Williams's house. The two houses were similar in design and in their English furnishings, except that Busby's home featured but one story. It also had an outbuilding for cooking, a safety feature that few homeowners seemed to have adopted. Of greater significance, it was built adjacent to the grassy plot where the treaty had been signed amid a great panoply of dress uniforms, ceremonial cloaks, flags, and tents.

"It is there that the troubles began," Busby said as he carefully replaced his bone china teacup on its matching saucer. Despite the warmth of the day, he was clad in dark brown trousers and suit coat with a lighter brown waistcoat. A neck stock all but concealed the white linen shirt beneath. Richard was far more casually dressed in the trousers and open-neck shirt he had been issued the day before, along with funds to see the Americans through.

They were sitting in the front parlor of Busby's home, a small mahogany table set between them to accommodate the dainty cakes and breads that accompanied the tea prepared by the ambassador's wife and served by his eldest daughter. All the windows and doors had been opened to welcome in the early summer breezes wafting across the Bay of Islands. Through the billowing curtains Richard could see the white buildings of the port of Russell across the bay. Atop the highest of the hills that served as the port's backdrop, Richard could make out a flagstaff flying the Union Jack. This flagstaff, Busby told Richard, was the fourth that had held that flag. Hone Heke had chopped down the others on three different occasions.

"Why?" Richard asked, struggling to maintain his concentration while thoughts of the tasks that lay ahead drifted through his mind. As a de facto representative of the U.S. government, it was incumbent upon him to give the ambassador his full attention, to absorb what information he could, and to pass on as much of it as he was able when the opportunity arose. Above all, he now had an intensely personal reason for trying to understand New Zealand.

"Until then, you see," replied the balding little man, his stern expression giving way to a charming smile, "the British and the Maori were getting along quite well. There were conflicts, of course, but most of those involved intertribal issues of little concern to us. Generally, we left the Maori to resolve their own arguments. We were their friends and allies, and we offered protection to those who sought it and prestige to Maori chiefs who accepted it. Indeed, the status of many chiefs and tribes was measured by the strength of their ties to the colonial government. Their prosperity depended on it, not to mention their *mana*."

"Is that not still true?"

Busby pursed his lips. "To some extent, yes. Witness the status of Chief Nene, with whom you seem to have forged quite a close bond—a most exceptional thing, I might add. No one needs to tell you that Chief Nene is a strong ally of Great Britain. But as you have witnessed, such loyalty to the Crown can come at a price. The good news for us, thus far at least, is that it is a price Nene and chiefs like him seem prepared to pay."

"Is it jealousy that drives chiefs like Heke to wage war against their own people, even their own tribe? Fear of losing prestige and influence?"

"Nowadays, perhaps. But as I expect you are aware, the Maori were waging war against each other centuries before Europeans stepped foot on this island."

"Yes, I am aware of that," Richard agreed, now fully engaged in the discussion. "Chief Nene made quite a point of it. What is it, then? Was not the Treaty of Waitangi designed to resolve differences between the British and the Maori and to formalize your relationship? And by so doing, to transform New Zealand into one big happy family? I don't mean to sound flippant, but that is essentially what Chief Nene told me. He and . . . others of his *iwi*."

Busby eyed Richard. "Do you think Chief Nene truly believes that? The part about one big happy family?"

Richard shrugged. "Whether he believes it or not is hardly the point. It's what he devoutly wants. He's sick of war, and he's sick of watching his people get slaughtered. He's sick of watching his *enemies* get slaughtered, for that matter."

"I pray you are right," Busby countered. "I pray all the chiefs come to view the treaty that way. The jury is still out on that, however. The treaty is still being signed, in fact. Copies of the Maori version are being carried to every part of the colony to secure the signature of every chief—or his mark, as is more often the case. There continue to be a few holdouts," he continued, "but we are making progress. Mind you, the issues involved are quite complex. One could write a book about them, and I imagine someone will, someday. For the moment, you need to understand that there are two versions of the treaty. There is the British version and there is the Maori version. Therein lies the rub, however unintentional that rub might be."

"Two versions? You mean the original treaty and the one translated from English into Maori, I expect. But don't both versions say the same thing?"

Busby held up an index finger. "Aha! That, dear sir, remains a matter of conjecture. Certainly the British had honorable intentions. The challenge of translating from English into Maori was taken on by your newfound friend Henry Williams, a man honorable to his core. Neither he nor anyone else in the colonial government set out to dupe the Maori.

Unfortunately, that is the way it seems to have turned out." Busby held up a hand to forestall a question. "If you please, Captain, I am almost finished. Then you may ask any question you like.

"The problem comes, you see, not from the actual wording of the document but from how those words are interpreted—that, and the nuances of the English language. The Maori are a proud lot who, like most indigenous peoples, prefer the spoken word to the written word. Some chiefs are very well educated—again, as you have seen for yourself—although most of them have little or no experience in reading or writing, certainly not in matters of the law. So it should come as no surprise that a Maori chief might not fully appreciate the difference between 'cede sovereignty' and 'grant sovereignty.' That is but one example of many, but it's a critical one. A Maori chief is not likely to listen to the counsel or opinions of another chief, whether he is an ally or not, and certainly not those of any *pakeha*."

Richard thought for a moment. "So, what I think you are saying is that a Maori chief would rather be wrong relying on his own counsel than be right relying on the advice of someone not of his tribe."

"Quite so. At least that is true of most of them. All this is compounded, of course, by the language barrier."

Although Richard's tea had grown cold, he took a sip anyway. "I'm stuck on two points, Mr. Busby."

"Just two? Congratulations. Fire away!"

"Why did the Maori want the treaty at all? Seems to me that they had things pretty much their own way before the treaty was signed. And how do they interpret what is in the treaty?"

Busby chuckled. "I sympathize with your confusion, Captain Cutler. It's all rather a mishmash, I'm afraid. As background, bear in mind that ten years ago, a year after I arrived in Paihia, thirty-four chiefs signed the Treaty of Whakaputanga. Outside this very room, mind you."

"I won't even try to repeat that word," Richard laughed. "Was that treaty a prelude to Waitangi?"

"In a sense, yes. It was a declaration of independence, one that in essence recognized New Zealand as a sovereign Maori nation."

"And this treaty. Was it accepted as legitimate elsewhere?"

"It was. All of the European monarchs agreed, including Queen Victoria."

"So . . ."

"So, when the British and Maori began negotiations for what was to become the Treaty of Waitangi five years later, the Maori believed they were negotiating as a sovereign nation. Alas, that proved not to be the case."

"As I said, I've heard some of this before, and no matter how many times I hear it, I fear I will still be confused."

"I understand. But to get back to your question, the Maori wanted the Treaty of Waitangi because they wanted British forces and British law to clean up that ungodly mess over there." He pointed in the direction of Russell. "And they wanted protection for their land and culture from interlopers, including British interlopers, otherwise known as land-grabbers. They trusted the British government to act in their best interests, in part because the treaty confers British citizenship on the Maori people. It is not unlike the tactics the Romans employed after subjugating a foreign people. *Civis romanus sum* may have sounded good in the beginning, but in the end, Roman citizenship bestowed precious little on the conquered people. When all was said and done, they remained the conquered people."

Richard shook his head, recalling the lessons he had learned as a schoolboy reading Julius Caesar's *Gallic Wars* and other Latin texts. He had struggled with the language, but some of the lessons stuck. "And the British? What is their position on the treaty?"

"The British government believes the treaty transfers sovereignty of North Island to the Crown in return for British protection, British trade, and, how shall I best say it, British *civilization*. And because of Captain Cook's wanderings around South Island those many years ago, the Crown claims sovereignty over that land as well. So today, as a result of Waitangi and HMS *Endeavor*, what we call New Zealand and the Maori call Aotearoa is indeed one big family. Whether or not it is to become one big *happy* family under British rule remains to be seen.

"Meanwhile, I am ashamed to report that British settlers are seizing lands from the Maori, either by paying a nominal sum for those lands or by taking them outright, pointing to the treaty as justification for their illegal acts. As you can imagine, the Maori feel betrayed—not so much by British settlers, despite their land-grabbing, as by the British government, which for reasons I cannot fathom refuses to do the right thing."

"God Almighty! What a mess."

"Yes, I believe He would agree it's a horrible mess, one that I am ashamed to say I had a hand in creating, although with an unwitting hand. And what we have seen in recent weeks and months is, I fear, but a prelude to what is coming. Our agreement started out as honorable and above board, but that is not how events have unfolded. Once the land was in hand, so to speak, greed, corruption, and self-interest took over, as they generally do in the course of human events. It's a tragedy, and there seems to be little to be done about it."

"What will come of all this, do you think?" Richard asked.

"Why, the answer is obvious, my good man. What will come of all this is war."

The knowledge gained on the previous two days weighed heavily on Richard's mind as he continued staring out the window of the major's antechamber. And there was more. At about mid morning he had met with Jack Brengle at the home of Henry Williams. Brengle had been rowed over from Russell to the beach in front of Williams's home to give his report. Richard was struck by the grin on his executive officer's face as he jumped from the bow of the wherry and strode up to the veranda where Richard was waiting to greet him.

"I have good news to report, Richard," Brengle had said as he was mounting the steps.

"I figured you did. That silly grin gave you away. I wasn't sure, though, whether you were smiling because you found a ship or because you passed a memorable night in one or two of those 'establishments' over there. Is it really as bad as they say?"

"Worse. Or better, depending on your preferences. If you like rum, fistfights, and whoring, Russell is the place for you. But never mind about that. I did not come to enlighten you on the sins and cesspools of Russell."

"What, then? You have found a ship?"

"I have indeed found us a ship. She's the *Sarah D*, out of Nantucket. Her master, a fellow named Josiah Redding, is willing to take on what's left of our crew in return for honest labor. As luck would have it for us, many of his crew have deserted, apparently to purchase more of what Russell has to sell. Redding claims he has neither the time nor the will to find them and bring them back. He had a look at the men this morning. He's impressed with Howe's experience in another Nantucket whaler, and with Payton, Sturgis, and Purslow. The others he thinks he can 'make do,' as he put it. I am less confident about Spaulding. Redding doesn't need a purser, unfortunately, and Henry Spaulding is no seaman."

"We may have to pay for Henry's passage, then."

"Possibly. So we're set. It took the price of one mug of ale to seal the deal."

Richard laughed. "I'll make certain the United States Treasury reimburses you for that ale, Jack. When does *Sarah D* weigh?"

"On Saturday. In four days."

"Well done, my friend. Well done. Have you told the men?"

"I have. They're elated and quite relieved."

"I imagine they are. And Jonty? Has he seen reason?"

Brengle's smile faded, and he shook his head. "He still insists on coming with us."

"*Us*, Jack?"

"Yes, Richard, *us*. If you go, I go. We have already discussed this, and it's settled," he said firmly. "As for Jonty, I suggest you have a word with him after you meet with all the men. They need to see you before they go. They need your blessing. You've become like a father to them over these past months."

"Of course. We will do that together later today after I meet with the major, or tomorrow morning at the latest. I will talk to Jonty alone afterward and make him see things my way. I must admit, I will miss the lad. I will miss them all. I've grown quite fond of them."

Brengle nodded. "You are still determined to return to the *pa*, then?" he prodded, and was surprised when Richard did not answer right away.

Richard was staring out across the bay, as if the answer could be found there. When he spoke, it was in a distant tone. "This may seem strange to you, Jack," he finally said, "but I hear voices calling to me. At night in dreams, of course, but sometimes during the day when I am fully awake. Am I going mad, do you think?"

"How can I say? Whose voices do you hear?"

"Yours. My mother's. Lang Weeks's. Jonty's. But most of all I hear Anne and Ataahua. Do you remember her wails as we left the *pa*?"

"How could I forget? Many in the *pa* wept that morning to see us all go, but Ataahua's keening was heart-wrenching."

"Yes, it was," Richard said simply. "I still hear it often." He looked at Brengle with pleading eyes. "I am being torn apart. How can I *not* go back there? I gave my word to a woman I have come to love, and who I know loves me. And I gave my word to Chief Nene. But I also swore an oath to my country as a naval officer. A ship is waiting to take me back to the life I once lived and loved, the life where my duty lies. But is that the life I now want?" He sighed deeply. "I don't know, Jack. I just don't know."

The only sound in the room was the ticking of a wall clock in the parlor followed by a sequence of eleven chimes. At their conclusion Brengle said, "I understand that you are being torn in many directions, Richard. And I wish I could help. But only you can decide which course to follow. Whichever you choose, I will be with you."

"I have always counted on your friendship and support, Jack." His voice was ragged with emotion. "But never more than now."

Brengle tried to lighten the mood with a grin and a joke. "Why do you think Secretary Henshaw was so keen to sign me on as your first officer? Military matters aside, someone has to keep you away from trouble. And those hussies across the bay are trouble with a capital T!"

"I have no wish to find that out," Richard said. "I seem to be able to make my own trouble!"

Three and a half hours later, while Richard paced back and forth in the major's antechamber, his impatience morphing into anger, the door to the inner office finally opened. The major's smartly attired orderly appeared in the opening and snapped a salute. "Major Blackwell will see you now, Captain Cutler," he announced.

Chapter 22

"My dear man, do come in," the impeccably clad British officer exclaimed as he pushed himself away from his desk and onto his feet. "I apologize for keeping you waiting. Urgent business in Russell, you understand. Affairs there are becoming a bit dicey. But you need not concern yourself with that, of course. Please have a seat and tell me what's on your mind. Before you do, might I interest you in a splash of Madeira?" He gestured toward a sideboard crowded with bottles. "Surely the sun is over the yardarm somewhere in our great empire," he chuckled. "I have sampled far better in my day," he added sadly, "but alas, it is what we have. Given the heroics required to procure anything of quality at this remote post, I suppose we should be grateful. So, a splash? It's the least I can do for keeping you waiting so long."

"Please," Richard said. He assessed the major as he strode across the room to the handsomely polished sideboard and selected a bottle and two glasses. He saw a clean-shaven man with reddish-brown hair similar in color to his own, although it was close-cropped on the sides. His crisp movements indicated a no-nonsense approach to business that bore a strong resemblance to Navy Secretary Henshaw's manner.

Similar in age, physique, and education, the two officers—one American, the other British—differed in both career choice and career perspective. While Captain Richard Cutler had joined the American Navy to serve country and family, Major Oliver Blackwell had joined the British army to serve himself. Or so James Busby had told him.

Holding a full glass in each hand, Blackwell walked back and handed one to Richard. "You navy chaps always seem to have the upper hand," he bantered pleasantly. "You take the fine wine, so to speak, and leave us poor army chaps with the dregs. Even when we manage to get something drinkable, the prices are shocking!" He leaned against his desk, his right foot crossed over his left. "Cheers, Captain," he said, raising his glass before downing a healthy slug. As he put his glass down, he tried to smother a belch.

Richard took a sip of what seemed to him an excellent Madeira. "Perchance, Major," he countered lightly, "that is because in the navy, an officer must draw from his personal resources to pay for the spirits he consumes. That is where his money goes. In the British army, an officer must pay for his rank, and the more he pays, the higher the rank. That is where his money goes. Which may explain why a senior British officer such as yourself can ill afford fine spirits." He smiled at Blackwell's sharp glance. The major was no doubt trying to decide whether he had just been insulted or was simply the recipient of the American's awkward attempt at bonhomie. "At least," Richard added in the same jovial tone, "that is how I understand it *used* to be in the British army. Procedures may well have changed with the times."

"Not at all," Blackwell bantered back, having made up his mind that the American meant no offense. "It's a bloody good system. Keeps the riffraff out of the officer corps, which is precisely where it needs to be kept. Unfortunately, we can't say the same thing for the navy, now can we?" He chortled at his own wit, then assumed a businesslike demeanor. "So, Captain Cutler, now that we have mocked one another's service in the time-honored fashion, how may I help you? What do you need from me? I assume it isn't Madeira."

Richard regarded him evenly and spoke straightforwardly. "What I need from you, Major, is all the powder and shot you can spare. All of it. I also need enough regulars to safeguard its transport to the *pa* of Chief Nene, a two-day march from here."

Blackwell raised his bushy eyebrows and astonished Richard by letting out a hearty guffaw. "I now understand why you have come to see me, Captain, and not Captain Tilney in Russell. I mean no disrespect, but do you have *any* idea what you are asking of me?"

"I believe I do, Major," Richard retorted. "I am asking you to send reinforcements to Chief Nene, who has been a staunch ally of Great Britain since the day you first set foot on these shores. He gave you the land on which this town sits. He has made many sacrifices in the name of the Crown, and he is about to be called upon to sacrifice a great deal more. His people are in dire straits, and if they are not resupplied in the near future, I fear the worst for them."

The major turned beet-red. "That may very well be true, Captain Cutler," Blackwell snapped, "and in fact I have every reason to believe it *is* true." He paused to regain his composure before continuing. "Sorry, old boy. Pressures of the job, you understand. Believe me when I say that I appreciate what Nene and his tribe have done for Great Britain, and for me personally. I am a great admirer of his, and I deeply regret his misfortune. But also believe me when I say that there is nothing I can do to help him."

When Richard sat silently, jaw set and eyes demanding further explanation, Blackwell said, "The sad truth is, Captain, that there truly is nothing I can do to help Chief Nene. Literally nothing. Not at this moment, anyway."

"Why the hell not?"

Blackwell snorted. "I shall tell you a dirty little secret, Captain, one known only to a select few individuals. Paihia, Russell, and the whole Bay of Islands are virtually defenseless. Defenseless and bankrupt. I have but ten soldiers under my command. Add to that number a few Marines under Captain Tilney stationed in Russell, and you have a scenario for disaster. We are making a big show of pitching tents during the day and lighting campfires at night, and we march the same men back and forth around the area. But it's merely a ruse meant to fool Hone Heke into thinking there are many more of us than there actually are. If the Maori have half a mind to attack, they will make short work of Paihia. Russell might hold out a bit longer. Easier to defend, you understand, standing as it does at the end of a long peninsula. But even there it would be just a matter of time. Too few soldiers up against too many Maori. The mathematics of defeat." He barked a laugh.

"How can that be?" Richard asked, dumbfounded.

"You tell me, old boy," Blackwell scoffed, "because I have no good answer for you. Three months ago, my superior, Lieutenant-Colonel Hume, was called back to Sydney with his 96th Regiment. I have no idea why. Perhaps the local exchequer could no longer afford them. More likely, someone in high places has his head stuck in the sand. Or up someone's bum. The pitiful group he left me serves more as a police force, and not a very good one at that!"

"Can you not ask Governor Fitzroy for help?"

"I have. Several times. But I doubt to any great effect. Auckland is as defenseless and bankrupt as we are."

"Can nothing be done?"

"Yes, something can be done. Something *is* being done, and this much the good citizens of Russell and Paihia know about. The governor has sent urgent dispatches to Sydney, all but begging for troops and ships for the defense of both Auckland and Russell. God be praised, a light has finally shone through the muck. Reliable sources tell me that Admiral Braithwaite is dispatching a squadron of five naval vessels to New Zealand. Two ships are bound for the Bay of Islands and three for Auckland. Each ship will have a full complement of Marines, as well as army units and supplies. Oh, sorry, Captain, I should explain that Admiral Braithwaite is—"

"I know who he is."

"Do you?" Blackwell asked in surprise. "Then you may also know him to be a fine commander-in-chief struggling to manage a situation that has become quite unmanageable, poor fellow. Be that as it may, a lead ship of the squadron, HMS *Resolution*, is due in Russell within a fortnight, maybe sooner. We await her arrival with great anticipation, as you would expect. She will have with her not only Marines but also a hundred men and officers from the 99th Regiment, and a battery of cannon to supplement the pitiful few we have."

"That sounds promising."

"Indeed. So here is my pledge to you, Captain. When *Resolution* gets here, assuming she gets here in time, you will have everything you need to resupply Chief Nene, including a ten-soldier escort.

"In the meantime, I am raising a militia of one hundred local citizens, and I am working with Captain Tilney to shore up our defenses. I appeal to you and your men to lend what help you can. I understand you have recently survived a dreadful ordeal in the bush, but I could certainly use your assistance. You are of course under no obligation to help us."

Richard picked up his hat. "My executive officer and I will do everything we can to help," he promised. "I will not commit the rest of my men, however. They have endured too much already, and they are due to sail for home in three days. I will not allow any interference with that."

"I quite understand."

Richard had originally planned to ask for Major Blackwell's help in tracking down Lieutenant Weeks and the five sailors who went with him into the bush. But he saw no point in it. He had asked the same of Chief Nene, and like Blackwell, Nene had no men to spare on what would seem a fool's errand.

Richard rose to his feet. "Thank you for your time and your honesty, Major. And thank you for your pledge. I will send my two Ngapuhi escorts back to the *pa* to inform Chief Nene. He will be most grateful. Good day to you, sir." After the two men saluted each other, Richard turned to leave.

"One moment, Captain Cutler, if you please. I have something further to say to you."

Richard turned back, eyes narrowed. "And what is that, Major?"

Blackwell smiled warmly. "Merry Christmas, Captain."

"Merry Christmas to you, Major," Richard said before opening the door to the office and walking out.

Richard had last been on a single-masted packet almost two years ago when he sailed from his mother's home in Hingham, across Quincy Bay, to Boston Harbor and the offices of Cutler & Sons on Long Wharf. Today's journey from Paihia to Russell was much shorter but no less satisfying. As the waterfront of Paihia faded astern and the swift little vessel passed a string of small islands that were the last vestiges of a lee shore, her mainsail and jib caught the full force of a strengthening westerly that sent her creaming on a broad reach toward the harbor that served as the centerpiece of Russell. Richard's joy at being back under sail was tempered only by his distasteful scrutiny of a town that by now had become the stuff of legend.

From out in the bay, the town looked much like a seaside Maine village shimmering under a summer sun. People on shore were going about their business in a casual stroll or a fast pace, or, for one individual Richard had no trouble spotting, in a drunken lurch. From such a distance it was difficult to judge whether the men he could see were townspeople or crews ashore from the flotilla anchored in the harbor: whalers, fishermen, and merchantmen of various rigs and flags. One of them, a black-hulled brig, her bow to the wind, was flying the Stars and Stripes from her signal halyard. Richard could not make out the lettering on her stern, but he took her for the *Sarah D.* From the look of her she had survived a number of cruises, and certainly the stench drifting up through her single black funnel amidships suggested the workings of a whaler. Whatever flaws she revealed from this distance seemed more cosmetic than dangerous, however, and that was comforting. Clearly, she could take on whatever the Horn threw at her.

When he got closer to shore, he noted a long, narrow vessel pulled up on the pebbly beach. The totem-like carvings along her two garboard strakes and the inverted rudder projecting high on her stern made her a *waka*, a Maori war canoe. This canoe, however, flew the black, white, and red flag that, Henry Williams had explained to him, identified her as a trader bearing the fruits of Maori labor to villages along the New Zealand coast and across the turbulent Tasman Sea to New South Wales.

Now that the packet boat was well inside the west-facing harbor entrance, Richard shifted his gaze to the north side of the harbor, where one- and two-story warehouses, ship chandlers, ropewalkers, sail lofts, and shipwright offices were interspersed with a liberal sprinkling of what must be taverns and brothels, judging from the deep guffaws and high-pitched squeals emanating from within even now at 10:30 a.m., two bells in the forenoon watch. Richard wondered briefly if any of his men were sporting in these houses of ill repute but quickly dismissed any concerns. They had been without female company for too long, and the voyage home would be a long one.

As the packet boat shortened sail and feathered up to the substantial wooden wharf at the east end of the harbor, Richard stood up in the cockpit to lend a hand fending off. As he did so, he looked down into water so clear he could see the seabed ten fathoms down. On impulse he dipped his hand into the deliciously warm water and swirled it around as a child would do.

"Thank you," he said to the sloop's mate and to her captain, an ex-navy man who claimed he had once served as a coxswain to an admiral of the White. Richard believed him. "For your troubles, Tom," he added, handing him two silver coins before leaping from the cockpit coaming up onto the wharf. Nearby, the mate was securing the boat to the wharf with a spring line. Richard handed him a coin as well.

"Thankee kindly, Captain," the boat's master called up. "'Tis not necessary, though. No charge for an officer, as I told ye. 'Twas me duty and me pleasure."

Richard waved that away. "Does this pathway go up there?" He pointed to the crest of Maiki Hill, which dominated the town.

"That there's the way, sir. Just remember to veer to yer right when you reach the ruckus. Don't be goin' down that northside street, sir. 'Tis no place for a gentleman. Follow the road to the right, as I said. She'll loop around a mite, but she'll take ye where ye need to go."

The day was sunny and warm, a perfect early summer afternoon. As Richard walked along the path, he gazed upon a community of stark contrasts that seemed at once to incorporate the best and the worst of the human condition. Shops and homes erected on the south and east sides of the harbor were substantial and picturesque, attractively set back from the harbor behind a stately array of *pohutukawa* trees arrayed with scarlet flowers. One home in particular caught his eye, a two-story affair that seemed more in keeping with the country estate of a wealthy merchant in Provence or Tuscany than a colonist's homestead. Inland and to the east of that building stood an attractive wooden church surrounded by a graveyard. Like many buildings on this side of Russell, the church stood out not because money had been pumped into it, but because it had been expertly constructed with loving care and good taste.

What Richard could see directly across the quarter-mile-wide harbor, on its north side, presented a far different picture. It was as if the hand of God had emerged from the heavens and pointed a long, gnarled finger at the north side of Russell as His thundering voice decreed, "Let the sins of Man be committed there." Richard chuckled at the mental image and at the thought of the good pastor of the lovely church trying to convince a Sunday morning congregation that leading a godly life begins with a repudiation of sin.

As he approached the well-maintained pathway leading up the hill, two women came walking toward him. Both wore loose white muslin dresses that gave them the appearance of sailboats floating down the hill. One of the women paid him no mind. The other, the one closer to him and the more svelte of the two, flashed him a roguish smile from under her broad-brimmed hat. He raised his hand in salutation and smiled back as she walked past him.

Richard had barely begun the ascent up Maiki Hill when he encountered a checkpoint manned by two Royal Marines. To the right of the checkpoint was an area of cleared land on which had been constructed a stockade to house military personnel in Russell. Although the stockade was nearly empty, according to Major Blackwell, its personnel had joined forces with local citizenry to shore up the defenses in and around the stockade.

At the checkpoint, a blue-uniformed Marine corporal challenged Richard to state his name and purpose.

"I am Richard Cutler, and I hold the rank of captain in the United States Navy." He produced the piece of paper that confirmed those two statements. "My purpose in coming here is to address the sailors in my command who are temporarily quartered up there." He nodded toward the top of the hill. "Captain Tilney has given me his permission to do that. He will confirm that statement, if you wish."

The sentry saluted. "That will not be necessary, Captain. We have already met some of your men." He winked at his companion. "Welcome to Russell." He stepped aside to let Richard pass.

On his way to the top of the hill, it occurred to Richard that an adversary who wanted to avoid the checkpoint and steal up the hill undetected would have no difficulty doing so. As he approached the top, he began walking between rows of crisp white military tents pitched on both sides of the pathway—almost all of them unused, he knew. He wondered whether they had convinced the Maori that there were many more troops encamped in Russell than there actually were. Based on his experiences in Chief Nene's *iwi*, Richard doubted that the Maori would be so easily fooled.

The ten surviving members of his crew were waiting to greet him at the crest of the hill by the flagpole. Standing at rigid attention before a much smaller stockade, the towering flagpole with the Union Jack fluttering at its peak, they made a fine spectacle despite the worn slop chest trousers and shirts they had been issued. Brengle stood out in front. Montgomery and Talmadge, the two remaining midshipmen, stood behind him, and the rest of the crew were behind them in a compact group. As if on cue, each crewman snapped a salute and kept his right hand up and steady as Richard neared the flagpole.

Brengle did not make eye contact. He kept his gaze dead ahead. "Crew assembled as ordered, Captain," he announced.

"Thank you, Lieutenant," Richard said in his command voice. Then, leaning in toward his executive officer, he said sotto voce, "I did not expect such parade ground formality, Jack. Nor do I require it."

"It's the men, Richard," Brengle explained in an equally low voice. "This is at their request."

"I see." To the sailors: "At your ease, men!"

The men complied, keeping their eyes front and center. Richard strode past Brengle to Senior Midshipman Talmadge. He offered him his hand and Talmadge took it. "Thank you, Tom," he said before moving on to Midshipman Montgomery. To Richard's relief, Jonty also took the proffered hand and shook it firmly.

Richard went on to the group of sailors and Marines and repeated the process, one by one, until he came to John Templeton, a tow-headed engineer from Boston. "Where did you get that nasty bruise on your jaw, John?" he asked him with a frown.

Templeton gave him a sheepish look but said nothing and returned his eyes forward. Boatswain's Mate Cyrus Payton, standing nearby, spoke for him. "He got it in a tavern brawl, Cap'n," he said evenly. "Wasn't his fault, though. We was all out celebrating his birthday when the fight broke out. He took one on the chin."

"Why did a fight break out?"

"Some bastard came up and insulted his mother. A man can't have his mother spoken ill of, sir. A man has to defend his honor. An' his friends have to help."

"Who were you fighting?"

Payton shrugged. "No one seems to recall, sir."

"Half seas over, were you?"

"No, sir. Full seas. Every blessed one of us."

Richard turned his face to hide a grin. When he turned back, his face composed, he said in a stern voice, "I cannot and will not condone alehouse brawling, men. You know that is my strict policy. We are guests here, and when we arrived in Russell, I asked you not to forget that. Apparently, you weren't listening." When his crew could not meet his eyes he added, his voice sterner still, "On the other hand, I will also not condone an insult to the mother of any member of my crew. So good job, lads. Well done. And by the bye, John, happy birthday."

Templeton looked up with a huge grin on his face. "Thank you, Captain. Thank you very much."

"You're welcome. Now take care of that jaw."

"Oh, yes, sir. I will, sir. Plummer and Sturgis here are taking right good care of me," he added. "A man couldn't ask for anyone better, 'cept maybe that fine lady of yours, sir."

That remark rendered Richard speechless, and it took him several moments to recover. Whether Templeton was referring to Anne or Ataahua he could not tell, and the uncertainty pulled at his heart. "Thank you, John," he finally managed. "She would be gratified to know you feel that way about her."

"I do, Captain. We all do."

Still uncertain which of the women who loved him Templeton had meant, Richard strode back to where Brengle was waiting. His heart was heavy as he gazed below at the peaceful town and harbor. The sun had passed its apex and was on its downward arc. Merchantmen in the harbor looked like model ships, and the people strolling along the curved pathway of the harbor looked like children. *So beautiful*, he thought. *This land is so beautiful.* At that moment, looking down on it from above, Russell seemed more a South Seas paradise than a hellhole. With a sharp exhale, he turned around to face the men. Brengle turned with him.

"Gentlemen," Richard said, struggling to keep his voice steady, "as I have said on several occasions, we have come a long way together since that fateful day when we lost our ship, our bearings, and too many of our shipmates. By the grace of God and by sheer determination, you and I have made it here, and from here you go home. I am indebted to each of you for your help in bringing us here. I am especially indebted to Lieutenant Brengle for his relentless efforts to watch over you and to keep us all alive. Now, however, the time has come for us to part company. You are sailing home, and I—"

"Excuse me, *sir!*" a deep voice interrupted.

Richard was startled to realize that it was Jonty who had spoken. The pink-cheeked boy who had sailed with him from Washington those many months ago had become a man somewhere along the way. Moved beyond words, he took a moment before answering. "Yes, Mr. Montgomery? You have something you wish to say?"

Jonty had remained at stiff attention since Richard's arrival. "I do, *sir!*"

"It's out of order, but if you have something to say, by all means say it."

"Yes, *sir!* Thank you, *sir!*" Montgomery snapped out. His voice broke on the last "sir," somewhat spoiling the effect, but he went on. "Begging your pardon, *sir*, we are not sailing home. We are not sailing anywhere. We are staying here with you and Lieutenant Brengle, *sir*. We go where you go, and we fight who you fight. We mean no disrespect, *sir*, but there is nothing you can do to dissuade us. Am I right, men?"

"Yes, *sir!*" a chorus of eight voices bellowed.

Stunned to his core, Richard looked askance at Brengle, who raised his hands in a gesture that said, "This is none of my doing." He stared at the young midshipman for several moments, a frown knitting his brow.

"What you say is duly noted, Mr. Montgomery, and very much appreciated. But what you are proposing is out of the question. Do you hear me?"

"I hear you, *sir!*"

"And?"

"Nothing has changed, *sir!*"

Richard took in the faces beyond Montgomery. "You men all agree with this?"

"Yes, *sir!*" eight voices responded.

"And if I order you to leave?"

"We stand with you now and always, *sir!*" Tom Talmadge cried out.

"Goddammit, Jack!" Richard spluttered to his executive officer. "This is mutiny."

Montgomery overheard him. "Yes, *sir!*" he bellowed. "Bloody mutiny, *sir!*"

Richard threw up his arms and stormed toward the pathway to the stockade. His crew, from Brengle on down the ranks, executed another perfect salute.

Eleven days later, as Richard was sipping beer in a tavern with his two midshipmen, word spread rapidly through the streets and alleyways of Russell that a Royal Navy frigate had been sighted to eastward sailing westward toward the Bay of Islands. "It's *Resolution!*" speculation ran through the town. "She is coming at last!"

And so she was.

CHAPTER 23

"TELL ME, MRS. CUTLER, HOW DO YOU FIND OUR FAIR COLONY?"

Anne looked at each of the others who had just taken their seats around the table before looking at Robert Fitzroy. He was a distinguished-looking man, and she had taken a shine to him the instant she met him, drawn to his gentlemanly manner, elegant appearance, and obvious sophistication.

"Well, Sir Robert," she replied seriously, "*I* found it when my husband's ship ran *into* it!"

The silence that followed was shattered when John Shilling, seated across the table from Anne, roared with laughter. Fitzroy and his wife joined in, and the four of them dissolved in helpless laughter until even the young Maori woman preparing to serve the meal was engaged.

"I say, Mrs. Cutler," Fitzroy gasped when the mirth had run its course, "that was a good one! A jolly good one indeed, madam."

"My word, yes, indeed it was," his wife agreed as she wiped tears from her eyes. "Sakes, Robert, we haven't laughed like that in an age, have we? Thank you, Anne, if I may take the liberty of calling you that?"

"Oh, please do. I already feel that I am among friends." Then, for no apparent reason, the smile faded from Anne's face and she seemed to withdraw into herself.

John Shilling regarded her with concern. "Are you quite all right, Anne?" he asked.

Anne nodded. "I am, Captain, thank you. A sudden memory, I'm afraid. I do apologize for ruining the mood."

"No apologies are necessary, my dear," Mary Fitzroy put in. "We quite understand. You have been through such an ordeal these past few months. Please forgive our jollity."

"Heavens, no," Anne insisted. "I started it, after all, and I must admit, laughter has not come easily to me in recent months."

"I should think not, dear lady," Robert Fitzroy said. "Let us have our dinner. We shan't make this a late night," he promised.

"Thank you. That would be lovely," Anne said.

Fitzroy nodded to the young Maori woman, who brought over a silver tureen, placed it carefully on the table, and began ladling out a thick seafood stew into four ceramic bowls.

The dining area of Government House was hardly what a British nobleman would deem lavish, Anne thought, but compared with what she had known thus far in New Zealand it was equal to the state dining room of Buckingham Palace. The long mahogany table was draped with crisp white linen, and silver candelabras flanked a silver platter bearing two loaves of freshly baked bread. Oil paintings of seascapes and dignitaries graced the walls, with pride of place going to a grand portrait of young Queen Victoria. The queen hung directly behind the governor's seat at one end of the table, as if to allow Britain's monarch to monitor the goings-on below her.

When the stew had been served and four glasses of claret filled, Sir Robert cleared his throat and stood. "Ladies and gentleman," he said solemnly, pausing a moment for effect, "the queen!" He raised his glass high.

Three chairs immediately scraped back. "The queen!" the others echoed in unison.

Finally, much to Anne's relief, she was able to eat. Since arriving at Government House the previous morning, hunger and fatigue had been her constant companions, notwithstanding Charles Scott's considerable efforts to see to her every need and despite the efforts of the Fitzroys' four young children to keep Jamie entertained. Now, as she breathed in the heavenly aroma of freshly baked bread and savory stew, she feared her empty stomach might give way to an unspeakable social gaffe.

"This is delicious," she remarked after tasting a spoonful of the stew. "It tastes like the sea. What is in it?"

"The sea!" Mary Fitzroy laughed. "It has oysters, cockles, and a local flatfish, much like our sole back in England. The vegetables are from our garden, and the seafood was donated from local *iwis*, God bless them. Kura here prepared and cooked the stew."

Anne smiled at the young Maori woman. "*I tunua koe i remai?* You cooked this? Thank you. It is delicious! *Mauruuru, he reka!*"

Kura flushed. "*Mauruuru, e te wahine atawhai,*" she said deferentially.

"My word, Anne," Mary Fitzroy gasped. "You speak Maori?"

"A little," Anne acknowledged.

"How extraordinary! Who taught you?"

"I learned it at the mission. Te Whina and Daniel MacKenzie taught me all that I know. I am fortunate to have had two such excellent tutors."

"How very extraordinary!" the governor's wife said, as if learning to speak the native tongue was unheard of.

"Indeed you are fortunate in your teachers," the governor agreed. "Your pronunciation and vocabulary are commendable," he added. "I have many questions to ask about your experiences, but I shall defer them for now. For this evening, please enjoy your meal. It's rather simple fare for Government House. Our budget for entertaining is a bit strained, I'm sorry to say. As you well understand, other expenditures are more important at the moment."

Anne laughed. "Please, Sir Robert, don't apologize. I am most grateful for your kind hospitality. The stew and bread are divine, and the company most entertaining."

As second helpings made the rounds, Anne asked the governor how he and Lady Fitzroy had come to be in New Zealand.

"Now there's a story!" Shilling remarked before Fitzroy could answer.

"Not at all," Fitzroy countered. "It' quite simple, really. I am a navigator and surveyor by trade. A few years ago, I was assigned to the sloop *Beagle* and commissioned by the Royal Academy of Science to chart Patagonia and Tierra del Fuego, which I did. From South America *Beagle* sailed here to New Zealand, where I continued my work and began writing the first volume of my magnum opus. Upon my return to England I was invited to present my findings to the Church Missionary Society. For better or for worse, they were sufficiently impressed by what I had to say to champion my appointment here to replace Governor Hobson, who had taken ill, God rest his soul. So here I have been for the past two years with my lovely wife and four children to watch over me."

"How fascinating," Anne said politely. "Our lives do take the oddest twists and turns, don't they?" Her voice faded with that last sentence.

The evening wore on in pleasant fashion, with various stories about life-changing events and adventures, until the plum pudding was served and consumed. When she noticed Anne's increasing difficulty in stifling yawns, Lady Fitzroy rose to end the meal.

"My dear," Mary Fitzroy said, "forgive us. You are tired, and understandably so. It will take many days for you to come right after all you have been through. Please rest tonight. Tomorrow is another day. I understand from Captain Shilling that you two are planning a stroll around the gardens tomorrow morning. I think you will find that delightful."

Anne, unaware that such plans had been made, looked at Shilling but covered her surprise. "I am looking forward to it. But for now, I must confess, I need to relieve Rachael with little Jamie, though I have no doubt that the two of them are curled up together fast asleep. Thank you, Sir Robert and Lady Fitzroy, for this lovely evening. It is one I shan't soon forget."

She stood up, and the governor and Shilling stood up with her. "Captain," the governor said after Anne had taken her leave and Kura was clearing the table, "Might I have a word with you outside?"

"Of course, Governor."

The two men stood silently beneath the waxing gibbous moon until the governor asked quietly, "Any word yet on the status of the MacKenzie mission?"

Shilling shook his head. "Not yet. I expect to receive word tomorrow. Chief Wherowhero's runners understand how vital that information is to us."

"Indeed. Missionaries have traditionally not met with any harm from the Maori. I pray it has remained that way, else we are witnessing a total breakdown of our society here in the colony. Care for a smoke?"

"Please."

Fitzroy withdrew two thin cigars from a pocket of his coat and handed one to Shilling, who turned it over between thumb and forefinger, then ran it under his nose, breathing in the rich, pungent aroma of Jamaican tobacco.

"By God," exclaimed Fitzroy, doing likewise, "this is one luxury I shall not do without, damn the circumstances." From a second pocket he produced a small tin container and drew out a wax match, which burst into flame when he ran it through a square of sandpaper inside the tin. He cupped the flame in the palm of his hand and offered it to Shilling. The match light illuminated Shilling's face as he took several deep puffs.

"I quite agree," Shilling said, blowing out a stream of smoke that quickly obliterated the sulfurous smell of the match.

"How long do you think we have?"

Shilling shook his head. "Hard to say. Weeks, a month maybe, two at the most. It depends on how quickly Te Rauparaha can gather together his Ngati Toa and his allies. Of course, that is assuming that they will attack us, which frankly, I doubt. Their interests are south of here, in the Wairau Valley."

"That is true," Fitzroy agreed, "but illegal land-grabbing has become a scourge throughout New Zealand, not just around Auckland. Te Rauparaha is as outraged as every other chief over what he views as outright thievery. Which, of course, it is. Whenever Maori warlords try to abide by the terms of the treaty, they are rewarded for their efforts by having their lands unlawfully taken and white settlers pointing to the treaty as justification for it!"

"I understand your frustrations, Governor. I feel them as well. But there's not much we can do about that now. We have our own to protect, and that includes Anne Braithwaite." He gazed out into the night and added softly, "She has come to mean a great deal to me in the short time I have known her."

"So I've noticed. Have a care, Captain. Anne is no simpering serving girl. She is a noblewoman, and she is still grieving for her lost husband. The extent may seem excessive given the time that has passed, but I find it admirable nonetheless. Incidentally, her name remains Anne Braithwaite *Cutler*."

Shilling frowned. "Have no concerns on that score, Governor. My intentions are strictly honorable. The last thing I want to do is add to her burdens. I simply want to see her away from here and safe. Which brings up the question, when will she—when will *we*—be permitted to sail for Sydney?"

"After the squadron gets here. The admiral is insisting that his sister be conveyed to Sydney in a Royal Navy vessel, and I have none to spare. Which is why I am of two minds in deciding to dispatch your *Hazard* to Russell."

Shilling shot him a quizzical look. "I beg your pardon, Governor?"

Fitzroy took a long pull on his cheroot and exhaled slowly, watching the grayish-white smoke curl upward. "I agree that Auckland is in no immediate danger, whatever the Ngati Toa may have in mind. We are heavily fortified here, and besides, Chief Wherowhero is currently in residence in Auckland. The Waikato Tainui are many and strong, and they will fight for us to a man. The Ngati Toa know that and won't want to tangle with our combined forces."

Fitzroy went on, "If the worst happens and a civil war breaks out—and I have concluded that it will, eventually—we need to make preparations not only to defend Russell but to evacuate the town if need be. In the meantime, we need to strengthen our communications."

Shilling nodded. "Agreed. It is what I have been saying all along. While our priority should remain Auckland, we must do what we can to safeguard Russell, hellhole that it is."

"It was the colonial capital for a year," Fitzroy reminded him.

"I know, and it has great symbolic value. Britain's flag on the hilltop there symbolizes our empire. I understand it's been cut down three times. Three times! What an insult to England! It must never happen again! When do I weigh?"

"By week's end, if it can be done."

"It can be. I will see to the preparations at once."

"Good. I have great faith in your judgment and your abilities, John. I always have. I will send a messenger posthaste to Russell to alert Major

Blackwell and Captain Tilney. This bit of news will please them. But before we set the wheels in motion, have that stroll with Mrs. Cutler in the morning. She is looking forward to it, as I sense you are. The fresh air will do you both good, and she could do with the company of an honorable British sea officer."

Anne transferred her parasol from her right hand to her left and rested her right hand in the crook of Shilling's elbow. "I have a bone to pick with you, Captain Shilling," she declared.

Shilling arched his eyebrows. "My word! Should I be worried?"

They were strolling through the well-manicured grounds of Government House, two acres of gaily colored flowers, bushes, and shrubs displaying the full bloom of a New Zealand summer. Never one to tolerate the layers of clothing considered essential by most fashionable women, especially during the warm season, she had accepted Lady Fitzroy's gracious offer of a sheer white linen dress and a tasseled silk shawl to drape across her shoulders.

She looked up into Shilling's eyes, a dark blue that nearly matched the color of his gilt-edged uniform coat. "Before I tell you, I have a very important issue to raise. I need to know if you have heard from the soldiers sent as a rescue party to the mission."

"Not yet, though I expect to receive word shortly."

"What about the men we left behind on the road? Corporal Congleton and the others? What about them?"

"The same. My best guess and hope, since they did not show up here, is that they were picked up by the rescue party and taken with them to the mission. They had the horses they needed to do that."

Anne shook her head. "I wonder. It seems unlikely to me. If they did not catch up to us or arrive here soon after us, I fear the worst happened."

Shilling agreed but said nothing to indicate that he did. He did not want to spoil the moment, and there was nothing to be done about it in any event. "We'll have to wait and see, Anne. I am as concerned as you are—I daresay even more so—but we are powerless to do anything further at the moment. Colonel Crenshaw has sent out every available man. In the meantime, we will pray for good news."

"You are a very pragmatic man, aren't you, John."

"I have to be, Anne. Every man in my position has to be pragmatic. It's the bane of command, I'm afraid."

They walked on in silence, each absorbed in private thoughts, until Shilling asked offhandedly, "What is the issue you wish to raise with me? I fear it may be serious."

"It's not serious," Anne said. "I should not have implied that it was. I am simply curious about something. Whilst I do recall your invitation for me to join you in a stroll this morning, I do *not* recall actually accepting it. Until you appeared on the veranda this morning, I was unsure that we even had such an engagement."

"Were you disappointed to see me?"

She looked up at him through her long eyelashes. "That, Captain Shilling, is not at issue."

Shilling grinned. "Fair enough. But to your point: I would have to be the greatest of fools to have stayed away," he said, adding in the same teasing tone, "It was an oversight for which I apologize, my lady. It was shameful of me to take anything that involves you for granted. But navy men are forever hopeful, you know."

She blushed. "Hopeful of what, may I ask?"

Shilling did not answer straight away. Then: "Anne, may I be honest with you?"

"I should hope so. I hope you have always been honest with me."

"I have been, and always will be." Anne was startled at his intensity. Tentatively he brought a hand to her cheek, brushed aside the auburn ringlets that framed her face.

"I don't know how else to say this except to say it. I have strong feelings for you, Anne, feelings I have not experienced for many a year, and thought never to have again. Though I have struggled to keep my feelings in check, because I have the deepest respect and admiration for you, I suspect you are aware of them."

She withdrew her hand and looked away. "John, go no further, please. I beg you."

"I'm sorry, but I must," he insisted. "I had not intended to declare myself yet, but my orders to leave Auckland have forced my hand. I could not bear to leave without first telling you what is in my heart."

She shook her head. "John, I cannot. I only recently lost my husband, whom I continue to love with my whole being. I am not looking for a new love."

"Nor was I," Shilling pressed, "and I believe for a similar reason. I know you still grieve for Richard," he said earnestly, "and of course you should. I understand that he will always be in your heart."

She shook her head. "How could you possibly understand?"

"Because I, too, lost someone very dear to me."

She brought a hand to her mouth. "Your wife?"

"No, my fiancée. We were only a month away from marrying when the fever took her. I had recently returned to Portsmouth from duty in Gibraltar. I thank God I was able to be with her at the end. My grief afterward was such that I volunteered for service here in the South Pacific to escape England. Your brother, bless his soul, found a spot for me without question.

"Indeed," he said with a sad smile, "it was your brother who introduced me to Lillian. Her father, Captain Mayes, was a man he much admired, a retired post captain up for a baronetcy. Lillian was one of the sweetest women I had ever met, and I knew immediately that I wanted no one else for my wife. Later, when we announced our engagement, your brother hosted a celebration for us where he publicly declared that under no circumstances would he miss our wedding, come what may. To my eternal sadness, he did miss it. So did I." Shilling's voice had become barely audible as he spoke the last sentence.

Anne felt a surge of compassion. "Oh, my dear John, I didn't know. I am so very sorry."

"No one here knows. It's not a subject I care to broach." He took a step away from her and reached for her hand. In a voice on the verge of cracking he said, "What I want to ask you, Anne, is this: Might I dare hope that at some point in the future, perhaps when you are settled with your brother in Sydney, that you might take it upon yourself to look favorably upon me?"

Anne could not resist a smile. "John, you need not be so formal. You sound like a character in a Shakespeare play. I already do look favorably upon you, and not just because you saved my life and the life of my son."

"Thank you, but that is not really what I meant."

"I know exactly what you meant. All I can say to you now is that I am open to the possibility, if and when the time is right. And I think Jamie would be as well. At least he laughs whenever he sees you."

"That's hardly reassuring. It's probably my uniform."

"That's part of it," she teased, "but not all of it. I do believe he likes you."

"I'm glad he does. Does his mother like me also?"

"His mother has already answered that question." She pulled her hand away and put it back in the crook of his elbow. "Come, John, let us walk a wee bit more, shall we?"

They walked in silence along a path that led to the edge of the compound bordering Queen Street and turned to go back. As Anne was about to ask him for the details of his upcoming voyage, they spotted a Marine orderly striding toward them.

"What is it, John?"

"I'll find out." He disengaged his hand. "Stay here, please."

When Shilling reached the orderly, the Marine saluted smartly and handed him a folded paper. As Shilling opened it and began reading it, the orderly saluted a second time and departed.

"John?" Anne called out as Shilling slid the message into an inside pocket of his uniform coat and walked back toward her. "It's good news, I hope?"

"The best. Daniel MacKenzie and everyone at the mission are safe and on their way here. They should arrive tonight or early tomorrow morning."

Anne's face lit up. "Oh, blessed joy! How wonderful! Daniel and Maude and Jonathan alive and on their way to Auckland! I must go and tell Rachael and Te Whina. They will be overcome with joy and relief! Please excuse me, John. I must find them!"

"Of course, Anne. Off you go."

She turned to leave, then turned back, stood on her tiptoes, and gently pecked him on the cheek before making toward Government House. She did not see him place his hand over the spot she had kissed. When she was safely out of sight, Shilling withdrew the dispatch and reread it, his lips curling in anger. He had not told Anne all it said. MacKenzie and the others attached to the mission had been spared, true, but not Shilling's men. The Marines he had left to protect the mission, and Congleton and the others who had bought Anne and the others time to flee to safety, had been slaughtered.

"Bastards!" Shilling swore under his breath. "Fucking bloody bastards. You'll pay for this!" He thrust the communiqué back into his coat pocket and made all due haste to the harbor to prepare HMS *Hazard* for sea.

Chapter 24

"I've got the deck, Richard," Brengle said softly. "Get some sleep. You've been on watch all night, and we'll be moving out in another two or three hours."

"Thanks, Jack," Richard responded equally softly, "but I'll stay put. Sleep is no friend of mine tonight. It may be my mind playing tricks, but the bush seems to be moving. And yet it's deathly quiet. Too quiet. Do you have a sense of it?"

At that very moment, in the far distance to westward, they heard what sounded like faint rolls of thunder. *Strange*, Richard thought, *to hear thunder on a clear night like this. An abrupt change of weather coming?* The sounds lasted but a short while.

Brengle heard it too and waited for silence to return before answering the question. "I do. I was thinking earlier about when we left the *pa* for Paihia. We made camp that first night not far from where we are now. That night, those hoot owls, or whatever they were, were raising such a din, it kept everyone awake. And the insects, my God, what a racket they made. Tonight, there's hardly a peep. Something's up."

"Agreed. It's like being out at sea when the wind suddenly freshens and backs, and the waves pick up and the barometer tumbles. You know that a bad storm is brewing. And no matter how hard you work to prepare the ship for heavy weather, you know you're about to get pounded. I have that same eerie feeling tonight."

"Me, as well. But I confess, at the moment I would give a year's pay to feel the pitch and roll of *Suwannee*'s deck under my feet, whatever the weather."

Richard clasped a hand on his friend's shoulder. "That's because you're a sailor, Jack. As am I. It's in our blood."

Brengle chuckled.

"What is it?" Richard half-whispered.

"I was just thinking that you must wish you had already accepted your family's offer to take over Cutler & Sons. You'd be well away from here. Will you accept the offer, do you think? Certainly, your salary will be higher."

Richard scratched his neck. "We'll see. If I do, you're coming with me."

"Indeed?! What makes you think I want to resign my commission?"

"A five-fold increase in salary, for starters. In any event, we'll be at sea soon enough, my friend, bound for home, and when we are, we'll—" He froze, his senses alert.

"What is it?" Brengle whispered.

"Shhh. Listen."

"I don't hear anything."

Slowly Richard pulled his revolver from its holster on his belt. "*Listen!*"

There it was again, a rustling in the bush, then the sound of a branch snapping. Brengle heard it and drew his own revolver.

Richard motioned with his hand: *Take cover behind the wagon.* Silently the two men crept to the four-wheeled military wagon laden with powder, shot, muskets, and two three-pounder cannons that was blocking the pathway. "Take starboard, Jack," Richard whispered. "I've got port."

"Should we alert the others?"

"Not yet. If there's trouble, one shot will wake them. First, let's see what stumbles out of the bush."

Kneeling back-to-back with Brengle, Richard peered out from behind the wagon, trying to see through the thick vegetation crowding the north side of the pathway where he had detected the sounds.

"Maybe it was an animal," Brengle volunteered over his shoulder. "A boar, maybe. They're big fellows."

"Maybe."

"Hold on. There it is again. Closer now. Coming from over there." Richard pointed ahead and to his left.

Brengle nodded.

Richard gripped the spoke of a wagon wheel with his left hand and held the revolver in his right, the long barrel resting on his left forearm. He eased back the hammer to full cock and took aim.

The footfalls, for such they clearly were now, were becoming more noticeable, as though whoever was making them no longer deemed it necessary to mask his movements. Richard held his breath and steadied his arm. Then, as a dark figure emerged onto the pathway from a growth of tall ferns and grasses, he swore under his breath and stood up.

"Who is it?" Brengle hissed.

"Payton," Richard spat. As he and Brengle stepped out from behind the wagon, the boatswain's mate hove into view. His bland smile turned into alarm when he saw the revolvers aimed at his chest.

"Evenin', Captain, Lieutenant. Didn't mean to startle ye. Lost me bearings, is what. Them trees are so bloody thick a man can't see where he's goin.'"

"What the hell were you doing out there, Cyrus?" Brengle demanded.

"I was on the seat of ease, sir, upon me honor I was. When I was finished, I thought to see how the horses were faring. They're not far from here, to the east," he added helpfully, as though the two officers had no idea where the horses were being quartered. "Josiah and Nicky are with 'em. They do love them beasts. They say no need to relieve 'em. They'll stay with 'em through the night."

"Well, thank you for that piece of information," Richard said, grateful they had with them two men who had a way with horses. "But goddammit, Payton, be more careful wandering about like that. You very nearly got your head blown off a moment ago." He motioned the man away. "Get some rest. We move out at two bells."

"Aye, aye, sir. I'm sorry, sir. I will, sir." Payton gave Richard a quick salute and headed toward the small clearing where ten British soldiers and *Suwannee*'s crew had pitched camp and were taking shifts on watch duty, two hours on, two hours off.

At two bells in the morning watch, the sky remained dark and clear, the only light coming from a universe full of stars and a sliver of moon. There was barely enough light to outline the dark tops of trees against the sky. Behind them, to the east, strands of pink and apricot and purple sky were heralding another summer day.

A half hour later, after a quickly downed breakfast of plain bread with sliced cold kumara and a tin cup of black coffee heated over a small fire, the driver of the wagon urged the team of four horses westward into the rapidly diminishing gloom. The wagon trundled along in the wake of ten red-coated soldiers and eight casually garbed sailors, all a-horse. In the lead rode Richard Cutler, Jack Brengle, and a lanky young army lieutenant named Paul Dickerson, who had made it abundantly clear that he was none too pleased with Major Blackwell for burdening him with this assignment. "Sending aid to them savages?" he was heard to mumble. "A bloody waste of men and weaponry." Richard wondered how many of those under Dickerson's command shared those sentiments. Most of them, he judged, given their reluctance to do anything beyond what they were ordered to do.

Five hours later, as they were approaching and passing landmarks along the route that Richard had come to know well during his months at the *pa*, he caught a whiff of smoke that had nothing to do with campfires. He glanced at Brengle, who nodded in reply to the unspoken question. Richard raised an arm, and the entourage came to a halt.

Lieutenant Dickerson rode up scowling. "Why the delay?" he demanded irritably. "We need to pick up the pace if we expect to be on the return run by tonight. I say we move on, now!"

"And I say we don't," Richard said curtly. "As I recall, Major Blackwell put me in charge of this mission. Please do correct me if I'm wrong."

Dickerson said nothing.

Richard passed word for Josh Sturgis to come up. The able-ranked seaman from Dover, New Hampshire, had been a mainstay of the crew since *Suwannee* sailed from the Chesapeake, and was acknowledged to have the best eyes in the crew. "Josh, see that tree yonder?" He indicated a towering tree a short distance away in the bush. "Climb up there and tell me what you see. Don't yell out anything. Come back down to report."

"Aye, aye, Captain." Sturgis dismounted, passed the reins of his horse to Brengle, and began picking his way through the bush. He climbed up the gnarled tree without pausing, as much in his element as a spider in its web, moving from branch to branch steadily and easily. When he had gone as high as he could, he stopped and peered into the lightening sky. Richard and the others below craned their necks and waited. Either Sturgis was trying to confirm what he was seeing, or he was waiting until he was able to spot something of consequence. After an excruciatingly long span of minutes, Sturgis finally descended. He dropped to the ground from the lowest branch and forced his way back through the thick underbrush until he was standing on the pathway. He stared wordlessly up at Richard on his horse.

"What? What did you see?" Richard asked anxiously.

Sturgis hesitated. "Well, sir . . ." He bit his lower lip, unable to speak.

"Spit it out, Josh. What did you see?"

Sturgus swallowed hard. "I saw the *pa*, sir, clear enough. It's still a ways off, but I saw it." He stopped.

"Damn it, man! Report! That's an order!"

Sturgis blinked. "I saw the *pa*, sir, but there was no one *in* the pa. And I could see inside it right good from that height." He pointed to the top of the tree.

"You saw *no one* at all?"

"No one that I could see, sir. That's because there ain't much left to see. It's been burned. The *pa*, I mean."

"*Burned?*"

"Yes, sir. That's what I've been trying to say. I'm sorry, sir."

"Bring up the detail as quickly as you can," Richard snapped to Brengle. "I'm going on ahead." He dug his boot heels into his horse's flank. The horse lunged forward.

"Come back, Captain! Don't go on alone," Brengle shouted after him. "Wait for us!"

Richard ignored him. He galloped on, eyes forward and mind awhirl as he whipped by the familiar landmarks. As he neared the clearing he knew so well, the acrid stench of smoldering wood coupled with the sickly sweet smell of blood assailed his senses.

Ahead, through the thinning stands of trees and bush lining the widening pathway, he saw the vast clearing and, close by, the smaller parcel of land where, on that first night, Chief Nene had hosted the *hangi*. Galloping past it, Richard kept his gaze frozen on the outer wall—what was left of it. At first glance, it looked as though sections of the wall had been blasted through or bashed in, leaving but one corner blockhouse functional. Patches of broken stakes and logs around the circumference of a once defiant fortress stood forlornly amid the smoky rubble. Even the soaring watchtower had been hacked down. *How?* he wondered. He already knew who. He cursed his delay in getting here.

When he reached the wall, he did not go through the gate. He had no need to. What remained of the gate was open, but there were many other openings to choose from. *Cannon*, Richard thought as he rode slowly ahead. *This has to be the work of cannon. Nate was right after all.*

As he entered the grassy space between the two walls, he drew his revolver and held it flat against his right thigh. He searched for bodies; finding none, he rode through the inner gate and halted where Chief Nene had first confronted him. A quick survey of the grounds revealed that few areas of the *pa* had been spared, including the *wharenui* high on the hill. He began to see bodies now, here and there on the slope of the hill and in the cluster of huts at its base. A few of them were showing small movements, but the blood and gore from smashed skulls made it clear that those still alive were near death. Nausea and uncontrollable rage overwhelmed him.

"Tane!" he shouted when he spotted the body of the young Ngapuhi warrior on the ground. Just five days ago he had wished Tane Godspeed when he raced away from Paihia to inform Chief Nene that help would be coming soon. Richard dismounted, knelt beside Tane, and felt for a pulse. There was none.

Hearing the sounds of riders approaching, he got to his feet and retraced his steps to the outer wall. Brengle and the six sailors were riding slowly toward him, their eyes fixed on the scene of carnage. Richard waved them over.

"Jesus, Richard!" was all Brengle could muster. He dismounted and motioned to the six sailors to follow suit.

Richard struggled to maintain a semblance of control. "How far behind are the soldiers, Lieutenant?"

"Not far." Hands on his hips, Brengle surveyed a vision of hell. "How do you want to handle this? Are there dead inside?"

"Yes. Some may still be alive. Our first duty is to tend to them as best we can. When the soldiers get here, tell Dickerson to establish a defensive perimeter of his choosing. Whoever did this—and my money is on the Ngati Whatua—may still be lurking in the bush close by. Call out if you need me."

"Where are you going?"

"Up the hill." He turned on his heel.

"Have a care," Brengle called after him.

Richard waved in acknowledgment but continued striding up the path to the *wharenui*. As he passed each of the unimposing huts that had housed the Ngapuhi, he whispered a name: Chief Nene, Manala, Hohana, Ihaka, Kaia, Tane, young Irangi, who had invited Jonty to slide down the hill with him on a *nikau*, so many others—all his friends, his family. He did not stop to look in any of the huts; several had been razed almost to the ground. His men would see to that. He set his sights on the single hut that, for whatever reason, had sustained minimal damage. It was the one he had called home during those many weeks, the one where she had first come to him. His intuition told him he would find her there.

She lay on the thick flaxen mat that had once cushioned their love-making. Her head was resting on a pile of cloaks, and her hands were clutching at her belly. The left side of her skull had been crushed, and her ebony hair was crusted with dried blood. Fresher blood splotched her body, which was covered only by a *piupiu* skirt.

Unable to speak, to think, Richard walked over to the mat and knelt beside her. He lifted her left hand tenderly in his and felt a thready pulse.

"Ataahua," he pleaded. When she failed to respond, he moved closer and spoke louder into her ear. "Ataahua. Please."

Her eyelids fluttered but did not open. He gently placed his hand on her cheek and begged her again. "I'm here, my love. I'm here."

Her eyes opened and focused on his face. "Richard," she breathed, her body arching in a sudden spasm of pain. "*E taku e aroha. Kua hoki mai koe.*" She was barely able to whisper the familiar words of love. A thin smile creased her cracked lips.

"*Ae, taku aroha,*" he managed in reply. "I have come back. I promised I would."

Her smile was as feeble as her grip on his hand. "Too late," she murmured, her smile fading.

"No, Ataahua!" he cried out. "No! It's not too late! You are alive and I will take care of you. You will heal!"

"Too late," she murmured again even more feebly.

"You mustn't die, Ataahua!" he choked. "I have come back for you. We will see the mountains and the snow together. Please, Ataahua! Believe in me! Believe in yourself. Please don't die!" He knew as he spoke that his words were both futile and false.

"Too late, my love," she rasped. Her eyes still locked on his, she slid her bloodstained hand across her belly, down to where the blood was most profuse. "Too late," she murmured. "Too late . . ."

Richard tore his eyes from hers and followed the movement of her hand. When he gently lifted her blood-stained *piupiu* to confirm the worst, hot bile rose to his mouth. He swallowed hard to force it down. Twice he made the sign of the cross over her chest. "Ataahua, my sweet love," he moaned. "I had no idea. Please believe me. I didn't know!"

"I did not tell you. I did not want to force you to come back to me." She gripped his hand with all the strength left to her. "*Tena ngana ki te maarama. Ka nui taku aroha ki a koe.*"

That declaration of love seemed to claim the last of the life force lingering within her. Her eyes closed, then fluttered open one last time.

"Richard," she whispered, "please, I must ask . . . for me."

"Ask anything."

"Bury me . . . and our baby . . . at our place by the river. *Ka mahia ko tenei . . . e taku e aroha nei.*"

He buried his face in his hands, frantically swiping at tears with his fingers. The voice of Jack Brengle issuing commands outside seemed sacrilegious.

He took her limp hand in both of his and kissed it. "*Ae, e taku e aroha. Ka mahia e ahau.* I will do it, my dear one. I will take you there, and our child." His voice broke on the last word. He kissed her hand one last time and placed it gently on her heart.

CHAPTER 25

MAJOR OLIVER BLACKWELL PUT DOWN THE REPORT, FORMED A STEEPLE with his fingertips, and settled it under his chin. The rigid lines on his face relaxed as he gazed up at the ceiling. The open windows on three sides of the office admitted a refreshing breeze that ruffled the papers. Jack Brengle thought for a moment that the playful zephyrs might have distracted the British officer. But he doubted it. The man was too conscious of his rank and duty for that.

As though aware of what Brengle was thinking, Blackwell dropped his hands and straightened his back. "Captain Cutler has read your report, Lieutenant?" he asked.

"He has, Major."

"And he agrees with your conclusions?"

"He does. We composed the report together."

"I see. Pity he can't be here to tell me that himself. We have important matters to discuss. Lives are at stake, and he, more than anyone, should realize that. Remind me: Where is Captain Cutler at the moment?"

"To the best of my knowledge, he is in Russell meeting with Captain Tilney and the others responsible for the town's defense."

"Well, I daresay that I should have been included," Blackwell snapped. "Damn it, man! I am the one most responsible for planning that defense, and we are in a most precarious situation!"

"Captain Cutler understands that, Major. That is why he is where he is. He means no disrespect, I assure you. He asked me to represent him here today."

"And this report . . ." Blackwell harrumphed. Before the major could comment further, Paul Dickerson interrupted with a derisive snort.

Blackwell's gaze swung to him. "You have something to say, Lieutenant?"

"I do, sir."

"Then say it."

Dickerson uncrossed his legs and leaned forward in his chair, signaling that he thought what he was about to disclose was of no small consequence. "Gladly, Major. While I do not dispute what Lieutenant Brengle's report says," Dickerson said pompously, "I maintain that he has omitted critical facts. So many, in fact, that I believe that the entire report should be called into question."

Blackwell stifled a sigh. "Get to the point, Lieutenant."

"Yes, sir. The point is that Captain Cutler frequently displayed poor judgment in the decisions he made and the orders he issued during the recent expedition. I would go so far as to say that what he did constituted a dereliction of duty that placed my men, his men, and the mission itself in jeopardy."

Blackwell arched his bushy eyebrows. "Lieutenant, we are not in a court of law, and this is not a legal proceeding. I am simply seeking information. Say what you have to say in plain language, please, without embellishment and personal opinions. Bear in mind that I hold Captain Cutler in high esteem. Few men could suffer through what he has endured and come out whole on the other side. He is an exceptional officer, which is why I offered command of the expedition to him." He left "and not you" hanging in the air.

Dickerson flushed. "I, too, hold Captain Cutler in high esteem," he said insincerely. "But as I have stated, I believe there were times during the mission when he acted in a manner unbefitting a military commander. If you will permit me to explain . . ."

Blackwell nodded and sighed. "Yes, yes, get on with it."

"I can offer three examples without any further thought," Dickerson said. "When we arrived at the native enclosure, Captain Cutler, who had ridden ahead and left his *entire* command behind, I should add, was nowhere to be seen. He was, in fact, in a hut tending to a woman.

A *native* woman! We should have left the place as soon as we realized that Chief Nene and his warriors had fled into the bush after what was likely a sudden attack at night. We could hardly resupply an ally who wasn't there, could we? Captain Cutler, however, would not hear of it. He insisted that he had other work to do before he could allow us to leave."

"What sort of work?"

"Your question brings up my second point. The next morning, I again urged Captain Cutler most emphatically to have the men mount up and move out. The Ngapuhi in the *pa* were all dead. There was nothing we could do for them. Again he refused, even though my men guarding the perimeter had reported hearing possible enemy movements during the night."

"You informed Captain Cutler of this?"

"Yes, sir."

"What did he say?"

"He *said* that he would not leave until he had carried this dead Maori woman to the riverbank and buried her. Moreover, he insisted on carrying out this procedure alone, even though his own men offered to help. Three hours were thus consumed, wastefully and dangerously, in my opinion. Had the enemy chosen to advance, those three hours could have been our last."

"I see. And your third example? Be brief, Lieutenant. We haven't all day."

Dickerson nodded. "When Captain Cutler finally returned to the *pa* from the river, he ordered the munitions we had risked our lives to bring there *blown up!* The powder, muskets, cannon, all of them destroyed. I agree that we could not allow those arms to fall into the wrong hands, but I believe *you* will agree we could sorely use them here in Russell. Had we departed the *pa* earlier, we would now have them in our possession."

Blackwell nodded reflectively. "Is that all, Lieutenant?"

"For the moment, yes, Major."

Blackwell's gaze shifted to Brengle. "Care to comment, Lieutenant?"

Brengle shook his head. "No, thank you, Major. Everything I have to say on this subject is in the report you have on your desk."

"Very well." Blackwell drummed his fingers on his desk before speaking further. Then: "Thank you, gentlemen. What you have written, Lieutenant Brengle, and what you have stated, Lieutenant Dickerson, will be given full attention and a fair hearing as soon as circumstances allow. For the moment, we have more pressing matters to consider.

"We must hope that Chief Nene was indeed able to flee the *pa* with many of his warriors. Until they come to join us, as surely they will if they are alive, we are without a valuable ally and have lost a critical tactical advantage. If Heke attacks us—and the information our Maori scouts are bringing back suggests he will, and soon—we will be on our own. We will not have a second front coming up behind Heke to squeeze his forces in a pincer. In addition, with Nene out of the fight, our intelligence capabilities are severely compromised. No one knows a Ngapuhi chief better than another Ngapuhi chief. Without Nene's scouts and runners to keep us informed of Heke's movements, we are like an army on the march without cavalry units to act as its eyes and ears." He smiled briefly. "Or as you would put it, Lieutenant Brengle, a naval fleet at sea without any frigates."

"Just so," Brengle agreed.

"So there we are," Blackwell summarized soberly. "Accordingly, I am ordering the evacuation of all remaining military personnel and supplies in Paihia to Russell. That will leave Paihia defenseless, but we have no choice. We must make our stand in Russell. Private citizens will have the choice of remaining in Paihia or going with us. If tradition holds, the Maori will not harm the citizens who decide to stay. Unless, of course, they take up arms against the Maori.

"On a final note, we have two naval vessels in the harbor. A third ship is due imminently. These ships have the guns to help defend Russell and the capacity to evacuate the entire population if need be. We will immediately start making contingency plans for evacuation."

"Yes, sir," Dickerson responded.

"Good. That is all. Lieutenant Brengle, if you would remain for a moment, please."

Dickerson stood, saluted the major, offered a stiff bow to Brengle, and left the room. When the office door had closed behind him, Blackwell said to Brengle, "Despite what you may think of Lieutenant Dickerson, he is a loyal officer and a good soldier. I had to give him his due just now, but I must confess that what he had to say about Captain Cutler gives me pause. It seems out of character for the man."

"I understand, Major," Brengle returned. "And it is not my place to question the lieutenant's competency."

"Only his tact."

A smile flitted across Brengle's face. "You could put it that way, sir."

"I believe I just did." Blackwell clasped his hands together on his desktop. "*Entre nous*, how *is* your captain, Lieutenant? Please speak freely. Nothing you say will be entered on the record. In any case, I have no authority over Captain Cutler. He is an American, after all, and I, obviously, am not."

"Yes, sir. Thank you." Brengle inhaled deeply and exhaled slowly. "To be frank, sir, he's in a bad way. It will take time to bring him to an even keel. He has a stout heart and mind, though, and he will come out of this eventually. I don't know how long it will take—several days, a week perhaps—but he will recover."

"I do not doubt it, given the man's character, but unfortunately time is in short supply here, and I need him on the front lines. May I assume that Captain Cutler's behavior is related to the native woman Dickerson went on about?"

"In large part, yes sir, it is."

"She was more than just an acquaintance, then."

"A bit more, yes."

"I see." Blackwell eyed Brengle closely. "So much more that he was willing to take the time to carry her body to a remote place and bury her there? And in so doing, put lives and the mission in jeopardy?"

Brengle did not blink. "That is not an easy question to answer, Major. Captain Cutler cared deeply for Ataahua, but he cared deeply for the entire *pa* as well. Despite what Lieutenant Dickerson alleges, however, Captain Cutler did not insist on anything. He in fact ordered me to take the men and supplies back to Paihia, leaving him only a horse and shovel. He assured me he would follow later."

"But you refused?"

"His men refused, sir. They heard what he said to me, and they refused to leave without him."

"Even when their captain ordered them to leave?"

"After what they have been through, they would sooner face a court-martial than abandon their commander," Brengle replied simply.

Blackwell shook his head. "My God, that's loyalty for you. I suppose their actions are pardonable given what you all have been through together. Frankly, I could use some of that loyalty from my own men. But Lieutenant Dickerson also chose not to leave with his own men and the munitions when he had the opportunity," Blackwell pointed out. "I wonder why. He would have been well within his right to do so, you know."

Brengle shrugged. "That, Major, is a question I believe is better put to Lieutenant Dickerson."

"Yes, quite," Blackwell sighed. "Lieutenant, this is not your fight. It never has been. You are free to leave at any time. But I assure you that if you and Captain Cutler decide to stay and fight for just a short while longer, Her Majesty and the empire will be immeasurably grateful."

Brengle gave Blackwell a meaningful look. "I know what Captain Cutler will say in response to that request, Major. And so do you."

A clamor outside drew Blackwell's attention to the harbor-facing window. What he saw brought a smile to his face. There could be but one reason why citizens of all ages were running pell-mell toward the waterfront. A look beyond the wharves out into the bay confirmed his suspicions. A naval ship was shortening sail as she prepared to round Tapeka Point and enter the bay.

"Curse me to hell and back three times," he exclaimed. "Her Majesty's ship *Hazard* has come to pay us a visit."

Midshipman Ian Gillman left his station by the foremast and strode aft to the quarterdeck where three officers were standing by a quartermaster's mate at the helm. He saluted his captain. "Lieutenant Bunting's respects, sir, and we are approaching Tapeka Point."

The acting commodore returned the salute. "Thank you, Mr. Gillman."

Gillman turned to face forward. He clasped his hands firmly behind him in timeless quarterdeck fashion and waited.

John Shilling turned to his executive officer. "The quarterdeck is yours, Mr. Philipotis. Take her in." Gesturing toward the sailing master, he added, "Mr. Sayers can offer advice on a suitable anchorage, if needed. I'm going below."

George Philipotis touched the forward tip of his fore-and-aft uniform hat. "Very good, sir."

Shilling proceeded down the aft companionway to his cabin on the gun deck. The Marine sentry at the doorway snapped to, stamped the butt of his musket on the oak-planked deck, and stiffly swung his right arm, flat palm down, across his chest. Shilling acknowledged the salute and stepped inside his private preserve.

He stopped at his desk on the extreme starboard end of the ship and took a moment to study *Hazard*'s wake through the stern galley windows between the sleeping and dining alcoves. A glance through an open gun port confirmed that land was fast approaching. Overhead, on the weather deck, he heard the shouts of boatswain's mates, the shrieks of bosuns' whistles, and the stamp of bare feet as sailors made ready to shorten sail. The voyage had been too short for his liking. Soon he would feel the ship swing into the wind and hear her remaining press of canvas shivering and flapping. And then the splash as her spek anchor dove into the depths, its chain and cable rumbling out the hawser hole until *Hazard* was secured to the seabed near the two other Royal Navy vessels. All the harbor's other seagoing craft—the armadas of merchantmen and whalers of many nations—had long since departed Russell for home or for less threatening shores.

Reminding himself that he had limited time before a midshipman hurried below to request his presence on deck, he opened the top drawer of his desk and removed the contingency plans he and his officers had prepared for the defense of Russell and the evacuation of its eight hundred citizens. Capacity was not an issue. *Hazard* and her two sister ships had ample space and stores to accommodate these people on the two-day sail to Auckland. The question was, would these people agree to abandon their homes and their livelihoods? Early indications suggested that many would not.

He opened the packet of papers and quickly reviewed them. He was well known for his attention to detail, and he would not lower his standards now, whatever the circumstances. This morning, however, he was annoyed to find his mind wandering. Yet he could hardly deny that the image distracting him was most welcome. Thinking of Anne's face brought him a sense of peace and comfort, and at the same time inspired a keen sense of excitement and anticipation. He wondered if it was the same for her when she thought of him.

Shaking off thoughts inappropriate for the moment, he tried to concentrate on the papers he had placed on the desk before him. It was no use. Again her image appeared, teasing him—perhaps loving him?—he could not tell which. Attention to duty was becoming nigh on impossible. Shaking his head, he smiled ruefully and returned the papers to the desk drawer. Then he straightened his coat, collected his hat, and retraced his steps up to the quarterdeck.

The people lining the shore to watch *Hazard* undergo the evolutions of anchoring in the outer harbor did not command Jonty Montgomery's attention. He had witnessed that spectacle countless times. This morning, he was drawn to what he saw in the opposite direction.

"You know, Tom," he confessed to his fellow midshipman as they walked together, "I have wanted to go in there ever since we arrived in Russell. I'd love to know who lives there and what happens in there."

Talmadge paused to study the elegant white stucco building that most of Russell's citizens considered the crown jewel of the town's architecture. "Someone rich, surely," he replied.

"Probably," Montgomery concurred. "But it's rather odd, isn't it, how many people come in and out all day, and how noisy it can be. And sometimes when I've walked past, the smell coming out of there was sickening. Worse than a seat of ease or a pile of rotting carcasses. What do you suppose makes that horrible stench?"

Talmadge grinned. "Well, why don't you go and ask him."

"Who?"

Talmadge pointed. "Him. That fellow in the garden. He acts like he owns the place. Go on. Go up and demand to know what goes on in there."

Montgomery looked dubious. "Oh, no, I shouldn't. We mustn't dally. The captain is expecting us."

"Oh, go on. The captain is probably still asleep." He nudged his friend with his hip. "Go on. Ask the fellow. Or are you chicken?"

"I'm no chicken!"

Talmadge grinned when Montgomery gathered up his courage and marched through the open gate into the well-kept grounds. When he waved at the man tending flowers, the man waved back, and that was all the encouragement Jonty needed.

Richard Cutler cracked one eye open to the brilliant sunshine streaming through the open window. Wincing, he quickly closed it. His head throbbed, and his stomach still threatened to rebel. Two days—or was it three?—had elapsed since he had gone over on his beam ends, stone drunk. He remembered the tavern, but not the people to whom he had been talking or the names of the giggling women who had approached him. He had done nothing untoward with any of them. Of that, at least, he was quite certain. His brain might have been awash in alcohol, but even drunkenness could not dull his unwillingness to buy what they were selling. He drank to drown his anguish, and copious amounts of rum and corn whiskey had done the job. What had transpired after he finally stumbled out of the tavern into the early morning rain, his right arm draped across Brengle's shoulders for support, remained a blur. Had he passed out? He could certainly recall the siege of vomiting followed by the savagery of dry heaves on his way to Johnny Jonson's Boardinghouse Grog shop, where Brengle had booked a room for him, and where Brengle had somehow managed to get him undressed and into bed.

What day was this? It had to be Tuesday, since yesterday, Jonty had assured him, was Monday. *Where is Jonty?* he wondered as he ran his fingertips over the three-day stubble on his cheeks and neck. "Christ, I'm a mess!" he muttered despondently.

Apart from Brengle, Montgomery and Talmadge were the only two of *Suwannee*'s crew who knew his whereabouts. During the previous two days they had brought him small plates of food, which he had ignored, and copious amounts of steaming hot coffee, which he craved. By now he was feeling better, more in command of himself. And he decided it was time to take the next step.

Hauling himself to his feet, he struggled into cotton trousers and a linen shirt. After waiting a moment for his roiling stomach to quiet, he left his room and strode out the front door of the boardinghouse—and into blinding sunlight that pierced his brain like a knife. Raising his right forearm to shield his eyes, he blinked and squinted until his vision adjusted to the searing glare. He saw little of note in the inner harbor; there was little there to take note of. But there, in the outer harbor, a navy vessel—a three-masted sloop by the look of her—had arrived. A ship's boat lowered from tackles attached to stays and yardarms was being rowed toward East Wharf and the modest stockade located near there. A sea officer—a lieutenant judging by the single gold-fringed epaulet adorning his left shoulder—was seated in the stern sheets next to the coxswain as eight sailors worked the oars.

"That was once me," Richard choked out, comparing the smartly turned out British officer to the man he had become.

With a surge of adrenaline, he resolved to change that. He walked the few steps to the pebbly beach, stripped off his shirt, waded knee-deep into the still water, and dove in. His naked chest rubbed against the stones and weed of the seabed as he kicked his legs and used great sweeping motions of his arms to propel him out into deeper water. Swimming was, for him, an exhilarating exercise. As a boy learning to swim in the waters of the Chesapeake Bay and Cape Cod, he had shrugged off the ancient sailors' superstition that learning to swim simply meant a slower death in the event his ship went down. Richard regarded swimming as both pleasurable and therapeutic, and never more so than today. The embrace of the warm saltwater brought his body aware and alert, even as his tortured lungs demanded air.

When the desire to breathe became overbearing, Richard planted both feet on the seabed and lunged up, up, until his head broke the surface with a mighty swirl of water. Released at last from the mire of terrible grief that had drawn him down and paralyzed him, he side-stroked toward the shore where Montgomery and Talmadge awaited him by a towering *pohutukawa* tree bearing the last of the summer's crimson blooms. When his toes touched bottom, he stood up and waded in to shore, licking the salt from his lips and using both hands to coax his shoulder-length hair away from his face.

"Glad to see you up and about, sir!" Montgomery called out as Richard sloshed out of the water.

"We thought you were a seal when you surfaced," Talmadge put in, grinning. "Or an orca, maybe. We've seen them swimming not far offshore."

Richard laughed. "Glad I didn't know that. God, that was heaven! I'll be doing it again tomorrow. Did you chaps think to bring coffee?"

"A full pot awaits your pleasure in your room, sir. Along with eggs, a loaf of bread, butter, and a slab of cold pork."

"You're a good lad, Jonty," Richard said, suddenly ravenous. "You and Tom are hereby promoted to the rank of admiral. Let's have at it, shall we?"

In his room, he changed into the only other pair of trousers he possessed, a gift from James Busby, and then asked after the other members of *Suwannee*'s crew and the progress of Russell's defenses.

"All is in good order, Captain," Talmadge reported. "Mr. Brengle sends his compliments and looks forward to your return to action. He—all of us—are very concerned about you. Even some of the British soldiers and townspeople have been asking after you."

"How gratifying to hear that I am well known in town," Richard said dryly. He accepted a sandwich of egg and pork from Talmadge and ate it hungrily.

"And sir?" Montgomery said when Richard held out his cup for a refill of coffee. "You have an invitation."

"Do say! So I'm still to be received, then. Who is it from?"

"A bishop, if you can believe it. A Catholic bishop from France is living here in Russell. Do you recall that building up the pathway from here? The one you said resembles an Italian villa?"

"Of course. It's a gem. The bishop lives there, does he?"

"No, sir. He lives close by, though. No one actually lives in that building because it's not a home. It's a business, a print shop."

"A print shop? Surely you jest, Jonty!"

"I do not jest, sir! And," Montgomery added proudly, "I met the bishop. I was reluctant to approach him at first, but Tom teased me into it. And I'm glad he did. The bishop's a kind man, and he gave Tom and me a tour through both floors. What a place! The press and paper and ink and just about everything else come all the way from Lyon—that's a city in France. And that horrible stench we sometimes smell coming from down that way? It's from a tannery in the back of the building."

"A tannery? Of all things! Might I guess that they use the leather to bind their books?"

Jonty smiled. "Yes, sir. You are correct. Every book printed there is bound in fine leather. One of the workers told us that it can take two or even three years to process the hides properly. After the books are printed and bound, many of them are given away free to Maori tribes. Certain books you have to pay for, of course. The books are written in French and English and Maori, and most of them are about Christ's teachings. Hundreds of them have been printed, and the ones Tom and I handled were beautiful, like something you'd see in a lord's library. Weren't they, Tom?"

Talmadge nodded. "They were."

"Think on it, sir! A printing press, all the way from France, here on the far side of the world!"

Richard gave Jonty an affectionate smile. The love of books was something they shared. "It is indeed noteworthy," he agreed, recalling with a sharp pang the beautifully bound Bible that Ataahua had brought from her hut to show him. "Perhaps I too will soon get to gaze upon this wonder. It was the bishop, I take it, who extended an invitation to me?"

"Yes, sir," Talmadge confirmed. "He is looking forward to meeting you. When he asked us how we came to Russell and we told him, he said he had heard remarkable things about us all, and about you in particular.

He said he is most anxious to meet a man who has so quickly become a local legend."

Richard hoped the legend wasn't based on his tavern exploits. "I'm hardly that, Tom. When and where am I to meet this paragon?"

"Tomorrow, at four bells in the forenoon watch."

"At his home?"

"Yes, sir. We can point it out to you from the window here."

"I shall be there if duty permits. By the bye, what is the bishop's name?"

"Pom . . . Pompy . . ." Talmadge looked at Montgomery, who said, "Pompallier, sir."

Captain John Shilling sat comfortably on the after thwart of the clinker-built ship's boat as the boat pulled toward East Wharf at the eastern end of the harbor. Although he had visited Russell only once before on a brief layover, he was well acquainted with its reputation, as was every other seaman in the South Pacific.

He wondered if Anne would be shocked if she heard about some of the goings-on there. She would never see them, of course. No lady would. The question and its possible answers brought a smile that he was careful to hide from the sailors pulling on their oars. Something unusual in the water ahead pulled him out of his speculations.

It was a big fish surfacing. No, by Jove, it was a man swimming! He had come up from the depths and was now side-stroking toward the southern shore. Shilling, a man who enjoyed a bracing swim, gave him a brief wave. The swimmer either did not notice or chose to ignore it.

"Toss oars!" the coxswain at the tiller ordered, and all eight oars snapped to the vertical. The ship's boat skimmed on momentum alone toward a stone-and-wooden quay. Just prior to impact, a bowman leaped ashore, fended off, then threw a line around a bollard and secured the craft to it with a clove hitch.

"I'll be back in three hours' time," Shilling told the boatswain's mate doing double duty as coxswain. "If I am delayed, I will send word. In the meanwhile, the men are free to wander about and have a nip of grog on me. Make sure they keep their wits about them. We're sitting on a powder keg here." He handed a fistful of gold coins to the coxswain, who stared down at them in surprise.

"The men and I thank ye kindly, Cap'n," he said.

Shilling walked the short distance to the Marmy barracks where Major Blackwell and Captain Tilney awaited him.

"Welcome to Russell and the Bay of Islands, Captain Shilling," said Tilney, who looked every inch a career Marine officer. "A good voyage from Auckland?"

"Thank you, the voyage was uneventful, and therefore good," Shilling returned.

Blackwell chuckled. "Understood. I assume your Lieutenant Philipotis filled you in on our discussions yesterday?"

"He did, and I believe I am well versed in our situation. I must say, however, that I am both distressed and concerned by the citizens I encountered on my way here. They seem unaccountably jovial. Are they truly so blind to the dangers they are facing?" His tone of mild reproof implied that the apparent complacency of the townspeople was somehow the fault of the other British officers. "As I understand it, my mission here is not to wage war but to assist in the evacuation of Russell. Is that your understanding as well?"

"It is, Captain," Tilney assured him. "And believe me when I say that we are doing our best to convince them that they are in grave danger. The problem is, most people don't believe the Maori will attack. Nor do they believe that we would abandon them should they be wrong. So, life here goes on as before. The taverns and brothels remain open for business, if you're interested."

"I am not, but I daresay my men will be," Shilling said. He was mulling over the ramifications of what Captain Tilney had just told him when Major Blackwell said, "I say, Captain, there is a chap recently come to Russell whom I am most keen for you to meet."

"Oh? Who is he?"

"He's an American naval commander, if you can believe it. He emerged from the bush several weeks ago with a group of sailors, all that remain of his crew. His ship foundered off the west coast a year ago. He has since made his way here, and his fantastic stories are well worth a listen. He has been most helpful . . ." He stopped. "I say, Captain, are you ill? You have suddenly gone as white as a ghost!"

Shilling shook his head. The words "American naval commander" had jolted him to his very core. "I am fine, thank you. A stab of indigestion is all. I would like to meet this man. Where might I find him?"

"I'm afraid I can't tell you that," Blackwell replied. "We don't know where he is. No one seems to know beyond his executive officer and two midshipmen, and they aren't saying much. In any event, he is staying out of sight."

"Where are the two midshipmen being quartered?" Shilling asked.

Blackwell and Tilney exchanged another glance. It was Tilney who answered. "Your best bet is to go up the hill. There's a small stockade by the flagpole. You should find at least one of the two up there. They're easy to spot. Damn nice youngsters."

"Thank you, gentlemen. I shall report back soon."

"Good luck," Blackwell called after him. "By the bye, the man's name is Cutler. Richard Cutler."

"Yes, I know, thank you," Shilling said over his shoulder.

As that conversation was taking place at the bottom of Maiki Hill, a conversation of a different sort was taking place on top of it, outside the small stockade adjacent to the flagpole.

"Welcome back to the land of the living, Captain," Brengle greeted Richard Cutler cheerfully. "I find it difficult to believe, but you don't look any the worse for wear."

"I find that difficult to believe as well," Richard laughed, taking in the eye-catching vista below them with appreciation. Finger-like peninsulas, secluded coves, and a scattering of emerald-green islets defined the shimmering blue waters of Te Rawhiti Inlet separating Russell from Paihia, where the work of transferring personnel and equipment continued. Richard's grin vanished as he leaned in to speak confidentially. "I apologize for my wretched behavior these past few days, Jack. I have acted shamefully."

"Ah, nothing out of the ordinary for you," Brengle responded lightly.

Richard grimaced. "Perhaps. But I am myself now. For what that's worth. Thank you for pulling me out of the abyss and standing in for me." He returned the waves of Garth Plummer and Elijah Howe, who were digging together in a second entrenchment looping around the stockade and flagpole.

"All for the love of glory, Richard," Brengle replied.

"Well, if so, you have certainly earned that glory." Richard's gaze swept over Russell's defenses. Their keystone centered on additional entrenchments around Christ Church and the town proper near the eastern end of the harbor. Although from where he was standing he could not see the main stockade at the base of the hill, he had noted similar work being done there on his ascent. He wondered if this herculean effort from teams of soldiers, sailors, and townspeople was worth it. Would Hone Heke really make war on the British Empire? True, he had rallied several powerful chiefs to his banner, and there was unrest among the Maori throughout North Island. But Great Britain was here to stay, and they knew it. Heke, an intelligent man, surely understood that the Crown was not likely to walk away from a colony it believed had been acquired through a legitimate treaty. Was all this posturing and all these threats worth the risk of sparking a civil war that would harm many innocent people, Maori and *pakeha* alike?

He lifted his gaze to the outer harbor where three Royal Navy vessels had anchored in a north–south line across the entrance. HMS *Hazard*, the small squadron's flagship, was positioned in the center facing north, her long bowsprit and jib boom pointed at *Resolution*'s stern fifty feet ahead. Fifty feet astern of *Hazard*, the 12-gun schooner *Duchess of Marlborough* aimed her bowsprit at the flagship's stern. Each vessel was held in place by anchors set out from bow and stern. The stern anchor was a kedge anchor, its rode linked to a spring line attached to a capstan amidships. With the click of pawls on the capstan, each ship could be repositioned to train her guns on any target on sea or land. Such concentration of firepower was a tactic that naval commanders, most famously Admiral Lord Nelson, had advocated for years.

"What do you think?" Brengle asked as he followed Richard's gaze.

"I think," Richard replied, "that the commodore of that squadron is an able sea officer. Who is he?"

"Major Blackwell tells me his name is Captain John Shilling from Auckland. Apparently he is held in high esteem by those he commands and by those who command him."

"Well, I should like to meet him. He is clearly a sea officer who knows his trade." Richard stared down at the town. "As to our land defenses, I would say that we have learned well from our Ngapuhi allies. What I see down there resembles what we saw in the *pa*."

"Exactly. Whether the enemy comes at us from land or sea, we'll have a reception committee ready to greet them. We'll beat the enemy at their own game, and then, by God, we'll leave. Right?"

"Right. I'm for leaving just as much as you are. There's not much more that honor can demand of us. And there's nothing to keep me here now."

Brengle looked skeptical. "We shall see about that, Captain. I'm going down to check on the men. Care to come with me?"

"I'll be along later, Jack. I'd appreciate a little time up here alone. That headland over there offers the perfect place to sit and reflect. Who knows how many more opportunities I may have?"

At ten o'clock the following morning, Richard Cutler presented himself at the home of Jean Baptiste Pompallier. The house had indeed been easy to find. It was the second-to-last building on the southern rim of the inner harbor, set between the Italianate villa that housed the printing operation and an impressive headland that jutted into the outer harbor. The last house on the pathway, he had learned, belonged to an English-man named Clenden who had formerly served as an American envoy safeguarding the interests of American whalers in Russell and was now, ironically, the town's police magistrate. A chance encounter with a local townsperson had provided that information as well as much more gossip about Russell. White-haired Ruth Wildish was a lively and very outgoing English widow. On learning that Richard was an American, she assumed he would be amused by the story.

Mrs. Wildish had also told him what she knew about Bishop Pompallier, Russell's most celebrated resident. Although she claimed to be Anglican by birth and upbringing, Ruth Wildish regarded Pompallier with affection and admiration. From his headquarters in Russell he oversaw the management of the press and all the other matters pertaining to the French Catholic Mission in the diocese of Western Oceania.

"He loves New Zealand and its Maori people," she said as their walk neared its conclusion. "What is happening here saddens him greatly. He is doing everything he can to prevent bloodshed, but even a bishop can do only so much."

"He won't sail to Auckland with the others, then, and stay there until the danger has passed?"

"No, he has said he will not leave. He cannot. These are his people, *pakeha* and Maori alike."

"What about you? Will you leave?"

"No indeed!" she said emphatically. "My beloved George and I lived here in Russell for fifteen years. My best memories of him are here. I cannot leave our home. It wouldn't be possible."

"What if there is trouble?"

"Trouble? You mean with the Maori? I doubt it will come to that. But if it does, I will take refuge either in Christ Church or the Catholic church. Hone Heke will not allow harm to come to anyone in either of those sanctuaries."

"How can you be so sure?"

She looked surprised. "Why, because Hone Heke has given his word on that, Mr. Cutler," she stated in a tone that settled the matter.

Pompallier's residence had been constructed in the manner of most New Zealand *pakeha* homes: simple in design, utilitarian in decor and function, but pleasing to the eye. The parlor where morning tea was to be served was adorned with an Ottoman rug, a sofa, and three high-back chairs of French provenance. A highly polished mahogany side table displayed Limoges plates depicting scenes of the French countryside—Provence or Lombardy, perhaps—and seascapes.

"This is a beautiful room," Richard said. Gesturing at the china and evocative wall hangings, he added, "These lovely things make me regret that I have been to France only once. Yours is certainly a beautiful country, Monseigneur."

"*Merci beaucoup, capitaine,*" the thin cleric replied, his delicate features lighting in a smile. "*Mais parlez-vous de la France ou de la Nouvelle-Zélande?*"

Richard gave him a bemused look. "I apologize. My French has never been very good. What did you ask me?"

"I was asking if you are referring to France or New Zealand?"

Richard smiled. "Both, from what I have seen."

"That is the correct answer, *capitaine. Maintenant, nous parlons en anglais, oui?*"

"*Bon. En anglais. Merci.*"

Pompallier chuckled. Richard sensed in him none of the pompousness he associated with Catholic clergy of high standing. In contrast, Pompallier seemed a simple man with simple tastes who wore a continuous smile. His elaborate clerical robes could not conceal the heart of a shepherd who yearned for little beyond the proper care of his flock. Richard was about to ask him a question about his background when there came a knock on the front door.

Pompallier held up a hand. "I apologize, Captain Cutler, but I have invited another to join us this morning. I do not normally do such a thing without proper notification, but this man, I believe, bears a message of some urgency. I hope you do not mind."

"Not at all," Richard assured him. He assumed the "matter of urgency" involved church business, thus his surprise when Pompallier returned to the room in the company of a blond, well-proportioned young man wearing the full regalia of a senior British naval commander.

"Captain Cutler," Pompallier announced. "I have the honor of introducing you to Captain John Shilling of His Britannic Majesty's Navy. Captain Shilling, please meet Captain Richard Cutler of the United States Navy. He is a newfound friend whose story, some of which I have heard from his young shipmates, I believe will be of great interest to you."

"Indeed, sir, I believe I already know some of the captain's story." He turned to Richard and held out his hand. "How do you do, Captain Cutler." Richard took the hand and shook it firmly, taking the measure of the Englishman just as the English officer was taking his.

"How did you find me?" Richard asked him offhandedly.

"It was no great challenge," Shilling deadpanned. "I put Midshipman Montgomery on the rack and forced the information out of him. He was blurting it out even before I started in on him. So here I am, at your service."

"May I ask what kind of service you are here to render?"

Shilling's expression turned stone serious. "You may, and I will tell you everything in due course. But first I must verify the facts as I understand them. I apologize for the intrusion. If you would kindly bear with me."

Richard nodded. "Of course."

Shilling cleared his throat. "Your name is Richard Cutler. You are a captain in the United States Navy. A year ago, your ship, *Suwannee*, foundered off the entrance to Kaipara Harbor, south of the Pouto Peninsula. From there you led the survivors of the wreck up the beach and, eventually, across the island to Russell. Are these facts correct?"

"They are," Richard replied, mystified. "Apparently my midshipman revealed quite a bit of information beyond where I was to be at ten o'clock this morning. I must have a word with him."

"No, Captain. What you must do now is sit down."

Richard bridled. "I beg your pardon?"

"Please sit down," Shilling repeated, not unkindly.

"Why?"

"Please, my son, do as he asks," Pompallier urged when Richard hesitated.

Richard looked at him askance, and then kept his eyes locked on Shilling as he slowly sank down onto a chair, his hands gripping the twin upholstered armrests. "What is it that you wish to tell me, Captain Shilling? Have you found the remains of my third lieutenant?"

Shilling shook his head. "I know nothing of your lieutenant," he said, "but I do know something of your wife."

"My wife? How could you possibly know anything about Anne?" He choked. "She was washed away and drowned when the ship sank."

"Indeed, Captain," Shilling said gently, "she did not drown. Your wife is alive and well and living at Government House in Auckland with your infant son, James. She will tell you all about it when she sees you. Just know that both of them are in good health and thriving. As soon as duty permits, I will take you to Auckland to be with them."

For long moments Richard stared blankly ahead, seeing nothing, hearing nothing beyond the rapid thumping of his heart, an odd ringing in his ears, and a concerned voice from far, far away beseeching him to say something, anything. The room was spinning around him, his upper body was rocking back and forth. When Pompallier leaned over to place a comforting hand on Richard's shoulder, the trance broke. Richard looked up at him wild-eyed. He seized the prelate's hand in both of his and kissed it again and again like a man possessed, until at last the dam burst, the tears flowed freely, and he was up, throwing military discipline and social protocol to the wind. He hugged the bishop as he would a savior, and he hugged Shilling as he would a long-lost friend. Then he slumped back into the chair and slipped away into a blissful sanctuary deep within himself.

CHAPTER 26

ONLY ONE ATTUNED FROM BIRTH TO THE SMALL SOUNDS OF FOREST and sea would have discerned the faint rhythmic dripping of water from 160 paddles and the wash rippling away from the hulls of two *wakas* skimming across the bay.

On that bay, in the dark hills rising above it, and in the boats themselves, it was as quiet as a tomb. Even when the prominent prows of the two war canoes loomed out of the murk to crunch softly onto the beach next to a third *waka*, there were few sounds to indicate what was happening. Two hundred warriors, one group led by a white-haired Ngapuhi chief named Te Ruki Kawiti and his trusted *ariki* Pamuka, the other composed of Ngato-Hine, Roroa, and Kapotai warriors from Wainanaku and Waikate, stepped soundlessly over the sides of the vessels into the shallow water. Most of them were armed with a musket and tomahawk, and each carried a heavy leather or wooden cartouche box slung across his bare chest and secured to a belt-like rope at the waist. A few of the warriors brandished an ax or a shovel. A few others, the more senior warriors, wielded a *tupara*, a double-barreled shotgun procured in trade or battle. One after another, the two hundred men stepped up onto the beach where Hone Heke, his fearless *ariki* Pokai, and an additional hundred heavily armed Ngapuhi warriors awaited them.

Heke was an imposing sight standing at the water's edge as he watched the gathering with a veteran's eye. He wore a simple light cloak of flax and bird feathers; on his head was a black-visored Royal Navy hat, a gift from Governor Hobson as a reward for being first among the Maori chiefs to sign the Treaty of Waitangi. His deep-set eyes radiated intelligence, and the brown skin on his face bore jagged lines, swirls, and circles, all in black, intriguing tattoos that continued on to other parts of his body.

When the warriors were assembled on the beach, Heke turned to Kawiti. "*Kua hui katoa nga taane?*" he asked him.

It was a rhetorical question. Heke could plainly see that the warriors were assembled.

"*Ae, rangatira nui.*"

Heke nodded. "*Kei te marama koe ki te mahere pakanga?*"

Another rhetorical question. Kawiti knew every element of the battle plan. A brilliant tactician who had long opposed British rule, he had helped formulate it.

"*Ae, rangatira nui.*"

The next words were not a question but a warning. "*Kia mahora: kaore tatou e whawhai ki nga tangata.*"

Kawiti nodded. He understood. Every warrior on that beach understood. Today, they would not wage war on civilians. Under any circumstances. On that point Heke was adamant.

"*He pai tena,*" Heke grunted. He motioned for the three hundred Maori to follow him.

Silently, they crept northward until the black mass of Maiki Hill was within sight. There, as planned, the force split. Kawiti led a strong contingent of Ngato-Hine and Roroa warriors southwestward to the outskirts of the sleeping town while Heke and Pamuka continued northward to Maiki Hill. At regular intervals each chief relayed his current position to the other by mimicking the *kou-kou* cry of the *ruru* bird. Their calls stimulated the real *rurus* in the bush to respond, but that did not concern the Ngapuhi. Kawiti was able to pick out Heke's call, just as Heke would recognize Kawiti's call.

Heke avoided the blockhouse and barracks of the stockade at the base of Maiki Hill. He avoided, as well, the pathway leading up to the flagstaff. He and Pokai and the hundred warriors they led stole through the thick underbrush on the eastern and southern slopes until the much smaller stockade and blockhouse guarding the flagpole came into view. There they took cover in a shallow gully high above the low-lying early morning mist. A lone sentry sat on a chair outside the stockade, yawning and occasionally picking at his teeth, clearly bored with the humdrum of duty.

The Maori had not long to wait. Within the half-hour, as the feeble dawn drew form and substance from the mist, rolling volleys of musket fire erupted from below to the south. The sentry leapt to his feet and called out an alarm. Moments later, a squad of four half-dressed redcoats emerged from the small blockhouse dragging a wide wooden plank, which they pushed across the deep trench encircling the hilltop. Another seven men emerged from the stockade led by a young lieutenant, who crossed the bridge and looked down to see what the ruckus was about. As they approached the edge of the hill to peer down at Mata-uhi Bay and the awakening town, Heke made his move.

"*Na, nga toa tao! Whakeetke!*" he cried into the early dawn.

Half his forces sprang from the gully and followed Pokai. When the young lieutenant whirled around, a bullet to his brain knocked him over backward. The troops under his command, struggling to make sense of what was happening, put up a fight but were quickly overwhelmed.

As the rest of the garrison inside the stockade ran out to provide reinforcements, the Ngapuhi who had remained in the gully sprang into action with axes, knives, and clubs. In a matter of minutes, the fighting was over. Heke held the hill. Not one Maori had been killed or seriously injured. The only British soldiers who remained alive were two who had chosen to flee rather than fight.

Aware that the lower stockade would soon be alerted, Heke commanded, "*Haki! Inaianei!*"

The real work of Heke's mission now began in earnest. The warriors brandishing shovels formed the first wave to attack the towering flagpole. Furiously they dug around the pole, deeper and deeper, wider and wider, until they had gone beneath the iron barricade protecting the base of the massive wooden pole.

Then the axemen took over, two at a time, eight blows per man, hacking, chipping, and chopping, blow after splintering blow. With an almighty thundering *crack!* the flagpole and its oversized Union Jack came crashing down to earth for the fourth time.

Yet another restless night. When sleep did come, it was in small snatches of dreams or, more commonly, nightmares. *This blasted waiting*, Richard thought as he lay on a blanket on the churchyard grass. When, oh when, would the local authorities finally order the three ships off and away, with or without the citizens of Russell? Anne was alive, yet there was no way to get to her. He wondered if John Shilling was experiencing the same frustration, for the same reason. He doubted it after their conversation yesterday, though he had a lingering suspicion that there was more here than met the eye. Not that he could find fault with either of them, whatever the facts might turn out to be. What he had felt for Ataahua and the love they had shared was real and too meaningful to deny. Why should it be any different for Anne, a widow, or so she thought, thrown together by Fate with a handsome Royal Navy officer?

Not that Shilling had given any indication that his relationship with her was anything but aboveboard. He had simply recounted to Richard the facts of how he came to meet Anne at the mission station and how he had whisked her away to the safety of the colonial capital. He had not sought praise or gratitude from Richard. It was a matter of one military officer reporting to another military officer of equal rank on the successful conclusion of a mission.

"I did what Admiral Braithwaite demanded of me and what Governor Fitzroy expected of me," he had concluded. "However, I must confess to you, man to man, that because I believed Anne was a widow, I allowed myself to develop feelings for her." He sighed. "You need have no worries on that score, however."

"You are quite certain of that, are you?" Richard had pressed, unable to stifle a surge of jealousy.

Shilling stiffened. "Of course! Are you suggesting that anything improper occurred between Anne and me?"

"I am not suggesting anything of the sort, John. I have known you a short time, but long enough to recognize a man of honor. You would not lie to protect me or Anne. I do believe you."

Shilling flushed but quickly recovered. "All of this is not to suggest," he said with more than a trace of remorse, "that I am blind. I am not. I see Anne for the marvelous woman she is, and I will confess that there were times when I wondered if there might be a future for us. But those were reveries of a lonely man, nothing more. And I knew it." He smiled sadly. "Anne was always kind, as a true lady is, but she never wavered in her devotion to you. When a dashing officer expresses an interest in a lady, and the lady informs him that she is still grieving for her husband, it would take a far less intelligent man than I not to get the message."

"Anne told you that?"

"In those exact words. She is still very much in love with you. Besides," he added, "there is a child involved in this, a child who looks remarkably like you. So you see, there's absolutely no reason for you to fume. All I ask is to be present at your reunion," he joked. "God knows I would not want to miss that."

Richard's expression softened. "Thank you for telling me this, John. You are a good man."

"Opinions differ on that. By the bye, I can tell you one more thing with absolute certainty."

"What's that?"

"You are one very lucky bastard!"

Richard smiled before a flash of memory cast him back to an afternoon outside the *pa* when Jack Brengle, speaking for the crew, had said similar words to him concerning another woman.

Now, restlessly trying to find a comfortable spot on the churchyard grass, Richard knew he was facing more hours of numbing idleness and tedium. He had made friends in Russell, but Russell was not where he needed to be. Giving up on sleep, he threw aside his blanket, got up, and stepped to the fence surrounding the grounds of Christ Church. He could not see much through the mist, but he could make out the dark outline of someone familiar standing nearby.

"Good morning, Jack," he whispered. "You're up early. It's not yet two bells."

"Good morning, Richard. Something woke me. Something feels a bit off. Do you hear that?"

Richard listened for a moment and shook his head. "All I hear are bird calls. I believe they are owls, what the Maori call *rurus*. What of it? Beyond the fact that they seem unusually active tonight."

"That's just it." Brengle strained to listen. "*Why* are they so active? And is it just the owls making those sounds?"

Richard frowned. "What are you getting at?"

"Do you remember our expedition on Pine Island off the Florida coast? Our orders were to attack the Seminoles who were harassing mainland settlers."

"I do, and I recall you saving my life. Or me saving yours, I don't remember which. I also recall that those clever bastards turned the tables on us. We didn't attack *them*. They attacked *us*."

"Right. And do you recall the night before that attack? How the hoot owls were so active? And how the Seminole warriors used the owl calls to signal each other? We ignored those sounds, and men died as a result."

Richard listened more intently, then slowly nodded. "You think the Maori are up to the same sort of mischief?"

"I think there's a damn strong possibility. They're certainly as clever as the Seminoles."

Richard listened a moment longer. Weeks had passed in Russell without incident. During that time the men had grown more and more complacent, and with that, more restless and irritable. Could the day of reckoning truly be upon them? "I suggest we wake the men," he said. "But quietly. If you're right and we're about to have a fight on our hands, we don't want the enemy to know we're on to them."

When Heke attacked, Captain Shilling was leading a troop of bluejackets and Marines from HMS *Hazard* to Christ Church to finish digging a trench outside the five-foot-high fence that surrounded the Anglican church. Then, and only then, Major Blackwell had insisted, would Russell finally be as secure as it could be. With the British dug in at all three stockades and the guns in the ships in the harbor run out on both the port and starboard sides, Hone Heke would accept the fact that he had been outmaneuvered and checkmated, and would slip quietly away into the bush.

Shilling doubted that Blackwell was right on that point. What little he knew about Heke suggested he was not the sort of commander to show his hand unless he held all the aces, as he had during the British rout from the mission. Shilling and Anne had narrowly escaped with their lives. Not so his men, savagely killed and then mutilated—deaths Shilling remained determined to avenge.

When a crack of musket fire erupted not far away, Shilling dropped to a knee. He could not pinpoint where the shots were coming from, but it was somewhere ahead on the edge of town. He motioned to his men to lie flat and waved up Sean Wiggins, his sergeant of Marines and a hardened veteran of heated campaigns.

"Sir!" Wiggins breathed when he had slithered up to his captain.

Shilling pointed in the direction of the musket fire, which by now had become sporadic. "Take two men over there and see what you can see. Fire your revolver three times in the air if you need us to come up. Understood?"

"Sir!"

"Have a care, Sergeant. Don't forget we're on a war footing. Those are not rowdy merrymakers out there. They are likely seasoned Ngapuhi warriors who would as soon kill you as not."

"Understood, sir!"

Wiggins carefully worked his way around and was soon swallowed by the early morning murk.

"Seems you were right, Lieutenant," Richard remarked to Brengle after the initial blast of musket fire. He tightened his grip on his revolver and waited with the rest of his men for the next blow.

It came with an ear-splitting *crack!* followed by a thud that shook the ground. Richard looked up into the lightening sky. The crest of Maiki Hill rose above the mist, stretching high into the sky. Silhouetted at the very peak against the pale dawn was . . . nothing. Nothing at all. The flagpole was gone.

"Jesus Christ! How did they manage *that*?" he wondered aloud, his tone mixing disbelief, admiration, and fear.

"The stockade up there must have been taken," Brengle said, equally stupefied. "Heke holds the high ground!"

Their trance ended when Jonty Montgomery came running up from his station at the church. "Sir," he reported breathlessly. "Captain Shilling is here with men from *Hazard*."

"How many men?"

"I don't know, sir. More than a few."

"Very well. God knows we can use them, whatever their number. Jack, you are in command here. I am going to talk with Captain Shilling. Send Jonty if you need me."

"Aye, Captain." Brengle turned to direct his full attention to the quarter-mile stretch of open land north and east of the church that was coming into focus as the sun rose and the fog lifted.

On the south side of the church, Richard met John Shilling. "Good morning," he said to the British officer, who was faultlessly clad in full undress uniform and armed with revolver and cutlass. "How many men do you have?"

"Forty-five," Shilling replied. "You?"

"Eleven, including myself. Plus a hundred local militia. I don't think we can count on them," he added. "When the chips are down, they won't put up much of a fight."

"It's not their job to fight. It's ours. How many Ngapuhi are out there, do you think?"

"Hard to say. I don't know Heke, but Chief Nene once told me that a Ngapuhi war party typically numbers three to four hundred."

Shilling nodded. "So, counting my men, your men, a squad of Marines from the other two ships, the soldiers in the main stockade, and the town militia, we have an equal number. We may have the same quantity," he added ruefully, "but not the same quality, as you correctly point out."

"Right. So, we're outnumbered two to one and the enemy holds the high ground. The odds are definitely in our favor. We have them right where we want them."

Shilling's chuckle was brief. "You know, Richard, these townsfolk are fools to believe they won't be harmed if they don't carry a weapon. That might be true it this were Nene and his ilk, but I fear Heke is far different. I suspect these townsfolk won't change their tune until Heke has them for evening tea, literally. But I suppose we must try to save them. As we are the senior officers in the field, I suggest we start moving as many people as possible to the harbor stockade—as a precaution, we'll tell them. From there, if need be, we can quickly get them into the boats. Can you form a detail?"

"I'll put my two midshipmen on it. If anyone can convince these reprobates to wake up and try to save their skins, it's Jonty Montgomery and Tom Talmadge."

Hone Heke nodded contentedly as he stood next to the three-pounder cannon and looked down on the arena of battle, such as it was. He had achieved his primary objective of chopping down the hated flagpole in a remarkably short time. The capture of the blockhouse and its single cannon had been a necessity, nothing to gloat over. He understood the tactical advantage taking the stockade had given him, but he would not press either his advantage or his luck. There was no need. Kororareka was his for the taking, but for what purpose? He would gain little and risk much by attacking the town. Worse, it would have the opposite effect of what he wanted to achieve. It would rile up the *pakeha* against him and make his strategy harder to implement. He had already made his point and delivered his message.

What he had done was nothing more than a symbolic gesture, but it was a critically important one. No one needed to remind Heke that he and his allies did not possess the wherewithal to force the British from Aotearoa. Too many chiefs had been duped into believing the pledges of the Crown and the assurances of the missionaries that they would protect Maori integrity and culture and property. He understood how these chiefs had been taken in. He was one of them. He, too, had once believed those wondrous visions of harmony and prosperity for all New Zealanders. But those visions, he had concluded, applied only to *pakeha*.

Since the signing of the Great Treaty, many Maori had seen their land taken from them and their status reduced to little more than slaves.

These abominations had to stop. Heke spat on the ground. And stop they would. Maori *mana* was more powerful than British guns. If the northern chiefs could not drive British soldiers from Aotearoa, they could drive terror into the hearts of white settlers and convince them that their future lay elsewhere. If a former colonial capital could be so easily threatened, and its symbol of authority so easily chopped down, surely the land-grabbers would see the futility and danger of trying to eke out an existence on these islands. Fearful for their lives and their livelihood, they would leave of their own accord. With no colony to police, British soldiers and European missionaries would soon follow. Aotearoa would once again be left to the Maori. The prospect of ultimate victory caused him to smile.

His smile faded moments later when the sporadic gunfire of the past hour suddenly increased in tempo. As did the shouting and cursing in both Maori and English. The sounds were coming from the south and east, the area where he had ordered Kawiti to create a diversion to allow Heke to do what needed to be done. What he was now hearing was no diversion. It sounded more like an outright assault.

This was what he had feared most. Kawiti was a superb leader, the best Heke had, and he could not win without him. But like his *ariki* Pamuka, Kawiti had fire in his veins and hatred for everything British. Would that hatred cloud his vision and cause him to defy Heke's wishes? If so, this mission was in serious jeopardy. He called over Pokai and ordered him and four warriors down the hill with all due haste. Each warrior carried a musket.

Brengle had maintained his position by the fence and was first to sound the alarm. "Here they come!"

"Make ready!" Shilling cried out. Forty-five sailors and Marines took aim at the screaming, half-naked warriors running toward them. Leading them were two Ngapuhi, each wearing the cloak of command, each running with teeth bared and nostrils flared, exhorting their warriors onward as they pumped their long-handled spears up and down in the air.

"At my order!" Shilling cried.

"Hold!" Richard Cutler shouted. He was standing between Shilling and Brengle studying the open field with his miniature spyglass.

"What the hell?" Shilling demanded. "Damn it, man, they're almost upon us!"

Richard handed Shilling the glass. "Look behind them!"

"*What?*"

"Look behind them!"

Shilling raised the glass to his eye, and what he saw made his jaw drop. The attackers were themselves being attacked! Streaming out from the blockhouse and barracks came soldiers from the 96th Regiment of Foot led by none other than Major Oliver Blackwell. They, too, were screaming. Amid the unholy din and chaos, the Ngapuhi did not initially hear or see them. But when the front rank of redcoats dropped to a knee and started firing in a disciplined sequence, they turned to face the unexpected onslaught. Within seconds the two forces were entangled in fierce hand-to-hand combat.

"*Hazards*, to me!" Shilling cried. He was first out of the opened gate, cutlass in one hand, revolver in the other. Sergeant Wiggins and the rest of his troop followed close behind.

"*Suwannees*, to me!" Richard echoed the cry. Ten Americans raced through the gate to join the fray.

It was a frantic melee, a deadly contest of will, strength, and brutality. The Maori, more experienced in close-quarter combat, initially took the upper hand. They fought off the 96th Regiment with clubs and tomahawks, bashing skulls and tearing flesh and muscles with surgical precision until the ground was slippery with blood and gore. The redcoats fought back viciously, plunging steel into soft tissue, stamp and parry, stamp and parry, lunging with bayonets, piercing brown skin again and again until brown disappeared beneath red. Screams and grunts of impaled men fouled the air.

The tide of battle shifted when the British and Americans raced down the hill and joined the fray. Sandwiched between two enemy forces, and realizing they were now fighting a battle for survival, not conquest, the Ngapuhi fought all the harder. As the battle raged on, both sides began flagging. Swinging an ax or musket was demanding too great an effort, picking up a rock and hurling it at point-blank range almost as much. Still the killing and maiming raged without pause and without mercy.

With no more bullets in his revolver, and no time to pause to reload, Richard had only his fists and feet, and these he brought to bear with savage fury until a blow to his back sent him sprawling face-down onto the ground. Struggling to turn over, unable to defend himself, he gazed helplessly into the dark eyes of a tattooed demon with an ugly iron blade poised over Richard's heart. Richard closed his eyes to the inevitable.

"Hey! Chief!" he suddenly heard Shilling shout. "You! Look at me, you bloody bastard!"

The warrior turned, saw what was coming, and flipped his spear to the horizontal to ward off the blow, too late. The well-honed steel of Shilling's cutlass sliced down through the wooden shaft as though it were matchwood and slashed into the Maori's upper left arm, nearly severing it. Blood spurted from the severed artery as Shilling yanked the blade out and thrust it deep into the man's intestines. "That's for my men you bastards slaughtered!" he raged.

When Shilling put the sole of his boot on the warrior's chest and pulled back on the haft, the man looked down stupidly at his gaping wound, then crumpled to the ground.

Wails of "Pamuka!" went up all around them. The battle was waning. Both sides had suffered casualties. There was no clear victor, though with the loss of their leader many Ngapuhi started retreating toward Maiki Hill, leaving five freshly arrived warriors to fight on.

Shilling reached a hand down to Richard and hauled him to his feet. Before Richard could thank him, four bullets tore into Shilling's body— two hit his chest, a third his right thigh, and another his shoulder. It was as though he was facing a firing squad.

Retaliation was swift and brutal. Two Ngapuhi were seized, wrestled to the ground, and savagely beaten. A third was bayoneted in the stomach and back. Two others were gunned down.

Dazed, Richard bent over Shilling, unsure what to do but almost certain that Shilling was already beyond any help but God's. The men who were not chasing after the retreating Ngapuhi crowded around.

"What can we do?" Jonty said, sounding very young.

"We must get him to Dr. Pryce in *Hazard*. See to it, Jonty. Take two men and get Captain Shilling to his ship. Smartly, now!"

"Aye, Captain." Montgomery pointed at Nick Purslow and Sergeant Wiggins.

"I've got him!" Wiggins said. He lifted Shilling gently and cradled him in his arms. As the sergeant turned to go, Shilling reached out and gripped Richard's wrist with the strength left to him.

"You are on a fool's errand, my friend," he rasped. "My wounds are mortal. Thank you for your friendship. May God go with you. And please speak of me to Anne!"

Richard nodded but could not respond. He motioned to Wiggins to get on with it, never taking his eyes from Shilling until the post captain was lifted into a ship's boat.

The battle now essentially over, Major Blackwell ordered his soldiers to return to the blockhouse and barracks, pack up their gear, and report at the beach no later than noon to escort private citizens to the boats. *Hazard* and her two sister ships were weighing anchor that afternoon and setting sail for Auckland. Citizens would be given two choices: go or stay. There would be no further delays. The decision was final.

Minutes passed slowly in the church compound where most of the soldiers had gathered, and where many citizens lingered. The fifteen redcoats and Marines who had been seriously injured were, like Shilling, transferred to a naval vessel. Those dead or beyond hope remained at the church, tended to by women from the town. Jonty was crushed to find the body of Thomas Talmadge among the dead. The senior midshipman, his best friend, had been clubbed down and his skull cracked open. Blood and gore matted his curly hair. Montgomery had been fighting at his side earlier in the battle and had nearly met the same end. A bullet fired into the eye of the Maori warrior attacking him had saved him. Montgomery was too stunned at the time to thank Jack Brengle.

Across the field the Ngapuhi had raised a white flag, signaling their intent to attend to their own fallen.

Despite that flag, the men of Russell remained vigilant. Sporadic firing was continuing from the hills. Several random shots had struck the south wall of the church, leaving bullet holes and ricocheting into the cemetery or thudding against the wooden fence. Not far away Richard spotted a familiar figure—a bespectacled man dressed in white cloth and a black neck stock. He was walking with a determined air toward Maiki Hill, unescorted and under no flag of truce.

"Well, I'll be damned," Richard muttered.

"Who is he?" asked Brengle.

"That's Henry Williams, the missionary you met in Paihia."

"What the hell does he think he's doing? Settling the issue all by himself?"

Richard nodded. "I would imagine that is exactly what he is thinking to do. He claims to be a friend of Hone Heke. I suspect he's going up there to try to put an end to this madness."

"Can he do that?"

Richard shrugged. "We'll see. There's no way to stop him from trying."

At first, it seemed he had succeeded. The sporadic firing ended. Relief and hope spread through the town as people shared rumors that Russell would be spared and they would not have to evacuate after all. Citizens who had gone to the beach to line up for transport to one of the three ships in the harbor decided to turn around and go home.

Suddenly, all that changed. A few minutes before noon, Russell was rocked to its core by a stentorian explosion. Flames spewed high into the air over the blockhouse and barracks of the main stockade. Burning embers fell onto the thatched roofs of nearby homes, the fire on one roof leapfrogging to another and another until the entire east side of Russell was ablaze.

The who, what, and how of the explosion were unknown, though it hardly mattered. Pandemonium had been ignited, and the conflagration rapidly swept through every nook and corner of Russell. Adding to the clamor and chaos, *Hazard*'s starboard battery of eight 32-pounder guns suddenly opened up in a perfectly timed sequence, one discharge of orange flame and white sparks followed by another, the muzzle of each gun aimed high to deliver its payload against the distant hills where Heke's force had taken refuge.

Citizens of Russell sprinted, screaming, toward the beach and the boats, quickly filling each beyond capacity. After rowing each heavy load out to one of the ships and unloading their cargo, the oarsmen backed oars and returned to the beach to take on another load. Many of those who could swim simply plunged into the harbor and swam for their lives.

Expecting a countercharge against their exposed position on the beach at any moment, Major Blackwell and Captain Tilney deployed their soldiers and Marines on the beach in defensive positions. As time passed, no attack came. The Ngapuhi had vanished—into thin air or into their *wakas*. Ordered nonetheless to provide cover for the evacuation, military personnel were among the last to leave the beach. As Richard clambered up the steps built into *Hazard*'s hull and stepped onto her weather deck, First Lieutenant Philipotis touched the edge of his hat in respect to a superior officer.

The lieutenant's grim expression foretold the inevitable answer to Richard's unspoken question. "Captain Cutler, it is my sad duty to inform you that Captain Shilling is dead."

CHAPTER 27

Auckland, New Zealand

March 1845

FOR RICHARD CUTLER, BEING A PASSENGER UNDER SAIL WAS BOTH A JOY and a cure. Freed from the burdens of command, he allowed the wind, sun, and sea to have their remedial effects. This morning, at the dawn of his first full day at sea in a year, was no exception. He gazed up from his spot at the starboard railing amidships, taking in the three towering pyramids of white canvas, their leeches shivering in the brisk southwesterly. *Hazard* was sailing full, through cobalt seas on a course shaped for Hauraki Gulf. Astern, *Resolution* and *Duchess of Marlborough* kept pace with the flagship. But the exhilaration that filled him was only temporary.

The services for the dead had been brief, as prescribed by scripture and custom, and as necessitated by the summer heat. Three hours earlier he had stood in silent witness as all twenty-one bodies, wrapped tightly in canvas strips and weighted down with grape shot, slid one after the other down a plank and plunged feet-first into the Pacific Ocean. On the weather deck crowded with sailors and civilians, the living had watched silently as each body was committed to the deep and acting captain George Philipotis read the burial rites for the next soldier, sailor, or Marine. When God was called upon to receive the soul of Thomas Talmadge, U.S. Navy midshipman, Richard glanced at Jonty Montgomery, who was standing at attention in front of the American contingent. He was not surprised when he saw, not a boy overcome by emotion at the loss of a dear friend and the sole American among the dead, but a mature junior naval officer paying tribute to another naval officer who had committed his life to ship, captain, and country, and who had died in the performance of duty. As Talmadge's body slid from under the flag and disappeared beneath *Hazard*'s bubbling wake, Montgomery turned aft and maintained a crisp salute until the service had ended.

As a senior naval officer, John Shilling was entitled to have his body conveyed to the naval base in New South Wales for more formal funeral rites presided over by a Royal Navy chaplain. But Shilling had declined that honor. As a young officer years ago, he had been appalled to learn that the remains of Admiral Lord Nelson were transported in a barrel of brandy from Trafalgar to the quays of London, and from there on to St. Paul's Cathedral. Such deference seemed pointless. As he lay dying in his after cabin, Shilling had insisted that he be buried at sea with his shipmates. And so he was, to the mournful tattoo of pipes and drums as his body slid into the deep.

"You all right, Jonty?" Richard overheard Brengle ask the midshipman as the two passed by each other on deck.

"I am, thank you, sir," Montgomery had replied matter-of-factly before continuing on his way forward.

Richard walked up to Brengle. "We'd best keep an eye on him," he remarked. "He's taking it harder than he lets on." He nodded in greeting to three former Russell residents strolling by, one of whom he recognized. "Good morning, Mrs. Wildish," he called out to her. "Nice to see you aboard and safe."

"And you, Captain Cutler," Ruth Wildish called back. "This is all pleasant enough, though I must confess, I am already looking forward to the return voyage."

"It shan't be long in coming," Richard assured her.

"Best not be, else I'll have something to say about it. And you know me well enough by now to know that what I'll have to say will not be pleasant."

"Yes, ma'am."

She turned to rejoin her companions, then paused to look back. "That was a most appropriate service, Captain," she said. "Most appropriate indeed. I deeply regret the loss of lives on both sides. So sad. So unnecessary."

"I would not choose to do battle with that lady," Brengle joked to Richard as they watched Ruth Wildish disappear forward. "Give me Heke any day." He added, "Do you truly think she will have a quick voyage back to Russell?"

Richard shook his head. "Not likely. I fear the sack of Russell will have serious repercussions. The British cannot afford to let it stand. In any case, there isn't much left of the town after the fire."

"I agree. I still wonder about that explosion. It was ill timed, to be sure."

"It was," Richard concurred. "It had to be the munitions stored in the stockade, but who or what set it off is a mystery. It may have ignited a war that neither side wants but neither side can avoid. Russell is too valuable for either side to lose."

"Especially now that blood has been spilled." Brengle paused a moment, then: "If this wind holds, we should reach Auckland sometime tonight. I can't begin to imagine what that must mean to you."

Richard looked toward the distant shore a few miles off to starboard. Since those terror-stricken moments before the wreck of his ship, this was his first opportunity to observe the coastline of New Zealand from the sea. *Ataahua was right*, he thought. *This land is a paradise.* Long stretches of blinding white sand set off by majestic bluffs stretched to north and south. White-capped turquoise seas surged up to break on the far distant shore. The subtropical vegetation dotted with stands of cabbage trees that grew inland was the very image of the South Seas islands palms that had stirred Richard's imagination as a boy.

"I'm having a hard time imagining that myself," Richard said softly, almost to himself. "She was dead in my mind for so long, Jack."

Hazard trembled as her bow struck a large cresting wave, and the spray of seawater brought him out of his reverie. Richard brushed the droplets off his white shirt. "I don't know how tomorrow will go. I ache to see Anne and take her in my arms. Of that much I am certain. As for the rest, we'll just have to wait and see. I really don't know what else to say. My mind's a bit muddled at the moment. At times I think that this is a dream, that none of it is real."

"It will go as it should the moment you see her," Jack reassured him. "Meanwhile, try thinking with your heart rather than your brain."

"You think I haven't done that?" Richard pulled a watch from the inside pocket of his coat and checked the time. "Please assemble the men in the after cabin, Jack. The captain has given us leave to use it. I need time with them, and I need to assure them that as soon as possible after we reach Auckland, they will be heading home. They will not be involved in any further conflicts. This morning Mr. Philipotis informed me that an American warship is either sailing to Auckland or is already there."

"Did he say which ship?"

"*St. Louis*, a 20-gun sloop. I believe she's out of our East India Squadron."

"What is she doing in these waters?"

"I don't know. Perhaps looking for us, although that seems unlikely after all this time has passed. Regardless, she is the men's ticket home."

"Your ticket home as well, I trust."

Richard smiled. "Just so. By way of Sydney, I should think."

Anne Cutler gratefully accepted a second cup of tea from Rachael. She took a sip and sighed contentedly, happy to be sitting here in the flower garden at Government House. The day was sunny but not hot, warm in the sun and coolish in the shade, the promise of transition from summer to autumn. The trees protected them from the wind that had sprung up last night, the rustling of their leaves like soft music.

"Another cake, my lady?" Rachael held out a plate of plump fruit cakes topped with orange glaze.

"Thank you, no, Rachael. They are utterly delicious, but two is my limit. I expect Master Jamie might care for one, though."

At the mention of his name, Jamie looked up from his seat on the grass and banged one of his wooden blocks representing warships.

When Rachael came over with the plate of cakes and leaned down to offer him one, Jamie grabbed one in each hand and stuffed them into his mouth one after the other. His mother burst out laughing.

"Well, we are in a jolly mood this fine morning," Daniel MacKenzie laughed as Te Whina hurried over to clean up Jamie. He inhaled deeply. "And it is a fine morning indeed. The *tuis* started singing before five o' the clock. 'Get up, get up!' Perhaps they know that this is a very special day."

"I heard them," Jonathan Riggs said grumpily, playing along. "I was not quite ready to rise, either. Still, such a melodic song."

"Melodic is the very word I was looking for," MacKenzie said. "I believe Captain Shilling is particularly fond of *tuis*," he added.

"I have heard him say that very thing," Riggs confirmed.

"Gentlemen! Gentlemen!" Anne interrupted, pretending to be angry. "Stop this tomfoolery! Do you think for one moment that I am unaware of your little game? I seriously doubt that Captain Shilling could identify a *tui* if one landed on his shoulder." She took another sip of tea before adding in a low tone, "Though you and Jonathan are my very dear friends, Daniel, neither of you knows my heart as well as you think you do."

MacKenzie blushed. "I apologize, Anne. We meant no harm. You know that you are very dear to us as well."

"I do know, Daniel," Anne said. "Your arrival here in Auckland lifted an enormous burden from my heart."

"We merely thought," MacKenzie went on, "that is, we assumed, that your spirits would be high on learning that *Hazard* was sighted at dawn off the volcano—Rangitoto Island, isn't it? We were simply trying to lift your spirits further still."

Riggs nodded. "We apologize if we have upset or offended you. Please forgive us."

"You have done neither, Jonathan," Anne said. "But you *were* having fun at my expense. Rather than being miffed, though, I am grateful that you care." She was about to comment further when a bold knock on the front door echoed down the central corridor leading to the open back door.

After a moment, Charles Scott emerged from the far side of the building and began hurrying toward the rear veranda, hands waving in agitation. Anne rose to her feet and intercepted him.

"I will answer it, thank you, Charles," she said a little breathlessly.

Scott stopped short. "Madam?"

"I will answer the door," she repeated. "I believe I know who has come to call, and if I am right, I should like to be the one to greet him."

Scott sniffed. "As you wish, ma'am." He turned on his heel indignantly and strode away.

Anne walked through the open back door into the hallway. "Coming!" she called out. "Just a moment, if you please!" She walked briskly down the corridor that bisected Government House into living quarters on one side and administrative offices on the other toward the heavy wooden door that opened to the front veranda and the pathway leading to the city's main thoroughfare.

Before opening the door, Anne paused before a mirror to straighten her dress and scarf, pinch her cheeks, pat her hair, and allow her heartbeat to return to normal. Satisfied all was in order and that her nerves had calmed, she gripped the door handle and pulled the door toward her. When it opened, her world crashed to a halt. For a few short seconds she stood rooted to the spot, unable to think or speak. "Oh, my God!" she sobbed. "Oh . . . my . . . God!"

She reached out to touch him, to confirm that he was real and not an apparition. Her legs buckled. He stepped forward and gripped her arms.

"Anne," he rasped, his voice laced with emotion. "Oh, sweet Jesus! Anne. It *is* you!"

Epilogue

The sails whipped in the rising wind with sharp snapping sounds. On deck, a solitary figure stood looking beyond the ship's railing toward shore, the thick collar of his woolen coat turned up against the wind and spray. Once *St. Louis* rounded Cape Reinga at the far northern tip of New Zealand, she would head into the darker waters of the Tasman Sea, away from New Zealand on a course bound for New South Wales.

His heart was full as he watched the New Zealand coast slip past. His elation at being back in the arms of his beloved Anne had not abated. Their reunion was at first clouded by the loss of John Shilling, a man, Richard knew, whom Anne would forever hold in her heart. But as the days progressed, they resumed their life together with the old love and passion. For Richard, however, the great joy he found in her arms was at times overshadowed by the secret he had buried deep inside and would take to his grave. The heartache might ease, but it would never go away.

The fierce love he felt for his son, this small replica of himself who babbled "papa" and grabbed at his coattails, helped to fill the hole in his heart. Fatherhood completed Richard's life as he had never imagined it could. And if thoughts of another child, one who was not born, sometimes crept into his mind, they were quickly banished.

As *St. Louis*, with the remainder of his crew safely on board, made her turn westward and sailors adjusted sails and rigging to the new course, he heard what sounded like a keening wail off to port. It was there, legend held, at Te Rerenga Wairua, that the souls of dead Maori dove into the sea and swam beneath it to their ancestral homeland at Hawaiki. The keening was hauntingly reminiscent of a beautiful Maori maiden bidding farewell to her lover as he left her *pa* for the last time. A shiver ran down between his shoulder blades, and his eyes prickled with moisture. Or was it just salt spray in his face and the whine of the wind in the rigging?

"Are you quite all right, Richard?"

The gentle voice beside him, so dearly familiar, brought him back to the present and the happiness it held, but he realized that he would never be entirely free from that beautiful, mystical place known as Aotearoa, the Land of the Long White Cloud.

He looked down at the dear face smiling up at him. "Yes, my love," he replied. "I am quite all right." He leaned in to kiss her, then shrugged off his coat and settled its warmth comfortably over her shoulders. He offered her his arm, she took it, and together they strolled forward along the weather deck toward their future.